I Haven't a Clue

JUDY DEHNE

PAGE PUBLISHING, INC.
Conneaut Lake, PA

First originally published by Page Publishing 2020

ISBN 978-1-6624-1781-8 (pbk)
ISBN 978-1-6624-1782-5 (digital)

Printed in the United States of America

Dedicated to my beautiful daughters, Heather and Page. Who never stopped believing in me.

Chapter 1

The clouds are just as ominous as the thoughts in my head. The thunder rolls much like the pain in my heart. The lightning is bright and breaks into the sky as though it is either angry or afraid. I know those strikes and streaks for I feel them deep inside my soul. I once dreamed of running away, but unfortunately, only my body would be leaving. My mind and soul would remain trapped by my own doing. Now my thoughts of freedom are like the bolts of lightning. Quick to come, quick to harm, and just as quickly gone, with only the rolling thunder to remind me that I will never be able to leave. As I lie there beside him, I hear the breathing. It's heavy and steady but roaring in my ears. I want it to stop. I'm not sure if it's mine or his that I want to end. It's as if I am at the edge of a high cliff overlooking the raging ocean. The noise is so loud, and my head feels the pressure until I am sure it will explode into tiny shards of glass, as if it were a mirror suddenly smashed. Just make it stop. I need the silence. I cry silently for the quiet.

He knows I am awake. Still I am lying in a dreamlike state. I am neither sated from a long sleep nor restless from the lack of it. I am just here. The alarm will soon go off, and the day will begin. It will not be as loud as the alarm ringing in my mind. Leave.

The alarm does go off with its buzzing. It's loud and very annoying. I want to throw it across the room and hear it smash against the wall like the waves on the rocks below the cliff I am standing on in my dream state. I lie here motionless as he hits the button on the alarm to end its ungodly noise. He turns to kiss me good morning, and I remain unmoving and pray I am really dead.

He is kissing my face. His breath reeks of stale whiskey, and his body smells of another woman. He tells me he knows I am awake and how much he hates it when I ignore him. He is kneading my breast as though they are balls of soft dough. His thumb is rubbing across my nipple. I hate him, but not nearly as much as I hate my traitor body. My nipples are hard under his thumb. He slowly moves his hand down my stomach and stops just before where he will enter me. He takes my hand and puts it on his hard shaft. I have no control over my fingers, and they curl around it naturally. He groans in my ear as if in pure ecstasy. I begin to rub him, and he begins to grind against my hand. He knows I am moist and ready for him because I am looking directly into his bloodshot eyes. He smiles at me, and I see his yellow teeth from all the cigarettes he smokes at work. I want to vomit and fuck his brains out both at the same time. I wonder how I can have these two strong feelings at opposite ends of the spectrum. He thrusts into me with one hard fast stroke. I welcome him by arching against him. I lose all control. I am clinging to him, digging my nails into his back, aching for more. I know he is ready for his release because he is stiffening above me. I am silently begging him to slow down and wait for me, but it is too late. He floods me with his hot sticky come. He has no idea what real love is, and it surely isn't his unwanted come shooting into my body. I hate him for what he does to me and how he makes me feel. I loathe everything about our so-called marriage. He rolls off me, taking me into his arms as if he just gave me the most wonderful, earth-shattering lovemaking session ever. Not even realizing that I feel empty and alone.

Before he gets off the bed to take his shower, he reaches over and grabs me by the arms. He shakes me like a rag doll. Laughingly he says he is just checking to make sure I am alive. Someday when he shakes me, I hope he snaps my neck.

I hear the shower and know I must get up and get everything ready for him. He will want his clothes laid out as if he were a two-year-old. His breakfast must be ready. His coffee hot, his toast lightly buttered, his eggs poached, and his juice cold. I must be sitting in the chair next to his. I think I need to take my pills prescribed for me to stop the raging in my brain and the anxiety in my chest.

It's done and ready as he enters the breakfast nook. He bends to kiss me, and his breath is now minty from the mouthwash he has used. His eyes aren't as bloodshot, but there are still a few red lines in the whites. They remind me of a road map in the atlas sitting on the shelf in the library. I wonder what I'd find if I were able to travel those red lines. Would I enter deep into his mind, finding his darkest secrets? Would they reveal how he really feels? Would I find a raging ocean or a calm, serene sea?

He will leave just enough money for me to buy food for our dinner tonight. He instructs me on what to make for food and says to be sure it is on the table at seven thirty. I will be meeting his sister, Haven, for lunch today. After eating his breakfast, he gives me a deep kiss and tells me to enjoy my day with Haven. He reaches for his briefcase and heads for the door. I wait for the door to close before I rise and remove the dishes from the table. I look at the butter knife, wondering if it would puncture my skin and plunge deep into my heart. I calmly load the dishwasher, pretending I am smashing every dish against his handsome head. Wishing he could feel my pain.

Chapter 2

I spot Haven sitting under the red-and-white striped awning on the veranda at the local café. She looks absolutely radiant in a cool blue top that matches her lovely eyes. The town clock in the square rings out one single chime. Everyone in the small town knows it is noon and not one o'clock. The time has been off for at least the past twenty years after the clock was struck by lightning. No one seems to care. I wave.

"Hello beautiful." She stands up to give me a tight hug.

"Oh, Haven, that baby looks as though he is going to pop right out."

She sighs deeply. "I hope it comes before I am done with lunch, I'm so tired of carrying it."

"I hope not, girl, I'm hungry."

The waitress brings us both a glass of water with a slice of lemon.

"I ordered you a glass while I was waiting."

I order a taco salad, and Haven orders a chicken/peach salad.

"Have you decided on names for the baby?"

"Mathew only picked out names for a girl. He is positive I am having a girl, and I think it's a boy."

"I hope you have twins." She just gives me a deadly stare. I am surprised to find out that she wants to have another baby right away and gasp.

"Don't you want children?"

She is aware that my marriage to her older brother is not made in heaven. "I haven't given it a lot of thought as our lives are so very busy." She knows I am lying but doesn't push me any further. The town clock chimes two. "I must leave soon so I can buy Mack's dinner for tonight."

"I am so full I will probably just roll home and take a nap." As I look in my purse for my money, I realize Mack didn't give me enough for groceries and my lunch. Haven quickly reads my dilemma and grabs my check.

"This lunch is on me today." I start to protest, but she just shakes a finger at me. "You can buy me a case of formula for the baby when I have it." We hug and say our goodbyes.

I decide to walk the three blocks to the market. The sunshine on my face feels wonderful. I wish I could have worn short sleeves and shorts, but the bruises would only draw stares. I feel almost alive and decide I hope Mack actually makes it home to enable us to enjoy our meal on the patio. The store is crowded, and I realize even with all the people in the place I know very few. Mr. Tittle is behind the meat counter and smiles as I walk toward him.

"What may I get you on this beautiful day?"

"Do you have any other New York strip steaks besides those in the case?"

"I have some one-inch steaks in the back."

"Two, please."

Mr. Tittle goes into the back just as I notice a man at the end of the aisle staring at me. When I make eye contact with him, he smiles broadly and winks. I can feel myself turning red and turn away. He quickly closes the distance between us.

"I'm sorry for being so forward and hope I haven't offended you."

I smile at him and quietly say, "No problem."

"Do you, come here often?"

I answer before thinking, "Every single day."

He smiles again, and I notice his teeth are very white and very straight, and he has dimples to die for. I am embarrassed and feel like a young schoolgirl. Mr. Tittle comes back with my steaks and asks, "How are these?"

"They are fine."

Mr. Tittle wraps them for me. As I turn to leave, Mr. Stanger touches my arm. "You have a great day." I continue my shopping, and as I walk slowly down each aisle, I am disappointed not to see Mr. Stranger anywhere. I check out and at the door look back to see if maybe I will be able to see him at least one more time.

I feel an excitement I haven't felt in a very long time. What has come over me? For Pete's sake, I'm a married woman. I usually take the bus from the market to my street corner. It is only six blocks, but carrying a couple of bags of groceries can make it difficult. I decide I need to walk off my feelings. As I am walking, I can't help but think of Mr. Stranger. Wow, what a nice-looking man, and he seemed to be so open and friendly. I wonder what it would feel like to be naked under his body. To feel his skin on mine. What would he do if I began to rub him through his tight blue jeans? I'm beginning to perspire, and I have a tingling deep within my lower belly. I want him. I want to feel him buried deep inside me. I begin to tremble uncontrollably, and I am wet. My breath is coming in short puffs, and I think I might pass out from lack of air. I have to take another pill when I get home to calm myself down. I unlock my front door and carry my groceries into the kitchen and place them on the counter. I can't even put the food into the refrigerator. I have to take a shower, I have to cleanse my mind of this craziness, and I have to find my bottle of pills.

I practically run into the master bathroom, frantically looking for my pills. Where on earth did I put them? They are not in the medicine cabinet or in any of the drawers. Forget the damn pills, I will feel better after a long cool shower. I begin to strip my clothes off. As I take my bra off, I look into the full-length mirror. My nipples are hard, and I touch them with my fingertips. It seems to send a streak of heat straight down my stomach and into my moist inner soul. I continue to undress, and still I stare at my body in the mirror. I gently touch myself. I wonder if Mr. Stranger would touch me the same way. I insert my finger, and it feels so good I can't seem to stop myself, and I can't stop watching my reaction to my own touch. I stand with my legs spread with my fingers working in my hot inner being, practically steaming up the mirror. I can hear a far-off ringing. Is it an alarm from my body, telling me to stop? Is it God condemning me for my actions? I climax, and as I watch my release in the mirror, I snap back into reality. It's the phone in the bedroom ringing. I whip open the bathroom door and charge for the phone, answering it breathlessly.

"Hello, what took you so long, darling?" Mack asked in a honey-toned voice. "Why the hell are you out of breath? Are you daydreaming of how you will feel when I fill that hot pussy of yours with my big cock?" Still talking in that sickening sweet voice he uses when he thinks he is being sexy.

"No," I answer far too quickly and far too loud. "I was in the basement when the phone rang, and I ran up the steps to get it." I try to calm my voice. I suddenly feel ashamed of my self-satisfaction and nakedness. I try desperately to control my breathing and my emotions, hoping Mack won't guess as to why I am so worked up. How could he know? But he seems to know everything I think and do during the day when he is not home.

"I'm glad you called, will you be home early enough to eat on the patio?"

"That's why I called. I am working on a murder case and have a ton of research to do. I'll be very late. Don't worry about dinner or waiting up for me." I am praying he doesn't hear the relief in my voice.

"I'm glad you called or I would have done both." I hang up the phone, and I wonder which young intern he will be fucking tonight. I am not jealous of his extramarital activities. I am jealous that he is free to do as he pleases while I am trapped. I begin to laugh uncontrollably and reach a low degree of hysteria. I go lie on my back on the bed and begin to cry. I cry myself into a stupor and then into a restless sleep. I dream of Mr. Stranger standing over me laughing at my body. It is as though he is staring into my soul. I hate him and wish him dead.

Chapter 3

I slowly wake to the darkened bedroom and realize that I am alone and naked. For a split second I have no idea where I am or why I have no clothes on. It all comes rushing back to me, and it overwhelms me until I feel as though I am drowning. The shame, the excitement, the longing, the loneliness, and the hatred. Always the loneliness and always the hatred is with me. I dress and turn on the bedroom TV. The local newsman is talking about another murder in his nasal twangy voice. Why can't they find newspeople with sexy or husky male voices, instead of little skinny nasal twerps to read off a screen in front of them? A photo of a handsome young man flashes on the screen, and nasal man is saying he is the person found murdered in the city park earlier today. The face looks familiar, but I seem to be in a deep brain fog and can't place it. They switch the picture from him to Chief Detective Timothy Mackenzie. Of course Mack would be handling the case. He handles all the homicides for the small town of Flag Lake. This makes five in the last two years. No suspects, no real leads, and many hours of banging his head against a stone wall, when he isn't banging the new assistant, secretary, officer, or waitress in the local bar.

Poor Mack, all that hard work and research into the cases and for nothing. I turn the TV off and walk into the kitchen. I put the groceries away and pour myself a glass of wine. I decide to sit on the patio and sketch while I enjoy the wine we would have had with our steaks. It's really a shame Mack won't be here with me. I laugh out loud at the very thought of wanting him to be here. I prefer the lone-liness to his constant belittling and badgering. Nothing I do is right. Nothing I do to please him is what he wants except for when we are in our bed. He knows he can manipulate me into doing whatever he wants and that my body will react on its own free will. I find that I really don't feel like sketching or doing anything creative. I just sit and stare into the darkening sky, sipping my wine and wondering how it would be outside the fenced-in yard. The ten-foot privacy fence is more to keep me in than to keep others out. The yard is beautiful with its blooming flowers and fountains. The gardener does a wonderful job of keeping it perfect. I often sketch or paint a bloom from one of the many flowers. But this evening I have no desire to make them come alive on my canvas.

I finish my wine and go inside to find something to eat. I really don't feel like cooking anything and choose to eat an apple. It's tart and crisp, and the sound it makes as I bite into it reminds me of what a skull must sound like when it is cracked open by a blunt object. I envision it lying open with the blood oozing from the gaping hole. The white brain matter with tiny red veins running through it like the meat of the apple I am eating. The juice runs down my chin, and I wipe it away with my hand. I stare at my fingers, half expect-ing them to be red like blood. I try to break the thoughts from my head and pick up a magazine on the kitchen counter. It's a detective magazine that Mack subscribes to, and it has many detailed stories of murders and how the detectives solved the cases. I find it amusing how all the articles in the magazine are solved with such ease, and every detective is highly decorated for his achievements. Not so in real-life Flag Lake, South Carolina, where murder cases remain open for years, and there are no decorated detectives with their pictures hanging on the walls in the courthouse.

Chapter 4

It's been over a week since the murder of the young man in the park. It's also been a week since Mack has forced me to make love to him. He has not come home before ten at night, and he is up and gone before six in the morning. It is nine o'clock on this Sunday morning, and I am lying in bed, listening to his breathing. He is still asleep, and he moans softly while he pulls me closer. I wonder how disappointed he will be when he awakes and finds it's me he has reached for and not one of his willing bitches. The phone interrupts my thoughts of Mack and how it would feel if he were completely out of my life. Would I still live in fear, or would I finally find peace? Someday I will know the answer to that plaguing question. Someday soon. Mack reaches for the phone as I pray a silent prayer that it is the police station calling him to come into work. I lay motionless as I listen to his side of the short conversation. I realize it was Mathew and that Haven has gone into labor. He wants us to meet him at the Memorial Hospital in Portsmith. Flag Lake only has a small clinic to handle emergencies and appointments for the common cold and flu. The doctor only comes in once a week in the morning and otherwise the nurse practitioner sees his patients.

Mack insists we take a shower together to save time. Save time my ass. He just wants to fondle me and watch me struggle with my emotions and feel my body react under his skilled hands. I end up giving him the oral sex he wants while the hot water is beating against my head and back. He holds my head in position until I'm not sure whether I am drowning or suffocating from my face being pushed into his lower stomach. Thank God his release is quick to come and I can spit the shit out into the shower without him really knowing whether I swallowed or not. He prefers I keep his "love juice" inside me no matter what. I have no idea how I haven't gotten pregnant these past three years of marriage. We quickly dress and grab a cup of coffee to go. He decides to take the convertible for the fifteen-mile drive to the hospital. The day is beautiful, and the fresh air makes me feel alive. I have my auburn hair pulled back into a simple ponytail, and a few stray hairs whip into my face. Mack traces my jawline as he drives and wraps his fingers around a strand of hair. He gently pulls to get my full attention.

"You will behave yourself while with my family. You will not embarrass me with idle chatter of arts and other stupid crap that no one cares about."

I wince at his cruelty and doubt I will be the center of anyone's attention.

"I promise not to talk unless talked to."

We arrive at the hospital, and Mack has a cigarette before entering the building. He pops a Tic Tac into his mouth, but I can still smell the vile odor on his shirt. I want to tell him it would take more than just a Tic Tac to make him smell good. Of course, I keep my thoughts to myself. This is to be a glorious day for Haven. I love her more than anyone. She is the sweetest woman that I have ever known, and I don't know what I would do without her in my life. We stop at the main information desk to ask for directions to where Haven and Matt would be in the delivery section of the hospital. We are informed they would be on the third-floor maternity ward. As we take the elevator to the third floor, Mack suddenly pulls me into his arms. "I hope soon it will be Matthew and Haven coming here for us. I want us to be the parents." I shudder in his arms, and he believes it is because I am pleased with the idea. However, I'd rather die than give birth to a baby that came from his loins. As the elevator door opens, I am released from his embrace, and we walk slowly out of the elevator.

Mack takes my hand as we ask the nurse at the counter where we can find Matthew and Haven Bricks. She says they are in room 16 just down the hall. I want to ask if she thinks Haven will be in labor a long time but stop myself, knowing Mack would not approve. After all, what the hell would just a nurse know about the length of labor? Haven is lying in bed with a cute pink gown on. She has the IVs and monitors all hooked up to her, but she still looks beautiful. I go to her bedside and give her hand a squeeze.

"You look wonderful."

"I doubt I will when another contraction hits me."

Matthew stands at the foot of the bed, looking worried and proud at the same time. Mack slaps him on the back.

"How are you holding up, Buddy?"

"Truth? I'm scared as hell. I want to go into the delivery room, but I'm afraid I'll make a fool of myself and pass out or punch the doctor."

Haven giggles. "You'll be fine. That's why you went with to the Lamaze classes." He manages a weak smile.

"Christ that was bad enough without actually going through the real thing." Just then Haven is hit with a hard contraction. She lets out a small scream, and Mack comes unglued. His face turns nearly transparent.

"Just how long has this been going on, and why isn't a doctor in here to administer some sort of pain medication?"

"I'm having the baby natural, and this is what happens during a natural delivery."

"Well, this just isn't right."

"Please, will you take Matthew and go downstairs for some coffee and maybe outside for a cigarette. Maybe spike the coffee or something to calm you two down." Neither of them like the idea but leave anyway, grumbling to each other as they're closing the door behind them.

After they leave, Haven sighs. "I'm sure Matthew will drive me nuts while in the delivery room."

"Can I get you anything and somehow make you more comfortable?"

"Maybe a small glass of ice chips."

Before I can give the glass to her, she goes into another contraction. This time it's longer and much harder.

"I feel wet, like I've peed the bed."

I press the call button for her, and the nurse comes in immediately. I step behind the curtain as Haven is being checked. The nurse confirms her water broke and the baby's head is right there. She leaves the room only to return in a moment with a doctor who looks to be about twelve years of age.

"I'm Haven's doctor. I'm Dr. Joseph Steinhoff. Everyone calls me Dr. Joe." Haven is having another contraction just then, and he goes to check her. Looking at her over the end of the bed, he says, "Let's get this party started. Where is your husband, is he not coming into the delivery room with you?"

"I sent him for coffee, and he is probably outside on the patio having a cigarette with my brother." The doctor frowns and she adds, "He doesn't smoke, but my brother, Mack, does."

"Sorry but there just isn't time to run around the hospital and look for him now. You'll have to deliver the baby by yourself."

I have no idea why, but I volunteer to go in with her. "I delivered puppies once."

The doctor laughs and hands me a gown. "Well, I hope she has a healthy baby and not a litter of cute puppies. Although that may just get me into the medical journals if she does."

Chapter 5

Twenty minutes later, Haven gives birth to the most precious baby girl I have ever seen. I cry like a small child who had been hurt when they laid her on Haven's chest to meet her for the first time. I'm happier than I have been since the day of my wedding. In that second, I wish it were me instead of Haven. I stay with Haven in the delivery room while they finish cleaning the baby and doing the postdelivery things they do to the mother. Haven chatters to me about how easy the birth was and how she can't wait to get pregnant again and maybe have a little boy. I just smile and say I can't wait to hold her and to spoil her rotten. It seems to only take a few seconds before they are wheeling Haven and her sweet baby girl out of the delivery room and back into their private room. She is holding her baby girl, and I'm walking next to the bed.

As we enter the room, I see the thunderous look on Mack's face, and all my happiness flies out the window. He practically screams at me, "What were you doing in that delivery room? You had no right to be in there, and what were you trying to do, steal Haven and Matt's baby?"

Matt rushes to Haven's side and starts to cry with pure joy. He apologizes for not being with her and hopes she will forgive him. She hands the baby to him and tells him she was fine with him not being in the delivery room because she had me in there to comfort her. Mack is still raving about how insensitive I am for shoving myself into their special moment. How it always has to be about me. Haven finally realizes what is going on and becomes angry herself.

"Shut your fucking mouth, I am thankful she was with me. Matt would have died in there watching it, so it all turned out for the best."

Mack shuts up, but I can see it isn't over for me. He goes to Haven and kisses her cheek. "I'm sorry, you know I love you. You know how protective I am of you and how selfish my darling wife can be."

Haven just rolls her eyes. The baby starts to cry, and a nurse comes in to tell Haven she needs to feed her baby. Haven is going to be breastfeeding, so I suggest to Mack that we leave and let the family have some time together. He agrees, and we leave after giving hugs and kisses to the new family.

I don't see the slap to the face coming when the elevator door closes. I'm stunned that he would strike me in a public place. I just stand there looking at him like it's the first time I have ever seen him. He doesn't say a word but just grabs my arm and leads me out of the elevator like a naughty two-year-old child. I follow beside him silently, trying not to burst into tears. Once again I have angered him without even trying. I know more is to come. Once in the car, his ranting starts again. He demands that I make sure I apologize to Haven and Matt for being so thoughtless and rude. I vow that I will and ask if he thinks we should send flowers to Haven and the baby. He says he will take care of it because I will surely fuck that up too. I'm surprised when he pulls into the café parking lot and stops the car. I wait for him to get out and come around to open my car door. He hates it when I get out on my own, like a bra-burning bitch. Any woman that thinks she can just do as she likes is a bitch and needs to know her place. It's as if he thinks I will start off running if I get out of the car without him there to guide me.

We sit at a small table in the back of the café. His back is against the wall so he can see everyone in the café and those coming and going. I find it amusing that he thinks everyone is out to get him because he is the chief deputy detective of the small town of Flag Lake. Of course, being able to see everyone, he'll know just when to put on the charm and impress the local ladies. He is such an ass. I wish I could let them all know how mean and cruel he really is. I wish I could show them the bruises. I wish they could hear his words to me when I have upset him, but most of all, I wish one of them would cut his bastard heart out of his body and leave him to die on a cold damp street.

He orders coffee for both of us. I'm not very hungry but also know he's not interested in what I want or how I feel. The waitress comes back and brings our coffee. He orders a hamburger and french fries for himself and a light salad for me. He winks at the young waitress, and I wonder how many times he has made love to her over the weeks she has worked at the café. She looks to be his type. She is young, blond, maybe in college, or maybe a single mother trying to make ends meet. You can tell she finds him attractive, and she knows I mean nothing to him. We eat in silence, and he nods to several who come in to have their lunch. I wonder what his plans are for the rest of the day but know better than to ask him. After we are finished with our meal, he pulls my chair out, and I get up while he throws a tip on the table. I notice the tip is nearly as much as the check is. The waitress must be a special piece of ass to him for him to leave that much for a lunch tip.

We leave the café and are headed for the car when he announces, "I will be dropping you off at home and heading for the rifle range. I'll pick up something for dinner, and we will go see Haven and the baby in the evening. I think it will be nice to see them and the grand-parents with their new grandbaby."

I am relieved that he will not be home for the afternoon but also know it's not the rifle range he is headed for. The waitress must have stirred him up, and he must go find a willing whore to satisfy his sexual hunger. *Better her than me,* I think to myself.

Chapter 6

Once at home I change into shorts and a sloppy shirt and grab a Diet Coke out of the refrigerator and head for my studio. I haven't worked on anything for a while, and today I actually feel like painting. I always have a canvas ready, and my paints are always at hand. I stare at the blank canvas and know exactly what I will paint. I choose watercolors and begin to sketch an outline of what it will be. I have the music on softly and am singing along to the Carpenters, feeling free and wonderfully alive. My studio is the only place I feel safe and happy. It is the one place his being doesn't pour into. The one place he never enters, whether it is physically or in my head. It lets me be me. I paint for over an hour before the phone breaks into my world. I absently answer it, and there is only breathing on the other end.

"Who is this?" Still no voice answers me, only heavy, sick-sounding breathing. "Whom are you looking for?"

A man's voice says, "*You.* I am looking for you, and you will know when I have finally found you."

I slam the phone down and run downstairs to check to see if the windows and doors are all locked and the drapes pulled. I make sure the alarm system is turned on. Mack will think I've gone mad to have everything turned on and locked when he gets home. I won't tell him of the phone call because he will be angry and ask who I am trying to fool. He will tell me he knows it's my lover and that I am only afraid that he will come home early and catch us. No, I will not tell him of the phone call.

I slowly climb the stairs and enter my studio. I feel ill. I feel as though I am going to throw up and my hands are shaking. Why is this happening to me? Why do I keep getting these phone calls, and it's always when I am happy and feel alive? It's as though someone is in my head and can tell my moods and my fears. I hope he does find me. I hope he kills me. I hope he puts an end to this nightmare. I stare blankly at the canvas and the beautiful painting I have started. It is of Haven holding her new baby girl. I start to cry, and I know I can't finish the painting today. I know I may never finish the painting. Mack would not approve of me giving her one of my mediocre paintings. He thinks I can't do anything. I turn off the overhead light and the music then quietly close the door behind me. I am closing the door on my happiness and go downstairs to start a pot of tea.

I notice it has started to rain as I wait for the water to boil, and I wonder what time Mack will be home and if he really will bring something for our dinner. I continue to stare out the kitchen window at rain dripping off the eaves and off the trees in the backyard. It is a silent sort of comfort that comes from each drip. The teakettle begins to boil, and I look for my tea in the cabinet above the stove. I don't hear the car in the drive or the garage door open, but I do hear the cursing from Mack as he has to unlock the door and turn off the alarm system. I wonder what excuse I can get away with today. A phone call from a heavy-breathing man just won't cut it. I decide to tell him I was in my studio, and I can't always hear the doorbell or door open. He may buy that one.

He comes into the kitchen, and I expect him to explode at me for locking him out and turning on the alarm. To my surprise, he says, "Smart move to lock everything up and turn the alarm on. With the new murder in town, it isn't wise for you to go anywhere alone and not to walk outside the house until I find the culprit who is killing." Once again I am his prisoner. I wonder if he will let me visit Haven and the new baby. I don't bother to ask because I know the answer.

He sets a small bag on the counter, and I notice that is contains sub sandwiches. They are not my favorite, but it beats having to make a meal in the mood I am in.

"Why don't we eat early tonight and then we won't be so late seeing my new niece?"

"Good idea, when would you like to eat?"

"I'd like to lie down for an hour or so before eating." He places the subs in the refrigerator. I finish making my tea and go into the library to find the book I had started a few days before. He follows me into the library. "Maybe I wasn't clear enough for you. I would like for us to lie down for an hour or so before we eat." I want to protest, that I just made tea, but know it would be fruitless to try to convince him otherwise. I take the cup of tea back to the kitchen and dump it in the sink while he goes directly to the bedroom. As the tea is slowly going down the drain, I feel as though my soul is being sucked along with it. Down into the abyss of loneliness.

I walk into the bedroom, and he pats the bed beside him. I cross the room and notice he has opened the drapes, and the rain is coming down harder and beating a steady rhythm against the windowpane. The droplets are like tears running down the face of the innocent about to be punished for a crime not committed. I start to lie down, and he reaches for me. His hands are hot and sweaty and remind me of a man who has worked hard all day in the sun. They make me shiver as if I am very cold. He laughs.

"Hold on, we have all afternoon to make each other feel good."

His kiss tastes of cigarettes, and I want to demand he at least brush his teeth. I don't because I know it would anger him, and I don't want to anger him any more today. He is kissing me deeply and is pressing me down into the bed. I am nearly choking from his tongue and his weight on me. I unconsciously struggle, and he raises above me.

"Would you prefer your lover to me?"

I am breathless, and he takes that as a submission to his caresses. His hands are under my shirt, and he is pulling it over my head. He puts his face into my cleavage and begins to suck gently. He rolls me to the side and unhooks my bra and pulls it free from my breasts. He begins to suckle my breasts.

"I hope this will be our son doing this soon." I think I will die before I allow that to happen. Yet I am responding to his sucking and his hands. I reach for him, and he is hard. He groans, "I want you now." He is close to violently removing my shorts, and he strips my bikini panties from my body. He opens his belt and unzips his fly, and his cock springs from his pants like a jack-in-the-box. I have to stifle a giggle with a groan. Lord help me if I should laugh while he is raping me. He doesn't even pull his jeans off. He just plunges into me like a teenage boy hurrying before being caught by the girl's father. His strokes are fast, deep, and painful. Painful because I don't want them. I don't want his seed in me. I don't want a child from him, but most of all, I don't want him.

He pays no heed to my stiffened body and keeps on driving into me. Driving into my soul, taking my dignity with every plunge. He is pounding into my body, only caring for his own release. When it comes, I lie still under him, praying he will be sated and not want to repeat this ungodly coupling. After what seems a lifetime, he rolls off me. He stares at the ceiling and begins to laugh. I turn toward him and wonder at what humor he finds in what he just did to me. He looks over at me and says, "Wow, that has to be the best we've had together in a very long time." I mistakenly don't answer, and he grabs a piece of my hair and cruelly pulls it so my face is within an inch of his. "It's the best, don't you think?" he snarls. I am wincing from the pain of having my hair pulled, and I groan a low guttural groan. He lets go of my hair. "You bitch, you don't deserve my lovemaking. I should bring a homeless bum into the house and let him at your useless body. Then maybe you'd appreciate what I do for you."

"I'm sorry, I was just enjoying the after tremors I always get when you are done loving me."

Kissing me, he says, "I knew it was awesome for you." He slowly removes his clothes. "Get under the covers and we will nap together." I suddenly feel extremely exhausted, and I do fall into a deep peaceful sleep. Only to wake up to his fingers inside of me, stoking me gently. I open my eyes to his face above me smiling down at me. I smell the cigarette on his breath and know he has been awake for a while or maybe never fell asleep at all. His kiss tastes bitter and stale. Yet my body is reacting to his fingers without my consent. My mind is practically screaming no, yet I am moving in rhythm to his stroking fingers. My climax comes fast and hard, and I shudder under his manipulation of my body. He continues to kiss me, and I am waiting for him to rise above me and take his pleasure deep inside me. To my surprise, he kisses me gently.

"Are you okay?"

"Yes." For once I answer him truthfully.

"Let's grab a quick shower and get ready to leave to see Haven."

"Do you want to eat the subs before we leave?"

"You eat while I take a shower and then you can shower while I eat."

Sounds good to me as I won't have to share a shower with him and worry whether I will have to perform oral sex again.

We finish our showers and the subs. Mack seems to be in a very peaceful mood. It feels too good to be true, and I worry when the bomb will be dropped. We drive to the hospital with very little conversation. I am lost in thought when I hear Mack calling my name.

"Elise, have they picked a name out for the baby?"

"Matthew only picked out girl names, so I'm sure they have one by now."

"I hope they somehow include my mother's name. I have always loved my mother's name."

"Rebecca is a very regal name and fits your mother quite well."

Jokingly he says, "They could always name her Marion Louise after your mom."

I laugh with him. "I think not."

We arrive at the hospital, and Mack has a cigarette while I browse in the gift shop. I am holding a tiny pink unicorn when he enters the shop. He takes it from me. "I think it is the perfect gift for the little princess upstairs." He is just full of surprises this afternoon. I am still waiting for the bomb. As we enter the elevator, I remember the last time we are in it and unconscientiously touch my cheek. He sees the absent movement. "Get over it." I quickly remove my hand and look away from his cruel eyes. So much for the peaceful feeling.

Chapter 7

As we walk into the room, I can hear the laughter and the chattering. Both sets of grandparents are there, and they are cooing and talking baby talk to the precious princess all at once. You'd think there wasn't another baby anywhere in the whole world. I decide that the princess will be the most pampered little girl ever born. They barely stop their cooing to welcome us into the room. Mack gives his mom a hug and shakes hands with his dad and nods to the others in the room. He takes the baby from his mom, and he is talking to her and telling her what a lucky little girl she is. He looks so relaxed and a natural with the baby. It makes me for just a split second wish he had a child to love. It's a fleeting moment, and I check to see if anyone may have seen my longing. I hand Haven the tiny unicorn.

"This is the perfect gift for our baby girl."

Mack asks, "What do you plan on naming this little beauty?"

Haven answers with, "Well, it was the very first name we picked out together." All eyes are on her and Matthew, waiting for them to reveal the name. "What do you all think of Rebecca Elise?" she asks with a joy in her voice. Mack's mom begins to cry, and I am just dumbfounded. Why would they use my name?

"Oh, Haven, I am honored."

Then I see the rage in Mack's eyes. He stares at Haven and snidely asks, "Did Elise push her ugly name on you?"

She is hurt, and it shows in her eyes. "I love her, and I love her name, and I can't think of anyone I would rather name our baby after."

Mack has no alternative other than to say, "I was only kidding." I know he meant every word he said.

I love his sister so much. We visit for about an hour until the nurse comes in to shoo us all out. After hugs and kisses, we all leave in a group. Mack's parents suggest we all stop at the Round Up for a quick cocktail before going home. After all, this is a celebration. I can tell Mack doesn't care to but agrees to go so as not to spoil the happiness shared by the others.

Chapter 8

The bar is nearly empty, and we are seated at a table toward the back of the place. Once again Mack sits with his back against the wall. He is sullen, and I'm not sure if it's because he doesn't want to be at the bar, or if it's because of the name Haven and Matt picked out for the baby. He didn't say a word to me while we were driving to the bar, and I didn't initiate any conversation. The grandparents are so happy and are chatting about the baby and how glad they are she had an easy time in delivery. Mack's mom reaches over and squeezes my hand and thanks me for going into the delivery room. Matt's parents both say they are so grateful that I was available. Mack turns to me and says, "Yes, she is such a lifesaver when it makes her the center of attention." Everyone turns to stare blankly at him. I want to crawl under the table and somehow melt, seeping into the dirty cracks in the floor.

The waitress comes and saves us all from the awkward moment Mack has created. Everyone orders a mixed drink except for me. I order Diet Coke. Mack's mom quickly asks if I am pregnant, to which I answer, "No, not that I know of."

With mischief in her eyes, she says, "Mack, maybe you should get on the ball to change that status."

I look at Mack and can sense that he is angry and is thinking I am talking of our love life with his mother. I answer, "Maybe someday, we are trying." He seems to be pleased that I have said we are at least trying to have a baby.

The conversation turns to the new murder in Flag Lake. Mack is pleased to be the center of the conversation and happy to tell what he can about the poor man. His father asks if the man is a local, as the name has not been released yet. Mack tells the eager ears that the man is in his early thirties and has just moved to the area. He continues to tell them that he has spent the last few days checking into the man's background to see if there is any connection to a mob, gangs, drugs, or other organization that would have caused him to be murdered. So far, it seems he is a clean-cut young man just trying to start over in small town America. He tells them he can't say too much more about the case as it is an ongoing investigation.

His mother asks him if it's true that a group of young children found his body and that his skull was smashed in. He tells her in his most authoritative voice that, yes, a group of ten-year-olds found him, and yes, his head was smashed in. She then gently reaches across the table and tells him that Flag Lake is so lucky to have him on the case. I have to stifle a giggle. Really? He's worked all five murder cases without any success, so just how lucky are the citizens of Flag Lake having him in charge?

He of course eats up the attention and sits there like a male peacock showing off his colors. His own father spoils his preening.

"I hope you have better luck with this one than the last four."

I actually choke. "My soda went down the wrong pipe." Too late, Mack gives me a look of pure contempt. The bomb will fall in the car when we leave. I wish now I had ordered a mixed drink. Maybe even a double.

His mother adds, "How awful for those children to have had to see something so traumatic at such a young age. It will probably scar them for a very long time."

"I've arranged for them, along with their parents, to receive counselling from the local shrink."

She seems to be pleased with his wise actions. "You are such a good person. You are always thinking of others' welfare."

I am, on the other hand, thinking of what a momma's boy he is. Throw in a cruel fucking jerk and you have the famous detective of Flag Lake in a nutshell. I remain silent and only half listen to the rest of the conversation. It is not until I hear Mack speak my name that I come out of my own little world.

"Are you ready to leave and go home? After all, I have a long day tomorrow working on the murder case and all the other things that are thrown onto his desk in the course of the day." I agree it is time for us to leave and wait for Mack to help me with my chair. I hug his mother and Matt's mom. I know better to hug the other two men at the table. Even though they are my father's age and are more of a father to me than my own, I know Mack would read something sexual into the hugs. With goodbyes out of the way, we leave, letting the others there enjoy each other's company over another cocktail. I'm sure they are discussing that precious granddaughter of theirs. They will have her whole future planned before the evening has come to an end and they go their separate ways.

Mack opens my car door and waits patiently while I get into the car. He seems to anyone watching the most considerate husband on the planet. Once he enters the car, the bomb begins to explode.

"Just what the hell did you mean by laughing at me in front of my parents and Matt's?"

I know better than try to lie. "I wasn't laughing. I really did choke. I'm sorry." As I am fastening my seat belt, he reaches his hand out in a snakelike movement and places it around my throat. The pressure starts out light.

"I should kill you right here in the car and dump your ugly body in the lake on the way home." He increases the pressure and continues with, "You ungrateful bitch, one of these days I may just choke you to death. It would serve you right and give me great pleasure to see the life drain out of your deceitful eyes as I squeeze my fingers around your white throat." His tone is evil and menacing. I neither move nor do I cry out in pain. I just sit there thinking how it would be if he would just once follow through with his threats.

The ride home is done in complete silence, with only the sound of the windshield wipers whishing back and forth, wiping away the rain from the glass. It is calming, and I fall into a dreamlike trance watching them move back and forth. It seems almost sexual. I begin to daydream about Mr. Stranger. Just as quickly as his face appears in my thoughts I am jerked back into reality. I suddenly remember the picture of the murdered man on TV and know that he is Mr. Stranger. Oh my god, that beautiful man must have been murdered right after I met him in the grocery store. I can't remember what the time was when I was in the store. No, wait, it had to be shortly after one o'clock. He was probably murdered while I was masturbating in bathroom. What if he was killed just as I climaxed? I want to ask Mack if they know what time he was murdered, but I don't want to bring up the subject. Not now, not while Mack is angry over my actions at the Round Up. I feel as though my evil actions somehow was involved in his murder. God help me, I am losing my mind. Was it his murderer who called me and said he was looking for me? Was I next on the list to be murdered? No, it couldn't be, because I have had the phone calls before. I always thought it could be one of the convicts Mack actually did put away trying to get revenge and that I am an easy target. I feel the emptiness and loneliness creeping up inside me. It's a feeling I have no control over, and the hurt is deep. I am so engrossed in my thoughts I fail to realize we are home and that he has pulled the car in the garage. Mack slaps me on the back of the head.

"Stop daydreaming about your lover, we are home. Get out of the fucking car and go into the house."

"Aren't you coming in too?"

"What the hell do you care if I'm home or not?"

I pathetically answer. "I care."

"You only care because you can't call your lover and talk to him, or maybe even have him come over."

"Don't talk so crazy. With all the surveillance cameras on the property, something as small as a hummingbird couldn't escape being on video."

"Just get the hell out of my car."

He doesn't have to tell me twice and I practically jump from the car. I am opening the kitchen door as he is backing out of the garage. I hear the garage door shut and breathe a sigh of relief knowing he won't be home until late. He is angry and worked up and will find his relief with one of his whores. Maybe the cute blond waitress.

Chapter 9

It's only a little after eight and so I decide to relax a bit before trying to sleep. I start water to make a cup of tea and find the cookies in the pantry. I feel I need something sweet to help stop the nagging feeling of emptiness and loneliness that has taken up space in my soul. I know guilt will be added to those feelings after I eat a package of my favorite cookies. I really don't care right this second if I gain 150 pounds. I want to dunk my cookies into my tea. I plan on using a full teaspoon of sugar in my tea and maybe a touch of sweet cream. That should put me into a sugar coma. Hopefully it will help me fall asleep. With my tea made, sugar and all, cookies in hand, I head for the library. I will enjoy my sweet treat and read the book I have started and can't seem to get back to. Mack won't be home until late, and I will have eaten all the evidence. He would be appalled to know I ate like this and also that I had the nerve to eat in the library. Why, a crumb might fall onto the plush carpet, or I might spill my tea on the leather couch. If he only knew.

I turn the lamp on next to the leather couch and grab a fleece blanket to curl up in, finding my book on the desk where I had left it earlier in the day. I settle onto the couch with my tea, cookies, book, and blanket and start to feel at peace. The book is about a city girl going to Cajun country. Really well written and humorous yet serious. I finish my cookies and my tea and think I should take the plate and cup back into the kitchen and put them into the dishwasher but want to finish the chapter I'm on. I'm awakened to a stinging slap to my cheek. I jump, and the book drops off my lap.

"You fucking piece of shit!" he is yelling at me. "How dare you eat and drink in the library. How dare you turn into a fat cow." He yanks me off the couch by my hair. He whirls me around so my face is within an inch of his angry, distorted face, holding me firm by the hair. All sleep has fled from my brain as I stare into his fiery eyes. At that precise second, I'm thinking he may be the devil himself. "Look at you, thinking you can sneak in here and eat and drink your fucking tea. Who the hell do you think you are? The queen of Sheba? Did you honestly think you would get away with disobeying my orders to keep your shit out of my library?" He's raging at me all the while spitting foul-smelling whiskey breath into my face. My hair is pulled so tight away from my face I'm afraid to answer for fear the movement of my mouth would pull chunks of my hair out. He thrusts me away from him and onto the sharp corner of the coffee table. I feel it bite deep into my side. The pain is so sharp and deep I'm sure he managed to crack one of my ribs. I gasp for air and try to get up off the floor. He comes around the table to grab me once again by my hair and pulls me up. The pain shoots through me, and that is all I remember until waking up in our bed. I must have passed out with him still hanging onto my hair. My first thought is *Why didn't he just kill me when he had the chance?* But that would be too easy of a death for me.

I lie there, not moving, trying to sense if he is lying beside me or even in the room. I gently feel my side and find it to be tightly wrapped. Did he do this himself or did he call a doctor? I would have laughed at the last thought if the pain would have been any less. I open my eyes to find him standing over me with a smirk on his face. I thought, *Oh dear god, this isn't over yet.*

"How do you feel?" I don't answer but just turn my face away. He bends over me and yells, "Look at me, you stupid bitch!"

I turn to find his hands clutching a glass of what looks like bourbon. He holds it as though it will leap from his hands if he loosens his grip. I have no idea how much time has lapsed since I passed out but know it must not have been too long or he would not be still drinking. Seeming to read my mind, he states it is only one in the morning and that he plans on calling into work and taking a vacation day. That in itself should be a red flag, but my mind seems muddled, and things seem to be moving at a very slow pace. Even though I know, I try to ask him what happened, only to find my tongue thick and dry in my mouth. It feels as though I have slept for a week breathing only through my mouth. I try to swallow away the feeling, but I have difficultly even doing that. I have no saliva in my mouth and manage a weak-croaking sound deep in my throat.

"Oh, does the stupid bitch need a drink?" he asks with a sneer. I nod, and to my horror, he grabs the back of my head and thrusts me upright with such force that the pain feels like a hot sword piercing through my side. I grasp the blanket and open my mouth to groan. He isn't done with me yet and forces the glass of bourbon to my open lips and pours it into my mouth. I instantly choke on the burning liquid and start to cough uncontrollably. Dear Lord, please let me die now for I can't bear the searing pain in my side or him. I'm sure I'm going to pass out again and pray for the peace it would bring. He laughs at me and thrusts a bottle of water into my hands. I'm too weak to get the cap off. I finally let it lie on the bed and try to ease myself back down.

"You really are pathetic tonight, my dear," he says in a jesting tone. He opens the bottle for me and warns me, "You better not spill that shit on the bed, or I will drown you with the rest of the bottle."

I manage to take a sip, soothing my burning dry throat. I want to scream for him to just kill me. Instead I just remain silent waiting for him to continue his torture. Surprisingly he informs me, "I won't be sleeping in the bed with you tonight and probably never again." Bending over me, he says, "Your eyes deceive you, and I can see that that would please you immensely." He jumps over me like playing leapfrog to his side of the bed and pounces on his knees like a little boy who was excited over receiving a new bike on Christmas Day. Dear God, please let me die. I vow I will kill the bastard if I manage to live to recover. He finally crawls from the bed. "I'm going downstairs. By the way, how many of those fucking anxiety pills can you take before you die?" He laughs as he closes the door, and I think, oh shit, he gave me an overdose of my own medication. People will think I drank and took and overdose, and the bastard will be freer than he is now. Without a wife to curb his ambitions, his sexual desires, because she committed suicide. I played right into his hands.

I wake around three in the morning when I try to turn over to my left side. A shooting pain brings me wide awake and gasping for breath. Shit, I haven't died in my sleep after all. I try sitting up and find I can, but the pain is excruciating and makes me feel as though I may vomit. The fear of wetting myself in the bed wins out over the pain and I try to stand. I hang onto the bedpost and take my first halting step toward the master bathroom. I slowly walk to the dark-ened room, taking baby steps, expecting to collapse in a puddle on the middle of the floor. I manage to make it into the bathroom and switch on the light. My reflection in the mirror will frighten even the bravest of heart. I have a gash on my temple above my right eye and the blood dried around my eye and onto my upper cheek. Making it look as though someone had tried to pry my eyeball out of its socket. I have a bruise on my right cheek and decide the gash was from Mack's college ring he wears on his left hand instead of a wedding band. My hair is in a disarray of snarls, sticking to my head in places and standing out in others. I closely resemble a madwoman who has escaped from an asylum. I gently lower myself down onto the toilet and pee. I feel so weak and tired, I doubt I will have the strength to get off the toilet and walk back to my bed. Once more in an upright position I decide I might as well try to clean the blood from my face. I run warm water and cup my hands to fill them and bend to splash my face. Bending over is a mistake as a wave of dizziness assaults me. I grab the counter for support and take deep breaths, which is also a mistake. Dear god, there is that searing pain in my side again. Surely I will die before the morning. Finding it nearly impossible, I manage to reach for a washcloth hanging on the towel rack. I gently begin to wash my bruised and cut face. I look like death warmed over and feel even worse. My head aches, and I'm sure I'm a crystal glass that is about to shatter from the sound of a shrill voice. I feel the side of my head where my hair is matted and find a lesion there too. I take the warm, wet washcloth and press it to the cut, bringing it away to find it bloodstained. I tenderly try to brush the hair on the other side. I can't endure standing much longer and turn to walk into the bedroom. I leave the light on in the bathroom so I can see to walk to the bed.

Before I reach my destination, the door opens, and Mack strolls into the room like a cat who has just cornered a mouse. He seems proud of his accomplishments.

"I thought I heard you moving around up here. Oh my, you look like shit, tsk, tsk. What have you done to yourself, my pretty? You won't be going anywhere until you are all healed up. You should really be more careful while taking prescription drugs and drinking. One never knows how one's mind and body will react to those." He's smiling and using an overly friendly tone.

"Leave me alone, Mack, haven't you done enough? I believe I have a cracked rib, if not a couple, and I have a large cut on my head and one above my eye. I suppose you will tell everyone I inflicted this all on myself while you were out saving the town? Who was she this time, Mack, the waitress, a new office employee, one of your old girlfriends? Who did you fuck after you dropped me off? Or maybe, none of them were available, and it was just more than you could handle. No one wanting the great Tim Mackenzie."

"You are pushing the limits, Elise. I should show you what a beating really is like. I should just put you out of my life for good. Maybe I will." He is coming toward me. I try to shield my face as he raises his hand to strike me. He stops suddenly and instead encircles my shoulders and helps me to the bed. He gently helps me lie down. "I'll bring you some tea."

I wanted to tell him to be sure to add enough pills this time to kill me but hold my tongue. I vow in my head to kill the bastard if I survive this ordeal.

He brings me a cup of chicken broth instead of the tea. "It'll help you heal, don't you want to get better fast?"

I'm thinking, *Yes, I do, and then I plan on slitting your throat the very next time you fall asleep.* Spending the rest of my life in a prison cell with Big Barbara couldn't possibly be as bad as existing here with him. As I drink my broth, he sits on the edge of the bed.

"You know, Elise, I love you, and I wish you would stop doing things like this."

I feel like throwing the hot liquid in his smiling face and yelling, "You did this, you asshole! You must have hit me or kicked me while I was passed out to get these kinds of injuries." I say nothing and just let him go on and on about his everlasting love for me and how he couldn't wait until I was better so we could go visit little Becca.

"Is that what Matt and Haven decided to call the baby?"

"I don't give a rat's ass what they call her, I plan on calling her Becca. And I'm going to try to forget they chose your fucking name for her middle name." I didn't say anything more. I finished my broth. "Just rest the remainder of the night."

I sink deep into the pillow and must have fallen into a deep dreamless sleep before he even left the room. I awoke to Mack singing "Come and Get Your Love" by Redbone. For a split second I had forgotten what happened to me, until I tried to get up and suddenly was sure a Mack truck ran me down the night before. Mack comes into the bedroom carrying a breakfast tray with a rose and a pot of hot coffee. There is scrambled eggs and buttered whole-wheat toast. He knows I hate whole-wheat toast and eggs period. He is just doing this to make me seem ungrateful and bitchy if I say anything. He fluffs my pillows and pours me a cup of coffee. I take a sip, and then I try to eat the eggs without gagging. I take a bite of the toast and wish I had at least a bit of jelly to add to the tasteless shit. But then jelly will just add inches to the belly, isn't that how the saying goes. Mack sits in the chair next to the bed and sips his coffee while closely watching every bite I take. I begin to wonder if this will be my last meal. Geez, maybe I should have had it blessed before I started to gag the crap down. I think to myself, *Maybe I'm just overthinking the situation.* While he is sitting there silently glaring, I decide to go over the facts.

Chapter 10

He's angry over me going into the delivery room. He's angry over the name they picked out. He's angry over everything. He's just angry. The house phone rings and interrupts the silence and my thoughts. It usually is his mother or the station calling. I pray it's the station calling him into work for something only the infamous Mack can handle. Much to my regret, it is his mother.

"No, Mom, I'm at home today. Elise took a tumble down the basement stairs, and I decided to stay home and keep an eye on her. No, she's just fine. She has a few scrapes and bruises, but she will live. Oh yeah, I forgot we even had that. It's in the attic. I'll get it down immediately. What time will that be? Sure, we wouldn't miss it for the world," he's saying with a big grin on his face. I have eaten all that I can, and as he hangs up the phone, I lift the tray off my lap and wince from the pain in my side.

"Well, sweetness, we are going to be at Haven's this afternoon when she comes home," he announces as he stands up to retrieve the tray from the side of the bed. I want to cry and tell him I just can't go, but I know that is not an option. He looks at me and says, "You'd better suck it up, buttercup, After all, if you weren't so careless with your pills and booze, you'd have never taken that tumble down the basement stairs." Ah, so that is the story he plans on telling everyone. "Get your fat ass out of bed and take a shower so you will at least look halfway presentable." He is whistling as he leaves the room.

I struggle out of bed and begin to unwrap my ribs. Holy shit, I am bruised all down my side and onto my hip area. He truly did a number on me. I manage to make it to the shower, and the hot water actually feels good. Hurts like hell when it hits some of the bruises, but then it feels good on others. It's almost like a "hurts so good" experience. As I am drying myself off, I have to hang onto the bathroom counter as every time I try to bend over to dry my legs, I nearly take a header onto the tile floor. Not sure I will survive this afternoon. I am nauseous, and I suddenly have to throw up. No, no, no, please God no. It doesn't help to pray, and I hang onto the back of the toilet as I spew the eggs into the bowl. My head is spinning like a top, and I sink down onto the cold tile floor. I just have to rest a minute and get my balance.

Mack comes in to see me lying on the floor, and I can't stop the flow of tears running down my cheeks and dripping onto the blue tile. Instead of helping me up, he steps over me and starts the water for his shower. Finally looking at me with disgust, he says, "Oh, for Christ sake, Elise, I'm done with your bullshit, get your ass up and get dressed or I swear I will get you up and throw you back down the stairs."

I pull myself into a sitting position. "I can't get up without your help." Instead of helping me, he gives me a sharp kick to the calf of my leg.

"I said get up, Elise, I mean it."

I reach up and grab the counter and manage to rise to my feet. I'm afraid to take a step for fear I'd collapse again but more afraid not to. I carefully walk to the bed and sit down. I beg God to just let me die. What did I ever do to deserve this pain? I must have been a terrible person in a previous life. That made me giggle thinking maybe Mack would get his karma in the next life.

I slowly begin to dress, and as I do, I begin to think of poor handsome Mr. Stranger. Would he have been kind to me? Would he have made love to just me, and would I have satisfied him? Would he have really laughed at my body like he did in my dream? I doubt it. After all, these are my thoughts, so to me, he would have been the most handsome, loving man ever.

Mack comes strolling into the bedroom from the bathroom just as I was smiling to myself. "Oh, honey, I know you love what you see, but I doubt you could take all this with your body so beat up." Using a sarcastic tone while holding onto his cock, he says, "Don't worry, baby, I'll give it to you tonight after we get home. By then you will be begging me for it, like you always do." He bends to kiss my neck. I find him so repulsive I can't help the shivers that ripple down my body. He just laughs and starts to dress.

He had gone into the attic while I was showering and brought down the family bassinet that was encased in plastic. Both he and Haven had been placed into the lovely hand-carved oak bed when they were brought home from the hospital. It was given to us because everyone just assumed Mack and I would have a baby first. I personally am happy to get it out of the house as it is an ugly reminder of how much I hate Mack and how much I don't ever want his child! I ask if he has brought down the baby blanket that was lying next to it. He says he'll get it now. I'm just relieved he didn't tell me to go get it.

We have a few hours before we are to leave for Haven's, and to my surprise, Mack suggests I rest those hours before we leave. I finish with my hair and makeup and relish the idea of just being able to lie down. I take my pills and settle on the top of the bed. I can hear Mack on the phone talking to the police station. I only hear bits and pieces of the conversation, but apparently, they are combing the entire town for clues on who may have seen anything or heard anything in regards to Mr. Stranger's murder. I fall asleep thinking, what a shame that such a beautiful man had to die so violently. My dreams are of peace and of being held in the arms of Mr. Stranger. Unfortunately, I am awakened to Mack's voice saying, "That must have been one hell of a dream. You were moaning like you were having the best sex ever. Too bad your lover can't see you now, I'm sure he would be repulsed at the very sight of you. Get up, it's time to leave."

Chapter 11

The trek to the garage and the ride over to Haven's nearly makes me pass out. We drive in silence except for Mack screaming obscenities to the drivers he doesn't see fit to be on the road. Once we pull into the driveway, I know the lecture would begin.

"Don't you even try to be the center of attention with your fucking 'Oh poor me' act. I swear, Elise, I will have you committed for a drug overdose if you try any shit today," he warns through gritted teeth. I never respond, and he yells, "Do you fucking hear and understand me, you stupid bitch!" I just nod and wait for him to get out and open my door. I struggle to get out, trying to look as normal as possible. Mack takes the bassinette out of the back of the car, and we start up the driveway. Mack's dad comes to meet us and holds the door open for Mack and me. His mother quickly comes over and starts to undo the plastic from around the bassinette. Mack instructs me to help her. As I'm helping hold the plastic, his mother looks at me for the first time.

"Oh good lord, child. You look horrid!" she exclaims in an alarmed voice.

Mack says, "Well, that's what happens when you mix anxiety pills and booze. You fall down the damn basement steps."

His mother just looks at him like he's nuts. She takes my hands and begin to check me over. "When Mack said you were hurt, I never dreamed it was to this extent. My god, girl, where else are you hurt?" She begins to frantically run her hands over my back, and when she comes too close to my side, I flinch. She immediately pulls up my blouse and cries in alarm, "Jesus, Mack, why the hell didn't you immediately take her to the emergency room? Are you that damn dumb?"

Mack yells back with such venom I thought he was going to explode. "Me, dumb? That stupid bitch is the one who fell and the one who insisted on not going into the emergency room. She didn't want the whole town to know she is addicted to booze and pills."

His mother responds just as venomously, "I doubt that was the real reason, and don't you ever talk to me that way again. I'm driving her in right now, she needs medical attention, and you need a brain, my dear son."

"No, really, I'm fine," I plead. But Mack's dad takes over.

"Oh no, you're not, now let Rebecca drive you in."

"What about Haven and the baby?" I ask weakly.

"Don't you make no never mind about Haven and the baby, they'll be here when we get back," Rebecca states firmly.

Mack stays with his father while Rebecca drives me to the ER.

"I'm fine, honest. Mack is going to be upset that you drove me to the doctor when this is supposed to be Haven's day."

Rebecca isn't listening to me and is driving as though the devil himself is after us. Once at the ER, she jumps out and runs in to get an EMT to assist me out of the car and into a wheelchair. The doctor on duty is a nice-looking young man in is early forties. After the initial introductions, he carefully begins his examination. He asks Rebecca to please leave the room for a few minutes while he does a more complete exam. Once she is out of the room, he turns to me and says, "Do you want to tell me what really happened to you?"

"I tumbled down the stairs while on my anxiety pills and bourbon."

He gently takes my hands in his. "I've been a doctor long enough to know the difference between someone getting the snot beat out of them and falling down a staircase."

I start to cry and, between sobs, manage to squeak out, "Please, you have to believe me."

He states in a no-nonsense tone, "Normally I would report this to the authorities, but seeing your husband would be investigating this, I'll keep quiet. But if you ever come into this ER with injuries like this again, I will go to the County Sheriff's Department, do you understand?"

I nod and respond with a weak "Thank you."

He calls Rebecca back into the room and explained that the x-rays show two broken ribs, a concussion, and two lesions to the head. Not to mention the many other bruises to my torso and extremities.

"I'll prescribe a strong painkiller and bed rest for at least the next five days. No getting up except to go to the bathroom, and then you are to be assisted. Your concussion is severe enough that if you bump your head just a little, it could start a brain bleed that would kill you. No lifting anything heavier than a fork full of mashed potatoes, drink plenty of water, and stay in bed. Is there anyone who can take care of you for the next few days?"

Rebecca responds, "She will be staying at my house."

Chapter 12

We leave the ER two hours later. "I am so sorry for spoiling the baby's homecoming."

"It's okay, I'm sure there will be many more babies' homecomings to attend." I'm secretly was afraid of what Mack will say and what he'll do once we are alone. As if reading my mind, she states firmly, "Don't you worry about Mack, I'll take care of him." As we turn into Haven's driveway, I notice the garage door is open, but her minivan is not parked in it. Rebecca toots the horn to get the attention of the men inside the house. Mack comes out with a sneer on his face. Rebecca gets out of the driver's side. "She has two broken ribs and a concussion that is so bad that if she even thinks of bumping her head a little, she will get a brain bleed that will kill her almost immediately."

Mack's mouth hangs open in surprise. "You have got to be shitting me."

"Yes, so she will be staying at our house for the next week so I can baby her and make sure she is taken care of properly. I will not have any argument from you, do you understand, Timothy?" He just glares at me and nods. "Now come along, dear, let's get you settled on the couch." She gently helps me walk to the door. "Where is Haven's minivan?"

"They were delayed at the hospital. Something to do with lost paperwork, they should be here any minute."

With Rebecca's help, I am propped up on the couch with a glass of water and a blanket over my legs. Once she and Gerald are out of the room, Mack looks at me and said, "You really are a fucking attention-seeking bitch, aren't you?" I don't answer him, and he continues with "I should just punch you in the head and watch you die." Just then there is a horn honking in the garage.

"They're here, they're here," Rebecca exclaims, clapping her hands. Gerald swings the kitchen door open to the garage and rushes out. Haven is practically carried in by her father, and Mack ushers Matt in, patting him on the back with every step. Rebecca brings the baby in and is crying with joy. I lie on the couch with tears streaming down my face. Everyone is laughing and talking all at once, oohing and ahhing over the baby.

Haven notices me on the couch and gives out a small scream. "Oh god, what the hell happened to you?"

Wiping a tear from my face, I say, "I fell down the basement steps."

"Well, you look like someone beat the stuffings out of you. Dear lord, how did it happen?" She sits next to me.

Mack takes over from there. "She apparently decided to go down into the basement after consuming her anxiety pills and half a bottle of bourbon. You know what a total dumb bitch she can be," he adds for good measure.

Haven glares at him. "Careful, bro, I suspect you pushed her with your quick temper." Mack doesn't say another word, while his mom proceeds to clue Haven and Matt in on my injuries. Haven agrees that it is a wise idea for me to stay with her mom.

The rest of the evening goes past in a flash. The rest take turns holding Becca and changing her. Mack even sings to her while holding her. It is a bittersweet time for me. I wants to hold the baby so bad, but I don't think I'd be able to without dropping her. Mack finally agrees to run home and get a couple nightgowns for me and a robe. Only because Haven insists that he do it. I am finally escorted out into Gerald and Rebecca's BMW, and we are headed to their house on the shores of Flag Lake. Mack promises to stop by after work the next day and see how I am. By the look on his face, I can tell he hopes I die in my sleep that night. I won't put it past him if he thinks he can sneak into his parents' house and smash me in the head during the night. I believe he would. The grandparents chat about Becca and how they plan to surprise the kids on her baptismal with a trip to Belize for a week. Of course, they would have to take care of the baby. Maybe they would share her for a day or so with Matt's parents. But seeing how they still work and aren't retired, it would be hard for them to actually keep the little thing overnight. I have to laugh to myself at how well they have planned it all out. It's as though they had planned all this the day Haven told them she was pregnant.

Chapter 13

Once at the house, I'm taken directly to the downstairs guest room. It's a lovely room with pale-yellow walls and brighter yellow drapes covering the patio doors. The doors lead onto a private deck that overlooks the lake and is quite beautiful in the evenings. Rebecca helps me into a nightgown and promptly puts me to bed. She makes sure the TV remote and my phone are near at hand. She then quietly closes the door and says she'd bring me a tray of food for dinner in an hour or so. The drapes are open and gives me a beautiful view of the beach and lake. A teenage couple walks barefoot through the sand, stopping to steal a kiss. A cool breeze comes through the screened doors, and it feels wonderful. I feet at complete peace. A feeling I don't always enjoy. I must think of some special way to thank my in-laws for their kindness. The unfinished painting of Haven and Becca will be perfect. I'll have to finish it and give it to them when Mack is not around. He won't dare say anything about it once they hang it up. I was just thinking of how to accomplish that when Rebecca comes into the room with a tray of the most wonderful-smelling food. She has mashed potatoes and gravy, a most scrumptious-looking piece of beef roast, and tiny glazed carrots. I giggle when I see the mashed potatoes.

"Mashed potatoes because the doctor stated that I was to lift nothing heavier than a fork full of mashed potatoes?"

"No, Gerald loves them, and he likes the carrots too."

I don't hesitate to dig in as I remember I haven't eaten since this morning, and I'm ravenous. She sits with me as I eat, and out of the blue she states, "I don't think for a minute that it was pills and booze that made you fall down the steps." I nearly choke on a bite of half-chewed beef roast and just stare at her. "I know you better than that, and I also know my son. He was probably being a pain in the ass, and you just were in a hurry to get away from him and slipped on the stairs. I know how annoying he can be when he has a drink or two in him. I know you don't even like bourbon."

"Thank you, I wasn't drinking but honestly don't remember all the details as to what really happened. One minute I was up and the next minute I was coming awake in our bed all beat up."

"Well, the main thing is that you are okay and will heal in peace here at our home."

"I'm sure Mack will be here tomorrow after work, and he will come to his senses and see that this is the best place for you. Is there anything else that you might need while I'm in here?" she asks kindly while standing and reaching for my now empty tray.

"A drink of water with lemon please, and then I think I will try to get some sleep." She bends and gives me a motherly kiss on top of the head and promises the water in a flash. "I do have to go to the bathroom." She gently helps me from the bed and watches me as I walk to the bathroom. She's discreet enough to close the door part-way while I ease myself onto the seat and do my toilet. She's at my side to help me up and back into the bed. "Thank you for the water, lovely dinner, and kindness." She quietly leaves me alone to try to rest or to just think.

She comes in around ten to give me my painkillers, and I fall into a deep sleep shortly after she closes the bedroom door. I awake to a shrill scream that sounds like it's from someone being brutally beaten. Over and over the scream intrudes my sleep. The sound of Rebecca's voice gently calling me brings me fully out of my sleep.

"It's just a bad dream, honey. You are safe now," she's saying as she's rubbing my forehead.

"I'm so sorry for waking you, I have no idea what has come over me."

"It's okay, Elise, after what you've just gone through, I can understand a bad dream. I'll get you some warm milk to help calm you down. You can have another painkiller if you need one."

I hate milk in general and hope I don't spew the warm yucky stuff up. I just don't have the heart to tell her I hate the stuff. She arrives with a tray, and on it is a large cup of warm milk and a few Oreo cookies on a plate. Great, two things I don't like at all. I'm probably the only person on earth that hates Oreos and milk.

"Here you go, this will help you calm down. There is nothing like a cup of warm milk and a few Oreos to make the boogeyman stay at bay." I just nod and reach for the wretched stuff, hoping my facial expressions won't give my true feelings away. After choking down both, I'm ready for a trip to the bathroom again and maybe get a bit more sleep.

She actually turns a night-light on for me so I will feel safer and offers to stay until I fall asleep. I feel like a three-year-old and am a bit embarrassed.

"I'll be fine, and I hope I didn't wake up Gerald and the neighborhood with my ungodly screeches."

"Gerald is still snoring away, and the neighborhood is fast asleep." She quietly closes the door, and I try to remember what my dream was. It doesn't take me long to conjure up the frightening images of my dream. I'm standing over Mr. Stranger with an iron bar, and I had bashed his beautiful skull in. Mack is standing next to me, encouraging me to hit him again to make sure he is dead. Mack says he doesn't deserve to live for what he had done to me. I reach for a Kleenex to wipe the tears that are now rolling down my cheeks. I can't remember what Mr. Stranger had done to me in the dream, but I'm sure it didn't deserve me bashing his head in. Why would Mack be so adamant that he did something and that it warranted me killing him so violently? It takes forever for me to fall back to sleep.

Chapter 14

After two days of Rebecca babying me, I'm sure I'm ready to go home. My head doesn't hurt anymore, and my side is feeling much better. I'm almost happy to see Mack after he's done with work and am hoping in a way that he will insist I come home with him. To my surprise, he takes one look at me and says, "You still look like shit."

"Well, thank you very much, that's what I was aiming for."

His mother is right behind him. "For Christ sake, Mack, you sure can be an asshole. I thought I raised you better than that. Just what the hell is wrong with you?"

"I always call a spade a spade when I see it, and she looks like shit." He shrugs his shoulders. After that, I decide to stay at least one more day under the care of Rebecca. Mack stays and sits with me for a short time before going into the kitchen and getting something to eat. I want to sit at the breakfast nook and be with the rest of the family, but Rebecca says no to the idea. I sit in bed with a tray over my lap, eating the spaghetti and feeling sorry for myself, while they are in the kitchen. I'd have gotten up and marched in there, but I'm really not too sure of myself after Mack told me I looked like shit. Maybe he knows something about my body and looks that I don't.

He comes back in and starts to tell me about the murder case. "I found out something very interesting about you that day." He cocks his head and is smirking.

"What? What are you talking about?" I ask, surprised and a little bit afraid of what he might say. I'm thinking of the dream. Did he see me bash Mr. Stranger in the back of the head for real?

"Mr. Tittle said you were talking to the victim while ordering the steaks for our dinner that night. Just what the hell were you talking to a stranger for, Elise, and what the hell were you telling him? Did you tell him what time to meet you at home? When I would be at work and the two of you could get it on?"

"No, oh god no." I can feel my face flush. "He just happened to be in the store at the same time and came up to me and asked if the store was a good place to shop. Honest, I hardly spoke to him."

"Really, because Mr. Tittle said he was touching you on the arm and you seemed to know him. Just how well did you know him, and where did you meet him the first time?" His sarcasm fills the air.

"I never met him before that minute, and I don't remember him touching me at all." I can feel the burn of Mr. Stranger's fingers on my arm where he had held it.

"Bullshit, Elise. I can tell by the look on your face that you know him and that he means something to you. So why don't you come clean and tell me what the hell you know about him?"

"I don't know him at all, I never met him before that second in the meat department. Why won't you believe me, Mack?"

"Because you are a fucking liar, Elise. Always have been and always will be, that's why."

I don't know what to say or do to make him believe that I don't know the man. I try not to cry or show any emotion. I don't want to give him any more ammunition against me.

"Maybe I should drag your ass down to the station and into and interrogation room. Maybe then you'd be embarrassed enough to tell the truth."

"Please, Mack, please don't and please believe me." I begin to feel drained.

"Not only that, but the checkout man said you left and looked back as if signaling someone. He also said the victim left shortly after. He didn't see you get on the bus at the corner but thought you walked home. Why would you walk home, Elise? Did you go to the park and meet him there before he was killed?" He's close to screaming. I'm thankful the door is closed, so his parents can't hear our exchange.

"For Christ sake, Mack, no, no, no."

"Oh, shut the hell up, you lying bitch. I know you are connected to this guy somehow, and when I find out, I may just throw you down the fucking basement steps. Do you know how embarrassing it is to have to type a report about a murder and have to include your wife in it as a possible witness or suspect?"

"I'm sorry, Mack, I had no idea who he was or had any idea what would happen to him."

Just then his mother comes into the room. "Would you like some cake and ice cream?" I was never so happy to see her in my entire life.

"Yes, please, that sounds so good."

Mack just sits there and glares at his mother as if she had asked if I wanted to smack him in the head. Which I wanted to do, only more like smash him in the head with the piece of iron I had used on Mr. Stranger in my dream. He stands. "I better leave and go back to the station and write out a couple of reports."

"Can't you stay long enough for coffee and dessert?"

"No, Mom, I have to do a lot of work yet before my day is over." As she is leaving the room, he leans close to me and takes my face in his hand and pinches my cheeks together. "This isn't over yet, you lying fucking bitch." He leaves the room. I lie there, trying my best not to look upset or cry. What the hell am I going to do? What if he really does follow through with his threat and drags me into the interrogation room at the station? I hate him, and I really wish he was the one who died in the park and not nice Mr. Stranger. Always he brings the loneliness and the hatred. Always he brings the clouds and the darkness to my mind. Always he brings the smell of death whenever he approaches. Why can't I just be normal?

Chapter 15

A couple of days later, Rebecca drives me to the doctor for my checkup. She drops me off at home. She comes in to be sure I'm going to be okay alone. The doctor says to take it easy for a while yet. No heavy lifting and avoid exercising and bending over as much as possible for at least two more weeks. The concussion will take a while to heal, and if I experience any dizziness, nausea, or blurry vision, I'm to call for an ambulance immediately. It's not anything to play around with. Rebecca calls Mack on the way home and forward the doctor's orders to him. She adds "no sex" on her own, which I'm happy for, and I'm surprised at her firm tone of voice. I thank her for her concern, and she finally leaves me in the library where it all had begun. I look at the book still on the floor and decide I will probably never finish it. I go to the kitchen and grab a Diet Coke and head for my studio. I notice an unopened letter addressed to me on the counter. I find it odd that Mack wouldn't have opened it as he always opens all the mail to ensure I'm not hiding something from him. Why not this one. There was no return address, and the envelope is typed on a typewriter and not printed out from a printer. I carefully tear the edge off the envelope to open the letter. Inside is one piece of paper with the letters written in red ink.

> You, I Want You, And When I Find You, It
> Will Be Over!

I start to shake uncontrollably and have to hang onto the counter for support. Who is doing this to me and why? Could Mack be playing some sort of sick game to scare me? It has to be him, or he will have opened the letter. I check the envelope for a date stamp only to find there is none. It's as if whoever sent it brought it into the house and personally laid it on the kitchen counter. I slowly get control of myself and begin to check the alarm system. It had been on when Rebecca dropped me off, and I turned it back on when she left. It has to be Mack. I bravely make up my mind to ask him about it when he comes home. Should I also ask him about the phone calls? I don't know what to do. I reread the letter to see if I can recognize the printing. I go to the desk in the library to find something that Mack would have printed something on. I find a sheet of paper that he had started a list of things he obviously plans to take to his grandmother's cabin when he goes with Matt. His printing is nothing like that in the note. It scares me even more to think it may be someone other than Mack.

Mack arrives home an hour or so later. Instead of going to my studio, I sit at the kitchen table and try to think of who would be trying to scare me. I try to think of old boyfriends from high school that were a bit off kilter, or maybe someone I met in college. No one comes to mind. I have no enemies that I know of. I got along with most of my classmates in high school and in college. Those that I actually interacted with. I was sort of a loner in both schools and didn't date much or go to frat parties. My close friends, I still keep in touch with, and they would never do anything like this to anyone. I'm at a loss as to who would be this mean. Mack walks into the kitchen and sees me sitting there.

"Are you all better now that Mommy babied you for a fucking week?"

I look at him and reply, "Yes, not that you really care whether I'm better or not."

"Oh, you are wrong, Elise, I care very much." He comes up behind me and slides his hand down over my breast. "Mommy said no sex, but I'm thinking if you lie on your back, I can fuck your pretty pussy without you even moving a muscle. Not like you move anyway when I am making love to you. See, your nipples are already hard. Come on, my dear little whore, and let Daddy take care of you. My mother had you long enough."

He starts to pull me along by the arm. He takes me to our bedroom, and he begins to undress me. He's actually gentle in removing my T-shirt and pants. He unsnaps my bra and pulls it from my breasts. He groans deep in his throat as he bends to kiss each hard peak. He sucks each nipple, and I throw my head back in abandonment. It feels so good. I don't want it to feel this good. I don't want anything having to do with him concurring my body to feel good. He slowly lays me on the bed, leaving my legs to dangle off the side. He kneels down and begins to rub between my folds. I immediately respond to his touch and become wet.

"That's what I like, you getting all hot for me, Elise. Just for me." His voice is deep and throaty. He replaces his fingers with his tongue, and I let out a moan as he slowly licks and sucks the nub that feels on fire with desire. I climax in what seems to be seconds after his tongue starts to work on me. He stands and removes his pants and lifts my legs up off the bed and around his waist. He plunges into me with one hard thrust, and although my side hurts, I respond to each and every thrust. As the plunges become deeper and harder and my side begins to hurt with a piercing pain, my mind begins to scream, *Stop, you are killing me!* Yet I match every thrust by grinding my hips against him. I can't control the shattering climax that shoots through my whole being. My body seems molded to him as he pumps over and over into me. I feel as though I've soared above the bed and never want to come down. With one last plunge he goes deep into me and spills himself with hot milky spurts. I wonder why it feels so wonderful this time and what's different. Why doesn't it always feel this good, and why don't I feel the loneliness and hatred I always feel when he rapes me? I realize that this time he didn't rape me. This time I wanted to feel him explode inside me. I wanted to feel satisfied, and I actually felt as one with him. After his orgasm is finished, he lets my legs down easy, and I feel numb from the neck down. All I want to do was lie here with my legs off the bed and let his sperm slowly leak out of me.

Mack picks my legs up and swings them onto the bed.

"Get some rest, you whore. You spread your legs too easily to be anything but a slut. You know that, don't you, Elise? You know that you are a fucking slut, don't you? I married a whore and a slut."

So much for the best feeling ever. So much for being lifted high and soaring in ecstasy. The feeling of hatred begins to seep into my soul along with the feeling of guilt. How can I abandon myself and let myself be used by him? Why did my body deceive me once again? I vow as I lay there naked that I will never allow him to treat me like this again. I will never be his slut or whore or anything thing else. Now, I'm afraid. Afraid of the storm that's building deep in my heart and soul. So afraid I begin to tremble with a fury I can't control.

Chapter 16

I want to scream. I want to cry. I want to murder my husband. I want to see him lying on our bedroom carpet slowly bleeding to death. If only I had the nerve to make it happen. If only I had a way of just completely letting go and making him *gone*. My thoughts are interrupted by Mack cursing as he's stomping up the steps.

"What the fuck is this, Elise?" He's waving the envelope I left in the kitchen. "Is this some secret code from your lover? Just what does this mean? You had better tell me the truth or I swear I will choke the life right out of you." He's screaming so loud the windows seem to be rattling. I look at him and the letter now being shoved into my face.

"I don't know, Mack, I found it on the counter, and because there was no address, I thought you left it there."

"Why in the hell would I leave you a stupid note like this? Why would I write anything to you?" He rounds the bed. I feel a weariness deep within my bones. I'm not sure I can withstand any more of his verbal or physical abuse. If he decides to hurt me, I doubt I could defend myself in any way.

"Please, Mack, believe me, I have no idea where the note came from. I checked the envelope over and over and I tried to think of anyone who would do this. Please, Mack, tell me it's just a bad joke you are playing to scare me."

He looks at me as though I had grown a pair of horns. "No, bitch, it isn't me. No, it must be your friend. When I find out who he is, I will kill both of you and bury you in the backyard." He swears and gets up abruptly and marches out of the bedroom, slamming the door so hard I'm sure the neighbors hear it four blocks away. I slowly get up and go into the bathroom. I turn the shower on and stare at myself in the mirror. I don't like what I see. A woman who looks mentally beaten, pathetic, and lower than low. What happened to the woman who was so full of life and happiness? Where did she go? The one I see looking back at me is not me. It's a perfect stranger, and I don't like her.

I take a long hot shower and afterward I go directly to bed. I take a painkiller, hoping I will fall into a deep dreamless sleep. I do fall asleep, but it isn't dreamless. I have the same nightmare I had while at Mack's mom's. Only the characters are switched, and it's Mack lying with his head bashed in, and Mr. Stranger is standing beside me, encouraging me to finish him off. Mack is staring at me and slowly asks me why I would want him dead. I wake shivering like I've been lying on a bed of ice. I turn the light on, half expecting to find a bloody iron bar lying on the bedroom floor. I drag myself to the bathroom and splash cold water on my face until the dregs of sleep leaves me. I don't want to go back to sleep and dream the same nightmare. Even though it is only four o'clock, I make myself stay up and get dressed. I would love to have some coffee, but that would mean going into the kitchen and making a pot. I would undoubtedly wake Mack, and I'm not in any frame of mind to deal with his bullshit and abuse this early in the morning. I'd forgo the coffee and just go to my studio.

As I enter the room, I begin to relax and already have forgotten the dream. Well, almost forgotten the dream. It will stay with me a long time. I stare at the sketch I had done earlier of Haven and Becca and once again feel at peace. I work on the canvas for several hours before I hear Mack in the kitchen. I know I'd have to face him sooner than later, so I put my art supplies away and head for the kitchen. I'm pleased with my accomplishments on the painting, and I'm not about to let Mack kill my good mood. I enter the kitchen, prepared for him to bring up the note from last night. He turns when I enter the room.

"How do you want your eggs and toast this morning?"

"I think I'll just have white toast."

"You know it's impossible to have white toast, don't you?"

I laugh. "Okay, how about coffee and white bread made into toast?"

He laughs and pours me a cup of black coffee and takes out the white bread to make my toast. I sit on the stool next to the bar and sip my coffee, waiting for him to bring up the note or some other topic that will result in an argument. He finishes making his eggs and comes to join me at the bar. He's unusually quiet, and I'm sure he's about to explode. After a few minutes of silence, he says, "I was thinking of the note, and I am afraid someone may have hacked into our security system. I'm going to call the company and have them check it over to be sure it's okay and then change all the codes."

"I thought maybe it was someone you had put away, and now he is seeking revenge. I would be an easy enough target."

"Yes, that is my very thought."

We continue our breakfast in a comfortable silence. "I'm going into the department and checking on who may have been released lately. I want you to keep everything locked just to be on the safe side. If the system has been breached, maybe it was a onetime deal." I'm torn whether to tell him of the phone calls and that they have been happening for quite a while. I decide to wait to see if it happens again. He can easily go through the phone records and check that out. He probably has an ongoing report of the phone calls coming and going from the house anyway. He won't trust that I won't be a good little wife and not talk to strangers. I'm surprised he allows me to have a cell phone. I'm sure he monitors that too. My studio is my only reprieve from his prying eyes and ears.

Before he leaves, he tells me not worry about anything. He is going to assign one of the young officers to do an extra patrol on our street. I thank him, and he is out the door. I go back to my studio and begin to paint again. I love how the painting is turning out and think that Rebecca and Gerald will love it. I have captured the look of a new mother loving her newborn and the look of contentment on the baby's beautiful face. I even have Haven in her pink gown she was in when they wheeled her into the delivery room. Being happy with my work, I go down to the kitchen to get a Diet Coke before continuing. I notice the mailman has delivered the mail through the slot in the front door. I casually walk over and start to pick it up. I freeze in my tracks as I see the envelope lying on top of the rest of the mail. Same red ink, same printing is on the front of the envelope as the first one. I am shaking but decide not to touch it. I leave it there as though I haven't seen that the mail has been delivered. Mack can get the mail and open the envelope. I don't want to touch it or see what it says inside. I quickly grab for my cell phone just as the house phone rings. I jump a mile with the deadening sound. Jesus, I am like a cat caught in a kennel full of pit bulls. I decide not to answer and wait for it to go to the answering machine. When I hear Mack's voice, I quickly pick it up.

"Mack, thank God it's you," I say breathlessly into the receiver.

"What the hell is the matter, Elise?"

"There is another envelope on top of the mail, I'm not touching it until you get home."

"I'm on my way." He slams the phone down in my ear. I go back to my studio to put my things away. No more peace. I'm not sure what I dread most, the message in the letter or what Mack's reaction will be to it. Either way it's surely not going to be a pleasant experience for me.

Mack gets home twenty minutes later and comes into the house like a bull on a mission to destroy everything in its path. He practically runs to the front door and picks up the envelope. I notice he is wearing plastic gloves. He must think there may be fingerprints on it. He carefully tears it open, and there is one sheet of paper enclosed. I stand like a statue while he reads its contents out loud.

"Ha ha, bitch, you're scared now. It won't be long until you are gone. Oh, and by the way, not even your bigwig detective husband will be able to help you."

I start to shake uncontrollably and have to sit down before I fall down. Mack comes over and sits beside me.

"I'm taking the letter and envelope to the lab immediately to be tested for fingerprints, fibers, or anything else that may have been left by the asshole who was doing this. I'm also pulling all the video recordings from the cameras all the way around the house. I'm sure to find something on the tapes or on the damn letter itself. Please make sure the alarm system is on, and don't let anyone in. The security company will be out tomorrow." He leaves me sitting in the chair, and I can hear the garage door shut behind him. I grab a Diet Coke and open it in a daze. I want to talk to someone. I need to talk to someone who will understand. I feel trapped and so alone. I have no real friends to confide in, and I will never tell Haven. Not now, not with her being so excited with her new baby. I slowly walk to my studio and decide to try to paint or maybe sketch something else. Something to keep my mind in a sane place.

Chapter 17

The next couple of days fly by. Mack has every available man, woman, and child working on the murder case, and those left over are working on trying to solve the mystery of the envelope. He makes no mention of me and the stranger in the grocery store. I guess he finally doesn't think I'm somehow involved in the actual murder. My only part in the tragic scene has been he talked to me in the store and made me feel feelings I hadn't felt in years.

Rebecca calls Mack in the evening and tells him that she'd be over in the morning at eleven to pick me up so I can go see Haven and the baby. She plans on picking up Chinese, and we'd have lunch with Haven. I'm so excited to finally get out of the house and to spend time with Haven I almost jump up and down when he tells me the news. He thinks it's a great idea. Once again I'm afraid of both shoes crashing to the floor. He has no idea I've finished the painting and plan on giving it to Rebecca when she comes to pick me up. I'm praying Mack won't insist on staying home until she gets here, or say he'd just take me to Haven's himself. The feeling of utter relief practically overwhelms me when he agrees to let his mom pick me up. He says he's working on a pretty promising lead on the murder case and would have to spend all day interrogating a suspect they had picked up yesterday. I'm too relieved to ask him about the suspect. I'm afraid he'll change his mind about letting me go. Things are beginning settle down here at home, and I don't want to rock the already leaking boat.

Mack leaves for the office around six, and I finish my coffee with a sense of real calm and peace. I'm excited to see the baby and wish I have a small gift to give her, but I have nothing and no way of getting anything for her. I guess me just loving her would have to do for now. I go into the studio and package up the painting and bring it downstairs just before Rebecca is about to arrive. I'm afraid Mack may pop in, and then I'd have to deal with his outrage that I'd think one of my paintings is good enough to give to his mother as a gift. She arrives right at eleven, and I'm ready for her. She immediately sees the package.

"What's in there?"

"Just something I painted for you, but it's a surprise. I'll give it to you once we are at Haven's."

She carries it to the car as I turn on all the security alarms, etcetera. We chat as though we haven't seen each other in years. It feels wonderful to be out of the house and to just enjoy another person's company other than Mack's. She has already picked up the Chinese carryout, and it makes the whole car smell delicious. I don't realize in my excitement to leave the house I had forgotten to eat. Geez, I hope she bought enough. I tell her that much, and she laughs so hard she says she can hardly see to drive. We arrive at Haven's, and I volunteer to carry in the food while she grabs the painting. Haven meets us at the door with Becca in her arms, smiling from ear to ear. She looks adorable, and motherhood seems to fit her well. I can hardly wait to set the food on the kitchen counter and take that sweet baby from her mother. She is wide awake and looks at me like she really can see me. I state that I'm sure she's looking right at me. Haven says she thinks her eyesight is coming along quicker than normal and is sure she follows things around the room.

We settle around the kitchen table, and Rebecca gets down paper plates and glasses for ice tea. She starts to serve the food as we talked about Haven's experiences being a new mother. It feels so good to feel loved and wanted. We eat, laugh, and when I say I'm painting again, Rebecca jumps from the table so fast she nearly tips her chair over and exclaims, "Oh my god, my painting, I want to see my painting."

Haven looks at her in surprise. "What painting?"

"I painted a painting for your mom to thank her for taking such good care of me while I was under the weather."

Rebecca comes into the kitchen carrying the package and sets it on the end of the table and begins to unwrap it. When it's completely unwrapped, but only she can see it, she sobs, "Oh, Elise, it is beautiful, and I love it." Haven gets up and goes to look at it, and she just starts to cry.

"I didn't paint it to make you two cry, I painted it because I just had to try and capture the love you share with Becca."

Rebecca lays the painting down on the table, wipes the tears from her eyes, and came over and gives me the biggest hug ever. The biggest hug she can give without squashing her granddaughter. Haven does the very same thing. "You have such talent."

Rebecca starts to chatter about where it will hang and how she can't wait to show Gerald. She's sure all her neighbors will be so jealous and want an original from her talented daughter-in-law. She says if I paint for them, I'd charge them an arm and a leg, because my work is priceless. I laugh and assure them I don't think Mack will appreciate it if I did. He's always saying how mediocre my work is. I think Rebecca is going to come unglued over that admission.

We spend the rest of the next few hours talking and taking turns holding Becca. Poor Haven only gets to hold her when she's breastfeeding her. I'm sorry when it's time to leave. I don't want to return to the cold emptiness of my house. I want my house to feel full of love and happiness like Haven's does. Yet I dread the thought of having a child to make that happen. Rebecca drops me off at the house, and as she hugs me goodbye, she once again thanks me for the painting. I tell her Mack knows nothing about it because I'm sure he'd not have approved. She says it will be our secret until it's hung for all to see. I feel a deep emptiness as I look out the door and watch her car drive away. I lock everything up and head for the kitchen. I'm sure Mack won't be home for supper, and I'm filled to the gills from the Chinese food I scarfed down at Haven's. I take a Diet Coke out and decide to just go out on the patio. Only to remember Mack warned that I can't leave the house to even sit in the backyard without someone with me. Shit, I'm trapped again. I go to my studio and decide to do another sketch. I will just wait to hear from Mack.

Chapter 18

I'm pleased when Mack drives into the garage. I'm standing in the kitchen when he walks in. He's ecstatic and just bubbles over with energy when he comes bursting through the door.

"We got him, we got the son of a bitch who has been doing the murders for the last four years." He grabs me in a bear hug and swings me around the kitchen. "We got him, we got him, we got him!" He kisses me deeply. Even though his breath tastes like a stale cigarette, I get caught up in his excitement. My side hurts, and I wince at his tight squeeze. He looks at me then and sets me down. "Christ, Elise, I'm sorry, did I hurt you?"

"I'm fine, please tell me all about him and the case."

He takes a beer out of the refrigerator and sits at the table and begins to fill me in on what he can.

The guy is a local bum sort of fellow who lives in a shack near the river, just out of town. He's in his fifties and always seems nice to me and is always surrounded by the local kids. He has even taught many of them how to fish for trout and to hunt small game. I find it hard to believe that he's the killer. I don't say anything like that to Mack, but I think, *Oh no, you have the wrong person.* I can feel it deep down in my soul. Mack gulps his beer down in two swigs and goes for another. I can see the relief on his face and am happy for him but not for the loner he's accusing of the murders. Mack assures me that he has confessed to all five of them.

I finally ask, "Did he give a reason for killing them so brutally?"

"No, he said he just had to do it." Then he quickly adds, "Killers like him don't need any goddamn reason for murdering their victims, they just enjoy the kill."

I think to myself, *No that isn't true,* and I still doubt Mack has the right man. Mack suddenly gets up and grabs me by the arm.

"Go get your best dress on, we're going to go out and celebrate," he says as he kisses me again.

I think, *Great, we are celebrating an innocent man's demise.*

We drive to Portsmith with Mack talking nonstop about the capture of the poor innocent man. I haven't seen him this happy since our wedding day. I guess trapping an innocent is a high for Mack. First me and now this poor soul. In a way I begin to think of the poor man as a kindred soul. We'd both spend the rest of our lives in a prison. His would have four walls and mine would have a whole world open to see but not to be free in. The slap to the back of the head brings me out of my daydreaming and back into reality.

"Elise, what the hell is the matter with you? Do you enjoy pissing me off by not answering me when I ask you a direct question?" he snarls.

"I'm so sorry, Mack, I was daydreaming about how pleased the town will be with you capturing the murderer. How the families of the victims can finally have some closure."

"Yeah, you're right, that should make a lot of people happy, including the fucking mayor who has been up my ass for the last four years. I can't believe he was reelected for another term. Man, I hate that bastard." There's enough hatred in his voice to scare the hell out of most people. No wonder the poor man confessed.

"I'm sorry, what did you ask me?"

"Oh, I asked if you enjoyed your day with my mom and sister. What did you guys do and talk about? How is that little cutie pie? Has she grown at all?"

"We mostly talked about the baby and how much she has grown. She looks at you as though she can see clearly already. She is adorable."

"Now that I caught the murderer, we will be able to spend more time with the little princess."

I can't help thinking, *Great, more time to be tortured.*

We arrive at the best restaurant in Portsmith. I hadn't realized he had made reservations before he came home from work. The Old Barn is just that. It had been an old barn that the owners converted into a beautiful club. The restaurant is located in what is the old hay loft. Open barn beams and crystal chandeliers make the decor in the place unique, and it's always packed with the crème of the crop. We are seated in a semiprivate area in the restaurant. The crystal lighting and the lace tablecloths along with the long-stem wineglasses, roses, and chilled wine make me believe Mack had actually taken time in requesting all this. We really are going to celebrate his victory, and maybe, just maybe I can enjoy a lovely night out. The waiter pours each of us a glass of white wine and hands us menus.

"No need for menus, we know what we will have." Once again a tiny bit of my freedom is stolen. "The lady will have the baked trout covered with creamed asparagus, a side salad with ranch dressing. I will have the New York Strip steak, medium, smothered in mushrooms and onions with extra au jus, with a side salad and french dressing. We will both have water."

The evening starts out beautiful, until the mayor of Flag Lake, along with other town officials are seated at the only other table in our secluded area. Now, it all becomes very clear to me. The infamous detective is about to gloat to the mayor of his accomplishments. I feel like crawling under the table. Of course, they all come over to congratulate Mack on the wonderful arrest he has made that day. He can't have puffed his chest out any further if he'd been the only rooster in a coop full of horny hens. Jesus, does he not have any conscience? The mayor seems to be pleased and beams at Mack as though he's a good little boy who has recited his part perfectly in the school play. I sit there with what I hope looks like a sincere smile on my face and say all the right things a proud wife should say about her asshole husband.

Thankful when our food arrives, I turn my attention to my plate. I love trout, but Mack knows I hate asparagus to the point of gagging. I try to scrap the green slimy spears off my fish and just eat the sauce and trout. To me it seems to have seeped into the fish and just spoiled the taste of the whole dish. I drink two glasses of wine and am about to drink the third when Mack announces loud enough for the whole place to hear, "For Pete sake, you are drinking your wine like it is water. You know you can't handle half a glass, much less three." Embarrassed, I take a drink of water instead. "Eat your asparagus, Elise, it's the best part of the dinner."

I want to answer that if they are that great he can eat them for me. "Yes, just saving the best for last." I put them into my mouth and abruptly leave the table, heading for the ladies' room. As I'm nearly running from the table, I can hear Mack's laughter. Needless to say, my dinner ends up in the porcelain throne. As I return to the table, the whole table next to us is staring at me with concern. I have no idea what Mack might have told them, and I really do not want to know. We sit in almost silence, listening to the next table talking of town business. No one mentions Mack again, and he must have gotten bored because he suddenly asks, "Are you ready to leave?" I nod, and we get up to leave. He of course goes over to the mayor's table to says goodbye. I once again just stand there with my arm through Mack's like the trophy wife I'm not.

Chapter 19

It's a beautiful evening, and it's nice to be out of the house. I almost feel free. We drive with the top down and drive to the downtown section of Portsmith. We park in the parking lot next to a busy nightclub.

"Let's live it up a bit, baby."

As we enter, I can hardly see for the cloud of smoke that hangs over the tables and bar. Apparently, it isn't a city ordinance here to not smoke in the premises. The thick cloud stings my eyes and make it hard to breathe. Mack leads me to a table toward the back of the place. He sits against the wall, and I sit next to him. A waitress about sixteen comes to take our drink orders. Mack tells her "Two bottles of Miller Lite" and winks at her as she writes it on her little pad. She makes a point to wipe the already clean table, just to lean over and show off her perky little boobies. Christ, they are making the wait staff at these places younger and more promiscuous as each day passes. Mack notices the look on my face.

"Jealous?"

"Do I have reason to be?"

He laughs and squeezes my hand. "Not if you are a good girl and keep giving me what I want."

My thoughts turn to the trout in the toilet and I laugh. He's sure I'm thrilled at his statement. We have a couple of beers, and Mack announces he wants to dance. This is a first for him. Wow, locking up an innocent man brings out all sorts of surprises in the day. It's a slow soothing sort of song, and the singer has a great voice.

The song is "Can't Get Enough of Your Love Baby" by Barry White, and the singer sounds remarkably like Mr. White himself. With few couples on the floor, I'm able to see the singer clearly over Mack's shoulder. He not only has the sexiest voice, he is unbelievably sexy as hell. I could have creamed myself right there on the dance floor. We are dancing next to the small stage, and I make eye contact with the singer. Holy shit, a hot lightning bolt just went down from my hard nipples through my stomach and ended up lodged somewhere in my wet inner being.

Mack pulls me closer and whispers, "I love it when you are getting ready for me while we are in public."

I think, *Oh hell no, not you, but the singer can fuck me right here on the dirty dance floor and I would beg for more when he's done.* I just growl deep in my throat. Mack nibbles my earlobe and lets out a groan as he pulls me close enough to feel his hard dick pressing into my lower stomach. Great, we must look like a couple of horny teenagers grinding on the dance floor. Get it together, Elise. I pull slightly away from him and try to compose myself to resemble more of an adult woman dancing with her husband. It works until I make eye contact with the singer again. With knees that feel like Jell-O and my inner core overflowing with molten lava, I'm having a problem even moving my feet to the beat of the music. Thank God the song finally ends and I manage to wobbly walked with Mack to our table.

Mack's cell phone rings just as we sit down, and he has ordered another beer for himself. He can't hear and excuses himself and walks toward the door, leaving me alone at the table. The waitress brings Mack's beer and hands me a note and nods toward the singer. I open the note, and all it says is "Hey, beautiful, call me anytime," with his phone number on it. I quickly put the note in my purse before Mack returns and sees me reading it. He will surely kill both the singer and me if he sees it. Mack comes to the table to announce we have to leave. Something has come up at the jail that needs his attention. I know better than to ask about the situation, as he seems agitated.

The drive home is in complete silence. He pulls into the garage, and I get out of the car. I'm turning the security system back on when I see the note on the table. I already know it is another one meant for me. I open it and read the boldface letters: "SOON VERY SOON." For some reason, this time I don't feel afraid. I feel nothing but tired. I decide to just leave it on the counter, and Mack can deal with it when he comes home. I go into the bedroom and grab a nighty and head for the shower. My clothes reek of cigarette smoke, and I suddenly feel dirty. The steam from the hot shower fills the bathroom, and the hot water hitting me feels like a mini massage. I think of the singer and his beautiful voice. Would he sing to me as he conquers my body? The water may have been hot but not nearly as hot as my thoughts. I'm afraid to wash myself for fear the touch of the loofah against my skin will make me come instantly. I just let the water do its job. As I step onto the bath mat, I look at myself in the fogged-up mirror. I imagine him behind me toweling me off. I can almost feel his penis brushing against my ass, trying to enter. When I bend to dry my feet, I swear he actually enters me, and I climax. What the hell is happening to me? I hate it when Mack touches me, but I can come with only my mind. Am I that big of slut that I can masturbate in my head and make myself climax? I wonder if Mack will be jealous of my overactive mind if I tell him? I put my nightdress on and slip under the covers. Sleep comes quickly and so does the dream.

I'm making love to the singer. I'm in my own bed, and he's above me. Only his face is all bloody, and he has brain matter oozing from just above his left ear. He's smiling at me with perfectly straight white teeth. He doesn't seem to realize he's already dead. He bends to kiss me, and when he opens his mouth slightly, blood runs out from between his lips and drips onto my face. I turn my head and see Mack lying next to me. He's propped up on his elbow, smiling at me. "Look what you've done again, Elise. Look what your hot pussy has caused. Another one is dead because of you."

I begin to scream. I wake up to Mack shaking me.

"What the hell is going on in your ugly little head?" I try to get away, but he has me trapped. He's pushing me into the bed, and I can't breathe.

I finally scream into his face, "Let me go, I'm suffocating!" He lets go of me and sits back.

"What were you dreaming? I found the note on the counter. Is your lover coming for you soon, Elise? You know I will find out who he is, and when I do, I will kill him myself. You will not get away with having a liaison with a man right under my nose. I will kill both of you. In fact, I will enjoy watching the life seep out of your body."

I have to get away, and I have to get away soon. Right that second, I have to get out of the bed. I'm shaking from the dream. Maybe I'm shaking because I had sex with the singer in my mind and it felt delicious. Maybe I'm shaking because I'm afraid I had really killed him. I get up and go into the bathroom to splash water onto my face. The cold water helps to settle my brain but not my shaking body. Mack comes in to use the toilet, and as he is standing there straddling the toilet, I think of the trout again. Why? Why would the thought of the trout in the toilet come to my mind at this point in the night?

Chapter 20

The next few days go by in a blur. Mack is so horrid words cannot describe him. Things are not turning out the way he had hoped it would after getting the poor man to confess to the murders. It turns out the poor man isn't so poor after all. Mr. James Flemmings is a very wealthy man. He may have chosen to live out his retirement in a shack alongside a lazy river, but he could have lived in a mansion. In fact, he owns one in upstate New York. Mr. Flemmings, who only uses Flem as his last name now, fell off the grid after his wife was killed in a car accident. He had owned a financial business a block off of Madison Avenue in New York for years and was worth a fortune. Not having any children to leave his legacy to, he sold the business after his wife's tragic death and moved out of the city. He became a recluse, and all his hard-earned money was in several Swiss bank accounts just building up interest. His investments would make a person's head spin. Mr. Flemmings has hired the best lawyer out of New York money could buy and now reneged on his confession to the murders. Stating he was browbeat and threatened by the detectives to confess to the crimes. It would be the trial of the century, next to O. J. Simpson's.

Mack comes home every night after ten with alcohol on his breath and perfume on his body. His clothes look as though he has taken up street fighting for a hobby and lost every match. I've never seen him like this before. Every little thing I do irritates him to the point I fear for my life. I'm thankful he comes home late and leaves early. Even his morning routine has changed. He no longer wants me to be anywhere near him. I lay his clothes out at night, and he grabs his coffee on the run. He tells me to stay in bed and not to get in his way or he will strangle me. Most of the time when he's home, he stays in the library. I'm not allowed in the room, so I have no idea what he's doing in there.

Once again I am lying in bed asleep yet awake. I am listening to the breathing. It's heavy and loud. It seems to be coming from the shadows that cover the walls and ceiling of the bedroom. They are looming over me like a black shroud with arms extending toward me. I feel as though they are beckoning to me. I feel afraid. If they touch me, will I be pulled into the abyss of my mind, never to return? A part of me wants to reach out to see if they are real and if I will actually be consumed by them. If I allow myself to go with the shadows, will I be free? I hear a soft moaning, and the shadows seem to fade as the moaning gets louder. As I come out of my dream, I am aware that it is me moaning. Mack is holding me down, and he is looming above me.

"If you must moan, let me give you something to moan about."

I am fully awake now and begin to struggle.

"I bet you don't struggle under your lover when he is fucking you, do you, Elise?" He is grinding against me through my night-gown. I feel his heat and his weight, and I want to vomit. He kneels over me and grabs my gown by the neckline and, in one swift jerk, tears it right down the middle. He grabs my panties and pulls them to my knees. He is now frantically trying to enter me, but my legs are caught together by my panties.

"Spread your goddamn legs, Elise." He growls at me.

I say nothing as I try to take my foot and shove my panties off my legs. I manage to get it off one leg, and now I am spread eagle for him to enter. He pushes hard into me, not caring that he is ripping my flesh. I was not ready for him, and he is hurting me. I cry out in pain. Still he does not stop. He keeps plunging deep inside me, and with each thrust, I feel as if I am being shredded. I hear myself begging him to stop. Except for the pain, it's as though I am not in my own body but watching myself being raped. I hear him grunting with each thrust, and I think of a pig rutting in a trough. It disgusts me to the core. Finally, he stiffens above me and finds his release. It's only then I realize my face is wet with the silent tears I have shed.

He rolls off me and says, "Shut up, you sniveling, ugly bitch. Do you think I enjoy your body? Hell, I feel more pleasure jacking off in the shower than I do when I fuck you. Don't worry, I won't be home much of this weekend. I will be working on the case." He sits up on the edge of the bed. I want to ask him if it's the murder case or a case of whiskey or maybe her name is Casie and he just calls her Case, but I say nothing. I feel relief that he will be gone. I only wish it was forever.

I turn my head and see it is just past six o'clock. For a Saturday, that is early for even Mack to be getting up. I lie still and hope he has forgotten about me. No such luck, he looks at me and says, "I want my breakfast like normal, so you better get up, Elise. You have had it too easy these past couple of days. I'm going to go in and take a shower, and I expect it to be on the table when I am dressed." So the routine is back and he will be his normal asshole self. I wait for the shower to start then get up and slip on my bathrobe. I begin to do my routine, like a good little maid. He will have everything just the way he likes it when he enters the kitchen. I wonder if there is a taste to arsenic and where it can be bought. I wonder how much I would have to use and if I would get caught. Who would catch me? Mack would be dead. I laugh out loud at my thoughts. If only I had the guts to pull something like that off.

Chapter 21

With his eggs poached, his toast buttered, and his coffee hot, I pour myself a cup of coffee. I hear the Saturday paper hit the doormat with a thud. I open the front door to get the paper. The paperboy waves as he sees me and speeds off on his bike. Tossing papers toward the neighbor's front doors. He rarely hits the mats when he throws them. I unroll the paper, and there on the front page screaming at me is a picture of Mack and Mr. Flemmings. Headlines are shouting, "Local Detective Beats a False Confession Out of a Millionaire." My hands start to shake, and I can hardly see the words under the headlines. I'm afraid to have Mack see the paper. I hear him enter the kitchen, and he calls out, "Is that the paper, Elise? Bring it here, I want to see what shit they dug up to print today." I slowly approach the table and place the folded paper next to his plate.

He sits down and opens it as he takes a drink of coffee. He spits his coffee onto the front page and begins to rave. "Those dirty son of a bitches, how in the fuck can they print these lies and get away with it? I have a notion to go down to the damn paper and give them a piece of my mind. How would they like to be arrested for slander? What a bunch of stupid assholes they have reporting the news in this one-horse town." His face is red with rage. I'm sure his head is going to explode at any second. With one angry swoop, he shoves all the dishes off the end of the table and onto the floor. He stands up and glares at me. "I suppose you think this is all a fucking joke and think it's funny? I can see it in your eyes you are happy they are belittling me and saying I have no idea how to do my job. Well, Elise my dear, you can go straight to hell with the rest of the peons in this hellhole of a town. I for one am not going to stand for this sort of treatment. I will show all of them I am right in this case, and I will prove it. You all can go to fucking hell!" He yells so loud I swear the windows rattle.

Grabbing his briefcase, he storms out of the room and into the garage. I hear the engine to his police cruiser start and the garage door open. I wait for the door to close again before I begin to clean up the mess he has made. I think to myself, *It's a good thing I didn't waste the arsenic on his breakfast this morning.* I have to smile at the idea. I also have to smile at the fact that I do think it's funny the way the town has turned on him. One minute he's a hero catching the bad guy, and as soon as they find out the bad guy is rich, Mack becomes a villain.

After cleaning up the mess, I take a long hot shower. Since the bad guy has been caught, I'm allowed to go about my daily chores. I'm once again allowed to go to the grocery store and buy what we need. Even though Mack is being a bear, he leaves me money every morning for groceries for meals he never is home to eat. Today, I'm looking forward to going out and seeing people. Even if they are only the employees at the local store. Maybe I could meet Haven and Becca at the café for lunch. I haven't seen them since our lunch together with her mom. I feel relieved and happy. Then I remember it's Saturday and Matt will be home. Lunch will have to be another day, but I could maybe stop at the sidewalk café and have a cup of cappuccino by myself. It would feel good to just watch the passersby. I take a few extra minutes and put a touch of eye makeup on and lip gloss. I brush my hair and decide to leave it hang loose down my back. I pick out a light-blue long-sleeved cotton blouse with a tiny darker blue pinstripe that is fitted through the waist. I wear jeans and slip-on sandals to complete the outfit. I like what I see in the mirror and feel good about myself.

I decide to walk to the café as it is a glorious morning. The sun is warm, but the breeze makes it comfortable. There are few peo-ple on the street, and they are leisurely strolling along, enjoying the beauty of the morning. Listening to the leaves rustling in the trees and the birds singing their songs gives me a sense of peace, and I wish it would last forever. I'm surprised that the sidewalk café is almost empty. I sit under a striped umbrella. I turn it to let the sun shine on the table, making it bright and cheery. The waitress comes to take my order and smiles at me with a warm, gentle smile. I think she loves days like this and is enjoying being able to serve the customers in the beautiful weather. I order a medium caramel mocha cappuccino. She brings it while I'm watching couples window-shop across the street. A new boutique had opened a couple weeks ago, and I think I might just treat myself and go in to explore. I'm sipping my cappuccino when I hear a familiar voice.

"Hello, beautiful."

I look up to see Matt standing there with a big lopsided grin on his face. Surprised, I immediately looked around to see if Haven and the baby are with him.

"May I join you?" He doesn't wait for an answer and pulls the other chair out from the table and plops down.

"Where is Haven and the princess?"

"They're at home. I had to come into town for a few things at the grocery store and decided I needed coffee to make it through the day." He sighs deeply. "Princess has turned into a vampire and thinks nighttime is the only time to be awake and to voice her opinion. And boy, does she voice her opinion. I never knew how loud a baby could be and how cranky they get when they are not getting what they want. Unfortunately, no one knows what she wants, and no one is getting much sleep because of it." He lays his head on the table. I can't suppress a giggle, and he looks at me like he is going to cry.

"Oh, Matt, I am so sorry. I can't imagine how hard it must be to have to work during the day and not get sleep at night. How is Haven holding up?"

"Oh, she seems to be reveling in motherhood, and it doesn't seem to faze her." He takes a sip of his jumbo cup of black coffee.

"Well, hopefully it's a short-lived stage Becca is going through and it will end soon." I'm trying to be as consoling as I possibly can looking into his bloodshot drooping eyes.

"Where is Mack?"

"He has been working nonstop on the case and rarely has time to eat or sleep either. I am just getting some groceries but thought it is such a beautiful day I'll try to get some sunshine and enjoy it."

He looks around as though he just realized it's daytime. "Oh yeah, it is really nice out, isn't it? I guess I drove here in a daze this morning. I hope the case is going better than what the papers are writing. Mack is sure getting the shitty end of the stick on this. I don't think I could handle it, and I'd probably crack under all the pressure. He is so lucky to have you to come home to and to stand next to him through all of this bullshit."

I just shake my head but say nothing. I'm thinking I wish he would never come home, and no, I don't stand with him on this at all. My silence is taken as a positive response to his statement.

We make small talk for almost an hour, and then we walk to the grocery store, but only after Matt has a refill on the coffee. I tell him I think I'd slosh if I drank that much and that you'd have to scrape me off the grocery store ceiling from all that caffeine. He just laughs at me.

At the store we part and do our own shopping. I buy just a few items for a fresh salad as I have plenty of food from the meals I didn't prepare for Mack this past week. He has at least called me daily to say he wouldn't be home for dinner so I don't have to prepare anything. I usually eat fruit and a glass of lemon water. When I pull out my wallet to pay for my groceries, a piece of paper came out of my purse with it. At first I don't recognize it, but after unfolding it and seeing the phone number, I remember where it came from. I can feel my face becoming flush and quickly shove it back into my purse. I'm being silly, reacting to it as though everyone around me knows how I had originally received it. When I look up, I realize the cashier is staring at me as though I'm mentally challenged, and she looks as though she's about to ask if I need help counting out my money. That makes me blush even more. I apologize, pay for my things, and walk out of the store.

Chapter 22

I decide to walk back to the boutique and nose around for a short time. I enter, and the tiny bell on the door makes a cheery tingling sound. A very attractive woman in her forties comes to greet me.

"Welcome to Forgotten Treasures, I am the owner/operator, Jordyn Kent. May I show you around? Are you looking for something specific for maybe someone special in your life?"

What a wonderful, cheerful voice she has.

"No, I'm just browsing."

"Much of the items I sell are on consignment and are created by local artist."

I'm surprised at the quantity and the quality of many of the items. I wonder if she'd be interested in any of my paintings. I walk over to where she has several paintings displayed, and I decided I'm as good as or maybe even better than most of the artists she's showing. She has followed me.

"I paint, and are you in the market for more painting to show, or do you have all you need?"

"Oh my, yes! I am kind of short in that area and could use more to fill up the wall. When would you be able to bring some in for me to choose from?"

"Not until next week, but I'm not sure you will like them."

"Look around you, we have all levels of talent here. What might be sophomoric to one is a masterpiece to another. Don't worry about it, I'm usually a pretty good judge on what will sell. I sell on a 60/40 percent rate until I am sure they are going to actually sell, and then I go 50/50. Hope that is all right with you?"

I think of all the paintings just sitting in my studio not bringing in any income and agree that it sounds like a great offer. We agree on Tuesday morning for me to bring in a few of the paintings because the store is closed on Tuesdays. I leave the store feeling higher than a kite.

I swear I'm walking on air thinking of which paintings I would take to show her. Jordyn is the kind of woman I immediately like and don't feel threatened by at all. I have a feeling we are going to become great friends. I enter the house through the front door and nearly shit my pants. Mack is standing in the foyer with a menacing look on his face. He literally slaps the grocery bag out of my hands, and it hits the floor with a thud. I instinctively step backward until my back hits the closed front door.

"Why the fuck were you so long, Elise? You and your lover have a little tryst this morning? Wasn't my cock enough for you? You had to go out and get some more?" I just stand there, trapped with no place to run. "Answer me, you fucking whore!"

I want to scream back, "No, I'm not like you, who can't be satisfied fucking just your wife!" Instead I whisper, "No, I went to the grocery store, and I had a cappuccino at the café. Matt stopped and we sat together. You can call and ask him if you don't believe me."

Grabbing my face with his right hand, he slams my head against the door. I think for sure my jaw will break under the pressure. "Maybe I should circumcise you like some tribes do in Africa. They use a clam shell, I could use a rusty jacket knife and then just let you bleed to death."

I'm sure he's Satan himself. After tightening his grip even more, he lifts my body off the floor. I dangle there pressed against the door, tears rolling down my cheeks. He lets go so abruptly I crumble to the floor in a heap. Big mistake on my part and I feel the heel of his foot grind into the back of my hand.

"I should break all your damn fingers so you can't hold his cock, so you can't hold a paintbrush, so you can't hold a fork to eat. I should just kill you now." He growls at me like a vicious dog. He turns and walk nonchalantly into the library as if he has just squashed a bug on the floor.

I slowly bring my hand up to my face and kiss the back of it like a mother would her hurt child. I have no idea what possessed me to do it, but it seemed to make me feel better. My face feels numb, and I'm not sure I have the strength to get up and take care of myself. I wish I could have marched into the library and kick him in the balls and watch him sink to the floor in pain. Instead I force myself to stand. With my legs feeling heavy and my hand already starting to swell and bruise, I walk to the bathroom. I step across groceries that are spewed across the foyer floor, not caring if they lie there forever and rot. I look at the stranger in the mirror and see the red marks on each side of her face. They would bruise quickly. This pitiful creature staring blankly back at me couldn't possibly be me. No, she has to be a stranger, someone I don't know. I run cold water and begin to splash it on my face and let it run onto my hand. It increases the pain tenfold. I fill the sink with cold water and ease my hand into it. Thank God it's my left hand and not my right. I stand there with my hand in the cold water until it feels numb. When the water feels like it's warm, I take out my hand and gently dry it. It's swollen to the point that I can hardly move my fingers. Thankfully, so far my face is red but not badly bruised.

Two seconds later I hear Mack at the door. "You have a mess to clean up out here, my dear Elise. Want to get your pretty ass out here and act like a fucking wife for once? It looks as though half of my dinner is lying on the floor. I'm not liking this at all, so you best quit sulking and get out here." He growls through the door. I pray for the strength to continue once I open the door. I walk out and met by a smirking Mack.

"My, my, you just don't learn, do you?" He's slowly walking around me.

I don't say anything and just walk to the groceries on the floor. I slowly bend to pick them up, fighting off the nausea I'm feeling. I carry them into the kitchen as Mack follows.

"What's the matter, Elise? Not feeling the happiness after making love to him? You don't seem to be as chipper anymore. Oh, my poor, poor Elise, what a shame." He's laughing at me.

After putting the groceries away, I go up to my studio. I close the door and slide to the floor. I lie there like a two-year-old sobbing until I can hardly breathe. First, I think of just ending my life. I think of my anxiety pills and how easy it would be to take the whole bottle. Falling into a deep dreamless sleep, never to awake again. Never to have to endure Mack's torture. How simple it would all be. I can almost hear him laughing after finding my dead body. No, I won't give him that pleasure. I begin to plan his murder.

Chapter 23

It's nearly five before I'm able to compose myself enough to come out of my studio. I go into the bedroom and look at the bed. If I could just lie down and sleep, I'd feel so much better. Maybe I'd wake up and it would all be just a dream. A nasty nightmare, but only just that, a dream. I take clothes and go into the bathroom and prepare to take a shower. I turn the water on and am about to step into the hot steaming shower when I hear the bedroom door open. Mack comes strolling in like a cat who knows the mouse is cornered and is about to give up its life. Fear shoots through me. I'm shaking, and I feel like I'm about to toss my cappuccino in the toilet. He walks into the bathroom.

"Mind if I join you?"

I can feel fear seep deeper into my body until it's slamming full force into the hatred that's waiting. Why must it always be those two that I feel? The hatred and the fear seems to merge into one being. Always in the shadows of my mind, building stronger with each second. Could I kill him in the shower and wash the evidence down the drain? Would I be free then? He doesn't wait for my answer but undress and step into the shower, reaching for my swollen hand as he goes. I flinch when his fingers curl around the swollen flesh. He doesn't seem to notice and brings it up to his lips and kisses it gently. Oh, dear Lord, does he think we're going to make love after what he just did to me? Making love isn't the exact term I would use to describe it. More like a slow rape.

"Relax, Elise, and I'll wash you."

Oh, hell no! I scream in my head.

He pours shower gel onto the sponge and gently starts to wash my body. He toys with my breasts, and they of course respond to his touch. I want to cut them off and shove them down his throat to choke the life out of him. He doesn't touch me intimately but continues down my legs and then my back and shoulders. He turns me and hands the sponge to me and says, "Now it's your turn."

I take the sponge and begin to wash him. He has turned his back to me, so I do his shoulders and back and buttocks then down his legs. He turns as I'm kneeling to wash his lower legs, and his hard cock brushes against my face. He grabs my head and forces my face into his groin. Rubbing his penis into my face.

"Take it, Elise." He groans.

I think, if I do this, maybe he will leave me alone for the rest of the night. His release is strong and quick, so is the yank on my hair.

"Swallow it, Elise, or I swear I will pull every hair from your ugly head."

I nearly choke as I try to catch my breath from the sudden pain inflicted on my scalp. I slowly stand up.

"I am done." I turn the shower off and step out onto the bath mat.

"Now that is how a good little wife is supposed to be."

I quickly dress. He dresses in his detective apparel. "I won't be home for dinner and don't wait up."

The relief that washes over me is like a waterfall tumbling into a raging river.

"Does that please you, Elise?"

"Then I won't make anything to eat. I'll just make myself a quick salad."

"Suit yourself, I'm eating with the mayor. He has invited us to his house for a nice cookout. It's really too bad that you are not feeling well and won't be able to attend." He smirks and calmly picks an imaginary piece of lint from his shirt.

"I'm sure you will enjoy yourself without me."

"It will be a long night, so please don't go into the library and fall asleep and make a mess. You know how I hate it when you invade my sanctuary."

Mack leaves a short time later. I notice he's taken the convertible, so that means he's out to impress someone. I go into the kitchen and grab my go to drink, Diet Coke, and decide on just what I would eat. I stare into the refrigerator for what feels like a month trying to make a healthy decision. Nothing looks good to me. I pull out the crisper and think maybe a spinach salad. It isn't top on my list of things to eat. I want comfort food, and spinach is about as comforting as a bed of nails to lie on. I finally decide on buttered noodles and a small ham steak. Not exactly healthy but better than the pound of chocolate and caramel I would prefer to eat. As the noodles are cooking, I sit staring out the window, wondering if I could really pull off a murder. What a morbid thought to have while waiting for one's dinner to get done.

I'm finally finished with my mediocre meal and have drunk all my soda, when the house phone rings. I feel a pang of fear run down my spine as I pick up the receiver, half expecting it to be the voice on the other end that warns me that soon it will be my turn. I shakily answer, "Hello."

"Hi, chickie."

I'm so relieved to hear Haven's cheery voice I could have cried.

"Hi, Haven, how are you?"

"I'm great. I'm calling to remind you of Becca's christening next Sunday at the church in Portsmith. We've added another person as a godparent for Becca. It's Cameron James. He is an old college buddy of Matt's, and apparently they made a pack years ago that they would be a godparent to each other's firstborn. I know Mack will sputter about having to share the duties, but he's not the only one in this world that loves that little girl. Cam was over the other night and held her almost all the while he was at the house. He's really a great guy, and I think he will fit right in with the rest of our loving family."

"That sounds wonderful, I can't wait to meet him." All the while thinking this is going to be a disaster.

"He and Matt played together in a band while in college for about a year. After college they sort of went their separate ways, only connecting now and then. Cam joined the Navy and then became a vet. Cam still plays occasionally but had opened a practice in Portsmith."

"How exciting to be able to do two things you really love to do."

We chat for a bit, and she tells me all about Becca and how cute she's getting. I personally don't think the little princess would get any cuter. She laughs and says I should keep her for a night when she doesn't sleep and make my decision on cuteness then. After our goodbyes, I clean up the kitchen, grab another soda, and head for my studio.

Chapter 24

I decide to do some sketching and take out my pad and set of pencils. I turn on the TV for noise and sit in my comfy chair and begin to sketch. I only half listen to what's on the television. I know it's *Date Line* or *48 Hours* or something like that. They're telling a story of a young man who had been killed nine or ten years ago, and now with DNA, they are sure they finally found his murderer. Wow, how technology has changed crime solving, and yet Detective Mack can't catch a killer if it was tied to his leg. I giggle to myself at the thought of killers tied around Mack and him not being able to see them.

I start to get some of my paintings ready to take to the shop on Tuesday. I find a few I had stacked against the wall that I particularly like. One is of a vase with tulips in it. Very simple but still very elegant. Another is of a basket of kittens being carried by a big old yellow lab. I always thought that would be nice in a child's bedroom or playroom. After picking out four more, I wrap each in brown paper. I will carry them down to the car on Tuesday individually so as not to damage them. I'm very anxious about getting Jordyn's opinion on my work. I really need something positive in my life right now, and I think Jordyn could be just the thing. I finish getting the paintings ready and looked at the clock. Where has the time gone, it's already ten o'clock.

I switch channels on the television to watch the local news. I'm shocked to see a dinner party, not just any dinner party, but the one the mayor is throwing. Live news of the event of the season, as the news woman explained. She's saying anyone who is anyone is at attendance at this wonderful fund-raising event being held at the mayor's mansion. He is raising money for the new addition that is to be added to the small clinic right here in Flag Lake. With this new addition, many new medical services will be provided for the small town, and this will eliminate having to travel to larger cities for medical care.

The camera scans the crowd just then, and lo and behold, there's Mack with his hand on a very attractive young brunette's shoulder. They look as though they could be husband and wife. Jealousy runs through my body. Anger hits me full force. I feel cheated on. More so than if he'd have been making love to the woman right there in plain sight. How dare the bastard go to an event of such importance without his wife? Just another way of letting me know I mean nothing to him, and he is showing it to the world. The anger builds inside me until I'm sure I would explode. I'm sure that when he gets home, he'd find tiny pieces of my body splattered on all the walls throughout the entire house. If he were here right this second, I would run him through with the french knife in the kitchen. My anger seems to seep out of the pores of my skin. I could no longer see the television screen clearly. I walk over to the set and slam the brass candleholder next to it through the screen. Only then do I feel any relief from the intense anger that has built up. As I look at the tiny shards of glass on the tiled floor and the cracked screen, I could almost smell his death.

I realize my anger has reached a new level. It scares me to think I'm capable of allowing myself to lose control like that. Holy crap, I actually broke the television. I unplug it and pick the small flat screen up and carry it out of my studio, down the steps, and out the garage door and dump it unceremoniously into the trash bin. Feeling void of emotion, I go back up to my studio and begin to clean the glass off the floor. A splinter slices into my finger, and I unconsciously put it into my mouth, tasting my blood. I wonder what it would be like to bleed to death. Knowing you were slowly dying yet not being able to do anything about it? I secretly wish Mack would bleed to death while I watch. Hatred has overcome the hurt and anger. After I finish with the cleanup, I decide I would just go to bed. Maybe read a bit of the book I will probably never finish. I close my studio down and close the door.

Chapter 25

I change into my pajamas and go down to get a cup of herbal tea. I pick out a lavender/lemon flavor that boasts of being a relaxing, sweet-tasting tea. As the water boils, I walk into the forbidden library to search for my book. I'm sure I left it on the end table. I switch the light on and am surprised at what a mess there is on the desk. I absently walk over and look at the paperwork lying all over the desktop. Newspaper articles of the murders and also police copies of the crime scenes. I don't want to look at any more pain and hatred, so I go to get my book. I go into our bedroom to drink my tea, read my book, and try to and relax. I don't want to think of Mack or the party he's at or the woman I had seen on the screen next to him. I don't want to think of the mess in the library or anything associated to Mack. Please, just let me relax, forget, and maybe sleep. I drink all my tea, and the book seems to get more boring with every page I turn. I really find it hard to concentrate on the book, and relaxing seems to be next to impossible. I should take my teacup down to the dishwasher so Mack won't come unglued that I actually drank a beverage in the bed. As I'm holding the book that I had taken from the room, I wonder about returning the book too. How foolish to be afraid to go into the library and retrieve my book. This is my house too, but then Mack never enters my studio, so maybe I should just give in and let the library be his. I try once more to get into the book without much success. I decide to go back into my studio. Maybe I could find peace once more.

This is the only room in the house that I love. I look out the window and think of how peaceful my life was before Mack became so obsessed with catching the murderer or murderers. I stare at my sketchbook and decide to sketch something to eventually paint and, who knows, maybe sell in Jordyn's shop. I have no problem thinking of something to work on and begin with a simple outline. Before long I have done a large pencil drawing of a child walking down a lane with a faithful dog at her side. I could just imagine Princess splashing in the puddles with her dog faithfully tagging along beside her. Both filled with unconditional love and innocence. I hear the garage door open and I'm surprised that Mack would be home so early. I just assumed he would be later. Fulfilling his sexual desires on the woman at his side at the party. I decide to go meet him before he has a chance to come searching for me. I turn the light off and close the door. I meet him on the stairs as he's coming up. He seems just as surprised to see me on the steps and awake as I am to see him actually home. He reeks of whiskey, cigarettes, and perfume.

"What the hell are you doing up, Elise? I thought you'd be fast asleep seeing how sick I told everyone you were." He sounds as if he actually believes his lie.

"What are you doing home so early, Mack? Didn't your little whore put out tonight?" My voice is as sweet as honey dripping from the hive. His body language goes from relaxed to tense and stiff in a matter of a split second.

"What little whore, Elise? Oh, did you see me on the news? She really is a beautiful, intelligent woman. She's the mayor's niece, and she will be joining my office. Are you jealous, my dear little wife?"

"No, not at all. In fact, I feel sorry for her." I turn to go back to our bedroom.

"You bitch!" he yells. "I should push your sorry ass down the stairs and just get you out of my life for good."

"Oh, Mack, can't you think of something more creative than that? You already told everyone I fell down the steps. What would your excuse be this time? I was running into your arms and tripped and fell?"

He reaches out and grabs a handful of my hair so quickly I didn't have a chance to escape his grasp. "You are pretty mouthy tonight, my dear. I may have to teach you a lesson on manners and how to treat your husband." Tears involuntarily fill my eyes, and I cry out in pain. "Maybe you should think twice on what you say to your loving husband, you stupid ugly bitch. Now say you are sorry for your mouth and get your ass in bed and be ready for me while I make us a couple of nightcaps." He shoves me toward the bedroom door. I'm not sorry for my mouth, and I sure in hell wasn't going to have sex with him after what he did this evening. No way am I going to lower myself to his level and allow him to use me like he normally does. He would have to kill me before I would give in to him. Maybe just maybe I'd kill him tonight.

I walk into the bedroom and look around for a weapon to use on him. I spot the poker from the fireplace, the candelabra on the mantel, or maybe I could convince him to have kinky sex and choke him with his own belt. I decide the latter would be bad because I am sure he'd strangle me first. I walk in front of the fireplace and loosen the poker from the rack. I don't want to be holding it when he comes in the door, but I don't want to be in bed either. Being in bed would really give him the advantage. I want to be prepared for the fight I'm sure we would have when he finds I'm not going to give in to his insatiable sexual needs. I stand next to the fireplace, trying to be nonchalant. My whole body seems to be shaking. I'm not sure if I would be standing when he enters the room or if I'd be a crumpled mass of Jell-O lying on the carpet. My heart is pounding in my chest so hard I can feel each beat in my temples. My stomach is in a tight knot, and I'm not sure if I'm going to vomit or just pass out. I wait there for what seems to be an eternity. I look at the nightstand and find the clock. I have stood there for a half hour, and Mack has not come up yet. I decide I would go find where he is and maybe I'd have my confrontation in another room of the house, but I'm sure I'd have one. I quietly walk down the stairs and approach the kitchen. He's nowhere in sight. I turn and go to the library. I find him slumped over the mess on his desk, with his head resting on his arm. His hand loosely gripping the glass of whiskey. He's mumbling in his drunken stupor, but I can't understand what he's trying to say. I think about ending his life in the forbidden library but decide against it. I need an alibi or at least a better plan than to smash his skull in with a poker. I turn and leave the library and go upstairs to our bedroom. I know I will sleep little that night for fear of him entering and raping me again and again.

I wake in the early morning after a very sound and peaceful sleep. I feel refreshed and calm. I lay there enjoying the peace and quiet, wondering what the day would bring. In an ugly flash, the memory of the past night comes crashing into my thoughts. The feeling of hatred and dread fills me with a thickness that weighs on me. It feels as though a pile of bricks has covered the blankets on my bed. I remember the fear of the conflict I was sure would happen last night. The bile rises in my throat, and I feel as though I'm drowning in my own bed. All I want to do is to bury my face in the pillow until I suffocate, drown, or just die. I decide lying in bed and feeling sorry for myself would be something that Mack would relish, and I refuse to let him rise above me. I make up my mind that I will no longer let him use me, humiliate me, hurt me, either mentally or physically. I will fight back and prove to him I am a strong person and that he will never break me. I get up and go into the bathroom. Looking into the mirror, I see a stronger me, much like the old me. It's amazing what a good night's sleep can do and how good you can actually look when you make up your mind to do something about the situation you are in. I wash my face and put on makeup and prepare to get dressed.

I hear Mack on the stairs and think I'm prepared for the bullshit he's going to toss at me this morning. He walks into the room and stares at me as if seeing me for the first time in his life. I face him stolid and unforgiving. I wait for him to begin his vitriolic tirade, but it doesn't come.

He slowly eases himself onto the bed and states in a weak, pathetic voice, "My god, Elise, I feel like I've been drunk for days."

I say nothing as I finish dressing and silently leave the room. I decide he could wallow in his self-pity and hangover all by himself.

Chapter 26

I go downstairs, pour a cup of coffee, and decide to make some ready-to-bake cinnamon rolls. I suddenly want something sweet and gooey to eat for breakfast. Why not start my day with a treat to myself. Lord knows I have had very few these past months. I'm sure he'd be down after he's had a shower, and then all hell would break loose. I'm hoping he would take his time and let me enjoy a roll and a cup of coffee before he begins his never-ending mental and physical abuse. I'm surprised when he doesn't show up. I'm able to enjoy two cups of coffee, and I've eaten three of the small sweet treats before I hear him come down the stairs. I'm well prepared for him. I'm not in the mood for his didactics. I'm done being told when to jump, how high, and how often, as though I'm a child incapable of thinking for myself. No, I would force myself to be callous and to stand up to him.

He walks into the kitchen dressed, clearly on his way out the door. I don't say a word, and neither does he as he pours himself a cup of coffee. He takes a sip and turns to look at me. I feel like a deer frozen in the headlights. I could feel the strength drain out of my backbone. I feel my self-esteem crumble as his bloodshot eyes stare into mine.

"You look good enough to eat this morning, Elise." He has a half grin on his face. I shudder at the thought and what may come next. "Unfortunately, I haven't the strength or the energy to do anything. I don't think I have the constitution to even stay in an upright position for very long this morning." He sinks into a kitchen chair.

"As good as those cinnamon rolls smell, I think they would kill me if I tried to eat one. God, I feel horrible. I know I fell asleep in the library, but I don't even remember coming home last night. I honestly can't remember anything after the first drink at the mayor's party. I wonder if I was drugged." He's talking more to himself than to me.

I stay silent for fear of what I might say if I start to talk. I'm waging a war within myself. Should I tell him what I saw on the local news? Should I tell him what he said regarding the beautiful woman he was talking with? Should I tell him how he pulled my hair and demanded I be ready for him when he came to bed? No, I won't say anything. Let him think I don't know about the woman. Let him think he went right into the library when he came home. I don't need to tell him anything. Let him figure it out for himself.

"When you are feeling better, you maybe should call Haven to go over the details for Becca's baptismal."

He mumbles something to himself. "When is it?"

"Next Sunday in Portsmith."

He rises from the chair and refills his coffee and walks out of the kitchen and into the library and slams the door. I hear the lock turn on the library door. Does this mean he will be staying in there all day and not go into the department? Still, relief floods through me, and I feel as though I had just won first prize in a contest. It doesn't matter if the contest only exists in my thoughts.

I refill my coffee cup and think about consuming another cinnamon roll and decide against it. I take my coffee and go outside onto the patio and sit in the garden, listening to the early morning noise of the backyard. The sun is warm, and the air smells of rain and flowers. I seem to have forgotten how wonderful the outside and sunshine can be. I have a feeling of renewal, almost a rebirth. Why hadn't I decided to stand up for myself earlier? Why had I waited so long to find my inner strength? I tip my head back and stare into the bright blue sky, letting the sun beat down on me. It's a deep feeling of relief that I feel. I finish my coffee and decide to go back into the house and ask Mack if he has any ideas of what he may want for our dinner and if we could eat on the patio.

As I approach the library door, I hear him talking to someone on the phone. I assume it is either his work or maybe Haven. I'm about to turn around and not knock on the locked door when I hear him say that "it should be a wonderful time." I gently knock on the door, and I heard him walking toward it. I'm expecting him to be angry and upset over another person being a godparent for Becca, but when he opens the door, he has a genuine smile on his face. He's just saying goodbye to whomever was on the other end. He looks at me and asks, "What do you need, Elise?"

"Do you want something special for dinner tonight, and could we eat on the patio if it doesn't rain?"

He calmly pulls me into his arms. "You decide, Elise, and yes, it would be nice to eat out there. I plan on working in the library for the rest of the day. I have some loose ends I have to clear up before my meeting in the morning with the mayor."

This shocks me. This is such an aberration from what I'm used to. I'm afraid to ask him if Haven mentioned the other godparent. He gently holds me for a bit longer and then lets his arms fall to his side.

"Go enjoy your day, I have work to do." He turns and shuts and locks the door behind him. He knows I will not bother him and wonder at the locked door.

The rest of the day goes by peacefully, and I spend much of my time on the patio sketching and just enjoying the sunshine. Around five o'clock I start the grill and prepare the salad and baked potatoes. I clean the patio table off and set the table for the two of us. It starts to cloud over, but it's still warm and pleasant. I go to the library door and knock, telling him through the door, "Dinner will be ready in ten minutes." I'm answered with a growl of disdain. I feel defeated again but decide I'm not going to take no for an answer. "Suit yourself, but I'm eating out on the patio if you decide to join me." I turn to walk away as the door swings open, and a disheveled Mack stands in front of me. He looks as though he had drunk a couple bottles of bourbon. I can tell he had run his hands through his hair so many times it's standing in all different directions. His shirt is wrinkled, and I'm not sure if he had taken a nap or just did a strenuous work-out in it.

He sees the surprise on my face and growls, "This case is going to kill me yet."

I gently take his hand and say, "Take a break and have something to eat, maybe drink a glass of wine, and try to put it out of your mind for a little bit. Then if you must go back into the library, perhaps you will see it more clearly."

"Yes, maybe you're right. Let's go eat, and I need a glass of wine. Thank you, Elise," he whispers.

We eat in near silence, and he returns to the library as I clean up the mess. I watch TV for the rest of the evening and decide to go to bed around ten. He comes into the bedroom shortly after and col-lapses on the bed, practically snoring before his head hits the pillow.

Chapter 27

Monday starts the usual routine. I make his breakfast, and he leaves. I go to the market and have my cappuccino without meeting or seeing anyone I know. I decide not to go to the shop and see Jordyn. Although I really am excited and anxious about her seeing my work and starting a great business/friendship, I don't want her to think I'm desperate or too pushy. When I get home, I go to the studio and start to paint. It's after three when I realize I forgot to eat anything, and I'm famished. I go down to get a Diet Coke and maybe an apple when the house phone rings. I don't even think twice about answering it and pick it up. Only after I say hello do I feel the old sensations return.

"My, have you been happy the last couple of days. That's how I like them, happy." His voice is a monotone. "I want you to always be happy, right up until you breathe your last raspy breath. Right up until your eyes become dulled with the look of death. Yes, happy, that's how I want you to be."

"Who are you? Why are you doing this to me?" I cry into the phone.

"All in good time, my sweet. Be patient, you will find out soon enough." He's laughing as he hangs up.

I slam the phone down and start to cry. Why me? Who could be so cruel? Mack has to be behind this. I'm sure of it. The calls only come when I'm happy or I'm daydreaming. It's as though the caller is in my head. Mack is the only person I could think of that has that sort of mean streak in him. It takes a while for me to get myself pulled together, and after I do, I don't feel much like painting. I close down my studio and go out onto the patio. That's where Mack finds me lying in a recliner sound asleep.

The kick to the chair brings me out of my dreamless nap. I jump out of the chair, ready to run, when I hear him cuss. "For Christ sake, Elise, you have to be more careful. I came through the house and out here without you even hearing me."

"I'm sorry. I must have fallen asleep. What time is it? Mack, he called again, you have to check the phone records." The words came out in a rush. "I was enjoying the afternoon when he called. I came out here to settle down, and I must have fallen asleep."

He stands there staring at me as if I've lost my mind. He calmly asks, "What the hell are you talking about? You have never mentioned anything about phone calls. I thought your lover only sent you notes. What time did he call, Elise?"

"It was after three. I was hungry and went for an apple and Diet Coke when the phone rang."

"Elise, it's nearly six, and I checked the phone records before I left the office. You must be mistaken about the time, or the call never took place. It would be just you to try to put your pathetic self in the limelight again. I doubt anything you say is true. I'm thinking you are writing the notes, claiming to have conversations with someone, just to get some attention. Really, Elise, you are something else."

I know at that moment the old Mack is back, and I'm in for more vicious calumny.

"Now, get your ugly ass into the kitchen and prepare me something to eat."

Instead of meekly obeying his command, I look at him with disdain. "I'm not hungry. You're a big boy, if you are so damn hungry, make yourself something to eat. I'm going to go take a bath and then do nothing." I walk past him and into the house, never looking back. I see him standing there on the patio in the reflection in the mirror. I stifle a laugh at the complete look of confusion on his handsome face. I hurry up the stairs, grab my lounging clothes, and go into the bathroom and lock the door. I hear the bedroom door hit the wall as he flings it open. I feel his heavy steps coming toward the locked bathroom door. I can almost feel his heavy breathing through the closed door. He twists the knob with such force I think it might twist off and break in his hand. He begins to pound on the wood until the whole door shakes.

"Open this door, or I swear I will tear it off the hinges!" he screams at the top of his lungs.

I sit on the edge of the whirlpool tub and watch the hot, steamy water running in to the cold porcelain. I neither feel afraid or any dread from him pounding on the other side of the closed door. I almost wish he could break it down.

After I don't open the door or answer him, he stops the ungodly pounding and softly says, "I swear I will kill you when you come out." I hear him stomp out of the room.

I slowly sink into the hot water and think, *Not if I kill you first.*

I stay in the tub until the water cools and I feel like a wrinkled prune. I stand up and step out of the tub. I turn the water on in the shower and step into it. Feeling it beat against my body like tiny needles piercing my skin. I welcome the tingling and pain it inflicts on me. After washing my hair in the shower, I turn the water off and step onto the floor mat. I stare at myself in the steamed full-length mirror. It brings back the memory of my masturbation while dreaming of Mr. Stranger. I'm tempted to do it again to see if I can bring myself to the same pleasure. My imagination also brings back the memory of how violently he died. I decide it won't be right if I actually did pleasure myself while he lies dead in an unmarked grave. So I just dry myself and dress. I brush through my wet hair and pull it back in a ponytail. Looking at my neck, I think that it makes it easier for Mack to slit my throat with my hair out of the way. I pick up my wet towels and hang them on the towel bars near the tub. It's time to face the music on the other side of the bathroom door. I finally unlock the door and walk into the bedroom. I have no idea what I would be walking into. I'm not expecting Mack to be standing next to the bed naked. I realize then that he always reverts to sex if he can't get his way with me in any other fashion. I walk past him and start toward the door.

"Not so fast, Elise. You honestly didn't think you were going to get me all worked up and then not give me what we both want, did you?"

I stop and look at him. "I don't want you if that is what you're thinking."

He shoots toward me like a flash of lightning. Before I can make it through the door, he has me in a bear hug. His lips are on mine, and he's forcing his tongue into my mouth. He lifts me off the floor and walks to the bed. I'm thrown onto the bed with such force I'm sure the bed breaks under me.

For once in my life my body doesn't react to his touch. I start to push him away from me. I use all the strength I have trying to get him off me. He raises his head and says, "Oh, so you want to play rough." He pushes me down even harder onto the bed. To both of our surprise, I'm not giving up. I manage to bring my knees up. It's all I need to make him lose his grip for just a split second. I take that advantage and push him with all my might. He loses his grip on me altogether, and I manage to bring my feet up and shove him off the bed and off me. I turn and crawl across the bed and grab the glass lamp on the nightstand. I yank it so hard the cord comes out the socket and whizzes past my head. I throw it into his face. He's so surprised at my violence he misses catching it, and it hits him full force on the forehead. It shatters, and the pieces of glass fly all over the bedspread and carpet. I don't stay long enough to see if he's injured. I run out of the room and down the steps. I can hear him following behind me, screaming obscenities along with threats against my life. I don't bother to stop and run out the front door and onto the sidewalk. He grabs his robe and follows. He catches me as I'm running up the next-door neighbor's walkway. I have no idea what he will do as he stands there grabbing hold of my arm. I look at the neighbor's large window, praying someone is watching.

"Wrong neighbor to pick, Elise." He snarls through clenched teeth. "They are out of town and called to see if they could get extra patrol to drive past their residence. You are dead meat. That is exactly what you are, an ugly piece of meat. I own you, Elise. You will never escape me."

I wish I were dead at that moment. Why didn't I pick the other neighbor or run across the street? I look into his eyes and think of a feral animal with rabies. Nothing is going to save me from his wrath. What will he do to punish me this time?

Chapter 28

I give up and walk beside him to our front door. The door stands ajar, and as I look into the foyer, I think of it as a torture chamber. I know just how prisoners of the Spanish inquisition must have felt when they were led down into the bowels of some castle to wait their torture and death. I follow seemingly calm on the outside as my insides turn into a molten pit of mush. He says nothing more to me as he marches me into the house like a naughty child who has run off against strict orders to stay put. I'm alarmed when he drags me along into the garage. As we go through the door. I try pulling away from him. He hisses through his teeth and says in a menacing tone, "I'd stop if I were you, Elise, you will not escape me. You better save your strength, my dear, because you will need all of it to survive." He hangs onto my arm and twists it behind my back as he opens a drawer and pulls out a rope and duct tape. I stare at them and then look into his evil face. Oh my god, he plans on tying me up and maybe suffocating me with the tape. At least, he will be silencing my cries and pleas with the tape. I really am a dead woman.

He drags me back into the house and straight up to our bedroom. Once again I begin to fight him. This time he is ready for me, and the blow to my head is hard, and the last thing I see is the smile on his handsome face as I slide into oblivion. When I awake, I'm tied to the bed spread eagle. I feel tiny shards of glass cutting into my legs where they landed on the bed. My mouth has duct tape over it. I lift my head and see him sitting in the chair next to the fireplace calmly drinking his glass of bourbon. I let my head fall back to the pillow. It hurts too bad to raise it. I think I probably have another concussion, and maybe this time it will kill me. I have to vomit. I will drown in my own bile. I pray for a quick, easy death. He rises and comes to the edge of the bed. Smiling down at me like a Cheshire cat.

"It took you long enough to wake up. At first I thought I may have killed you without having any fun. But then I could see your lovely breast rising and lowering as you breathed. We are going to have such fun. I can hardly wait. How about you, Elise? Oh my, where did all that fight go? Where did you learn to defend yourself like that? It really was very well played, except for picking the wrong house to run to for help."

He has stripped me naked while I was out, and now I'm defenseless and at his mercy. He crawls onto the bed beside me, cussing about all the glass on the bed. I pray a piece will slice off his cock. He straddles me and leans over. His face is only inches away from mine. I can smell the bourbon, and his eyes are shining with excitement. He's turned on to the hilt and is about to rape me. He gently kisses my cheeks and then runs his tongue down the center of my body, stopping just at the top of my navel. His hands trail over my breast and down my sides. I don't move, and I refuse to let him see my fear. He enters into me with one quick jab. It hurts, and I want to scream out, but nothing but a groan escapes from my throat.

"I know you like this. Doesn't it feel divine?" he states as he pulls the length of his shaft out of me and plunges into me until I'm sure I'm being ripped in two. I stare at him with hatred in my eyes. He keeps pulling out and plunging into me until I try to arch against him to push him off my body. "That's it, Elise, join in the fun and enjoy it." His release comes a lot faster than he wants. He's enjoying my torture. He rolls from being on top of me and curses as he steps on glass. He hops to the chair, and I turn my head to watch as he pulls a small piece of glass from his heel. I would have laughed out loud if my mouth isn't taped shut. He limps into the bathroom to clean up his foot.

As he's cleaning his foot, I become all too aware of the glass in my body. I realize if I move, they become very painful. I wonder just how long he will keep me tied to the bed—hours, days, or until I died from starvation. He comes out of the bathroom with his slippers and robe on. He walks to the bed and smiles at me.

"If you promise to be a good girl, I will let you go. If you try anything, I will kill you with my bare hands and throw you down the basement steps. Are you going to be a good girl and can I trust you to behave yourself?" he states in a nonemotional tone. I nod as tears of relief slowly slide down the sides of my face and into my hair. He slowly begins to untie me. "So foolish of you to run from me. Who would believe your bullshit? It's your word against a cop's." Once I'm free of the bed, I roll to the side of the bed that had less glass lying on it. "Oh, Elise, you are rather cut up from your stupidity. I'll bet you will think twice before throwing something made of glass at me again. You're just lucky I hated the lamp, or you really would be in deep trouble." He watches me struggle to get the tape off my mouth without ripping the skin off my lips. When the tape is off, my lips feel on fire, and I can't help but gasp for deep breaths of air. I never realized how good it feels to be able to breathe through both my mouth and nose. I walk into the bathroom and try to see the back of my legs in the mirror. He follows me into the room. "If you hold still, I will take the tweezers and pull out the pieces I can find." I slowly turn and want to scream for him to just get the hell away from me but doubt he would leave. I decide I probably can't pull them out without help, so I nod.

"Thank you."

He enjoys every time I jump or flinch when he pulls a piece out of my flesh. I'm sure he purposely digs deep into my meaty flesh when he doesn't have to. Blood is trickling down my legs onto the tile floor. When he starts to remove the slivers of glass out of my behind, he massages every spot that a piece comes out of. I'm sure he is going to force himself upon me again. I stand there, waiting for the assault. It doesn't come, and he finally says, "I think I have them all. Why don't you take a shower? You have a big mess to clean up in the bedroom. I really don't want to step on or lie on any shards of glass because of your stupidity."

I go back into the bedroom to grab some clean clothes and return to take my shower. He's examining the glass that he took from my body. He turns and with a half-smile, that I used to find very pleasing on him.

"I should make a cup of tea for you with these as you clean up the rest."

"No, thank you, I've had enough of your kindness for one day."

He laughs loud and spontaneously as he walks out of the bathroom. The hot shower that felt wonderful earlier now feels like real torture. I hurriedly wash myself and turn off the pulsating stream of pain beating on my body. As I carefully dry myself, I wonder if that's what it would feel like to be tasered. I finish in the bathroom and go into the bedroom to find it empty. I walk into the hall and get the upstairs vacuum and take it into the bedroom. I pick up the bigger pieces of glass and put them in a pile on the dresser. I strip the bed completely before I start to vacuum. I vacuum the bed first and then the carpet. I go over the carpet about ten times before I feel all the glass should be out of it. I run my hand over much of it, and it seems fine. I finish cleaning the mess up and put everything back where it belongs. I will go to the attic to see if there might be another smaller lamp for the nightstand. I really don't care whether there's spare lamp to use or not.

I go downstairs expecting Mack to be in the library. He's instead sitting at the bar in the kitchen reading a magazine. Without looking up, he asks, "Get your mess cleaned up, Elise?"

"Yes."

I take an apple from the crisper and a Diet Coke. I turn to go when he grabs my arm. I look at him, and he says with more sincerity than I've heard him use in a very long time, "I'm sorry I pushed you to revert to such violence. It won't happen again."

I stare at him and flatly state, "You are right, it won't. I will kill you next time."

He releases my arm, and I walk from the kitchen. My knees feel as though they will buckle with each step I take. I'm beyond afraid. Afraid he'll come after me, afraid I will actually kill him, afraid the judge won't see it as self-defense, afraid I will never find peace. I'm no longer hungry and set my drink and apple on the table near the stairs and climb the stairs and go to bed.

Knowing I will not sleep a dreamless sleep, if I sleep at all. I'm still wide awake when Mack slides in beside me. He doesn't try to pull me closer but turns his back to me, and soon I hear his gentle snoring. I lie there jealous of his ability to sleep. I wake to the sound of the alarm clock blaring in my ears. Mack reaches to shut it off and then turns toward me. I don't want him to be near me.

"It's time to start the day, Elise. I don't want anything but coffee this morning, so if you want to stay in bed a bit longer, you may."

"Thank you, I think I will."

I listen to his morning routine, and when he leaves the bedroom, I turn over and lie on my back staring at the ceiling. I hear him coming up the stairs, but I don't care if he knows I'm awake, sleeping, or dead. He pops his head through the doorway.

"I'm leaving, and I won't be home until late, so don't worry about making dinner or waiting up for me."

I raise my head and manage a civil "Okay, have a good day." He shuts the bedroom door, and I wait to hear the garage door open and close and the sound of the car diminishing as he drives away.

Chapter 29

I'm so excited for the day when I get up. Today is the day I'm taking my paintings to the shop. I watch the clock like a fifth grader waiting for the bell to end a boring school day. Finally, at nine o'clock, I go up to my studio and decide to use the tote I use to carry my paint supplies and canvas when I go to the park to paint. I grab my purse and notice a note on the table in the foyer. With shaking hands, I unfold the paper and read it.

"There is money on the dining room table for you to buy a new lamp for the nightstand. Have a good day, Love you, Mack."

I nearly faint. What is he up to? I go into the dining room and find $100 lying on the table. I take it and put it in my wallet, pick up my tote and purse, and walk out the front door to the bus stop. I originally was going to drive, but I feel the need to walk to allow myself to calm down. I feel an excitement mixed with a doom. What's going to happen next? What's Mack up to? I try to think of something happy as I ride the few blocks to my stop.

Jordyn is waiting in her shop. The bell above the door tinkles as I open it and step into the cheery store. The atmosphere is thick with happiness. I feel out of place and almost turn to leave, when Jordyn comes around the counter to greet me. "Good morning, I am so excited to see your paintings." She reaches out and hugs me. The anxiety is slipping away, and I return her smile with one of my own.

"I hope you won't be too disappointed."

She's taking my tote from me. She immediately starts to remove and unwrap the paintings. She doesn't say anything while she's inspecting each painting. My stomach rises up into my throat, and I realize I'm holding my breath. She turns toward me and takes my hands in hers.

"My god, Elise, these are spectacular. You have more talent in your little finger than most do in their entire bodies. I had no idea when you said you painted that I would be dealing with a professional."

I let out a huge sigh of relief. "I'm glad you like them, but do you think they will sell?"

"Sell? Sell? They will fly out of here. Now, let's go get a cup of coffee and discuss the prices of these gems." Taking my hand, she leads me from the store and across the street to the café.

Once we have our coffee, we settle down to business. The prices she suggests I think are a bit extravagant, but she assures me that they are a bit on the low sight.

"We will start out lower, and as they sell and the word gets out that I have a skilled painter on consignment, we will keep raising the prices." She's rubbing her hands together. I'm not too sure that that's really going to happen that way, but let her make tags for the paintings.

"Do you have time to help me hang them in the shop?" We laugh and talk while hanging the paintings. I feel so at ease with her it's as though I've known her for all my life.

It's after one when I think I better get home. I turn to leave and see the most beautiful lamp sitting on a table. It will go with the decor of our bedroom perfectly. I pick it up and see that it's marked at just $60. I decide it's the lamp I want. I take it to the counter and say, "I'd like to buy this lamp. It is a perfect replacement for the one I broke."

"It was handmade by another friend of mine." She wraps it, and when she hands it to me, she says, "It's yours as a welcoming gift." I start to protest, but she won't hear of it. She tells me she has another to match it if I want to buy the second one. I agree and walk out of the shop with two lamps for our bedroom. I'm so happy when I get on the bus to go home I'm sure I'm soaring with the birds above. I'm sure nothing can spoil my good mood. I'm looking out the window of the bus, and the day seems to be welcoming me into a new and wondrous world. The bus stops at the end of my block, and I step to the sidewalk knowing my life is about to change for the good. I feel as though I were floating toward the house. I suddenly think, *This is how a butterfly must feel as it flutters freely through the air, enjoying the freedom on a beautiful summer day.* I remember to turn on the alarm system, and I take the lamps to the bedroom to unwrap them and set them up.

I decide I'm not going to live my life in fear anymore. I've found the nerve to stand up to Mack. That didn't have the outcome I was hoping for, but at least I've found the guts to stand my ground. I make up my mind to be the woman I used to be. No more sniveling mass of gel. I will be strong. I enter the kitchen and grab another apple. I remember I had left one on the table next to the stairs last night. I put the new one back and walk to the table to get the apple and warm Diet Coke. The note is propped up between the two. I look at it with disgust and leave it there. I take the Coke and apple and go to my studio. I sit in my comfortable chair with my sketchbook and start to draw. I feel truly alive. I sketch a rosebush with beautiful butterflies floating above the bush and daintily sitting on the blooms. I get up and go to look out the window. It's still a sunny, pleasant day outside, and I'm still feeling elated with my new me. I decide to paint more of my troubles and fears away.

Chapter 30

It's already past six when I quit and go downstairs to scrounge up something to eat. A salad and a glass of ice tea. I'm sitting at the counter when I hear the garage door open. I'm surprised that Mack would be home so early. I have to mentally prepare myself for his many moods. I'm trying to remember if I dreamed he said he'd be home late or if he said it for real before he left. Either way, I'm sure I'm in for a battle of some sort. Mack comes into the kitchen and sees me eating a salad.

"Hey, is there enough in the fridge for another salad?" he asks as he walks past me. I swallow my mouthful of lettuce before answering him.

"Sure, do you want me to whip you up one?"

"No, I will, after I change out of these clothes!" he shouts as he runs up the stairs. He comes back down just as I'm finishing my salad and leans in to give me a peck on the cheek.

"Didn't you tell me you'd be home late tonight?"

"Yes, but I decided I had had enough bullshit for today and came home. Do we have any more ranch dressing?" He's looking for it in the refrigerator door. I get up and go to the pantry and bring out a new bottle. He goes about making his salad, making small talk about his day. He eats his salad in silence as I sip my ice tea. After he's finished, I reach for his dish, and he grabs my arm, and I freeze. I look at him, and he's smiling.

"I'm capable of cleaning up my own mess." He lets go of my arm, and I move away. He cleans up his mess. "Let's go watch TV, just not the news." He automatically walks past the table next to the stairs and see the note. He looks at me and walks past it without picking it up. I leave it there and follow him into the living room.

With Mack in this unusually calm mood, I begin to unwind myself. I had felt wonderful earlier, but when I heard the garage door open, I immediately went into defense mode. Mack stretches out on the couch and motions me to join him. I hesitate for a minute and then think why not enjoy the serene feeling Mack is offering. I lie down beside him, and he scrolls through the movie channels until he finds *On Golden Pond*.

"Is that okay to watch?"

"Yes."

Sometime during the first part of the movie, I feel his breathing become even and deep. I glance up to find his eyes closed, and his face has a gentle boyish innocence about it. That's the Mack I fell in love with.

I find it hard to keep my eyes open and fall into a peaceful sleep. I dream I'm lying on the wet grass. It's a soothing, warm feeling. The raindrops fall upon my body and my face. I can hear each drop hitting the blades of grass around me. It sounds as though a thousand little hands are clapping all at once and yet individually. The sky is dark except for the occasional brave bolt of lightning daring to break through the shroud of drops. The intensity of the bright streak shatters the droplets downward pattern, making them fall helter-skelter to the ground. Making the tiny hands lose their rhythm until the booming thunder shocks them back in time.

When I awake, I'm surprised that Mack is lying next to me, just staring into my face. He still has a boyish look about him, and I smile at him, thinking I wish he would always be like this. He says nothing and just tightens his hold on me and closes his eyes again, and I feel at that moment that he needs me. I continue to enjoy the feeling, hoping it won't end and we can be a comfort to each other forever.

The house phone rings and shatters the loving feeling that I'm having. I once again feel apprehensive. I let it go until the answering machine picks it up. Haven's cheery voice is about to leave a message when I quickly get up and answer it.

"Hi."

"Are you a real person?"

"Yes."

"I just called to remind you to be at the church in Portsmith promptly at ten thirty on Sunday for Becca's baptismal."

"We wouldn't miss it for the world." Hanging up, I turn to look at Mack.

He's sitting up and stretching when I walk over to the couch.

"How about I make us a nice drink?" I ask. I'm shocked when he declines.

"I will pass, I think I have been drinking far too much lately, and I need to stay more focused in my life. I'll just have a Sprite and maybe a few peanuts."

I go to the kitchen and get him a Sprite and myself a Diet Coke. I find the can of peanuts for him, and I grab the potato chips. I look at the Diet Coke and think, *You drink too much alcohol and I drink too much soda.* I replace the soda and take out a bottled water.

"Elise, just because I don't want a drink, doesn't mean you need to go without."

"No, I think I really prefer the water to a mixed drink or even a glass of wine." I hand him his Sprite and peanuts and go to sit in the chair.

"Please sit next to me."

I don't question his sudden change of heart and plop down next to him. We finish the movie in silence, with only the crunching of peanuts and chips to be heard between us. It's a pleasant sound.

We watch another old movie, and around midnight we both decide it's time to hit the hay. We put our snacks away and throw our garbage in the trash. He gently takes my hand, and we turn every-thing off downstairs and go upstairs to our room. I use the bathroom first, half dreading what might happen once we are in bed together. He goes into the bathroom, as I crawl into my side of the bed. I ask what time he needs to be up, and he says I shouldn't set the alarm. He had told the staff at the department that unless there's an extreme emergency, he's unavailable until Monday morning. He never seizes to surprise me. He pulls me close, kisses me lightly on the lips, and holds me gently as he falls asleep. It takes me longer to fall asleep, wondering which Mack I'd be facing tomorrow.

Chapter 31

The rest of the week is uneventful. Mack works in the library most of each day, and I work in my studio. We eat together, watch TV together, and go to bed together. It's the best week we've had in a very long time. Saturday seems to be flying by with Mack working in the library and me painting in my studio. We have a pleasant breakfast together and talk about the baptismal. We agree on not buying a present for Becca but opening up a savings account starting with $500. We could then add to it, besides buying her little things for her to open on her birthday, Christmas, etc.

Mack goes to the bank right after breakfast to set up the account. I stay behind and do a bit of housework. I see the note on the table and wonder if I should open it. I decide to let Mack and leave it where I had found it. Mack comes home with a bag of groceries and states he's going to grill out for supper and maybe we can just have a light lunch. I'm still not sure of his sudden change but decide to relish the moment and go with the flow.

Mack comes out of the library around one thirty and yells up the stairs, "Elise, are you hungry yet? I'm starved, and I'm going to make tomato soup and grilled cheese. Do you want some?"

"Yes, that sounds great."

I began to put up my brushes and pallet. He's singing as I walk into the kitchen. I feel as though maybe the old Mack is back. I begin to get the plates and soup cups ready and ask what he would want to drink. He decides on ice tea, and I think I might as well have the same. We sit in a comfortable silence as we eat our lunch. While we are cleaning up together, I ask, "Are you making any headway on whatever you are working on in the library?"

He just groans. "I have no idea. I'm not sure why I stay in this job. It consumes every second of my life. I have turned into an ugly ogre, and I don't like myself anymore. I sometimes feel like just falling off the edge of the earth."

I laugh. "Do you know the earth is round with no edges?"

He looks at me with a twinkle in his eye. "I'm sure it's flat in my head." He gently pulls me into his arms and kisses me with enough passion to melt the ice in the ice machine. My knees are wobbly when it ends. He gently smacks me on the backside and says, "Let's make this weekend ours." I nod as no words would come out of my mouth I'm so touched by his tenderness. "Now, let's get back to our dungeons and master what we're doing in there."

"My studio isn't really a dungeon but more of a place of peace."

"Good for you, Elise, the library is a room of chains that come alive and try to strangle me every time I open the door."

I'm seeing a completely different side of my husband. One who has broken himself just as much as he has broken me.

I return upstairs to my studio and begin to add to my painting. It feels so good to be able to not use my studio as a place of refuge. To be able to enjoy doing what I love without the feeling of dread hiding in the corners of my thoughts. Ready to surface and overtake my soul at any time. I feel loved, and I realize I do love this Mack. I'm not in love with him, but I do love him. I giggle out loud at that thought. Is it possible to love someone but not be in love with them? Yes, I conclude it's a possibility. I doubt I would ever be in love with Mack unless this new Mack continues living.

Chapter 32

I go down the steps a little after six, and I'm shocked at the cursing coming from the library. I stand at the bottom of the stairs and wonder who Mack is yelling at. I slowly walk to the library door and listen more closely. He seems to be talking to someone he knows, but I haven't heard anyone come to the house. It's then I realize he's yelling at himself and also answering himself as a different person. It reminds me of Anthony Perkins in *Psycho*, and I begin to be afraid. What should I do? Should I knock on the door letting him know I can hear him, or should I go back upstairs and wait until one of the Macks emerges from the room? I go into the kitchen instead and decide to bang a few pans, getting the steaks ready for him to grill. Mack appears just a few minutes later, and I ask him if he's finished for the day. He looks drained and as if he hasn't slept in a week. I don't mention that I had heard him carrying on a rather violent conversation with himself. I just continue to get the fixings for a salad out and the potatoes to bake in the microwave when the time comes.

"Mack, do you want a vegetable along with the baked potato and the salad?"

He looks at me like he has no idea what the hell I'm talking about, and the look scares me. He finally shakes his head and replies, "No, I think a salad, steaks, and potato are enough, unless you want one."

"No, I just wanted to please you."

He suddenly snaps at me, "Dammit, Elise, can't you just do what the hell you want to do for yourself, without always trying to please me." The sudden outburst takes me by surprise. Why it should, I have no idea. I don't answer him or look at him. He comes up behind me and gives me a hug. "I'm sorry." I lean back into him.

"It's okay."

He takes the steaks I had placed on a metal tray along with the tongs and starts toward the patio grill. I hand him some spices to add to the steaks. He just walks like a zombie through the door.

I set the table in the dining room and light the candles. He tells me to start the potatoes that the steaks would be done perfectly in just a few minutes. I start the microwave and finish setting everything out on the table. He comes into the kitchen just as the buzzer goes off on the microwave, announcing the potatoes are cooked. He sets the platter of steaks on the table, and I bring in the potatoes. He pulls out my chair and then pours me a glass of red wine.

"Why don't we do this more often?"

"I don't know."

We enjoy our wine and meal in a very peaceful atmosphere. It's almost as if we are meeting each other for the first time. The conversation is light, and the laughter comes easy. I lose the old sense of hatred, and it feels good to just relax. I only drink two glasses of wine, remembering the last time we went out to eat and how angry he became when I was going to drink three. He doesn't seem to notice, and as we finish our meal, he finishes the bottle of wine, pouring the last bit into our glasses evenly. We clean up together, comfortably working side by side.

When we are finished, he takes my hand and leads me into the living room. We sit on the couch together, and he turns on the TV. He picks a movie and gathers me close to him. With his arm around me and my head and back resting against him, I think, *What a wonderful day, why couldn't all our days together be like this one?*

It's close to midnight when he suggests we should get some sleep. After all, we are going to be spending tomorrow with Becca. He confesses he's very excited about seeing her again. We go up the stairs together and prepare for bed. Once in bed, he just holds me close, and we drift off to sleep, each with our private dreams.

Chapter 33

Something wakes me from a most pleasant sleep. I'm not sure if it's a noise or something more sinister. I just know I'm alone in bed, and I feel afraid. I lie there in complete stillness, waiting for whatever it is that woke me to become real. I wonder where Mack has gone. The bathroom door is open, and I can see with the aid of the moonlight that no one is in it. I slowly reach for the bedside lamp and switch it on. There's a folded note on the nightstand. I freeze, and feelings of fear and apprehension begin to fill my body. I slowly reach for it and open the folded piece of paper.

"I woke up and couldn't get back to sleep. You were sleeping so beautifully I didn't want to disturb you, so I went down to the library. I will wake you when it's time for breakfast and to get ready for the day. Love you, Mack."

I start to cry after reading the note. I'm not sure if it's from relief that it isn't from the monster stalking me or if it's from seeing the words "Love you" on the paper. The alarm clock says four o'clock. I turn the light off and try to fall back to sleep.

This time my dream is a haunting one. Mack and a stranger are fighting over Becca. They are each pulling on her. Each trying to wrench her from the other's grasp. She's crying, and she has blood on her tiny little body. I plead for them to stop, and they both turn to look at me. Just then I hear Mack's voice.

"Elise, wake up. You are screaming in your sleep."

I open my eyes to see him reaching for me. I practically jump into his arms and cling to him, sobbing like a child.

"It's just a dream, Elise," he's saying over and over.

I'm able to get control of myself and lean back onto the pillows. "I'm, sorry. I don't know why I have these nightmares, but I wish they would stop."

He looks at me and ruffles my hair like a puppy and says, "Maybe you need to go to the doctor and have it checked out." I'm beginning to think the same thing. But what type of doctor do I really need? A medical or psychoanalyst, that was the question. "It's six o'clock, if you want to get up and shower while I make breakfast." I just nod and swing my feet over the side of the bed.

I go downstairs in just my robe to the most delicious-smelling aroma. It's of fresh cinnamon rolls and bacon. Who wouldn't love that smell and coffee. Yes, I need coffee. Even though I had slept most of the night peacefully, the shower didn't seem to wash the dregs of sleepiness away. I need a cup of good strong coffee to wake up my mind and body. I take the cup of steaming liquid Mack hands me and take my first sip. It's hot and it's strong and burns a trail from the tip of my tongue to the bottom of my empty stomach. It's the best hurt I've felt in a very long time. I sit down at the bar and gladly dig into the hot bacon and a cinnamon roll. Mack laughs as I shove a whole piece of bacon into my mouth and happily crunch on it.

"Slow down, girl, I think I made enough for an army. You should have plenty here to fill you up."

"This is fabulous" is all I manage to say between bites.

Chapter 34

We are the last to arrive at the church. The morning congregation has all left, and so we have the whole place to ourselves. The grandparents are standing off to the side, jabbering as though they haven't seen each other in a month on Sundays. I see both Matt and Haven, who is holding the baby, along with another man standing with their backs to us in front of the minister. Mack's mom sees us first and calls out a greeting. Haven, Matt, and the other man turn around to say hello at the same time. I nearly trip over my own feet when I see who the third person to be Becca's godparent is. I do all I can do to keep my composure, and I'm sure my face is as red as the blood dripping from the statue of Christ standing next to the altar. It's the singer from the Old Barn, the night Mack and I went to celebrate his catching Mr. Flem.

It makes sense now. Haven had said he and Matt had played in a band together in college. Haven does the introductions.

"This is my brother, Mack, and his wife, Elise. This is Matt's buddy I told you about, Cameron James."

To my surprise Mack says, "Hey, man, I remember you from Haven's wedding. It's good to see you again. Weren't you at the Old Barn singing a few weeks ago?" They shake hands. He just looks at me with eyes of a Greek god and nods a hello. My voice sounds like Minnie Mouse.

"It's a pleasure to meet you, Mr. James."

"Please, call me Cam." His voice is the lowest, sexiest voice I think I have ever heard.

The minister asks if everyone is ready to get the show on the road, and we all nod and laugh. The actual rite only takes about ten minutes, but standing between Mack and Cam, it feels as if it's an eternity. I can't breathe normally, and I can't concentrate on the words to be repeated after the minister. I stumble on a few of them, and Mack nudges me in the side with his elbow. I would be hearing about this later. I feel it deep within my bones. After it's over, Rebecca announces that there's going to be a luncheon at their house as soon as we could all drive back to Flag Lake. We all start to leave the church at the same time. I'm still holding Becca and don't feel I will be able to control my shaking hands once I hand her back to her mother. When I finally do, I put my hands inside the folds of my full skirt, hoping no one will notice that they are shaking.

Mack admits he was very nervous during the ceremony and nearly couldn't say all the words. I tell him he did a lot better than I did. He laughs and agrees. The ride back to his parents' house goes smoothly. We all arrive at about the same time. It's then I remember the painting. Fear and dread begin to seep into my mind. I have no control over them. I'm feeling sick with dread. I'm going to be the reason Becca's day is spoiled.

Chapter 35

We enter the house, and I want to run and hide. I follow Haven into the master bedroom to help her change Becca out of her baptismal apparel and into a tiny pink dress with white tights and a pink headband with a tiny white rose on it. She truly looks the princess. She coos and gurgles all the while Haven is dressing her. Haven says she should be good for at least another hour before she would have to be fed. That should be long enough for all of us to finish our meal. Rebecca had a meal catered in especially for the big day and also so she could enjoy herself without the worry of cooking and cleaning up the mess. She had said she thought it would be more comfortable for everyone to be able to relax at the house instead of some restaurant.

Haven and I are just walking into the living room when I hear Mack say, "My god, what a beautiful painting of Haven and Becca." I nearly threw up from the bile rising in my throat. "It is superb, where did you find an artist to capture the look of love in their eyes like that?"

His mother turns and points at me. "Right there." Mack turns, and all the blood drains out of his face. I know I'm already as white as a sheet, but he matches my coloring to a tee. I just stand there rooted to the floor, waiting for the explosion to erupt. He doesn't move a muscle. Rebecca breaks the tension. "She painted it for Gerald and me for nursing her back to health. She did a wonderful job, didn't she?"

Everyone in the room all starts to talk at the same time. There were "It's beautiful," "It's fantastic," "What a wonderful gift." I still don't move, and I don't take my eyes off Mack. He slowly comes toward me, and I have the urge to flee. He reaches for my hands.

"I owe you an apology. That is great work. You did a beautiful job."

I can't hold back the tears that fills my eyes, but all I manage is a meek "Thank you."

He hugs me and whispers in my ear, "You are a true wonder to me."

The caterers announce that the meal is being served in the dining room, so we all begin to walk as a group to the table. I'm still shaking and unsure of myself or of how Mack is acting. Is it just that, an act, and he would lash out later when we're alone? I'm not sure I'd be able to eat without being ill.

The meal smells divine. The stuffed shrimp are to die for, and all the fixings are equally delicious. I eat way more than I ever thought I could. When Rebecca announces that dessert will be served in the living room with coffee, I'm sure I would burst out of my skirt. The small pieces of chocolate cake served with hot caramel sauce and sliced almonds are more than enough. I was thinking I'd only take a couple of bites to please Rebecca and then take my plate into the kitchen. I end up eating all of it, plus I drink a full cup of coffee.

I'm happy when Haven asks if I want to join her when she breastfeeds Becca. I walk along behind her like a fat little duck waddling to the river. I start to giggle, and Haven turns to ask what's so funny.

"I ate so much I am sure I am waddling like a fat duck."

"Believe me, you look slim and trim, just like you always do."

While she feeds Becca, she and I talk like we haven't been together for years. I confide in her that I had put some of my paintings in the little boutique owned by Jordyn. She's very pleased that I've finally come to my senses and realize I am an accomplished artist. We laugh at Becca's piggy noises as she nuzzles Haven's breast.

"I'm sure she will weigh one hundred pounds by the time she's a year old, if she keeps eating like she does." Haven laughs.

I carry Becca back into the living room just as Cam is walking out.

"Hey, beautiful," he says as his eyes stare directly into mine. I feel as though I've just been caught skinny-dipping in the old river. I can feel him undressing me with his eyes, and I'm not sure I don't like the idea.

I answer with a whisper, "She sure is a beautiful baby."

He puts his hand on my shoulder to keep me near him as he looks at Becca. I look at my blouse, expecting to see it smoldering where his hand is casually laid. "She is almost as beautiful as the lady holding her." He looks directly at me and winks. I can't think of a reply and take a quick step away from him and into the living room. Matt's mother comes forward and takes Becca from my arms, as Mack announces we are all going downstairs to the rec room to play cards. I'm not sure I'd be able to hold a hand of cards without everyone seeing how I'm shaking from my innocent yet seductive encounter with Cam. They all start to leave the room when Mack comes to me and says, "Are you all right, Elise? You look so pale, are you ill?"

I thought, *Pale? How could I possibly look pale when I am burning up inside?* "I think I gorged myself on your mother's lunch, and now I am a bit miserable." He accepts my excuse and takes my hand to lead me to the staircase. I ask if I could have a minute before joining them. "I think I would prefer to use the bathroom up here before I embarrass myself in the downstairs one."

Mack smiles his smirking little smile. "Oh yes, please use the one up here, no one needs to hear you explode."

"Gee, thanks, Mack, you make me sound like a stick of dynamite." I groan as I hold my stomach. He's laughing as he leaves the room.

I walk into the kitchen, and I'm surprised to find Cam standing there alone, looking out the patio doors. He turns when he hears me come into the room.

"Elise, you never called me." He's looking at me with desire in his eyes.

"Why would I, I am a happily married woman," I tell him as firmly as my voice will allow.

"Are you really, Elise?" He's walking toward me.

"Of course I am, why would you think otherwise?" I ask, trying hard not to keep my voice from giving out on me.

"Because of the sadness in your eyes, and the way you look at your husband with fear and not love." He gently runs his hand down my arm. My body reacts to his touch, and an involuntary shiver shocks my soul.

"I am too happy, and I don't look at him with fear," I state as though I were a five-year-old trying to defend myself for something I obviously had done. I take a step back and have backed myself into the island. He just keeps coming. We're standing so close I could feel his breath gently touching my face. Oh my god, he is going to kiss me. I turn my head away, and he laughs deep within his throat.

"Don't be afraid, Elise, I'm not going to do anything that you won't want me to. When I do kiss you, you will want me to. You will need me to." He gently takes my face in his hands. "Now is not the time, my love." He turns and silently leave the room. I walk blindly into the bathroom and stare at the stranger I see in the mirror. Am I that easily read? I'm suddenly sick. I throw up all the food I had eaten like a gluten earlier. I feel little relief from losing all my cookies to the porcelain god. I rinse my mouth out and splash a bit of cool water onto my face. I have makeup on and don't want to completely ruin it. Nor do I want to ruin Becca's day. I would simply ignore Mr. James for the rest of the time we have to spend together.

The rest of the afternoon goes by smoothly with a lot of laughter and love. Becca is doted on and held by everyone who are there for her special day. Mack holds her the most and seems to be truly enjoying himself with her. It couldn't have been a better day. Until Mack suggests it's time to go that I feel the tension seep into my body. Would Mack explode about the painting? Would I be punished for not telling him about the painting? Would he think I did it for attention? As we are saying our goodbyes, Cam comes over to us.

"Thank you for the invite to the house next Sunday." I look at Mack for confirmation.

"We are having a get-together on Sunday. Just Haven, Matt, and Cam are coming in for a cookout and a glass of wine." My stomach is in my throat again, and I only nod.

Cam shakes Mack's hand and leans in to plant a friendly kiss on my cheek. Oh good lord, now I'll be punished for sure, because a man kissed me innocently. Only I don't feel innocent at all. I feel as though I've just cheated on my husband. Good grief, I am spiraling out of control. I quickly turn and start out the front door. I need air. All the way home I wait on bated breath for Mack to explode. I sit there slumped in the seat, my head lolled on my neck as I look at the scenery we're passing. Not seeing anything, just waiting for the outburst to begin. I feel as though I'm a bowl of Jell-O not fully set being carried recklessly by a two-year-old on new carpet. Would I spill over the side and slide out of the bowl and plop onto the carpet or just slosh from side to side still contained? Would the two-year-old trip and throw me across the room to ruin all in its path? I know that somehow I would ruin the day.

Chapter 36

The outburst doesn't come. Mack jabbers about the day while he drives to our home. He's happy that we're part of Becca's day. Still I feel the unease. He says he likes Cam and is hoping he and Matt will bring their guitars and play and sing on Sunday.

We finally arrive home.

"You are awfully quiet, Elise, are you not feeling well?"

"No, I'm fine, maybe just a bit tired."

He pulls into the garage and smiles at me. "How about you go on inside and I'll drive to the root beer stand and pick up a couple of burgers for supper? You have to be getting hungry by now." He reaches over and touches my hair. I'm not hungry but agree to the burgers. I leave the car and go into the kitchen. I hear him leave the garage, and I turn on the alarm system. As I walk to the stairs, I see the note lying on the floor in front of the door. I leave it there. I'm not sure I can handle reading another threat. Mack could read it. I got upstairs to our bedroom and change into sweats and lie on the bed to wait for Mack to return home.

Mack comes home and calls for me to come to the kitchen to eat. I must have dozed off while I waited. I go downstairs, and as I enter the kitchen, I see Mack was reading the note. I shudder thinking of what it may contain this time.

He looks up. "Just more of the same. You have truly pissed off someone. He said it will be soon, Elise. I will get more police patrol for the house. Maybe you should just stay in the house for a couple of days again. I will take this to be tested."

I want to state the fact that I hate to be locked up in the house like a prisoner when some idiot is running free. I want to scream, "Why can't you catch him, or the right murderer for that matter?" Instead I say, "Okay, I'll just do some laundry and paint or read. Mack, I have something to tell you, and I'm afraid you will not be happy with me." I blurt this out before I lose my nerve.

"What the hell did you do this time?"

"I took some of my paintings to sell on consignment at the new boutique across from the café. The owner is a lady named Jordyn Kent. She seems really nice."

He looks at me like I just said I had cut up his mother and put her in the freezer. He shakes his head as if to clear it after being bashed in the skull. "Does she think they will sell?"

My words seem to gush from my mouth without any control from my brain. "Yes, oh yes, she was extremely pleased with my work. She said she was sure I'd be one of her best sellers."

"Good, I hope you do well." He has a genuine smile on his lips.

Without thinking I rush to him and kiss and hug him. "Oh, thank you for not being upset."

"I wondered when you were going to tell me."

"What?" I say, shocked.

"One of the guys in the office already bought one for his wife." He has a cocky grin on his face. "He rushed into my office and said your paintings were the biggest thing to hit Flag Lake since the William sisters sang back up for Johnny Cash in 1958." He's still grinning ear to ear. I'm shocked, thrilled, and apprehensive all at the same time. "Don't look so shocked, Elise. Not much goes on in this rinky-dink town without me finding out." He holds out his arms to me, and I willingly enter them and feel like I've just won the lottery.

Chapter 37

I realize I'm hungry and manage to devour the burger and fries with no problem. I feel better than I have felt in what seemed to be years. Mack seems genuinely happy for me, and we do truly have our weekend. I don't want it to end. It seems surreal, and I expect to wake up at any moment to realize I've been dreaming. I still have a nagging dread of Monday, but I want this day to stay the way it is and never end. Mack starts laughing, and I look up to find him staring at me.

"What? Did you say something and I was off in la-la land?"

"Something like that. I asked you if you were happy this weekend?"

"Oh yes," I reply. "I was just thinking I wish it could be like this every day. Happy and peaceful, with no tension, no hatred, no threats, no arguing. You know, I think we need to visit Princess more often. I think she brings the best out in both of us." I reach for his garbage, and he takes my hand. He slides off his stool and comes to me and kisses me gently. I can taste the fried onions he has eaten on his burger. It seems to just add to the intimacy of the kiss. When he releases me, I giggle.

"What?"

"You taste like the most wonderful fried onion I have ever had the privilege to kiss."

He steps back and, in an apologetic voice, says, "Oh geez, Elise, I'm sorry I will go brush my teeth immediately because I want to continue kissing you."

I finish removing the wrappers and I'm wiping off the counter when he comes back into the kitchen. He has changed into his blue silk robe, and I think he looks good enough to eat.

"I better go brush my teeth and change into something more comfortable too."

"Good idea, but don't take too long. I'll meet you in the living room." He growls deep in his throat. I practically fall up the steps I'm in such a hurry. I brush my teeth, wash in a few places, and add a dab of perfume. I put on my lime-green silk robe and hurry down the steps. I enter the living room and I'm surprised that he has turned on the fireplace and is standing in the middle of the room with two glasses of wine in his hand. I take one from him, and before I bring it my lips, the cell phone on the table rings. It breaks the mood instantly, and I let out a sigh of disbelief. He lets it ring until I say maybe it's important.

He picks it up and answers in a low, menacing voice. "Detective MacKenzie here." He listens closely and answers in a voice that could have cut through steel. "Shit, I'll be there in a half hour. Try to keep the twit calm until I get there." He ends the call and immediately throws the phone at the wall. I step back as he reaches for me. I'm not sure I'm not going to be next to hit the wall. He clings to me as if he were drowning. I'm beginning to have a horrible feeling that something terrible is happening.

"Mack, what is it. Who was on the phone?"

He pulls away and answers in a harsh, mean voice, "That was the sergeant on duty. Apparently, old lady Meyer has gone crazy and drove through the town square and shot out windows in the café and a few other businesses. She's claiming the devil has taken over the town, and she plans on getting rid of him all by herself. I'm sorry, Elise, I didn't want the weekend to ever end and surely not in this manner."

"It's okay, Mack, we will just have to make sure we have more of these days in the future." I give him another tight hug.

He goes upstairs and changes into his work clothes, while I wait on the couch for him to come back into the living room to say good-bye. He comes in, and I stand up for his embrace. He squeezes me tightly and nuzzles my neck and says in a very sad voice. "Without your sweet love, what would life be? Don't ever leave me."

I look into his eyes and say, "Let it be me. Are we Elvis Presley now?"

He laughs and answers as he's kissing my ear, "If that's what it takes to keep you happy, I'll sing Elvis to you every day."

He tells me to be sure and lock the door after he leaves and to turn on the security system and to stay in the house. For once I don't object, nor do I feel trapped. He walks into the garage, and I do as he says with the door and alarm. I then go back into the living room and finish my wine. I curl up on the couch in front of the fire and reflect on the weekend we had just had. Why is it so special from all the others? It feels wonderful to feel loved again. I hope it will last forever.

I must have fallen asleep because I wake up to being lifted off the couch. I come awake with a start and try to escape the arms around me.

"Hush, Elise, I'm just carrying you up to bed. You were asleep all curled up on the couch," Mack whispers in my ear. I relax against him and lay my head on his shoulder. He gently lays me on the bed and turns down the covers. I slip under them and wait for him to undress and join me. He slides in beside me and pulls me into his arms and sighs in complete exhaustion. It isn't two minutes and his breathing becomes even and deep. He has fallen asleep with me curled within his arms. It doesn't take long for me to follow in his footsteps.

I wake to him crawling out of bed. I ask, "Is it morning already?"

"Yes, Elise, it was four o'clock when I came home." He groans.

"I will go down and start coffee and your breakfast." I scoot out on the other side of the bed.

He's entering the bathroom and says over his shoulder, "That would be wonderful."

I make his usual breakfast, and I'm sipping my coffee when he comes down the steps. He doesn't say a word as he takes his first sip of coffee. He begin to eat in silence and then suddenly swears, "Damn it, why can't I catch a break in this fucking job?" I'm afraid to ask what has happened to cause this sudden outburst. He just looks so helpless and drained. I want to take him in my arms and just hold him like a child until he feels better. He finishes his breakfast and goes back upstairs to finish getting ready to leave. I wait, drinking my second cup of coffee. Then I remember he had said that Mrs. Meyer had shot out some of the store windows on the square. I think of Jordyn's shop and hope she had skipped it. I'm still thinking of her lovely shop being all shot to hell when Mack comes back in. He leans over me and kisses my neck.

"I'll be home late, so don't bother with a meal. I have a whole lot of shit to do today. The trial will begin on Wednesday." I just nod and about to ask about Jordyn's shop when he says, "You may want to go to your friend's store and help her clean it up. Old lady Meyer managed to shoot every front window in every store down there."

"Oh, poor Jordyn, just starting out and this has to happen."

"Well, hopefully she has insurance on the place. Most store-owners have to have insurance before they open." He finishes filling his mug with coffee and kisses me on top of the head and leaves.

Chapter 38

I finish my coffee and eat a piece of toast before going upstairs to get ready to go to Jordyn's shop. I'm just about to step into the shower when I have a feeling of dread attack my body like a flash flood raging through a canyon heading straight for an unprotected village. With my robe still on, I run down the stairs and check the security system. I don't remember resetting it when Mack left. I've reset it, but I feel no relief from the feeling of dread that has entered my body. I feel an overwhelming presence of evil. I try to shake the feeling off by trying to reassure myself that I'm just worried about Jordyn. Maybe it's because Mr. Flem's trial is starting in two days and I feel so sure he's innocent. I take my shower and dab a little makeup on. Just enough to cover up the dark circles under my eyes and take away the paleness of my cheeks. I add a bit of mascara and pull my hair into a single ponytail low over my neck. Dressing in jeans and a light sweatshirt, I'm ready to go. I take my purse off the hook and start for the door.

I'm not quite prepared for the devastation in the town square. Holy shit. The café has large shards of glass hanging still in the frame that once held colored-glass window. Completely in ruins is the front door to the supermarket. What the hell sort of gun did that woman use? I don't think an Army-issued M16 could accomplish all the damage that I'm seeing. Jordyn is outside her store, sweeping up the glass on the sidewalk, when I walk up to her.

"Hi." She turn and grins a wide toothy smile.

"Hey, girlfriend, did ya come to help? There's enough glass on the sidewalk to think someone was a bit angry."

"Mack said she was trying to rid the town of the devil all by herself." I reach for the dustpan to hold while she sweeps glass into it. I look for a dumpster or something to put the glass in when she points to a garbage can next to the door. I'm afraid to ask about the damage inside. She sees the look on my face and answers my silent question.

"It's not too bad. The bullets actually missed everything but a vase high on a shelf." I nod my relief. "It was a rather ugly vase I had made when I first started being crafty."

"Thank God it was just your ugly vase." She busts into a belly laugh, and I join in with her. We must have looked like a couple of fools, sweeping up glass and laughing so hard. "You do have insurance, don't you?" I ask after I wipe the tears from my eyes from laughing so hard.

"Yes, and there is a guy coming to fix the windows this afternoon. I'm just thankful there is no rain in the forecast." I agree as we continue to sweep up the mess.

After cleaning up the glass and making sure nothing is really ruined in the shop, we walk over to the café to help clean up over there. The owner is thrilled to get some help with the mess. Even though the place is shot up, customers and snoops have come for their cappuccinos and coffee. It surprises me that no one else is helping to clean up the glass. They literally step all over it to get to the counter and only seem concerned if they can't get their favorite rolls to go with their coffee. The poor waitress behind the counter must have apologized a hundred times to disgruntled customers that some of the equipment have been damaged by the bullets. I finally have enough and go to the grocery store and buy a piece of poster board and a marker. I make a sign that states, "Due to bullets ruining equipment, only coffee and cappuccinos will be served until further notice." It doesn't stop the customers and snoopy busybodies, but it does stop the derogatory remarks toward the haggard waitress. The owner is so happy that he gives Jordyn and me a card that says free cappuccinos for a month. We both say that isn't necessary, but he insists. Mr. Hawk insists it's the least he can do.

When everything is cleaned up, Jordyn and I have our first free cappuccino and sit at one of the tables. We talk about just how crazy a person has to be to think she can rid the town of the devil by shooting up businesses. I sense him before I feel him. I know who it is before I see the shadow looming over me. I know in an instant it's Mack. He takes a seat beside us and looks at the two of us as if we were suspects. I look right back at him and smirk.

"You look as if you think we did all this," I say, taking a sip out of my cup. He laughs.

"No, I know who did it and why. I was just thinking that I'd like to see the inside of Ms. Kent's shop. I was down here last night, but I didn't look inside. That's what the other detectives were hired for."

Jordyn gets up, smiling. "Well, let's go. We can use the door or the window to get in. I'll leave you to decide." We're laughing as we cross the street.

Once inside I could tell Mack is impressed with the contents in the shop. He looks in every nook and cranny. He expresses his appreciation over many of the pieces on display and says he's happy only a vase is broken. He thinks the bullet holes in the wall and ceiling added character to the place. He turns the corner and comes to where my painting hangs.

"Wow, Elise, these are beautiful. Did you only give her three to start with?"

Jordyn chimes in with, "No, she gave me six, but four already sold. Two the very first day they were hung up."

"I know one of my workers bought one."

"I'm just hoping she has more to bring in. I'm eager to sell more."

"I'm sure she does," Mack states as he keeps walking through the maze of displays. "Are these all local artists here?"

"Most of them are, I do have a few pieces from other friends located all over the world," Jordyn says, handing him a carved dragon. "That piece is from a friend who lives in Chicago. This is from a friend who lives in Oregon."

"Well, you have some very lovely things here. I can see why Elise loves this place."

I turn and look at him. "I never said I loved this place."

"You didn't have to, it's written all over your face, my dear."

After the tour of the shop, Mack gives me a quick peck on the cheek and says he has to be going back to work.

"You know there's no rest for the wicked. Take your time and enjoy your day."

I decide that is just what I plan on doing. I stay and help Jordyn dust and clean a bit more. The window guy has come to install new windows. He measures everything and leaves, but not before he buys my painting of the lab carrying the basket of kittens, and a crystal music box. He has a little girl at home that would cherish both of them. He's excited to hang the painting in her room and can't wait to give her the music box. I linger a bit longer and then decide to go home and get some more paintings ready and bring them back later in the afternoon. I would have invited Jordyn to the house but I know she can't leave with no windows or door glass to keep the place safe. Besides, it's a day of business as usual. Well, it is, sort of. People are coming in just to see what's broken, but they walk out after buying something, more often than not. I start for the bus stop, just as Mack drives up.

"Can I give you a ride somewhere, young lady?" he asks out the car window.

"I'm afraid my mother always told me not to ride with strangers."

"Good advice, little girl, but I'm just strange and not a stranger."

"Well, in that case, I guess it will be okay." I get into the car, and he drives me home. I tell him what I plan to do, and he says it's a good idea. He doesn't come in; he just drops me off at the end of the driveway. As he drives off, the feeling of doom engulfs me again. I can't seem to shake it.

Chapter 39

I open the front door and step on the mail. As I look down to see what we got in the mail, I notice that I've not only stepped on a few bills but a letter. The letter is covered in what looks to be dried blood. I freeze there in the open doorway. Who the hell is doing this? I carefully pick it up by a corner and look at the front of it. It's addressed to me, in bold block letters. I carefully carry it to the kitchen and put it into a baggy and then go back to close the door and reset the security alarm. I hesitate to call Mack, but this is different. The guy has escalated and added blood to the envelope. Maybe with the blood they could get DNA and catch this asshole. I dial Mack, and he answers after the first ring.

"Mack, I'm sorry to bother you at work, but I think this is important." The words seem to tumble out of my mouth.

"What the hell happened, Elise?"

"I stepped on another letter, only this time the letter seems to have dried blood all over it. I would have waited until you got home, but I knew this one was different. Maybe the DNA will actually catch whoever is doing this to me."

"Just leave it and I'll take care of it when I get home. I just don't have time right this second to come running home over a fucking bloody letter," he grinds out.

I know the old Mack has returned and that I should have never called him. All I can think to say is "I'm sorry." He hangs up the phone without saying another word.

I go up to my studio and begin to pick out paintings to take to the shop, but I really don't feel like doing anything anymore. I try not to let the letter and Mack's attitude bother me, but it's making me physically sick. I decide on six more paintings and wrap them and put them in my tote. I think I had better eat something before I return to the shop. I grab a Diet Coke and make a ham sandwich. I sit in the kitchen, staring at the enclosed letter lying on the counter. I have the strongest urge to just open it, read it, and then toss it into the garbage. I don't, but it's a hard-fought battle in my head to just leave it alone. I make up my mind that if I receive any more, I will read them and toss them and not tell anyone. It had been a mistake to tell Mack about the stalker. Is he a stalker at all? Maybe it's all in my head.

I finish my sandwich and decide to drop off the paintings at the shop. I figure the further away from the letter I am, the better I'd feel. Besides, being around Jordyn always makes me happy. She's like having a ray of sunshine on a very gloomy day. I pick up my tote and head out the door, determined to have a good rest of the day, no matter what.

I'm met at the door by Jordyn, who is just saying goodbye to a lady who had been shopping. Seeing my tote, Jordyn exclaims with excitement, "This is the artist I was telling you about. Come back on Wednesday and I'm sure you will find just the right painting you are looking for." The woman turns and looks at me and with a broad grin on her face.

"I will be back here on Wednesday as soon as the store opens for business. I am so happy I stopped today, I can hardly wait until Wednesday."

She leaves, and I notice the door to the shop has already been fixed, and one of the windows is being replaced at that very second. I comment on how fast the man is doing his job.

"Yes. He is working his handsome hinny off." Of course that makes me look directly at his behind, and I must admit, it is nice. Jordyn snorts when I raise my eyebrows, just as the man turns and smiles at me. I can feel my face turning a deep shade of red. We giggle all the way to the back room, just like a couple of schoolgirls being caught staring at a boy we liked.

Jordyn helps me unwrap the paintings and is very pleased with the ones I have chosen to bring in. I let her do the pricing as I have no idea what to charge or what they would be worth. I'm appalled at how high the prices are and express my concern that they would surely not sell at those prices. Jordyn laughs at me.

"You really don't know how talented you are, do you?"

"I guess not." I can't keep the worry out of my voice.

"No worries, girlfriend, they will fly off the walls just like the others did."

Once the windows and the door are finished being repaired, we decide to go to the café and have a quick cup of coffee. We sit outside so we can see if any customers come to the shop. We are only sitting there for less than ten minutes when a very impressive older gentleman walks into the shop. We both hurry across the street and practically run full force into him as we enter the store.

"Good afternoon, sir. May I help you find something? I am the owner of the store, and this is my dear friend Elise."

"Hello, I am Attorney Bixby, I am the defense attorney for the Flemming, or should I say Flem case that is about to start on Wednesday."

I freeze where I stand. I can't help but stare, and I feel ashamed at that moment that I'm the wife of the man who arrested his client. My first thought is to say, "He's not guilty, Mack has arrested the wrong man." Instead I say, "Very nice to meet you." I quickly move to get away before I embarrass myself.

He continues to speak with Jordyn, telling her he always buys a gift for his wife and his grandchildren when he's away on a business trip. Jordyn suggests a few items, which include my paintings that we had just finished hanging moments before. He picks out a trinket box for a granddaughter, a hand-carved airplane for a grandson, a wind chime for his daughter, and then a painting of mine for his wife. It's of a monarch butterfly on a lilac bloom. It's a smaller piece, but one of my favorite. He explains he will have to pack everything in his suitcase and can't fit much more into it. I'm happy he never asks about the creators of the pieces he has chosen, and Jordyn seems to know I don't want to be pointed out as the artist.

After he leaves, she and I talk for a bit longer, and then I decide I had better head home. I head for the bus stop with my empty tote. For some reason after leaving Jordyn's quaint little shop, my heart feels as empty as my tote. I can feel the fingers of sadness reaching deep inside me. I feel as though they are grasping onto my inner happiness and pulling it out of my heart and body. By the time I step off the bus, I feel like curling up into a ball and just sobbing. Why do my emotions swing from one extreme to another? It's apparent my anxiety pills are not doing their job, or maybe I need to add an antidepressant. Maybe I just need to say to hell with all of it and not take anything.

Chapter 40

I decide to quit feeling sorry for myself. I have a lot to be thankful for, and I need to look toward the future. After all, Mack has admitted to acting like an ass and has stopped drinking so much. He has been nicer this past weekend, and it feels as though there's a big chance our marriage is back on track.

I go directly to the kitchen and grab a water. *Lay off the Diet Coke,* I tell myself as I reached for the water. I really don't want the water, I want the Diet Coke, but if Mack could slow down on the booze, I could certainly slow down on the soda. I take a drink of the water and think it to be blah and not very satisfying. I find the little yellow lemon hiding in the refrigerator door and squeeze some into the bottle of water. I shake it and take a drink. Not all that much better, but not quite so blah either. I head for my studio.

I look at the painting I had started and decide to maybe add a bit more to it. I soon find myself so self-absorbed in painting that I nearly jump out of my socks when the house phone rings. I answer with a very shaky "Hello."

"Elise, are you okay?"

"Oh, Haven, yes, I am fine. The phone scared the daylights out of me when it rang. I was trying to add to a painting, and I was so engrossed in what I was doing that the phone scared me."

"You had me worried with the way you said hello."

"Sorry to alarm you, but when I paint, I sometimes get so wound up in what I am trying to create, I lose all track of the world around me."

"I thought I'd better call and see if I could bring anything for Sunday?"

"No, I can't think of anything for you to bring but that beautiful baby. Wait, Mack said something about Matt and Cam bringing their guitars so they could sing a few songs. If they wouldn't mind, that is."

"I think they'd be happy to do that. Matt doesn't get to jam with anyone too much anymore, and I know he loves to."

"Sounds like a plan to me. It should be fun, and I'm looking forward to it."

I can hear the baby in the background crying when Haven says, "Oh, oh, Becca is up and screaming, I'd better go."

I've forgotten about Sunday. I hope it goes smoothly and that Cam keeps his distance from me. I surely don't need Mack to think up more shit to torment me with. I must remember to ask Mack what his plans are for the meal so I can get the groceries needed and be sure to make it up ahead of time. I'd love to invite Jordyn, but I doubt Mack would approve of doing that. This is more like family. Even though Cam isn't really family, he's one of Becca's godparents.

I continue to paint until I can tell by the shadows on the wall that it's pretty late. I put my things away and decide to grab a bite to eat and then go watch the news. I enter the kitchen and see the bloody-looking envelope still lying on the cupboard. I had forgotten all about it while I was painting. I leave it there and prepare myself a salad with some fresh fruit on the side. I also take out another bottled water. I'm going to try very hard to cut back on the soda. I decide to eat in front of the TV. Mack won't be home until who knows when, so I might as well be comfortable. I flip on the local news, and right there in front of me is the attorney for Mr. Flem. He's talking to a reporter about the case. Or as he puts it, the lack of a case against his client. He seems pretty sure of himself and that it will be a very short trial, with Mr. Flem's name being cleared of any criminal charges. The reporter then informs her audience that attempts to speak with anyone from the prosecutor's office or the sheriff's department have been denied. She states that the trial is open to the public and that they are going to report live from the courtroom throughout the trial. I think that it will never fly in a bigger city, but here in the one-horse town of Flag Lake, South Carolina, most anything will be allowed in the courtroom.

I finish my salad and fruit, and I'm taking the plate into the kitchen when my cell phone dings. I look and it's a message from Mack.

"Don't wait up for me as I have a ton of shit to finish before I can come home."

I notice there's no "I love you" or anything else added to it. I finish cleaning up the kitchen and go back into the living room to finish watching the news and whatever else might follow. If nothing else, I can go to bed early and be fresh tomorrow to paint again. I curl up on the couch with a light blanket and start flipping through the channels. Finally deciding on a movie on Netflix.

By eight o'clock I'm yawning, and my mind is not following the movie at all. I decide to relax in a hot bubble bath with a few lit candles and a glass of wine. I go up to the bathroom and start the bathwater, and while the tub is filling, I go to get my wine. I light two of my favorite candles next to the tub. As I slip into the hot, steaming water, I see my reflection in the mirror. I look pale and thin. I wonder if that is how Mack sees me every time he makes love to me. Only he rarely makes love. It's a conquering quest for him. I sink into the water and lay my head back on the tub rest and try to think of nothing. The warmth soothes my body, and soon my mind is imagining what it will be like to have Cam make love to me. I'm sure he'd be gentle, bringing me to the brink of ecstasy, building me up and up until I will feel like my body is molten lava. My climax will be earth shattering, of this I'm sure. I finish my bath and take a quick cleansing shower before getting ready for bed. I turn on my relaxing sound machine to a babbling brook. I decide to open the drapes over the patio doors to let the moonlight in. As I lie there listening to the babbling brook watching the gentle shadows on the wall, I fall asleep in just a matter of seconds.

Chapter 41

I'm running through a dark forest toward a voice I could hear calling my name. The voice is raspy and gentle. It's pleading with me to come to him and that he needs help. As I run faster, I can feel the branches and leaves under my feet. They're cold and prickly, and I wonder why I don't have shoes on. I must not stop to find my lost shoes. I need to reach whomever is calling me for help. The faster I run, the further the voice seems from me. He's desperately begging me for my help. Is it raining or is it the tears running down my face? I can't tell. All I know is I'm getting very cold and becoming weaker with every step. Still the voice continues to call to me. The voice is also getting weaker. I must push on. I am now deep into the forest. It is dark and damp. I feel a chill through my body that is more spiritual than real. I wonder if any of this is real. I am so tired I can hardly run. I begin to stumble often. I finally collapse in a heap onto to the ground.

I can feel a warmth around me. It is a welcome warmth, for my body is chilled through and through. I lie there trying to absorb the warmth. I raise my head to listen for the voice, but it is silent. I know I have reached him, but I cannot find him. I begin to reach around me, and I feel him. I take his hand, and it closes around mine. I try to gain my strength to help him. Yet I do not know what he needs or what I can do. I try to speak, but no words leave my mouth. He only tightens his grip on my hand. I try to see him through the darkness. The moon breaks through the trees. and I can see all the blood I am lying in. I look into the man's face. I try to break away from his grasp, but he just hangs on tighter. I am crying now, "Please let me go." His face is unrecognizable. His eyes have been plucked out. I know without seeing that he has no tongue. Yet he is calling my name and asking for help. I begin to scream and pull away from him. I can't move. I am being held in place by a force I cannot see. I feel helpless and alone. My cries are becoming louder as I fight against the force.

I awake to Mack holding me down in our bed.

"Shut the hell up, Elise!" he is yelling into my face. "The neighbors will think I am killing you. Not that I don't feel like it right now. What the hell were you dreaming, did your fucking lover leave you?" He is shaking me violently. I am fully awake now, and I stop struggling against him. I look into his bloodshot eyes and smell his whiskey breath. He smells of some expensive perfume, and I finally come to my senses. I shove him away.

"Get the hell away from me!" I yell back at him. He lets go of me, and I get out of bed. "How dare you come home and into our bedroom smelling of another woman! Get the hell out of here! Go back to your whore. I don't need you or your help recovering from a nightmare." I am trying desperately to control my shaking voice.

I am still shaking from the nightmare and how vivid it played out in my head. Mack is sitting on the bed, watching me.

"How dare you yell at me in my own bedroom! How dare you say anything to me, you bitch!" he yells as he tries to stand up. I know I am about to be abused in the worse possible way. I can see in his eyes I have turned him on. He is about to rape me. Thankfully he is too drunk to stand. "I am the one who bought this house, and I am the one who feeds your fat ass. You are nothing, Elise. You are nothing but my bitch. Do you hear me, Elise?"

"I hear you. I hear, smell, and hate you, Mack. I will no longer put up with your bullshit. I will no longer sit back and let you hurt me." I walk to the fireplace and reach for the poker. He loses the smirk on his face and sits there like a stone.

"Do you really think you have the guts to smash my skull in, Elise? It takes a cold heart to kill, my dear, frightened bitch." He is laughing.

"If you even think of taking a step toward me, you will find out firsthand." My voice is much calmer than how I feel. Instead of taking that step toward me, he flops back on the bed and just lie there still as death. My first thought is to smash his head in with the poker. I just walk out of the room with the poker still in my hand. He does not follow. I doubt he can.

Chapter 42

Once downstairs and in the kitchen, I notice the envelope on the counter is gone. There's also a mess on the floor. It looks as if Mack tried to make himself a sandwich but it ended up on the tile floor instead of between the two pieces of bread that are still lying on the counter. I lean the poker against the cabinet and methodically clean up Mack's mess. I make a pot of coffee and sit at the breakfast counter, waiting for it to get done, and try to figure out the meaning of my horrid dream. Why am I having these terrible dreams? They are gory and vivid. I sit with my head in my hands trying to figure out my confusing life.

The coffeepot dings, and I pour myself a cup of coffee and go into the living room. I'm not in any condition to go to my studio, and I'm not about to go back into the bedroom. I pick up a magazine and start to thumb through it while sipping my coffee. I curl up on the couch with a blanket and decide to try to get a few more hours of sleep before Mack wakes up. I remember the poker in the kitchen and think why not leave it there, as a reminder to Mack that I no longer will be his pawn.

Something is being pressed into my throat. I reach out to push it away and feel the cold steel of the poker being pressed against my flesh. Mack is hovering over me with a menacing look on his face and an evil gleam in his dark eyes. I know at that moment I'm doomed. He has complete control over me.

"Don't you ever pull a stunt like you tried last night, you miserable ugly bitch." His tone is deleterious. I feel my stomach crawl quickly into my throat. The bile it carries is near to flowing into my mouth and dribbling out and down my chin. I don't move a muscle. I just stare fixedly into the glaring dark eyes. I know I'm his victim and helpless to do anything against him. After what seems to be an eternity, he lets up on the pressure, and I'm able to swallow the bile back down into my upset stomach. He finally releases me completely and caresses my face in a very loving manner. "Remember, Elise, I own you." He turns and walks away. "Get my breakfast ready like usual or I swear I will use this fucking poker on you and it won't be on your head. I'll make sure you will never enjoy your lover's cock for the rest of your life."

I feel defeated and slowly get up to do his bidding. I have everything on the table just as he likes it when he enters the kitchen. He sits silently and eats without looking at me or anything but the food on his plate. When he's finished, he calmly gets up and walks out of the room. I hear him take the stairs two at a time and wonder how he can even move after drinking as much as he had the night before. He returns and looks directly into my eyes and states. "Don't leave the fucking house today, Elise. That is an order I expect you to obey. I don't need to wonder what shit you are pulling while I am preparing for this case." I don't answer him. He walks up to me and grabs my face in his right hand. Placing his face an inch in front of mine, he grinds out very slowly, "Do you understand me, Elise? You are to not leave this house." I can't answer him with his hand holding my face, so I just try to nod. He continues to apply pressure to my face. "I should snap your neck." He lets his hand drop and leaves for the day.

I don't move until I hear the garage door open and close again. I turn the security system on and calmly pour myself a cup of coffee. I have lost whatever freedom I have gained. I'm right back to where he wants me.

Chapter 43

I make myself a bagel and cream cheese and have another cup of coffee, wondering what Mack has done with the letter I had put in the plastic bag. I figure he's thrown it out. At this point in time, I really don't care what he's done with it. I won't be telling him or showing him any more if they come.

After cleaning up the kitchen, I go upstairs. I think to myself what a bastard Mack really is. I have to change the bedding on our bed. It reeks of Mack and his night before. The stale smell of whiskey and perfume cling to the bedding and fills the room. I spray the mattress with Lysol and then spray the air in the room. I open the patio doors to let the room air out for a bit before I finish straightening it up. I hang the bedspread over the railing off the bedroom deck to air.

I go to my studio to see about getting some work done as I'm not going anywhere today. I doubt Mack will be home early or any decent time to eat. I'm relieved with the idea of eating alone without having to put up with his crap.

I don't feel like painting, so I begin to sketch. I know the pictures will fly out of my head today. They always do after a nightmare. It's as if my brain works overtime after one of the horrid dreams. My pencil practically flies across the page.

I finish the third sketch when I notice it's misting outside. I run to get the bedspread off the railing. Too late, it's already too damp to put back on the bed. I take it to the laundry room and hang it across the clothes bar. Its dampness matches my mood.

If I'm to be a prisoner in my own home, I might as well enjoy myself. I go to the freezer and grab the ice cream. I go back to my studio, eating right out of the container. I decide to try to finish the painting I'm working on. I hear the rain hitting the window before I hear the thunder. It's a loud rumble that seems to be coming from the belly of the earth instead of the sky. I go to the bedroom and I'm going to shut the patio door but instead step out onto the deck. The rain feels refreshing as I stand there, letting it beat down on my face. I'm getting drenched, but I don't care. I feel the freedom I wish I have. I'm so tired of the hatred and the hurt. I want the freedom I'm feeling to last forever. I think at that moment that the only way to achieve that goal is to be rid of Mack. Is murder my only choice? I will have to think of other options. Surely killing my husband is not the best solution to the problem. I must find a way before the situation escalates to the point that either I kill him or he kills me. I'm afraid the latter will happen if I don't take some sort of action.

I feel chilled by the rain, and I'm soaked to the skin. I love the feeling. I love the way the heavy clouds hide the lightning, but the thunder rumbles so loud it shakes my soaked body. I could have stood there forever if I wouldn't catch a cold. I slowly turn and step into the bedroom. I drip all over the carpet as I walk into the bathroom to remove my soaked clothes and dry off. I don't care. I feel invigorated, and nothing is going to change my mood.

I change into dry clothes and decide to just wash the wet ones I've been wearing. On my way back to my studio I notice the letter on the floor next to the front door. I pick it up and open it.

"It's getting closer, Elise. It will all be over very soon."

I tear it into pieces and throw it into the kitchen garbage. I feel nothing. I feel neither fear nor am I anxious, like I had been when I discovered the others. I'm numb to all of it now. I suppose I should thank Mack for making me insensitive to most everything that happens to me now. Oh, I'm sure if he threatens me again I will feel the rage and hatred. Those two feelings never really ever leave me.

I begin to paint again on my painting. I have no music or anything to listen to except the rain and the thunder. The clouds continue to roll in, and the rain comes down in sheets now. The wind has picked up, and the windows rattle as the rain and wind do their dance against them. I go downstairs to turn on the local news to see what sort of storm is hitting us. The local weatherman says we will be getting very high winds, and we are in a thunderstorm warning for the next three hours. He indicates that the lightning will be dangerous and to stay away from doors and windows for our own protection. I want to be out in it. I want to feel the wind and rain beat harshly against my body. I want to be lying on the grass next to the river feeling the charge of the elements around me. I settle for watching out the patio doors. I practically have my nose pressed to the window when I see the patio table with its expensive umbrella tip over and into the pool. I back up and laugh at the prospect of Mack fishing it out. He'd be so pissed he'd be tempted to demolish the whole backyard.

The wind, rain, lightning, and thunder continue into the late afternoon. The backyard is flooded, and I hear the sump pump kick in several times. I look out on the street in front of our house. The water has to be a foot deep rushing down toward the drains. It's as though an evil hidden force is pushing the water faster and faster. I stare mesmerized by the water and all the debris it carries with it. Maybe it's a good force washing away the evil on the streets and the town. Maybe it's God's way of cleansing the town of all the evil that lurks around every corner.

By the time the storm passes, it's after four o'clock. I'm famished. I have eaten the bagel and the ice cream, but I want something hot and filling now. I look into the refrigerator and decide to whip up a tomato hot dish. I haven't made it in years, and it's always been one of my favorites growing up. I'm happily mixing the ingredients together when I hear the garage door open. Shit, shit, shit. Mack's home. He hates hot dishes and will definitely want some other meal made and then forbid me to eat what I really want.

Chapter 44

He comes into the kitchen as quiet as a mouse. I wonder what he's up to. I don't have to wait very long. He takes one look at me and charges. I'm caught between the counter and the bulk of his body. He grabs me by the throat, and with his face inches from mine, he screams, "What the hell are you trying to pull, you fucking Bitch?" I don't answer him fast enough, and he slams my head against the cupboard door.

"What are you raving about?" I manage to strangle out of my closed throat.

"You know very well what I'm raving about, as you put it."

"No, Mack, I don't."

"Well, let me bring you up to date, dear. I took the letter you supposedly found into the lab. You know whose DNA was found on it?" He's pushing his body harder into mine.

"No, I have no idea."

"You should know your own DNA, Elise."

I look directly into his eyes, and I see a fury I have never seen before. I can't help the tears starting to fill my eyes.

"It's yours, you conniving piece of shit. Yours, my sweet little lying bitch."

I try to shake my head no, but that only brings another bang to the back of the head on the cupboard door.

"You have embarrassed me for the last time, Elise. If I have to keep you tied up in the basement, I swear I will. I'm the laughingstock at work. Everyone thinks I have gone daft. It's all because of you, you fucking bitch." He smashes my body harder into the cupboard.

He lets go of me so abruptly I fall to my knees. He ends his tirade by taking his foot and pushing me down. He stands there above me with his foot in the middle of my back.

"No, more shit from you, Elise, or you will be very sorry." He turns and walks out of the kitchen, and I hear the garage door open and close as he drives away.

I slowly get to my feet sobbing uncontrollably. I don't understand when or how anyone could have gotten that much blood from me to apply to the letter and envelope. The last time I bled at all was when Mack had tied me to the bed. It has to be Mack doing this to drive me crazy. He is malicious and nasty enough to do something like this. I have no idea why or what his motives could be, but I feel deep in my heart that it has to be him.

I sit at the breakfast counter and try to think of reasons behind his actions. I soon begin to doubt myself. Maybe it is me. Maybe I have a split personality and have no idea I'm really doing the things that are taking place. I have to giggle in spite of the situation. I'm really reaching for answers to even think of such a crazy idea that I have a split personality. Mack is bipolar that's for sure.

I decide to eat my hot dish and try to keep from falling apart waiting for Mack's return. I'm quite sure this ordeal is far from over. It's a waiting game now. I have to prepare myself mentally and physically for what might happen when he finally comes back. I try to think positive thoughts, but they are more like the storm that had raged earlier. They are dark and sinister. They are of pain, hate, murder, and more. Am I capable of murder? I'm beginning to think it's the only option I have, and that saddens me.

Chapter 45

I'm lying awake in bed, watching the shadows dance across the wall and ceiling, when Mack enters the bedroom. It's early for him to be home after the outburst earlier in the day. He doesn't bother to see if I'm sleeping before he switches on the overhead light. He walks to the patio door and closes the blinds. I think, *Yes, be sure they are closed before you kill me, you bastard.* He goes into the bathroom and returned in just his boxers. He turns off the light and crawls in beside me without saying a word. Soon I hear his breathing ease into a peaceful sleep. How dare he be able to put the day's events in a closed box and fall into a wonderful deep sleep? I pray at that moment he dies before the morning arrives.

The alarm goes off as it does on any normal workday for Mack. He rolls toward me and says, "Just coffee this morning, Elise. All I want is coffee. I have way too much going on this morning to load down on any kind of food."

I don't move or answer him. He rolls back and gets up and goes into the bathroom for his shower. I crawl out of bed, grab my robe, and head out of the room. I'm tired, so tired and weary. I feel drained, and when I look into the mirror, I can see that the events of yesterday and the lack of sleep have caught up with me with a vengeance. I splash cold water on my face, trying to get some color back into my cheeks. After failing miserably in the bathroom, I go into the kitchen. Thank God the coffee timer works, and the coffee is done. I pour myself a mug and hear Mack coming down the stairs, so I pour him a mug full. He takes it and says, "Thank you, I will be at the jury selection for most of the day today. I hope they find enough objective people to fill a twelve-man jury. The people picked will more than likely be people from out of town."

Mack leaves without a goodbye or saying another word to me. I feel relief that there had been no more confrontations regarding the DNA. I feel a sick sadness in my stomach and heart for Mr. Flem. He's going to be on trial for something he surely didn't do. I feel very lonely and wonder how Mr. Flem is feeling right now. Is he feeling fear, loneliness, or relief that the trial is finally starting? I doubt it will take very long. I only pray that he will be found innocent, because I know he is.

I stay in my studio for most of the morning. I finish the painting and decide to start some littler ones as pairs for the store. I just have to think of what would be good in twos. I sketch out a mare and a fowl and then a majestic stallion. These will look great together hanging in a study. I also think a set of four with the four seasons on them will work too. I set up the easel and find the canvases I will use for them. The mare will be a brilliant white, and the colt will be a paint. The stallion will be a shiny black. In my head I think a black and a white horse together will build a black-and-white colt. I have no real evidence that this is true, but in my head, it seems reasonable.

At noon I go downstairs and turn on the local news and decide to eat a bit of hot dish. I have made enough for a small army, and Mack won't be eating any of it. I take my bowl into the living room just as a breaking news flash comes across the TV screen. A reporter is standing in front of the Flag Lake courthouse, and a crowd of nearly five hundred spectators are gathered around her. She begins by saying what a day of turmoil and confusion this has turned out to be. The jury selection has to be postponed because Mr. Flem's lawyer never arrived at the courthouse. An officer has been sent to his hotel room. His car is still parked in front of his room, but when the officer had knocked at the door, there was no answer. The officer asked the manager to please open the lawyer's door after unsuccessfully trying to reach him by phone and knocking on the door. When the door was opened, no one was there. His clothes, laptop, briefcase, and car keys were all in the room. It was first believed he may have taken a walk, but two pair of shoes were found sitting neatly next to the hotel door. A pair of dress shoes and a pair of running shoes. Nothing seemed out of order or missing except for the lawyer.

The judge presiding over the trial postpones jury selection and states that the lawyer will be held in contempt of court when he decides to show up. Mr. Flem states in the courtroom that something must have happened to him, as he's a very reputable lawyer and won't pull something like this if it isn't warranted. The reporter says the judge has made a comment about no highfalutin attorney from New York is going to make a mockery out of his courtroom and get away with it. The sheriff has every available man out searching for the missing man.

I can't believe what I'm hearing and seeing. Mack is coming out of the courthouse just then. He's immediately swarmed by reporters and civilians wanting answers about the missing attorney. He brushes them off like they are pesky flies and gets into his car. I wonder where he's going and where Mr. Flem's attorney has disappeared to. The reporter says to stay tuned to the station as they will be reporting any new discoveries when they happen.

All I can think about is how upset, mean, and ugly Mack will be if this trial doesn't go the way he plans for it to. I won't expect him home before the missing man is found, and when he gets here, he'd be a bear. I'm bound to feel the blunt of his outrage.

Chapter 46

I turn off the TV and clean up after my lunch. I go up to my studio and begin to paint the background for the mare and colt. I have a hard time concentrating on what I'm doing and change the background twice before I decide I like it. I'm worried the painting will be three-dimensional if I continue the way I am. I decide to do the colt first. I want to be sure and capture its innocence and spirit. The eyes have to be very expressive to make him look real. I outline his little body, and by then I'm getting tired. I begin to put my paints and supplies away when the house phone rings.

I hesitate for only a minute before picking it up. The voice on the other end is full of laughter.

"You did it again, Elise. Another one is done in. You really are very good at what you do."

"What are you talking about?" I shout into the phone. "Who the hell are you?" My answer is only a devious laugh, and the phone goes dead. I'm shaking uncontrollably when I slam down the receiver, not because I'm afraid. No, I'm pissed. I'm so angry I want him to find me so I can meet him face-to-face. What on earth does this phone call mean? I finish cleaning up my things and go downstairs. I'm drawn to the living room and to the TV. I switch the set on and sit numbly on the edge of the couch.

It's the same reporter as earlier in the morning. This time she's standing near Mr. Flem's shack next to the river. I can see the water nearly overflowing the banks from all the rain we received yesterday.

It looks vicious and menacing as it rushes downstream. It look as though it wants to carry away all good in its dark swirling waters. She's saying that Detective MacKenzie will be giving a press conference in front of the courthouse along with the sheriff in just a few minutes. She continues to say the body had been found just outside of Mr. Flem's front door. Other than that, the police aren't giving out any details. I know immediately it's Mr. Flem's attorney. I feel my stomach do a flip-flop. I feel as though I've just gotten off a roller coaster and it has made me sick. I'm sure I'm suffering from vertigo. I can hardly walk a straight line much less run to the bathroom. I just make it there before I throw up my lunch, wishing I hadn't eaten anything. My god, does the caller think I have something to do with the murder? The reporter never said it was a murder, but I know it's another violent one.

I go back and sit on the couch, waiting for the news conference to be broadcasted. It shows the podium with all the microphones ready to go. After a few minutes of the cameras scanning the crowd, Mack and the sheriff approach the podium. The mayor is right behind them. I'm not sure if he's there to lend support or to chastise the sheriff department for not doing their job. He looks as though he could chew them up and spit them out as nails.

Mack begins with a "Good afternoon. Well, it isn't a good afternoon, as we are here to report that Mr. Flem's attorney, Mr. Bixby, has been found murdered just outside of town. His body was found earlier this afternoon by an officer going to check if he was at Mr. Flem's residence when he didn't show up in court this morning. We are sad to report that he was dead at the scene. An investigation into his death has already been started. The sheriff will try to answer any questions, to the best of his ability without jeopardizing the open case." He turns and walks away from the podium. Most of the questions asked by the reporters cannot be answered because of the case being new and open. All he does say is no suspects are in custody. I turn off the TV and know without ever seeing the body that he had no tongue or eyes left. It's as if the murderer is inside my head, and he doesn't want the attorney to see or say anything that will refer to the unsolved murder cases.

Am I responsible somehow for the murders? Am I the cause of them? How can I be? I don't know the attorney. I met him once in the store and that was it. Yet I feel deep down in my soul that I somehow am involved in the deaths of all these innocent people. I suddenly feel filthy. I feel as though I hadn't showered in weeks. I look down at my hands, expecting them to be crusted with blood and dirt. I'm slightly shocked to see the red smeared on them. Then I realize I haven't washed the paint completely off after painting the background on the canvas.

I practically run to the bathroom to take a hot, steamy shower. What the hell is wrong with me? Am I a psychopath? Am I killing people and not even aware of it? I strip off my clothes and step into the steamy hot shower. I don't care that the water is way too hot. I don't care that it's burning my skin. I scrub my body hard with a bath sponge and shower gel. No matter how hard I rub, I can't get the filth removed from my skin. It seems to be caked on me. Mud, blood, semen, it's everywhere. I fall to my knees in the shower and begin to sob and wail. I feel as if I'm drowning in my own tears. I've lost all control.

I have no idea how long I stayed crying in the shower. I feel weak and tired. I turn the shower off and step onto the bath mat. The bathroom is filled with a heavy misty fog. I wipe at the mirror but can't get it to clear enough for me to see my own reflection. The soft towel hurts where I rub my skin to dry it. I look down, and I'm red from head to toe. I had rubbed some areas nearly raw. I look at the now clearing mirror and I swear for a split second I see another figure behind me. I'm jolted into reality and realize I have had some sort of breakdown. I feel so tired and weak from the ordeal. All I want is to lie down and fall deeply into a peaceful sleep. Maybe I would just die. I finish drying, and without dressing, I walk into the bedroom and lie down on the bed. I don't care that I'm naked. The coolness from the silk bedspread gives me a kind of comfort. Maybe that's where the name comforter comes from, I absently think. I soon fall asleep.

I wake up to Mack saying in a very deathly voice, "Elise, are you lying there waiting for your lover, or did he just leave?"

I roll over and immediately know I'm going to be the subject of his rage and failure. I don't bother to answer, nor do I move. I don't care anymore what he does to me. He stands there looking at my nude body. He's staring with an expression of disbelief. I turn my head away and asked, "Why are you home at this hour, and why are you staring at me?"

"I'm tired of all the bullshit at the station, and you look as though someone threw you onto a vat of hot oil. What the hell happened to you, Elise?"

"I took a very hot shower, and I guess I scrubbed too hard with the sponge. I felt dirty after watching the news."

He goes into the bathroom without saying another word. He comes back to the bed with the body lotion. He removes his shirt and sits down on the bed. I don't want him to touch me, and I flinch when he reaches for me.

"For Christ sake, Elise, I'm not going to hit you. I'm going to put some lotion on you before you do actually chap." He begins to gently run lotion on my back and my thighs. He gently turns me over and begins to rub some on my arms. When he rubs it on my breasts, my nipples respond to his touch and become very hard. I know it's a mistake, but I can't help what they're doing. He begins to rub it on my stomach and then my upper thighs. He leans in and takes a nipple into his mouth and slowly circles my nipple with his tongue. My mind is screaming for him to get the fuck away from me, and yet I can't push him away. His hands are rubbing down my sides and finally finds what they're searching for. He begins to tease me with his fingers. Gently applying pressure in all the right places to make me squirm with need. His fingers enter me, and within seconds, he brings me to an earth-shattering climax. I want more, and he knows it. He removes his pants, but before he enters me, he spreads kisses and suckles my skin all the way down my stomach. I arch toward him, letting him know I want him. I know I'm his whore, and so does he. His tongue goes to the very place that needs it most. I spread my legs and let him do what he wants. I can't stop the moan or the hot explosion that goes through my entire body. I'm still shaking from the climax when he slams into me. I'm wet and more than ready for him. I match his thrusts one on one. With every thrust I push harder against him until he's so deep inside of me I'm sure we've merged into one. He spills into me with a vengeance and collapses on top of me. I feel drained. I don't have the energy to push him away from me. I'm not sure what I'm feeling. I'm not sure why I had responded to him. Do I need him? Does he need me? Were we both so detached from one another that sex was our only way we can feel whole? Only I don't feel whole, I feel torn apart. I had let him have me, and now I would pay for my foolishness.

He finally rolls off me and with a deep sigh starts to laugh. I don't want to know what's so funny so I just lie there unmoving. He turns to me and puts one arm over me and said, "Well, that was a nice homecoming. If you did this every day, maybe I'd be in a better mood."

"What, be your whore?" I answer as I push his arm off me and start to get up.

"Not so fast, you stupid bitch. You never answered me. Were you lying here waiting for your lover or had he just left?" I want to smack the smirk off his face. He had grabbed me by the arm to hold me in place.

"I was lying here waiting for you. You should realize by now, Mack, that I'm a one-man whore. Yours." I shove him off me and get up.

"You're a fucking liar, Elise. But I will let it slide today. I needed this, and I needed it bad."

I stand looking at him, and before I had a chance to think, I respond, "What, you couldn't get your new little brunette in the office to put out today?" Bad move on my part. He springs from the bed and slaps me so hard I see stars. He walks into the bathroom and slams the door. I put on a pair of sweats and a T-shirt and leave the room.

Chapter 47

I know the rest of the night will be full of turmoil and anger. He has failed again, and this means I will be punished for his lack of success. I'm sure the mayor gave him the business about the new murder. How the department can't solve the old murders and now there's another one. The town isn't over the last one of the stranger in the park. They surely would want answers and this to be resolved and resolved now. After all, there's still a murderer or murderers out there, scaring the shit out of these nice Southern town folk. Things like this happen in the big city, like New York, not a small town in the Carolinas. Yup, I'm in for a night of hatred and abuse. That is, if I let it happen.

I go to the kitchen and start to make chicken breasts in the broiler. I feel as though I need nourishment if I'm to fight and gain back what I had lost. My dignity is gone for sure. I make a salad for the two of us and put some frozen veggies in the microwave. It will only take a few minutes for the chicken to broil. I make a sweet-sour sauce to drizzle on the chicken when it's done. I only put it on two pieces and pour a lemon butter garlic sauce on the other two. It's just about ready when Mack enters the kitchen. He goes to the fridge and grabs a bottle of beer. He doesn't bother to ask if I want one. He takes a very long drink. Over half the bottle is gone when he finally comes up for air. I haven't set the table, and I'm about to when he reaches for the dishes. He suggests that we just fill our plates up and go sit in the living room to eat. I figure he'd want to watch the news.

We takes our plates in, and I sit on the big recliner as he plops on the couch. He picks up the remote and to my surprise starts skimming through the channels and stops on an outdoor show. Some meaningless show about duck people. I just look at him, and he shrugs his shoulders, and we eat in silence watching a family make a living off making duck calls and other duck crap. If I haven't been so fed up with his shit, I would have had to laugh at this.

We finish our meal in silence, and I take the dishes to the kitchen. I clean up the kitchen and go back to the living room. Mack is sprawled out on the couch snoring loudly. I take a light blanket and lay it over him. I turn off the lamp and turn the TV down to a low murmur and leave him there. I figure he'll be angry no matter what I do. If I wake him or if I leave him to sleep, I'd be doomed either way. I take a bottled water and go upstairs and crawl into bed. It's earlier than normal for me to be in bed, but I feel exhausted. I fall asleep, and for once it's a dreamless sleep. I wake to a sound downstairs. I'm sure Mack will come stomping up the steps anytime. He never comes. I think about going downstairs to see what he's doing but decide to just wait for him to come storming to me. I lie there and watch the shadows on the walls.

Chapter 48

Mack never comes to bed, and I fall back asleep. The alarm goes off, and I wake with a start. I reach to turn it off and curb the urge to throw the loud annoying thing out through the patio door. It will just mean another mess for me to clean up. I put my robe on and go into the bathroom to do my morning routine. I don't feel like being awake, and I don't feel like putting up with Mack's bullshit. As I enter the kitchen, I'm shocked to find Mack sitting at the counter sipping a cup of coffee. He gives me a weary look and says, "I was going to let you sleep."

"I set the alarm like a normal workday." I reach for a cup of coffee. "Do you want me to make you breakfast while you get ready?"

"No, I just need coffee to face all the shit that will be dropping on my head today. Maybe I should wear a hard hat today." No humor is in his voice.

"I imagine your day will be filled with a lot of bullshit. I don't envy you."

He just shakes his head and takes another deep drink of hot coffee. "I just wish I had some sort of clue as to who was doing these murders." I look at him, and I'm about to ask if he thinks Mr. Flem is innocent when he adds, "I was so sure Flem was the guy, because it all started right after he moved here. But now I'm not so sure. The murder of his lawyer has made me rethink the whole thing. I have file cabinets full of crap on the cases and yet no DNA, nothing to pinpoint who may be behind any of the killings. It's as though I am banging my head against a brick wall. Plus, I have the mayor breathing fire down the back of my neck. He acts as though the whole sheriff's department has their heads buried in the sand. The fucker couldn't find his ass with both hands, and yet he expects us to find whoever is doing the killing without anything to go on. I was hoping the motel surveillance camera would give us a break. But of course they are not really hooked up. They are just there to scare would-be thieves into thinking they are being watched."

"I'm sure this will bring half of the New York City investigators down here to help."

"I sure as hell hope not, Elise. That would mean I really am a failure, and I will lose my job. We'd have to move for Christ sake."

"Would that be so bad, Mack? We could move to Portsmith or somewhere else close and you could find another job."

"What the hell is wrong with you, Elise?" he practically yells at me.

"I'm sorry, I was just trying to give you another option."

"What kind of option is that? I'd look like I was running with my tail between my legs. No, I'll continue in this hellhole until I figure it all out." He leaves to get ready to face his demons.

"I probably won't be around all day and half the night."

"Hang in there."

He leaves without another word. I watch him drive down the street toward the sheriff's department. The phone rings as I'm walking back into the kitchen. I think about not answering it. I pick it up, and it's Haven.

"Hello, Elise."

"What's the matter, Haven?" She sounds upset.

"I was worried about Mack. I know he takes everything that goes on at work out on you."

"He's fine, and I can handle his mood swings."

"Good, do you want to meet me for coffee today?"

Seeing Mack hadn't given me any restrictions today, I answer with a "Damn right, girl."

"I will pick you up in an hour. That will give you time to get ready and for me to get Becca fed and ready."

"Is your mother going to be joining us?"

"No, not today. She has some sort of water aerobics class this morning."

Chapter 49

Haven pulls into the driveway right on time. I set the security system and run out to the car. I can hear Becca making cooing noises as I settle into the front seat. I can't see her sweet little face, because her car seat faces the rear. Haven seems happy to see me, and it makes me feel uplifted just to be in her company.

"Where are we going?"

"I thought we'd go to the café and then visit Jordyn's store. I haven't been in there yet."

"That is a great idea. You will love her."

"Then it's a plan."

The drive is short, and we park in the municipal parking lot. Haven seems a pro at getting the stroller out of the back of the van. She has it all set up, while I struggle to get the car seat out of the car.

"I know this snaps into the stroller, but how on earth do you get it out of the darn back seat?"

Haven cracks up and reaches in around me and undoes the latch, and bam, the car seat turns into a carrier that snaps into the stroller. "Just as easy as pie."

"Ha, I could bake a pie faster and easier than getting that contraption out and put together."

"Just wait until you have your own, Elise. You'll get the hang of all these new conveniences and contraptions or you'll drive yourself nuts trying." She's laughing at my pouting.

"I doubt it," I mumble to myself.

At least I know how to push the stroller and do so with pride. We order our cappuccinos and Bavarian creamed-filled rolls before finding a table at the edge of the patio. We have just sat down when I see Jordyn wave and start across the street toward us.

"Hi." I do the introductions, and Jordyn sits down with us. She of course takes over entertaining Becca. "We have plans of walking over to look through the shop."

"Great, it's been a bit slow this morning. I usually get a rush between eleven and one o'clock."

"I can't wait to see what all you have in there. If it's as good as Elise says, my husband will need another job to pay for all the things I'm sure I will buy." We're just finishing up our rolls when a customer goes through the door of the shop. Jordyn jumps up and heads back to the store.

Haven and I finish up our drinks and start across the street. Just as we're starting to cross, a car pulls up alongside of us. I see that it is Mack and immediately feel a cloud of doom settle around me. The passenger side window slides down, and I hear him say, "What the hell are you doing out of the house, Elise? I specifically told you to keep your ass in the house and not to even venture into the backyard. Yet here your ugly ass is parading through the town square." Haven immediately comes to my defense.

"For your information, jerk, I called and begged her to come with me to Jordyn's shop. How dare you call her ugly or any other bad names. And just why the hell should she be locked up like a prisoner? Today is a beautiful day. You really are an asshole, Mack."

I feel like I had just been caught cheating on my boyfriend, and my best friend is standing up for me.

"I just don't want her to cause any more embarrassment to me than she already has," he snarls at his sister.

"How the hell could she possibly embarrass you anyway?"

"Why don't you ask her and let her tell you about the shit she's been pulling. She's made me the laughingstock of the lab at work." His voice has enough venom in it to poison an elephant.

"I'm sure if you've been embarrassed, it was your fault, not hers. Go do something, Mack, and leave us to enjoy our day. I'll see that Elise gets back to her cell after we have finished our shopping." She shoos him away. I just stand there frozen listening to Mack and Haven argue. He rolls up the window and drives off. I know there will be hell to pay later.

Haven gives me a quick hug. "Is he ever nice? I wouldn't blame you if you divorced his ugly ass."

"Oh, he's been under a lot of pressure with the murders, that's all." I pray she doesn't ask what he means by my embarrassing him. Fat chance.

"Hey, what was he talking about anyway?"

"It's nothing, I just had him test something in the lab, and it turned out to be a big mistake."

"What was it?"

"Nothing really, and I'd rather just forget it."

We enter the cheery shop, and Haven sighs deeply in awe. "Oh my god, this is the most awesome place ever," she exclaims while turning in a circle. "I love it, and I've only been in the first two feet. This is just what this town needs. With all the negativity here, this is like a bit of heaven in the middle of hell."

I stand there with the stroller, just watching her walk slowly past the displays. She stops to touch a trinket here or run her hand over something. She's loving every second. I feel so proud to be a part of this place. Even though I have nothing to do with the shop, with the exception of my paintings being displayed. I still feel like I belong to the place. With Haven's approval of it, I feel as though I've accomplished something positive for once.

Haven finds my paintings, just as the lady from Monday is coming in through the door. Jordyn greets her with her happy "Hello."

"I sure hope that painter brought in more of her paintings. I've told all my friends about them, and they will be here in a matter of minutes." She strolls over to where Haven is standing and looks at her with a mock menacing look on her face. "I hope you realize young lady that I have first dibs on these paintings. I couldn't get one on Monday, but I plan on getting one or two today." Haven puts her hands up like she's ready to do battle over the paintings. They both start laughing at each other.

"I'm sure I can persuade my sister-in-law to paint me one if I asked her nicely."

"The artist is related to you? You lucky little shit. I only have dirt-dumb relatives."

Just then Becca gives out one long cry. Haven comes flying over and takes her out of the stroller. "Oh no, I think she has filled her diaper really good. Is there a bathroom or someplace I can change her without stinking up this lovely store?"

Jordyn points to the curtain. "Just take her back there. There is a counter you can use and spray if you feel you need to use it." Haven goes to change Becca, and I'm left all alone with the woman from Monday. I'm about to say hi when the bell jingles above the door, and five cackling women come through it.

"Oh Mary, you were so right. This place rocks."

I have no idea who says what as they all are talking and agreeing at the same time. Apparently, Mary is the lady from Monday. They come up to her, and she points to my paintings hanging on the wall. The little blonde with a huge red purse points to the painting of a vase with roses in it and yells, "That one is mine!"

The gray-haired one points to the fall scene of a river and says, "That one is mine." My head is spinning by the time they all pick out paintings. Jordyn introduces them to me and explains I'm the artist. They all gather around me and ask if I paint on commission privately. I say I never have before, but I guess I could. They want my card, which of course I don't have. Jordyn steps in at that point and tells them to just come in individually and she'd set up an appointment with me to go over whatever they need painted. I feel overwhelmed.

They all pay for their purchases and leave in the same whirl-wind that they have come in with. I'm in shock. Six of my paintings have just left the store with promises of commission work ahead. I feel the tears filling my eyes, and Jordyn comes over and gives me a big bear hug.

"You are the best thing to happen to my store."

"I'm in shock. I'd have never believed any of my paintings would really sell."

"Well, they are flying off the shelf. I hope you have a few more to bring down."

"I have been painting for years, just stacking them up," I tell her while I try desperately to control the tear starting to drip out of my eye.

"Good, if I could, I'd like to come to your studio and pick some out myself. Not that the ones you picked out aren't great, but I'd like to take a look if I could."

"Sure, but let me check with my husband when would be a good time for us to meet."

"Sounds like a plan."

Haven had started to come back into the shop from the back just as all the women were talking to me at the same time and turned right back around. She sticks her head out of the curtain and asks, "Is the coast clear? I just nursed Becca while the gaggle of geese where in here. She is sleeping now." She lays Becca back into the stroller and once again begins to check out the items in the store. She picks out a couple of things and asks about a few more. After paying for her things, I tell Jordyn I'd give her a call ASAP to let her know when she can come over.

"Please make it soon as I need your paintings in my shop!" she yells as we are already out the door.

I feel as though I'm walking on a cloud. I don't think anything will spoil my mood. Then I remember Mack's anger from before, and I know it will end and end as soon as he walks through the door when he comes home.

Chapter 50

I go directly to my studio and begin to rearrange my paintings. I try to sort them according to subject and size. Not an easy task as I have a lot of different subjects and some in at least three different sizes. Some I've forgotten I had even painted. Some make me laugh at their crudeness, but who knows, they may find a home somewhere. I look through several sketchbooks and decide to place them out of sight. I put them neatly in one of the two file cabinets I keep in the room and turn the lock.

I sense Mack's arrival before I actually hear him. I feel the same old overpowering sense of doom. I know I need to be on my best behavior and on guard. He isn't about to let the events of today go. No, he will be just as furious now, if not more. I slowly close the door to my sanctuary and quietly walk down the stairs to my evil destiny.

He's already in the kitchen when I walk in. He's grabbing a beer from the refrigerator. I don't say a thing. I wait for the tyrannical lashing to begin. He takes a long drag from the bottle, staring at me all the while. I take a seat at the counter, like a child who had just done an unbelievable horrid deed. He finishes his drink and walks to stand in front of me on the other side of the counter. I still remain silent. Not sure if that would piss him off more or calm him. I don't care, I'm not going to let him get the best of me. Not today, not anymore this week, not this year, not ever. Finally, he sets his bottle on the counter with a loud bang. Maybe it isn't so loud, but with not a sound in the kitchen except the humming of the refrigerator, it seems to vibrate through the room.

He still stands across from me when he finally says, "What the hell were you trying to prove today by disobeying my command?" I nearly snort at the words *my command*. I still remain stoic and quiet. He slowly drains the rest of the beer and throws the bottle into the glass recyclable bin. Turning, he snarls, "Answer me, you fucking bitch."

"I didn't realize you commanded me to do anything. Much less to remain your prisoner here in our home," I reply with the same sort of snarl he's using.

"Don't play games with me, Elise, I can guarantee you that you will not win."

"No games here, Mack. I am just talking to you."

"You always get my family to back your little shenanigans and take your side. I am tired of you making me the laughingstock and the bad guy with my family and at work."

"Pray tell, Mack, just how am I doing that? Your family knows you better than I do. They know what you are like. They know how obnoxious you can act. So please don't blame me for your family not standing beside you or having your back."

He stands there with a look of surprise and complete evil at the same time. "How dare you talk to me in that manner!" he yells.

"What manner, Mack?" I yell back. "It's the same manner in which you address me all the time, hostile and hurtful. Get over yourself, Mack."

He starts around the counter toward me, but I stand and push the stool between us.

"Do you honestly think a stool is going to save you?" he says, kicking the stool over and reaching for me. I run to the cupboard and take the French chef butcher knife from the rack. I turn to see him stop dead in his tracks. "Really, Elise, do you think you can stop me with a fucking knife?"

"I have no idea, but if you continue to act the way you are and come one more step, I guess we will both find out," I spit out at him.

He retreats and goes over to pick up the stool. I don't move. He sits with a sigh on the stool and asks me in a weak, tired voice, "How did we let our marriage fall apart like this?"

"I think it all started with the damn murders."

"I surrender, Elise, I will not yell or hurt you. I'm sorry I made such a scene with Haven, and I'm sorry for just now. You just have no idea what the hell happened today." He's holding his head in his hands.

"Why don't you tell me about your day? You used to tell me about your days and we'd either laugh or cry together."

He looks up, and for the first time, I see his bloodshot eyes and the look of defeat in them. He slowly begins to tell me what went on at work earlier today. "The sheriff has approved for an investigating team from New York to come in and take over the murder cases. Hell, they are not even from our state. I personally think they are FBI. He says not, but I'm not convinced."

"Maybe that is a good move," I interject.

"No, that means I am to turn over everything I have worked on to them and then take a back seat to everything that goes on from now on. I've worked my ass off for the last few years, and this just means I didn't do enough."

"Give yourself a break, Mack. Maybe new eyes and new tests will help. Everything you've done was not in vain. They will be able to see all the work you've done. Work with them, Mack, not against them."

"Easier said than done" is his sad reply. "Plus, we had a meeting with the district attorney, the judge, and the sheriff this afternoon. The DA wants to drop all charges against Flem. He said without any more evidence, there isn't enough to get any kind of conviction." His tone sounds defeated.

"Wait, I thought he confessed. I thought that was as good as a conviction right there."

"No, they say my interrogation methods were harsh and browbeating. It won't hold up in court."

"Oh, Mack, I'm so sorry."

"Don't be sorry for me, Elise. I don't want your pity, for Christ sake." He's getting another beer. "Want one?"

"Sure."

"Anyway, by nine o'clock tomorrow morning, Flem will be let loose, and they will hold another press conference. Not sure what they will say. Our chief detective beat the living shit out of our number one suspect, so we have to let him go. I was asked to make up a short spiel to address the public. I wanted to say that it was all bullshit, but I wrote up a couple lines just to appease the mayor."

Not sure what to say, I just sip on my beer. Finally I ask, "Are you hungry? I haven't eaten yet myself."

"No, I think I'd heave it up if I ate anything. I am finding it hard to believe that I can keep this beer down."

"Okay, I'm fine with nothing too." Sipping on the beer I really didn't want.

Chapter 51

The rest of the evening goes slow and smooth. We avoid the news like it carries the plague.

"I need to go into the library and put all the papers and files in there into some sort of order."

"Do you need my help?"

"No, no offense, but you'd drive me nuts."

I decide to just watch a senseless movie. I need something light and meaningless to put me into a better mood. As much as I hate Mack most of the time, I'm not without compassion. He doesn't want me to feel sorry for him, but I do. He did put everything he had into the murder cases to no avail. I find it hard to believe he hadn't had a break in any of the cases since the very beginning. Not a hair, fingerprint, or any DNA left at any of the murder scenes. It's as if something swooped down and murdered each one and then was gone. Whoever is doing the killing is very smart and knows just what to do to cover up the traces of himself. It's as if it's someone who knows the procedures used to find evidence. The thought strikes me. Maybe it's a police person or a lab tech or a doctor. For a split second, I think maybe it's Mack. Is he capable of doing the murders? I shudder at the thought, but it nags at me.

Chapter 52

I'm watching *Miss Congeniality* with Sandra Bullock when I drift off to sleep. I had known when I was lying on the couch that I'd fall asleep, and I had also known I'd dream. I'd known of what I would dream about, and I don't even try to stop the dream from coming. I'm not sure that you can control your dreams, but I sometimes feel I can. I believe the term for being able to do that is lucid dreaming. The ability to know you are dreaming as you are dreaming. At any rate, I go directly into the dream head-on.

I'm watching Attorney Bixby in his hotel room. He's talking on the phone to his wife. He's smiling and enjoying the conversation they're having. Nothing intimate, just a recap of the day they both had. Although he's still in blue jeans and a T-shirt, I can tell he's already settled for the evening. He hangs up the phone and looks out the window as if seeing something of interest outside. I wonder if he's seeing me spying on his privacy. He turns and picks up his briefcase. He opens it and takes a stack of papers from it. He's leafing through the papers, when he rises from the small desk and comes back to the window. He stares out into the darkness with blank eyes. Are you seeing me? He silently opens the door and with bare feet walks away from the motel room. He's following someone. I'm sure of it. I can't see who he's following, but I know by his body language it's someone he trusts. He isn't talking or looking at anything around him. He's just following. He walks calmly behind the person. He feels no fear of him and is not suspicious of why he's to follow him. I can't make out who he's following. He soon is at the edge of town. No one sees them leave the motel but me. No one follows out of curiosity but me. No one sees me.

He continues to walk to the edge of the raging river. He follows the river upstream, taking care not to fall into the swirling water. It flows wildly over its banks. It's still raining but not nearly as hard as it had earlier in the day. He neither feels the coolness nor the wet spongy grass beneath his feet. He's in front of Mr. Flem's cottage. He goes directly to the door and tries the knob. It's locked. He turns to the person he had followed and holds his hand out for the key. No key is handed to him. Instead the knife is plunged deep into his stomach. It misses the crucial organs to prolong his life. He falls to the ground and curls into a ball, holding his stomach. He tries to protect his heart with his arms and hands. Instead of stabbing him again, he is kicked several times. Each bringing a grunt of pain from the attorney. The assailant reaches down with black gloves and turns him onto his back. With his large smooth-looking boots, he steps onto his throat. Attorney Bixby opens his mouth to scream, but this only aids his attacker. He reaches into his mouth and pulls his tongue as far out as he possibly could. With one swift swish of the blade, the tongue is severed, and no scream of agony is ever to be heard. He then nonchalantly throws the severed tongue into the river. To be consumed by a hungry fish or turtle or other river creature foraging for food on this dark night. Looking directly into his victim's face, he slowly plucks out an eyeball. Slicing it free from the socket. He repeats his action with the second eye. He seems to be pleased with his work. He throws the eyeballs one at a time into the roaring river. He returns to the body, and leaning over it, he says something and makes the sign of the cross with the blade of the knife and slowly walks away.

I feel a strange peace blanket the dark night. I know I've just witnessed the murder of the attorney. I'm sure I know the murderer. Yet I don't recognize him. I somehow know I'm connected to him. I feel his anger deep inside me. The peace I feel is now suffocating me. I want to run to Mr. Bixby. I want to cradle his lifeless body in my arms and mourn him. I want to tell him how sorry I am he had to die. Instead I turn and walk away from the scene. Only when I feel the touch on my arm do I become afraid and start to scream.

"Elise, it's me," Mack is saying as he caresses my bare arms. I jerk wide awake and pull away from him. "You need to go to a doctor to address these nightmares you are having. You have been having them more frequently, and they are getting rather bothersome."

"I'm sorry, I know. I will call the doctor in the morning and make an appointment. If you think they are bothersome to you, try living through one."

"No, thank you, my real life is enough of a nightmare without having made-up ones. Do you remember what you dream?" he asks as he begins scanning the channels.

"Yes, most of them. But I really don't want to talk about them."

"The way you scream and fight when I wake you up, I doubt I'd want to know."

I'm thinking to myself, *No, not this one in particular.*

I get up, and trying not to walk like a toddler on wobbly legs, I walk to the kitchen and pour myself a glass of cranberry juice. The tart taste fills my mouth and reminds me of blood. I nearly spit it out into the sink. I swallow the first mouthful and dump the remainder of the glass down the drain. The metallic taste of blood seems to cover every taste bud in my mouth. I needed to brush my teeth and get the taste out of my mouth. I'm sure my tongue is cut. By the time I'm in my bathroom, the taste has subsided. I brush my teeth and rinse my mouth out with Listerine. Not my favorite flavor in the world, but it beats the metallic taste of blood or the tart taste of unsweetened cranberry juice. I go back into the living room and ask Mack if he has finished with gathering all the files.

He says, "I've gathered all the ones I'm going to let them hash over. I'm keeping some. Let the bastards research some shit on their own."

I don't say anything. I just nod. I don't agree with him, but I don't feel like I want to argue my point either.

Chapter 53

We sit and watch part of *It's a Hard Day's Night* starring the Beatles.

"Well, that sort of sums up my life," he states flatly. I have the urge to giggle but manage to contain it until he starts to laugh himself. Only then do I laugh with him. He switches off the TV and stands up and reaches for my hand. "Let's go to bed, Elise. I'm going to have a hard day's night all damn day tomorrow." We walk hand in hand all the way to our room. We don't need words between us; we just need us. He goes into the bathroom, and I change into one of my nightgowns. He returns, and I go into the bathroom to go pee. When I go back out, he's lying under the covers with his arm over his eyes. I slide into bed next to him, and he pulls me close. I curl up in his arms, and we both sigh and drift off to sleep.

Unfortunately the damn alarm clock blares its ugly *beeeeeeep* way too quickly. Mack groans as he reaches for it. He shuts it off and then shoves it off the nightstand to splat onto the carpeted floor. I move closer to him and say sleepily, "Thank you."

He snuggles my neck and says, "You are most welcome."

We lie there spooning for a few minutes longer before he nudges me and says we better get out of bed before we never leave it for the day.

He heads for the bathroom saying he doesn't want anything but coffee this morning. I put my robe on and head for the kitchen. I hear the paper hit the front doormat as I come down the steps. I open the door and pick it up. Pictures of both Mr. Bixby and Mr.

Flem are plastered on the front page of the paper. I fold it in half and lay it on the counter. I have no desire to read what's being written about them. I freshen up in the bathroom off the kitchen and think, I will never be ready to face the day. I pour my coffee and take out a bagel to toast. I'm not sure I really want to eat it, but I think I should maybe try to fortify myself. I'm sure I'd need some sort of substance when Mack opens the paper.

Mack comes into the kitchen, and I hand him a cup of coffee. He absently sits at the counter with a look of defeat on his face. I put my arm around his shoulder and give him a peck on the cheek. I'm not sure how he will receive my gesture of love. He looks down at me and says, "Thank you, Elise, I needed that more than you will ever know." He slowly unfolds the paper, and I wait on bated breath for an explosion. He says nothing. He reads the headlines and leaves his stool and tosses the whole paper into the trash. He comes back to the breakfast counter and sips on his steaming hot cup of coffee. After finishing his coffee, he heads for the library. He carries the first box out to the car without a word. The second box of files is carried with a bunch of mumbling under his breath. I'm going to offer to help carry them but sense he will only get angry with me. Not because of my offer to help, but because they have to be turned over to the other investigators in the first place. I ask instead if he will like a cup of coffee to go.

"Yes, Elise, I would. The swill at work is just that, swill."

I take out his travel mug and fill it to the brim with hot black coffee. Watching it swirl into the cup makes me think of the black raging water in the river, and I remember my vivid dream, and I shudder.

Mack takes his coffee, kisses my cheek, and leaves without another word. I listen to him leave and take my first bite of the bagel I really don't want or need to eat. I'm sure my day will not be pleasant. I take the paper from the trash and begin to read the article written about the murder of Attorney Bixby and what the author speculated happen to him. Nothing is written that I don't already know, and I know I can add details to it that no other would know. Yet I'm not sure how I know the things I do. It frightens me.

Chapter 54

I have nothing planned for the day. I finish my coffee, take out the trash, and sit at the counter wondering what I should do besides paint. I think about calling Jordyn and asking if she wants me to bring more paintings but decide against it. I don't feel much like doing anything.

I call Haven on a whim. Hoping she will have something cheerful to say and her mood would brighten my day a bit. To my surprise, she answers with, "Hey, I was just going to call you."

"Why?"

"I'm going to the Humane Society, and I wanted to know if you wanted to tag along. We decided to get a rescue puppy for Becca."

"Don't you think she is a bit young to take care of a puppy? How is she going to walk it?" I add laughingly.

"Both Matt and I feel the sooner we get one, the better it will be. I know it will be double work training a puppy and trying to take care of Becca, but we are sure it will be great in the end."

"Oh."

"No excuses, my dear sister-in-law. I'll be there in an hour."

I smile as I start upstairs to get ready.

Haven pulls into the drive and jumps out of her car. She comes flying to the door and nearly falls in as I open it.

"What's wrong?" I exclaim, fearing something had happened to Becca on the drive over.

"Oh my god, Elise. Did you hear the news conference? They have let Mr. Flem go, and a team of investigators are here from New York. What the hell is going on?"

"The sheriff decided to get a group to come down and help Mack solve the murders. That's all."

"Well, Mack must be livid. All Mack said during the press conference was that he appreciated the extra help in solving the cases. He said extra eyes and ears were needed. I'm sorry, Elise, but that doesn't sound at all like Mack."

"I know," I confess. "I told him last night to work with them, not against them. Maybe he is going to actually listen to me for once."

She looks at me as we are buckling the seat belts and start to laugh. "You don't really believe that, do you?"

I giggle and answer, "No."

We don't discuss it anymore as she drives to the Humane Society.

"What kind of dog do you plan on getting?" I ask as we're getting Becca out of the car.

"I don't know, maybe one that's house broken."

"I doubt that will happen." I start to push the stroller.

Haven starts to skip like Dorothy in the *Wizard of Oz* and begins to sing. "We're off to get a puppy, a wonderful puppy at that." I realize I'm in a good mood and begin to join in with her.

We stop at the Society's office first, and the kind lady asks enough questions one would have thought Haven was going to adopt a baby and not an animal. Where do you live, how long have you lived there? Do you or did you ever have any other pets while living there? Is your yard fenced in? How many children do you have? Is someone home most of the day? Who will be responsible for the animal most of the time? The list goes on forever, until she asks for references to go along with the hundred questions. Haven politely answers all the questions and gives Mack and I as references, along with a couple other friends.

Finally the paperwork is finished, and an elderly volunteer leads us to the kennels. Good grief, the place is wall-to-wall yipping dogs. They come in all sorts of shapes and sizes. They have Great Danes, Newfoundlands, Boxers, beagles, mixed breeds, and some that I have never seen before. Haven says she really wants a puppy that can grow with her daughter. The gentleman says that she's sure to find one in the other side, where they keep the mothers and puppies.

We go through a door, and there are at least fifty kennels with excited puppies jumping all over the place. How on earth is one to choose a pet? As we slowly walk past the pens, my heart feels broken for all these cuties without loving owners. Haven is quite a ways ahead of me when I spot a small black-and-white puppy huddled in a corner. He looks afraid and sad. The other puppies in his pen are playing all around him, but he's just sitting there as though he doesn't belong. I stop and kneel down next to the pen. The other four puppies don't seem to care I'm there or not. I begin to talk to the helpless-looking puppy. He raises his head and, with the saddest eyes I have ever seen, stares right back into mine.

The elderly gentleman comes back to me and asks, "Do you plan on getting a puppy too?"

"I hadn't planned on it," I answer honestly. "What's the story on the little one in the corner?"

"Oh, that's Squirt. He was found a couple of weeks ago lying next to his dead mother and two other dead puppies in the park. It seemed that someone killed the mother and thought he killed all the puppies too, but this little guy was still alive. He hasn't played since we brought him here," he adds with a sigh. I quickly call for Haven.

"Come take the stroller. I have some paperwork to fill out," I tell her when she walks over.

After filling out all the paperwork, I go back to the pen and tell the volunteer that I want Squirt.

"Are you sure? He probably won't live long."

"Why do you think that? Is he sick?"

"Oh no, he passed with a clean bill of health. He's just suffering from a broken heart. Can't always fix those."

"Well, I'm sure going to try." He hands me the puppy. Haven just stands there with a shit-eating grin on her face. "You knew all along, I'd get a puppy, didn't you?"

"Yup." She goes merrily off to fetch the puppy she has picked out. Mine is a mutt of unknown origin. The vet has put down possible Border collie and Lab mixed. Haven picks out a Douge de Boudreaux and pays for the breed through the nose. The volunteer says it's rare they actually receive dogs of that breed in there.

I tell Squirt his new name is going to be something that means brave. I settle on Warrior. Haven names her puppy Isabelle. It's only when we're driving home do I think of the outburst I'm about to receive from Mack. Holy shit, what was I thinking. He'll probably throw me and the puppy off the balcony or drown us both in the pool. Haven reads my mind and says, "He always had a dog growing up at home. He might be angry at first, but he will fall in love with Warrior."

"I sure hope so."

We stop at the grocery store before heading to my house. I need puppy supplies. I buy the best puppy chow, bowls, a bed and a blanket, a couple of chew toys, a ball, and a book on puppies. Thank goodness I have the cash on me. Mack isn't going to have any supper tonight! I can't wait to get home and try to make Warrior feel loved and wanted. Poor little shit.

Haven doesn't stay but holds Warrior as I unload all the things I had bought for him. When I take him from her, I feel as though I'm was bringing my baby home. He's the sweetest little guy I have ever seen. I take Warrior straight to the backyard to see if he has to do his job. At first he just sits humped over, but he finally does his job, and I pick the little darling up and bring him into the house. The phone rings as I enter the kitchen.

"Hello." Mack is on the other end of the phone.

"What you doing?"

"Well, I did something this morning I'm sure you will not approve of and I'm quite sure you are going to explode when you get home." I think it will be better to break it to him on the phone.

"What the hell did you do this time?" he screams into the phone.

"I bought a puppy."

"You what?"

"I bought a puppy, and I plan on keeping it whether you like it or not," I state in a firm voice. Even though my legs have turned to mush and my stomach is doing flip-flops. I'm hanging on to the dear puppy as though he would save me from the evil voice on the other end of the phone.

"What the hell gets into you? We need a dog in our chaotic life about as much as we need to buy an elephant. You are really stupid sometimes, Elise."

"Well I don't care what you think, I need this puppy, and he needs me."

"Whatever. I won't be home for supper." I could hear exhaustion in his voice. "Make sure he doesn't go into the living room or anywhere else that he can ruin the carpet. I got to go." He hangs up. I hug Warrior.

I spend the rest of the day playing with Warrior. He's so afraid and refuses to walk anywhere in the house without me right there. I pretty much stay in the kitchen on the floor most of the day. I take him outside through the patio door every half hour or so. He does his job and will come right back to my feet. If I try to run away, he follows as fast as his short legs will carry him. I think maybe I should have named him Tagalong. He finally curls up in his bed, and I go about my day. It's a short nap because the phone wakes him, and he barks as though he's about to eat an intruder. It's the cutest little bark I've ever heard. I answer the phone with a laugh.

"Do you think that mutt will save you from me? I will get to you both."

"Who are you?"

"You will find out soon enough, Elise." And the phone goes dead. I slam the receiver down and pick up Warrior.

"No one will ever hurt you again," I whisper into his fluffy little ear. I take him out the patio door, and this time when I set him down, he actually runs a ways away and pees. He starts to explore the backyard, and I sit down on the grass and let him go.

Chapter 55

By five in the evening I'm starving and decide to make a salad for myself. Warrior has eaten some of his kibbles and seems comfortable enough to explore around the kitchen and the bathroom. I'm not sure where I'll put him to sleep. I'm sure he'll cry if I leave him alone in the kitchen for the night. Mack will never let him in the bedroom to sleep with us. I'm not sure I'd like lying on the cold floor in the kitchen either. I guess I'll figure that out when bedtime comes.

I eat my salad and decide to go watch the news. I bring Warrior with me but keep him on my lap. The local news is just about to start.

Of course the news is going to be about the news conference and the release of Mr. Flem. I'm happy he's a free man, but I dread what the news will say about the police department in our small town. A part of me is mesmerized by the news story and another is appalled. I just want something positive to be announced. I need something positive for Mack. Life will be so much easier for us if he has something positive happen.

It covers the conference with the tenacity of a bulldog attacking a ham bone. The news reporter keeps using phrases that are demeaning and certainly don't paint a very pretty picture of the sheriff's department. If I'm upset by the coverage, I wonder what it's doing to the hardworking, dedicated force working around the clock to keep this town safe. He states in not-so-nice words that it's about time the town is getting help from more educated, competent, trained personnel. They're due to arrive from New York City around seven tonight. He's sure with these highly trained professionals the cases will be solved within hours.

That means that Mack won't probably be home before midnight and be leaving at the crack of dawn. I'm sure he will be impossible to please. I hold Warrior close and tell him that we'll be in for hell the next few days.

I clean up after eating and take Warrior outside again. He's so darn cute and is getting braver by the minute. He's a bright moment in my otherwise rather sad life. He's venturing farther and farther into the yard and will jump and run, playing like a normal pup. I hope his past will soon be erased completely.

I've taken Warrior with me to my studio. He sniffs at everything and barks at his reflection in the full-length mirror in the corner. He makes me giggle at his puppy antics. I'm very surprised to hear the garage door open. I feel sick inside thinking of what's about to take place when Mack walks into the house. Lord, please give me the strength I will need to face the devil himself, I silently pray.

I carry Warrior downstairs and enter the kitchen as Mack is struggling to get a rather large box in through the door. Warrior lets out a string of angry barks. He's struggling to get out of my arms. I'm not sure if it's to go hide or to take Mack's leg off. Mack looks up sharply and, to my amazement, laughs. I can't believe it.

"What on earth did you buy?" I ask as I come around the counter to close the door.

"I had to go to Portsmith to pick up the investigators, so I left early and went to the pet shop there." He props the box against the island.

"What is it?" I ask as I hand Warrior to him. Warrior immediately goes into attack mode. He growls and snarls and wiggles to be free. Mack begins to softly talk to him, and within seconds, the puppy becomes calm. I have never seen Mack so gentle with any animal. He coos and whispers to Warrior, much like he does when he holds Becca.

I take out a paring knife and begin slitting the tape from the box to get it open.

"What is this thing?"

"It's a puppy play pen," he exclaims excitedly. He puts Warrior down and proceeds to help me get the thing out of the box. "See, it folds up and has wheels on the bottom to help roll it from room to room." He rolls it to the center of the kitchen floor and opens it. It's much like a baby port-a-crib. Once set up, it's really something to see. The sides are made from a tightly woven wire mesh, so the animal can't chew through it. The bottom is the same until you place the mat on it. The mat has another mat that's placed on one side. The directions explain that it's treated with something that the dog recognizes as a place to safely urinate and do the other business. The urine is absorbed by a gel layer that is easily removed and tossed. Then replaced by a new one. It has a big enough space for the puppy to play and has a place to hang the feeding and watering bowls. Which can easily be removed to allow the pen to be folded without spilling everything. I can't believe they've made such a thing, and I'm really astounded that Mack spent the money on it. I put Warrior's bed in it and his toys. Then I place the puppy in it. He promptly pees in the designated area. Mack lets out a genuine belly laugh. I'm in a state of shock.

"Wait, I forgot the best part." He pulls another box out of a bag I haven't even noticed before. It contains a teddy bear.

"Won't he just chew that thing up in a matter of minutes?"

"I don't think so." He rips a Velcro strip open. He turns it on and then picks up Warrior. "Hold him up to your chest so he can hear your heartbeat." I do as he says and then he takes the puppy. "Now hold the bear to your chest for about thirty seconds." I do what he says, still wondering what's going on. "Now listen to the bear." I do and I'm completely mind blown. The bear has a heartbeat that's the same as mine. "I doubt he will chew up his momma," Mack says smiling. He puts Warrior in his bed, and I lay the bear next to him. Warrior immediately makes his couple of turns and plops down with his head resting on the bear. With an adorable puppy yawn, he shuts his eyes, and within seconds he's sound asleep.

I can't believe it. I go to Mack and give him the biggest hug ever. "Thank you so very much," I whisper with tears in my eyes. "You just never cease to amaze me."

"Well, I wasn't about to have to listen to a puppy whine and cry all night. Plus, I rather like you in my bed than sleeping on the cold kitchen floor." He gently kisses me. I giggle.

"Actually, that thought did enter my mind."

"I figured it did."

"Are you hungry?" I ask letting go of him.

"No, just tired. It's been a long, horrible day."

"I watched the news. It sure wasn't very complimentary of the sheriff's department."

"No, it really was worse than what it was on TV."

"Oh, Mack, I feel so bad for all of you." Tears just naturally fill my eyes.

"It'll be fine" is all he says as he reaches for a beer. We sit in the kitchen watching the puppy contentedly sleep, like a couple of kids. It's a peaceful feeling. It's a calm before the storm. A storm I can feel but can't explain. A storm so fierce I'm sure it will tear many lives apart. I shudder at the thought.

Chapter 56

Mack wakes the puppy up and takes him outside. He watches as the dog sniffs at everything and hops around in the grass more like a bunny than a puppy. I stand and watch from the patio. I can feel the tension that's racing through Mack's body. If only I can help. I think of my dream but decide not to bring it up. He will only become angry, and I'm not prepared for the devastation it will surely cause.

Mack brings Warrior in and says we'll take the pen up to the bedroom tonight to see how it works out. Mack folds the pen up, and I shut off everything downstairs and pick up Warrior. I'm not sure he'll be able to do the stairs, and I really have my doubts that he'll be a quiet puppy through the night. By the time I come into the bedroom, Mack has set up the pen.

"We are going to have to change our morning routine," he says over his shoulder. "You will have to take Warrior out right away, and I'll bring the pen down when I come down for breakfast. We will need another garbage can up here especially for the gel and his other deposits."

"I'll get the one out of my studio for tonight."

"Good idea." He takes Warrior and puts him into his bed, and I go to get the wastebasket. When I return, Mack is in the bathroom, and Warrior is drinking out of his water bowl. I bend over and pat his head.

"Be a good puppy tonight or we both may be thrown over the balcony."

Mack enters and with humor I seldom hear in his voice. "I'd never throw a helpless puppy over the balcony, but my goofy wife, now that's another story."

"Oh, I see where I stand." Mack comes over and reaches into the pen and runs his hand down the dog's back. He then turns and runs his hands down both of my arms. A chill of excitement races through me. I shiver at his touch. "As much as I'd like to fuck your brains out tonight, I doubt I could even get it up. I'm just too damn worn-out." He turns and walks to his side of the bed. I go into the bathroom, and by the time I'm finishing with my toilet and have my nightdress on, both puppy and man are sleeping. I gently crawl into bed and shut off the lamp. Mack doesn't even move.

I lie there just remembering the highlights of the day. Mack seems more pleased with the puppy than not. Becca gets her growing-up companion, and I get a dog as broken as myself. I sigh and drift off to sleep.

I awake to a little yip and a whine. It takes me a second to realize what it is. I quickly sit up and reach into the pen. Warrior nudges my hand and promptly falls onto the teddy bear, and I lie back down. Mack never moves a muscle. I look at the clock and I'm surprised to see it's close to four o'clock. I wonder if a teddy bear will work as good for a newborn baby. I'll have to be sure and tell Haven about it tomorrow.

Chapter 57

I awake before the blare of the alarm clock, so I silently get up and pick up a sleeping puppy. Grabbing my robe, I quietly walk out of the bedroom. I take Warrior out to the backyard immediately and stand in bare feet while he does his business. I'll pick up his mess later. The coffee is just beginning to perk, and Warrior seems content to chew on a toy. I wait to see if Mack wants food. A few seconds later I hear him yell down.

"I'll have the normal breakfast today! I'll need all the strength I can get to face those assholes all day long today."

"Yes, sir, I'll get right on it."

As I go about getting Mack's breakfast, I can't help wonder what it's going to be like for him at work today. I decide I don't think I can handle the pressure. My stomach feels queasy just thinking of having to stand up to the mayor like Mack does. I have everything on the table when Mack comes into the kitchen with the pen. I watch as he opens it.

"Do you think I can carry it up to the studio and set it up by myself?"

"It's really not that heavy, and the wheels help a lot. I'm sure you'll manage without a problem."

"Good, because I need to get some work done up there. Oh, I forgot to ask. Jordyn would like to come over and pick out some paintings for the store. Only problem it will need to be after the store is closed for the day or on a day it's closed. I told her I'd check with you when a good time would be."

"Elise, we are having company on Sunday, why not include her too?"

"Oh, I had forgot about Sunday. Do you think that would be okay?" I ask, unsure I'm really hearing Mack correctly.

"Why not? She's already met Haven and Becca. Maybe she can sing, and then we could have a regular jam session."

When he's done with his breakfast, he picks up Warrior and heads outside. I'm once again surprised. Not just with his acceptance of the dog, but also his calm mood. He's about to experience a very hard day at work and yet he seems calm and not at all worried. I begin to worry that he's surely about to explode at some time. I just hope he doesn't get too carried away at work and end up jeopardizing his job. Even though I hate his temper, I'd rather he take it out on me instead of losing it at work. I pray he doesn't lose it while trying to accommodate the investigating team sent down to help him solve the case. He brings the dog in and sets him on the floor and grabs his things and gives me a peck on the cheek, bends and gives Warrior a pat on the head, and is out the door.

Warrior and I finish our breakfast, and I decide to see if I can get the pen up the stairs to my studio. It's too early to call Jordyn or Haven, so I might as well see if I can get some painting done. The pen isn't as heavy as I think it will be. I'd have let him run free, but I don't want him underfoot while I try to work. I have to laugh at his antics trying to make it up the steps. His fat little puppy body isn't made to climb the stairs. Not just yet anyway. I manage to get everything set up, and with all the toys he has to play with, he seems content to stay in the pen while I work.

After about an hour, I take Warrior outside again. I look at the pool and think of how Mack had been pissed at having to drag the umbrella out of it. It's then I notice something at the bottom of the pool. I walk over to the edge to see what it is. I nearly fall in when I see what's lying on the bottom of the pool. It's a doll. Not just any doll, but one of my childhood dolls I haven't seen in years. In fact, I just figured my mother tossed it in the trash when I went away to college. It has to be another doll that looks like my Maggie. Who would do this to me?

Just as I'm about to get the pool stick, Warrior lets out a low puppy growl and starts for the back gate. I stand frozen to the ground. I'm not sure if I want to know if someone is there. Warrior is acting like a killer puppy, and I'm acting like a scared rabbit. I walk over to the dog and pick him up. He's still barking and acting all brave. I go to the gate, and even though I'm shaking in my bare feet, I open the gate. There's an envelope on the ground addressed to me. I look for whoever may have put it there, but no one is anywhere in sight. I think that disturbs me more than if I'd have seen someone running away. Or someone standing there ready to kill me.

I close the gate and put Warrior down. I open the letter knowing it will be another warning.

"Oh, Elise…Your puppy is so precious. Hope nothing happens to him."

That does it. Threaten me all you want. Scare me senseless, but don't hurt my dog. I'm really fed up with this asshole. I want him to fight like a man. How can I even begin to stand up against someone I cannot see? I take Warrior in the house. To hell with the doll in the pool. To hell with all this. I've had it. I tear the letter up and throw it away.

Chapter 58

I call Haven to ask her how Isabelle is doing. She answers the phone like a mother who has been up all night.

"Haven? Is everything all right?"

"Oh my god, I'm about to kill Isabelle, and I want to give Becca to the Gypsies." I can feel the exasperation in her voice and feel so sorry for her.

"Oh, honey, do you want me to come get one or the other?"

"Both would be nice." She giggles.

"Well, I'd probably do better with the dog." I remember the teddy bear and quickly add, "Haven, your brother bought the coolest thing for Warrior. You simply must get one or maybe even two. He also got a doggie pen."

"What? My brother bought something for the dog? Will wonders ever cease? What did he buy?"

"It's a teddy bear that emulates your heartbeat. I don't know how, but it just programs itself to your heartbeat. I held Warrior up to my chest and then the teddy bear. It calmed him right down, and he slept almost all night cuddled up on it. I thought it would be great for a newborn who wasn't sleeping too."

"Oh my god, where in the hell did he find it? I'm going to get two. What kind of pen?" she blurts out.

"It's a pen with a pee area and the bowls attach to the side. It folds up and has wheels on it. It's light enough for me to handle up the stairs. He got it at the pet shop in Portsmith."

"I'm getting dressed and driving to Portsmith. I can't do another sleepless night." She groans in desperation.

"I can watch Isabelle if you want to drop her off. I'm sure Warrior would enjoy a puppy playdate. He is getting much better with interacting with us."

"I'll drop her off in a little bit. Maybe you can wear her out and she'll finally sleep."

"I can't wait."

I call Jordyn to invite her over for Sunday. She's pleased and even says that she will bring her guitar too. I'm not surprised that she knows how to play. I tell her the time and make it a point to tell her not to bring anything else but her guitar. We'll supply all the food and drink. It's our pleasure. I hear the bell over the shop door tinkle and tell her to sell tons of things today.

I feel so much better after talking with both Haven and Jordyn I've forgotten the note. That isn't until the phone rings again. Thinking it may be Haven, I answer with a cheery, "Hello there."

"My, my, you are in a great mood this morning. I would have thought finding poor little Maggie dead in the pool would have dampened your mood. I guess I'll have to try harder." The voice is all too familiar.

"You are a coward, why don't you come out of hiding and meet me head-on?" I scream into the phone.

"Now that's the Elise I like to hear. The frightened one."

"I'm not frightened, I'm angry, you spineless jerk. I'm done with your bullshit. If you are going to kill me, do it like a man. Come get me." I slam the phone down. How dare he do this to me? I feel the bile rise, and I run to the bathroom and spew my breakfast into the toilet. That makes me even madder. The phone calls, the nightmares, the notes are all taking a toll on me. I feel sick nearly every day. Something has to give.

Haven arrives a short time later. She has Isabelle on a leash, and the dog clearly isn't having any of it.

"I am going to choke her before she learns to walk nicely on a leash." She's struggling to keep the dog from wrapping around her legs.

"Well, I hope she learns fast, because in another month, she is going to be bigger than you are."

"I know, but she is so damn cute." I take the leash and the dog from Haven. All the while Warrior barks at Issy. "Just go, we will be fine." I have to wonder, as she sprints to the car and the dogs begin to wrestle with each other at my feet, I may end up as a doggie snack if I'm not careful.

The time seems to fly by watching the two mutts play with each other. I take them outside and let them run around in the backyard. You'd never believe that Warrior is the same dog from yesterday. Yesterday he had been afraid and broken; today he is brave and happy to play with his best friend Issy. Issy is almost twice as big as Warrior and yet that doesn't seem to bother him at all. He dishes out the puppy bites as well as he receives them. I decide I have to be more like my little puppy. Maybe we are healing each other. What a pleasant way to spend the day. Watching two pups running around without a care in the world. At that moment, I want to be a puppy.

I take the pups inside and drag the pen downstairs. I place them both in the pen and expect more rough housing between the two. Instead they calm down and curl up together on the teddy bear, and after a couple cute puppy yawns, they both fall asleep. I begin to prepare a light lunch for when Haven and Becca comes back from Portsmith. I cut up some cheese and have some crackers along with a salad with fresh fruit. Now to just wait for Haven and the princess.

With both dogs contented, I have a few minutes to go sketch another painting. I think about turning on the news, but I really am sick of all the shit they're stirring up. I don't think I can take any more negativity right now. I bring my book down and sit at the counter and begin to sketch the two dogs curled up together. It will be a great painting. I may try to just paint Issy and Princess together. I can see the two of them walking together. Issy the size of a moose and Princess tiny and trusting. Makes me have a strange yearning inside. Do I want a baby? Oh hell no.

Chapter 59

Haven arrives later and comes in carrying the contraption I can't get out of the car. Inside is a screaming baby.

"What are you doing to my niece?" I cry as I go to rescue her from her evil mommy.

"She's just starving, that's all." Handing the baby to me. The pups are wide awake, adding to the din of noise with their own cries. "How was the beast?" Haven asks, walking over to pick up Issy.

"She was great, but you may want to take her out the patio door right away. She has been sleeping for a bit."

"Oh no, you don't get to sleep if I can't," Haven is saying as she puts Issy outside. She comes back and picks up Warrior, and he isn't happy. He tries to nip her hands as she carries him to the door. "You really are a Warrior, aren't you? Trying to eat your auntie when she's trying to be good to you is not nice." Both dogs take off running as soon as Warrior's feet hit the grass. She stands at the door and watches them do their business and play for a bit.

"I made lunch for us."

"Oh good, I'm as hungry as Becca. I better feed her first or she will never settle down." She takes Becca from me, and I retrieve the dogs from the backyard. "Can we eat out there? Maybe Issy will get tired and actually sleep." She's preparing to breastfeed Becca.

"Did you find the teddy bear and get a pen too?"

"I got two bears. One for the damn dog and one for Becca."

"That's a good idea. How about the pen?"

"Yup, I got that too."

We take our plates and go outside to sit at the table and eat our lunch as the pups play and Becca coos in her seat. Haven has set the seat down on the patio, and both dogs run up to inspect her. Issy seems to be telling Warrior that Becca is hers, and Warrior seems to understand her. They do the puppy sniffs and licks and then run off to play. It's a pleasant lunch.

Haven gets up and says she better get Becca home for a nap. If both child and puppy sleep at the same time, then she thinks she'd sneak in a nap too. She walks to the edge of the pool, and I remember the doll.

"Hey, Elise, did you have other kids over lately?" she asks. "There is a doll at the bottom of the pool."

I pretend I have no idea what she's talking about and try to act shocked. "Oh no, I wonder if someone threw it over the fence." I stare at my old doll lying lifeless at the bottom of the pool. "He must have one hell of an arm and should seriously think of becoming a quarterback or pitcher." I just stand there and stare at Maggie. Haven fishes the doll out, and I pray it doesn't have something written on it. I don't feel like trying to explain why this happened.

"It seems to be in perfect condition." She hands me Maggie. "I think you should dry it out and keep it here for Becca when she gets older."

"I will," I answer absently.

"Well, we better get going here."

I help her pack up Becca and put Issy on her leash. She isn't liking it at all, but when Warrior begins to walk beside her, she calms down and walks the short distance to the car like she has been leash trained years ago. I stand holding Warrior as Haven leaves with her car full. I turn and slowly go back into the house. The house doesn't seem so much of a prison anymore with the pup to keep me company. Maybe he's just what I need.

Chapter 60

Mack returns to his office after a quick lunch in the break room. The lunch consists of a stale sandwich from the vending machine and a very strong cup of coffee. Jesus, no one at the department knows how to make a cup of decent coffee. The sandwich probably had been sitting in the machine for a month or two. At least that's the way the damn thing tastes. Both food and drink seem to float at the very top of Mack's stomach. Mack thinks if a boulder can float in coffee, that's what's taking place as he opens the door to his office.

He has spent all morning going over evidence with the team from New York. He's surprised that they seem to actually appreciate all his hard work. He's also surprised that the leader of the team is a woman. A very attractive thirtyish woman who means business. The respect she expects from her team oozes from her very being. Nonsense is not a part of her vocabulary, and it isn't tolerated. Mack has never met a woman with so much confidence. He feels inferior next to her, but he'll do his damnedest not to show her that. After checking his voice mail and emails, he decides to go back to the conference room to see what they may have found in the boxes of paperwork. He thinks about calling Elise but thinks he'd rather not know what bullshit she may have dreamed up this time. He's sure that she can't or won't go through the day without claiming some crap took place. He's getting quite sick of her antics for attention.

Upon entering the conference room, he notices the box being gone through is one from the very first murder, and he has brought it in from home. Three of the investigators are trying to sort through it.

"Here, let me help you. I know the sequence it should be in, and I thought I had put it in the box in order."

"Oh, it probably was in order, but sometimes things will pop out at you if you go through it at random," the second in command states. Mack remembers his name is George something that ends in a *ski*. "But please join us, because I'm sure we will have questions for you." Mack notices that there's a fresh pot of coffee, and he figures he will need something to keep him going.

"Do you plan on working through the weekend?"

"No, we will fly back to New York after today and return again on Tuesday. We want to take some of the files back to New York and have some of our other analysts thumb through it. They work mostly on weekends, so we have something fresh to go on when we get back to work."

"I thought you guys worked around the clock on cases like this."

"Only on *Criminal Minds*, *NCIS*, and *CSI* do they do that. We actually put our families first." That comes as a shocker to Mack.

The mayor comes hustling into the room like his ass is on fire. Mack sees by the look in his eye he's in a foul mood. "I'm sure these people don't need your input into any of this. I think you have proven your incompetence to them by now," he states with enough venom to kill everyone in the room.

"Oh no, we need him in here. He has done some outstanding investigating, and his input is very much appreciated," George says with a slow, sure voice. "You can be very proud of his accomplishments here." This goes over like a lead balloon with the mayor.

"Well, if he's so damn good, I'd think he'd have solved the cases by now."

"Pretty hard to solve a crime when there is nothing left at the crime scene to go on," Mack snarls right back.

"Well, I for one am done with your incompetence and will suggest to the board that you be forced to resign."

"If you think I'm resigning because you think you can do a better job than me, you are badly mistaken, Mr. Mayor, sir," Mack states as he pushes his chair back and leaves the room.

Mack has had it. He decides to pack up for the day and go home. Fuck this place. It has been a very grueling morning trying to answer questions about nearly every piece of paper that has been in the first three boxes. He thinks that had been bad enough, but now the stupid fucking mayor has the audacity to cut him down in front of a team he and the sheriff thinks could do his job better. He's about to open his office door when someone calls his name.

"Mack, may I have a word with you?"

Great, now the sheriff is going to chew his ear off.

"Sure, what's on your mind?" Mack tries keeping his voice as normal as possible. He's sure the steam is shooting out of his ears like a broken hot water pipe on a cold day.

"I was thinking, maybe it would be best if you took a leave of absence for a while."

"Why the hell would you think I need to do that?"

"You've been under a lot of pressure lately, and with the investigators here now, I just think it best that you take a little break."

"Did the fucking mayor put you up to this?" Mack can no longer hold his temper.

"No, no, no, he didn't say a thing to me about it."

"Well, I don't need a fucking break, and I'm not taking one," Mack says as he storms into his office. The sheriff follows him in and shuts the door.

"Mack, you have no choice."

"What do you mean I have no choice?"

"If you don't request a leave, I will be putting you on administrative leave, with pay of course."

"What the hell is going on here? First the mayor says he will ask the board to ask for my resignation, and now you are putting me on administrative leave. Do you think I'm no longer qualified to do my job? I don't get it."

"Mack, it has been brought to my attention that you have been drinking a lot more after hours. I'm thinking the murders are just getting to you. Maybe a break from it all for a month or so will help you look at it with fresh eyes. Who knows, Mack, maybe the team will have found out who the killer or killers are by then."

"Who the hell has been talking shit about me? I have a right to know who is shooting off their big mouth!" Mack yells. "I haven't been drinking any more or any less than any other of the bastards that work for this department. You yourself have been known to tip a few back at the local bars. Hell, even the asshole mayor drinks. I don't see you two taking a leave. Maybe you two should go on a cruise or something together. You seem to have your head so far up his ass, people are beginning to think you are just another one of his appendages dangling out of his pants."

"That's enough, Mack. I am still your boss, and you will talk to me with respect."

"Oh, I'm sorry, did I hit a nerve?" Mack snaps back.

"Mack, besides the drinking, there is the episodes with the lab tests. I'm not sure what you were trying to do there, but testing envelopes for prints and then one with your wife's DNA on it, I can't be having my chief detective running around doing absurd shit like a lunatic."

"I know it looked bad, but my crazy bitch of a wife had me convinced someone was threatening her. I guess I wasn't giving her the attention she thought she deserved. Believe me, that won't ever happen again," Mack says with gritted teeth. "I had a long talk with her."

"Mack, I have no choice but to put you on leave, starting immediately."

"Do you want me to clear out my desk right away?" Mack is sneering.

"Now, that is uncalled for. Just go and take a little time off. I'm sure when you get back things will be better for all of us," the sheriff adds, getting up out of the chair.

"This is a bunch of bullshit and you know it." Mack starts slamming files into his briefcase.

"No, Mack, leave it all here. Just take whatever personal things you think you may need while you are out of the office. All the other stuff stays here," the sheriff says, holding on to Mack's arm.

"What the hell? Am I under investigation?" Mack asks, not believing what's happening.

"No, but we may need to see what you have been working on. That's all."

"Bullshit, I've seen how it works. You are doing an internal investigation. Have fun, Sheriff," Mack says over his shoulder as he walks out of the office.

Of course, everyone in the office is trying to hear what's going on. Sergeant Potts actually walks past the window at least three times. He keeps going to the copy machine that's near enough to the window to hear what's being said in the office. Seeing the fire in Mack's eyes and the disgust on the sheriff's face, they are all speculating what had been said in the office. Mack doesn't bother to say anything on the way to the elevator, and the sheriff walks after him without looking at anyone sitting stunned at their desks. The elevator door closes behind the two, but not a word is spoken between the two of them. Mack walks directly out of the front door of the sheriff's department and goes to his car.

"Fuck them all," he mumbles as he turns the key in the ignition.

Chapter 61

Mack doesn't feel in the mood to go home. He isn't in the mood to see Elise or anyone else for that matter. He decides to just drive. He drives to the local liquor store and buys a bottle of Jack Daniels, two packs of cigarettes, and a couple bottles of Coke. Getting back in the car, he drinks a long swig from the Coke and then fills it to the top with Jack. He pulls out of the parking lot and heads north. He drives for about an hour before he stops at a wayside and parks his car. He has finished the one bottle of Coke and opens the second. He rolls down the window and empties over half the bottle out on the pavement. He fills it with Jack and takes another drink. He gets out of the car and goes to the public toilet. After taking a piss, he decides to head to Portsmith.

It's still early, and not many people are off work and in the bar he chooses to have a couple drinks in. It's a little bar, off the main drag, and seems the perfect place to just sit and drink one's self into a coma. He chooses a booth in the back where he can watch the door and people as they come in. The waitress is a woman who looks as though she has just gotten done pulling a train of about thirty guys. She has too much perfume on, and her hair is messy. Her eye makeup is smeared, and Mack is sure she has a smelly pussy too. Probably had one too many guys last night. She looks at him and says one word.

"Cop." It isn't a question; it's a statement.

"No, just a guy wanting a drink or two by himself. Is there a rule around here against that?"

"Nope, name your poison. Oh, I know you're a cop because your picture has been plastered all over the boob tube for the last few months. You may be off duty, but you're still a cop."

"Jack and Coke. Heavy on the Coke," Mack says.

"Whatever your heart desires." She walks back to the bar.

"Bitch," Mack says as she walks out of earshot. She brings Mack's drink, and he says. "Make sure you keep them coming."

"Yes, sir."

Mack sits and scans his phone as he takes the first couple sips of his drink. Before he knows it, he's on his third drink and commenting on stupid posts on Facebook. Mack sits there all by himself, laughing at people's stupidity. Some of the posts are just so damn dumb. He finds it hard to believe how many people hash out their dirty laundry on this site. Mack hears a giggle and looks up to see a little hot blonde standing right in front of him.

"Hello, handsome, you seemed pretty glued to your phone," she says, swinging her long hair out of her face.

"Not too glued to it that I couldn't use your company."

She plunks her pretty ass down into the booth opposite of him and asks, "What ya drinking?"

"My poison, as the waitress stated, is Jack and Coke." He winks.

"Hey, Marcy, bring another round over here. please." She waves a ten-dollar bill in the air. Marcy obliges and takes the ten. "Keep the rest as a tip and start a tab for me."

"You come here often?"

"I own the place. I haven't seen you in here before. I've seen you on TV, but never in person."

"Apparently, everyone has seen me on the telly. I'm quite the celebrity," Mack says laughingly.

"Why, yes, you are. I hope you aren't driving back to Flag Lake tonight."

"I will have to, as I have nowhere else to stay," he says, raising his eyebrows.

"Well, when the time comes to leave, I'm sure we can find somewhere for you to stay. Can't have the fine detective driving drunk." She reaches across the table and rubs his hand.

Holy shit, I'm getting a hard-on already, Mack thinks to himself.

She seems to read his mind and says, "Try to save that for a little later, sweetie. I have to work for a couple of hours. I get off at eight, can you hold on that long?"

"For you, honey, I'll manage to hold on to it."

"The Viagra commercials say anything over four hours is dangerous."

"Oh, believe me, I don't need the little blue pill to please you."

She just smiles knowingly and licks her lips. Mack thinks, *Thank God I'm not seventeen or I'd have creamed my jeans.*

Chapter 62

I spend much of my day painting and playing with Warrior. When it's time to eat, I decide to pop a Lean Cuisine in the microwave and call it a meal. I haven't heard from Mack all day, but I haven't expected to either. It doesn't bother me one bit that he doesn't contact me. Warrior seems to take the place of the anger I would have otherwise felt from the neglect.

I turn the TV on and settle on the couch with Warrior sitting on my lap. He's chewing on a rope toy and trying his best to rip it apart. I settle on the local news. What crap are they reporting on today? Lo and behold, there's Sheriff Danking doing his best to run from a group of reporters. The questions are being fired at him faster than a machine gun. They're coming from all directions.

"Is it true that Detective Mackenzie resigned? Was he placed on administrative leave? Will he be coming back to the department in the same capacity as he is now, or will he be demoted? Whose idea was it for him to leave? If he took a leave, what was his reasoning? Is there something the citizens of Flag Lake should know about his leaving and the murders? Is he involved in any way with the unsolved murders?"

Sheriff Danking makes it to his car and turns and says, "This has nothing to do with the investigation nor is there any reason for the citizens of Flag Lake to be concerned." He gets into his car and drives away.

One of the reporters turns to the camera and states, "There you have it. No one is leaking any information on Chief Deputy Mackenzie's hostile walk out of the sheriff's department just after lunch today. It is said there was quite a heated exchange between the sheriff and the deputy just before Mackenzie stormed from the building and drove away. We will report the latest news on this incident as we are informed."

The first thing I think of is that someone is a snitch at the department. The second thought is, where the hell did my husband storm off to and why? Why didn't he come home? Where is he now at this hour if he isn't working? Like I don't already know. He's drinking and picking up some piece of ass to satisfy his hurt.

I switch the channel just as the phone rings. Not caring who the hell it is, I let it go to voice mail. It's Haven, so I pick up to answer.

"Hi."

"Wow, Elise, I just saw the news and wondered how Mack is." She's truly concerned.

"Well, I have no idea, because he chose not to come home yet."

"Oh, Elise, I'm so sorry. I would have thought he'd come home to have you lick his wounds."

"Don't worry about your brother, I'm sure he is just fine." A bit too much sarcasm is in my voice.

"I'm sure he just needed to be alone."

"I'm sure that's it, do you want him to call you when he gets home?"

"No, but tell him if he wants to cancel Sunday to just let us know."

"Okay, I will." I hang up the phone.

How sweet that Haven is concerned for Mack. She has no idea what he is doing right now to console himself. He will come home smelling of cheap perfume and booze and be an ass. I will not let him take whatever happened to him today out on me. No, I'm done being his escape goat and punching bag. I don't realize I'm hugging the puppy too tight until he cries and struggles to get free. Letting him go, I kiss him on top of the head and say, "Oh, baby, I'm so sorry I hurt you." Thinking of what Mack is doing and how he always chooses a slut over me makes me angry. I had hoped Warrior would prevent the old hatred from surfacing, but it's there.

Getting up from the couch, I take the pup to the backyard. It's beginning to be a beautiful evening, and I think of just sitting outside for a while. Instead, I go back into the house and change into my swimsuit. Maybe a couple of laps in the pool will release some of the built-up resentment and anger. I go to the side of the pool and dive in, not even checking the water temperature. It's cool on my skin and seems to seep deeper than just touching the skin. To my surprise, Warrior doesn't hesitate and does a belly flop right into the water. He does his little doggie paddle with ease. I call him, and he swims to me. When I hold him, he immediately struggles to get back in the water. I let him go and watch as he swims happily around in a large circle. I start to do a lap, and he follows me. When I reach the end of the pool, I set him back on the concrete at the edge of the pool. He runs alongside the edge of the pool while I swim. He waits for me to come up at the other end of the pool and flops into the water again. He seems to be born for swimming. I hope he learns to get out of the pool on his own. He's too little now and will drown if left unattended.

After a couple more laps, we leave the pool. He wiggles and shakes, takes a few steps, and wiggles and shakes. I wrap a towel around myself and grab another one to begin to dry the pup. He sits patiently while I dry him as best I can.

"You will have to go into the pen when we get in the house or the place with smell like wet dog."

I'm still rubbing his hair. With a sneeze, he runs away from me. He heads straight for the pool, and I run after him just barely getting to him before he flops into the water.

"Oh no, you don't, you cute little shit. You have had enough for the day. I can see you will need to be on a chain until you learn you can't just take a dip whenever you want to." Hugging him, I leave the backyard and take him directly into his pen. He doesn't seem to mind and starts to drink his water. He plops down on his bed and teddy bear and is asleep before I even walk away. I strip in the laundry room and place my suit and towels in the washer to be rinsed while I take my shower. I stay in the shower, enjoying the beads of water caressing my body. Unfortunately, all I can think about is Mack caressing some other woman's body. By the time I'm finished, the anger and hatred have returned.

Chapter 63

Mack waits in the booth for the owner to get done with her shift. He has found out her name is Heather. He tries to slow down a bit on his drinking as he wants to perform his best for her. Damn, he can't wait to bang her brains out. He watches her behind the bar, talking with her customers and laughing her cute little laugh. She's definitely a feely type of woman. She often will reach across the bar and touch a customer. It seems she treats both males and females the same. She's like a breath of fresh air. Cheerful, happy, pretty, and not at all like his bitch of a wife. Yes, it would feel great to be inside someone who actually wants him to be there.

At precisely eight o'clock, she walks over to Mack. "Hello, handsome, are you ready to take a short walk?" She gently rubs his arm.

"With you, honey, I'm ready to take a short walk, a run, and a jump. Your wish is my command." He gives her a sexy wink.

"Come along then, Detective, let's get to know each other better."

"You got it." Mack stands up and realizes he's drunker than he wants to be. He'd have to work harder to please her, and that is just what he plans to do.

They walk out of the bar together, and she starts to walk up the alley behind the bar. "Where are we going?" Mack asks, taking her hand.

"I live just up the way here about a block."

"I'd have thought you would have a room or something above the bar."

"Are you implying I have sex with men who come in the bar all the time? I don't make it a habit of fucking my patrons."

"I'm sorry, I didn't mean to imply anything like that."

"Good, because otherwise I'd have to let you drive home drunk." She's taking out her house keys. "We are here."

She opens the door to a Cape Cod-style house. When he steps into the house, it's as if he has stepped back in time. The whole decor is from the 1800s and beautifully displayed.

"Wow, your place is absolutely beautiful. You must make a damn good living to afford all of this stuff."

"I inherited a great deal of this from my grandmother, and most of these things have been in my family for years. Would you like a drink?" she asks while taking a crystal bottle out of the bar. She places two crystal cut glasses on the bar. "Bourbon okay for a starter?"

"Sure, but make mine short. I've drank quite a bit already tonight."

"You got it, Mack. May I call you Mack?"

"Everyone else does, so I guess it would be weird if you called me something else." He's examining the artwork hanging on the walls.

They settle on the Victorian sofa and sip their drinks. He's afraid to make the first move, so he waits for her to make it. She finally reaches over and takes his face in both hands and kisses him deeply. It nearly knocks his socks off. He isn't sure if it's from the drink or if it's from her. He follows her kiss with one of his own. It's delicious, and he never wants it to stop. He hasn't felt like this since he first met Elise. What the hell is happening to him? They spend the next half hour just making out on the couch like a couple of teenagers.

Finally after finishing their drinks, she gets up and takes his hand and starts for the bedroom. Mack thinks that the drink had really done a number on him as he feels dizzy and unstable on his feet. He's hoping to make this a night neither of them would forget. Now he feels he may not make it to the bedroom before he will collapse.

"What the hell was in that drink?" he slurs.

"Oh, just something to make you sleep for a while," she answers, giggling.

"But why?" he asks before he trips and face-plants on her bed.

"Good boy, Detective."

Chapter 64

Mack wakes up with a terrific headache. Heather is nowhere to be found. He slowly gets out of bed and tries to think of what the hell happened last night. He's naked, and as much as he tries, he can't remember anything after leaving the bar. Had he had sex with the blonde? Had he enjoyed it? He doesn't think he had drunk all that much. Hell, he drank most every night and a lot of times a lot more than he did yesterday. Plus, he's never had a headache like he has today. He doesn't even have a clue where the hell he is. He wanders into the bathroom and stares at his reflection in the mirror. He looks as bad as he feels. He takes a piss and then turns the shower on hot. He steps into the shower and feels as though he will pass out before he's finished. It's a very short shower. The longer he stays standing, the worse he feels.

He finds his clothes folded neatly on a chair in the bedroom. He knows he sure in hell didn't fold them. He would have been in too much of a hurry to fuck the blonde to carefully fold his clothes first. He dresses, and after checking to make sure his wallet and badge are in place and nothing is missing, he opens the bedroom door. No one is there. He wanders through the house and decides to leave and try to find his car. He opens the front door, and his car is sitting in the driveway. Checking to see if anyone is lurking in the neighborhood, he slowly walks to his car. The door is open, and the keys are in the ignition. Mack is thankful for that and decides to go home. He backs out and turns onto the main street. Driving past the bar, he thinks about stopping and telling Heather thank you for the night. But he can't remember anything about the night before. How do you thank a woman for a night when you have no idea what happened?

Mack drives home slowly, still racking his brain trying to remember what happened after he left the bar. Nothing. Had he been slipped a Mickey? She had seemed so nice at the bar, would she do something like that? Why would she do that? All his money, credit cards, etc. are still in his wallet. If she wanted money, she would have had the perfect chance. He sure in hell won't be able to arrest her without implicating himself. No, he must have just drunk a lot more than he thought.

He stops to have a quick breakfast before heading home. He has to have something in his stomach. His head still hurts like hell. Maybe food will help. Maybe he can get a couple aspirin at the café.

Chapter 65

I hear the garage door open, and Warrior begins to growl and bark. Easy boy, it's just your other master. The one who is an asshole. The one who doesn't care about anything but himself. The one who cheats on his wife all the time. The one who is no longer working for some reason. I just can't wait for him to come in. Just then he walks through the kitchen door.

"Hello, Mack, did you have an exciting night?"

"Don't fucking start with me, Elise, I am not in the mood." He heads for the refrigerator.

"I'll bet you were in the mood last night. Did your whore like the mood you were in?" I want to bash his head in.

"I wasn't with a fucking whore. I was passed out in a motel room."

"Really, and I guess I'm supposed to believe that."

"Believe what you fucking want. I don't really give a damn at this precise time." Mack growls while drinking orange juice from the carton. "I'm going crash in the library, and I swear if you or that damn dog make any noise to wake me, I will kill you both." Mack is just about out of the kitchen when I remember Haven.

"Oh, Haven said to call her if you want to cancel Sunday. She figured with all of the shit going on in your life, you may not be up to company. The whole world knows about your suspension. The TV made sure of that."

"It's an administrative leave, not a school suspension. You really are a stupid bitch." He quietly shuts the library door and turns the lock.

I spend most of the day in my studio. I'm excited for Jordyn to check out my work. I hope Mack doesn't cancel tomorrow. It's one o'clock before Mack comes staggering out of the library, rubbing his eyes. I have just brought Warrior down to go outside.

"What the hell time is it anyway?" Mack grumbles as he comes into the kitchen.

"It's one."

Mack stands in the doorway and watches as the dog runs to the edge of the pool and without any hesitation jumps right in. He swims around in a circle and looks at me as though he's asking why I'm still standing there. I hear Mack laugh and turn to see him coming outside.

"He doesn't seem to be afraid of the water at all. That could be a problem until he gets big enough to climb out on his own."

"I know, I went for a swim yesterday, and he jumped in after me. He didn't want to get out when it was time to go back in the house. I thought I'd pick up a chain for him so he doesn't drown himself."

Finally when he looks to be tiring, I reach into the water and call him. He comes right away, and I'm able to scoop him up. I set him down beside the pool to see if he'd jump back in. Instead, he shakes himself several times and takes off running. Mack grabs a towel to dry the mutt. It takes a minute before Warrior is tired of the chase and sits to be dried.

"I will get him a chain when I pick up the stuff for tomorrow's cookout. Make a list of things we need, and I'll go to the store after I take a shower."

"Okay, if you are still up to the cookout."

"Just because the mayor has it in for me, doesn't mean I am going to stop living, and it sure in hell doesn't mean I'm going to cow down to that asshole."

"What do you think you want to cook?"

"I'll pick up some good steaks, and we can have a big salad. How about a shrimp salad to go with and then some sort of fruit concoction for dessert. I like that strawberry shit you make with angel food cake."

"I'll make out the list."

"I'll check the wine rack and bar after I shower."

Chapter 66

Mack leaves for the store, and I go back to my studio to finish putting things away. I let Warrior run around on the tiled floor while I pick up things. He seems to be having a gay old time, when he suddenly goes to the patio door and growls his mean little puppy growl. I pick him up and open the door to look out. I don't see anything out of place and go back in and shut the door. Carrying Warrior, I go downstairs. He keeps growling and acting as though a monster is about to attack. I look toward the front door, and there's the note. I pick it. I begin to read it, and a cold chill runs down my spine.

"Elise, you should know better than to trust your husband. You know what he can do. Never mind, it isn't him you have to worry about, it's me. Time is running out. Slice, slice, and pretty Elise is no more."

I tear the note up and throw it into the trash. I look out the window to see if I can see anyone. I feel sick to my stomach and I'm shaking. Why would anyone do this to me? If it isn't Mack, then who could it be? I know nothing will show up on the security cameras, and Mack will just be ugly if I tell him. I'll just pretend nothing happened.

I'm still angry with Mack for not coming home last night, but I'm more afraid now. Mack is way too calm regarding his mandatory leave. I know he will explode, and it won't be pretty. I decide I won't rock the boat, but I'll be damned if he's going to rape me either. I don't want him, and he isn't going to spend the night with some whore and then use me.

Chapter 67

Mack goes to the hardware store to get a chain for the dog. When he walks in, you could have heard a pin drop the place was so quiet. People stop what they're saying and doing and just stare at him. He feels like a fish in a tiny bowl with a dozen cats watching his every wiggle. He walks directly to the pet department and picks out a chain and stake that would serve the purpose. After paying for his purchase, he turns toward the door only to have it blocked by three people. He's about to walk around them, when one looks at him and says, "So they are finally investigating your activities. It's about time they look at one of their own."

"Excuse me? Just what the hell are you implying? That the sheriff's department is crooked?"

The man moves aside and states loud enough for those around him to hear, "The mayor sure in hell thinks you are covering up for someone in all these murders."

"Well, the mayor doesn't know jack shit." He walks out of the door and to the car.

He opens his car door and throws the dog chain and stake on the passenger's seat. Crawling in behind the wheel, he does all he can to back the car out of the parking space and not ram it at top speed into the hardware's front windows. Mack has felt rage before, but this is crazy. He wants to kill the fucking mayor, and if he thinks he can get away with it, he would. How dare that bastard spread shit about the department. He needs to be dealt with.

Mack is so angry that he never really sees how people react to him when he's walking through the aisles of the grocery store. He pushes the cart as though it's loaded full of explosives. He practically throws the groceries into the cart. If he would have picked up eggs, they would have been smashed for sure. By the time he reaches the meat department, he's livid. The butcher asks what he can get for him, and Mack tells him he needs the best New York strip steaks he has. He wants six of them. The butcher shows him the cut and then proceeds to fill the order. Mack stands there waiting impatiently. Looking around, he wonders why the hell another grocery chain has never come into the village. This place is as old as the hills and needs to be updated badly. Hell, they still have the wrapping paper and string to wrap the meat. Taking his order, he goes to check out. Thank God there's no line and he's able to check out and leave without encountering another person. Still fuming, he drives home.

Mack enters the kitchen to the growling and yipping of Warrior. Reaching down to pet the pup, Mack is surprised that the pup nips at his hand and backs up and growls. Mack's already upset, and this is the last straw. With the toe of his shoe, he kicks the dog across the kitchen floor.

I enter the room as Warrior is flying across the floor yelping and crying. Running to the pup, I pick it up and start to try to calm the dog. "If I ever see you hurt Warrior again, I will fucking kill you."

"Shut the hell up, Elise, the little bastard bit me."

"He's a puppy, Mack, they have a tendency to bite."

"I don't give a shit if he is a puppy or not, he will never bite me again or I will choke him to death. Then I will choke you."

I got your shit for our cookout tomorrow."

"You can put it away. I'll be in the library. Just leave me the hell alone."

I put the groceries away, wishing Mack will die in the library.

Chapter 68

The rest of the evening and night goes smoother than I expected. I place the stake and chain in the backyard and chain Warrior. He isn't at all happy with the new restriction and lets me know with a lot of whining and yipping and rolling around. After about a half hour of trying to get loose, he finally lies down and takes a nap. While he's sleeping, I go inside. Mack is still in the library, and I'm not about to disturb him. I don't want to leave the kitchen in case Warrior wakes up and starts to cause a ruckus. I go through some recipes, looking for something that could be whipped up today and be ready for tomorrow. Mack has bought the fixings for a shrimp salad and the strawberry dessert, but I want to add to it. Settling on fire and ice recipe, I take the ingredients out of the refrigerator and begin to make the salad.

Warrior wakes up and comes to the patio door and barks to get in. I let him in and put him in the pen. He's content to chew on his toys and roll on top of his teddy bear. He sure doesn't look like he would have bitten Mack if it wasn't called for. I begin to wonder if Warrior senses something not right about Mack.

I watch a little TV and then decide to go up to the studio and then to bed. I just figure Mack would either sleep in the library or come to bed late. I'm finishing up in the studio when I hear him on the stairs. He goes to the bedroom and slams the door. I'm instantly angry. How dare he not come home all night and then think he's going to sleep in our bed and shut me out.

I go into the bedroom ready to do battle. Mack stands naked, looking out the patio door as if he's trying to impress the neighbors. Only with the trees you couldn't really see anything. He turns as I enter the room, and I realize he's drunk.

"There she is, the love of my life."

"I don't think so, Mack."

He may have been drunk, but he moves faster than Flash Gordon and has me pinned against the wall in a split second.

"You will never escape me. You will be what I want you to be, when I want you to, and for as long as I say."

"No, Mack, I won't."

He grabs my face in both hands, and I nearly gag from the smell of whiskey. Holding my face with his thumbs pressing into my neck, he bends his head to kiss me. He isn't expecting the knee to the groin and lets go and bends over in pain. It's all that I need to get out of his reach. He comes up and whirls to face me, ready to grab me again. He comes up short as he stares into the barrel of his own .38 pistol. The sheriff hasn't asked for it, but then it isn't the department's. It's his personal property. I carefully take the safety off, holding the gun in both hands.

"Take another step and I will put a hole right between your evil eyes. You will not stay out all night and then come here and think I will be a whore too."

"You haven't the guts to pull the trigger."

"Take another step and I guess we will find out."

Mack puts both hand up. "Okay, you win. Now put the gun back into the drawer before you really do shoot me or yourself."

"Oh, believe me, I won't be shooting myself." Hearing a sound behind me, I turn my head, and Mack shoots forward and grabs the gun. I don't struggle and give up the gun easily. I step back and see the fury in his body, but I don't flinch away. I stand straight and wait for the next assault. Expecting to be shot, I wait to feel the burn and pain of the bullet hitting somewhere in my body. I doubt he'd shoot me in the head and end it quick and neat. I could almost feel the bullet entering my guts and making an exit in the small of my back.

Instead he turns and walks to the open drawer in the dresser and puts the gun away.

He slowly turns, and still I don't move. "I promise you, Elise, that will never happen again or I will kill you, and your body will never be found." He turns and walks out of the room and down the stairs. I hear the library door slam shut. I gather up Warrior and get ready for bed.

As I'm brushing my teeth, I look in the mirror and see the dark circles under my eyes and suddenly feel sick. I bend over the toilet bowl and lose whatever food I had consumed that day. Warrior is in the pen whining as I'm puking my guts out. When I finish, I brush my teeth again and rinse my mouth out with mouthwash. I pick the pup up and tell him everything is going to be all right. I make sure his teddy bear is beating when I place him back in the pen. I close the bedroom door and slide between the sheets. I lie there for what seems to be hours just watching the shadows on the wall and ceiling.

Chapter 69

I wake to the screaming. Someone is hurt. Someone needs help. I begin to run from the room but find that I'm not in my own room. I'm in a motel running into the hallway. I have to help whoever is screaming. Oh dear god, I can't determine in which direction the screaming is coming from. It's a man screaming out in pain. He sounds as though he's being tortured.

I run down the hallway to the left of me. Opening doors as I go. No one is in the rooms. They are empty, and they are all covered in blood. After opening the last door in the hallway, I turn and start running back to the room I had come out of. I reach the room just as the door slams shut. I pull on the door handle, trying to open the door. I'm sure the man is in my room and needs my help. I pound on the door and beg to be let in. Still the door doesn't budge. I felt the warm liquid on my bare feet. Looking down, I see the blood oozing out from under the door. I try to move but seem to be glued to the carpet. Still the blood oozes from the slit under the door and covers my feet. I try the door one more time, and the knob turns easily. I slowly open the door but can't see anything for the room is dark and cold. I try the light switch next to the door, but it just makes a loud click in the deadly silence, and the room remains dark. With caution I step through the door and into the room. I stand, and as my eyes adjust to the darkness, I can see the form of a man standing on the other side of the bed.

I slowly walk to the lamp next to the bed and turn it on. I stare into the blank, cold eyes of the mayor. He isn't standing on the other side of the bed, he's hanging from the open beam. He's cut from the base of the throat to his groin.

"Elise, help me." I turn and run full force into Mack.

Chapter 70

"Oh my god, Mack, look, the mayor is dead. He's been murdered. Look at all the blood!" I cry, hanging on to Mack.

"Elise, what the hell are you talking about?" He shakes me until my head snaps back and forth. I look at him and panic. I try to get away from him, but he holds me tight. I turn to look behind me and find I'm standing in my own bedroom. The mayor is not hanging, and there's no blood anywhere. I hang my head and sob. Mack puts his arms around me and holds me tight.

"I heard you screaming, and Warrior was barking so loud I thought someone was trying to kill you. You need to see a doctor as soon as possible for these dreams of yours."

"They aren't dreams, Mack, they are full-fledged nightmares. They are so vivid I swear they are real."

"Well, they aren't, and it is getting damn annoying to have to wake up from a dead sleep to you screaming your lungs out."

I turn and pick up Warrior. Talking to him, I calm him down and decide to take him outside. I don't say another word to Mack but go down the steps and out into the backyard. The night air is cold and a chill runs through me. The dew on the grass is a direct contrast to the warm blood I felt on my feet only a few minutes ago. Is it really just a nightmare, or is there more to it?

I watch Warrior do his job and walk back into the kitchen. The clock says 2:30 a.m. I slowly walk back up the stairs and into the bedroom. Mack is sprawled out on the bed sound asleep. I put

Warrior in his pen and crawl into bed. Mack snorts and snores yet never moves a muscle. It must be nice to be able to fall asleep that easily. Maybe I should take up drinking. I try to calm my breathing and maybe fall back to sleep. However, every time I close my eyes, I see the vivid picture of the mayor hanging from an open beam. I vow to myself I will make a doctor's appointment first thing Monday morning. I fall into a fitful sleep, waking up often and each time feeling a fear I can't seem to shake.

Finally at six, I get up and take a shower. I'm just getting out of the shower when Mack enters the bathroom.

"Don't bother drying yourself because you are taking a shower with me."

I look at him and grab a towel. "Not today or any day." I begin to dry myself, and he grabs the towel away from me and shoves me into the shower.

"I said you are taking a shower with me, Elise, whether you want to or not. Now, you can play nice or you can play nasty. Either way, I will get what I want." He turns the water on so hot I think the skin will peel off my back. His hard-on is pressing into my stomach, and I want to throw up. Pushing me to the side of the shower, he lifts me up and sits me on his hard, throbbing cock. I have no control nor could I move if I wanted to. He drives into me hard and fast. With each pump, I want him dead. He finds his release and lets my body down. I step out of the shower feeling dirty and in need of another shower. It will be a cold day in hell before I walk back into that shower with him. I dry off and go into the bedroom and put my clothes on. I go downstairs and hook Warrior onto the chain in the backyard and go back into the house to pour myself a cup of coffee.

Chapter 71

The house phone rings, and to my surprise, Mack answers it. I can hear him talking to someone, and from his conversation, I know it is Haven. I walk into the hallway just as he's confirming the time for them to all come over. Apparently, they are to arrive around one and we'd eat at four, because after all, it is Sunday, and the others will have to go to work the next day. I've told Jordyn to come at one so we could go over the paintings before the others arrive. Oh well, I'm sure Haven will be a great help picking out paintings. I'm quite sure the men would rather sit outside and have a few drinks while the women are in the studio. Mack hasn't been in my studio for over a year, so I doubt he'd want to participate in choosing paintings for the shop.

Mack hangs up the phone and comes into the kitchen with the Sunday paper. He has a very grim look on his face, and I wonder what the hell is wrong with him. Surely the nightmare wouldn't have caused that look. Maybe he's feeling guilty for raping me in the shower. I nearly laugh out loud over that thought. He slips into a chair at the breakfast bar.

"Just a bagel this morning, Elise."

I don't answer him, but I do get the bagels from the refrigerator and the jam.

Waiting for the bagels to pop up, the nightmare enters my mind like a flash flood on a hot dry Texas road. I begin to feel ill, and as the bagels pop up, I run for the bathroom. I swing the door close and bend over the toilet and heave up the coffee from my otherwise empty stomach. I feel as though I've been sick for days. I'm weak and shaky when I come out of the bathroom. The toasted bagels smell putrid, and the thought of another cup of coffee makes my stomach roll. Mack never looks up. He just grunts as though he's thoroughly disgusted by what has just happened. I don't give a damn what he thinks. I have to make plans for my future, and that doesn't include him.

Chapter 72

Mack goes out into the backyard and begins cleaning the pool.

I make my side dishes and set out the picnic dishes to be used outside. I decide to add a candle and some flowers out on the tables. It will make it seem more cheerful. Lord knows with the tension, a little bit of cheer would be a blessing.

The morning flies by, and I'm shocked that it's going on noon when I look at the clock. I hurry upstairs to freshen up in case the company arrives early. Mack has cleaned outside and then went into the library and hasn't showed his face for the rest of the morning. I don't mind at all that he isn't around. It gives me time to think of a few plans to set into action to get out of this abusive marriage. It isn't that I haven't loved Mack, for I have, until all this bullshit started with the murders. He's changed so much that it's impossible for me to feel the love I had had for him.

I walk into the kitchen and pour myself a glass of wine. Then think better of it as I haven't eaten anything all day. I pour the glass of wine down the sink and replace it with a glass of lemon water. As I take a sip, it seems to soothe my thirst and doesn't seem as though it will upset my sensitive stomach. With everything that's happening, I'm not surprised that I have an upset stomach almost every day. I take Warrior and go to the backyard. The dog runs to the edge of the pool and runs as close to the water as he can without falling in. I watch, waiting for him to jump in at any second. He seems content to just run around it at full bore.

Chapter 73

I hear the doorbell a few minutes later and go back into the house to answer it. Mack yells that he has it, so I go back outside to get the dog. I can hear Mack making a big fuss over Princess and know that Haven, Matt, and Becca have arrived. I'm totally surprised to see Isabelle come charging through the open patio screen. Thank God I hadn't shut it or she would have plowed straight through it. Haven comes flying out to the patio yelling for Isabelle to stop, but it's fruitless. She stops and gives me a hug instead.

"I've given up on training that mutt. I'm enrolling her in a puppy school bright and early tomorrow. She only seems to mind when she is next to Becca."

I can't help but laugh at the defeated look on her face. The two dogs begin to play together, and we go in the house. We have just shut the screen when there's a loud splash.

"Oh crap!" I shout and run back out to find Isabelle in the pool. Warrior looks as though he may have pushed her or is telling her that she's in big trouble. Matt comes out in a flash and runs to the pool.

"I knew we were going to have trouble bringing that mutt." He's trying to get her to come to the edge of the pool. To everyone's amazement, she just pulls herself out of the pool and shakes all over Matt. She's one happy pup.

"Warrior can't get out on his own, so we bought a chain for him, until he has grown enough to get out like she did." The dogs go on their merry way, wrestling like the happy pups they are.

Jordyn pokes her head through the open door. "I found this handsome man out front about to ring the bell. But the door was open a crack, so I just shoved him through it. I hope you don't mind?"

Mack is the first to rush over to her and take the bottle of wine from her. "You didn't have to bring anything."

"It's nothing fancy, just grocery store wine."

Cam hands him another bottle of wine and then walks to me without saying a word to Mack and hands me a bouquet of daisies. "These are for you." He gently kisses my cheek. I can feel my face turn bright red.

"Thank you, but you didn't need to bring anything either." I'm just happy Mack has gone into the kitchen when Cam kissed my cheek. I'm not sure what reaction he'd have had.

Taking the flowers inside to look for a vase, I ask if anyone wants a drink. I'm followed in by everyone. I put the flowers in a vase as Mack fills everyone's request for drinks. I place the flowers on the stand in the hallway, thinking how thoughtful Cam is. Maybe he and Jordyn will hit it off. That would be great, and I'm hoping to be a matchmaker as the day goes on.

Everyone returns to the patio and sits around the table. Mack has Becca and is talking to her in all sorts of silly voices. She seems to be eating it up and is gurgling and cooing right back at him. He looks so relaxed with her in his arms. I wonder how he can change moods so quickly. Jordyn suggests that we go through some of the paintings. Haven jumps up.

"Not without me you don't."

We all look at Mack to be sure that he's all right with Becca. "What? You don't think I can handle this little cutie? Besides, I have her daddy right here to help out."

Once in the studio, Jordyn immediately starts to go through the paintings. "This is a lot harder than I thought it was going to be. You have so many great ones here I will have my car loaded to the hilt when I leave here. You are fantastic."

"Well, some are when I first started, and they are pretty crude."

"Oh my god, girl, you have no idea of your talent."

It takes about a half hour for Jordyn to decide which paintings she wants. She says she will be coming for more in a week or two. "Oh, here," she says, digging into her shorts pocket. She hands me a check. I stare at the amount.

"Why so much? Is this for some that haven't sold yet?"

"No, that is your cut for the ones that have already gone out the door."

"My god, Jordyn, this is for ten thousand. I thought maybe five thousand at the most. Holy shit, are you sure?"

Haven hugs me. "Put it away and don't tell Mack how much it is. He doesn't need to know."

I just shake my head and head for the bedroom. I go to my nightstand and pull out a little locked box. It contains a few pieces of jewelry my grandmother had given me. I unlock it and place the check in it. Locking the lid, I return to the studio and begin to help package up the paintings to be carried down to Jordyn's van.

Chapter 74

The afternoon passes with wine and laughter. Mack starts the grill. I, with the help of Jordyn and Haven, begin to bring the other food out. We place it on the side table inside the screened-in gazebo. The meal is delicious. I eat more than I have in a couple of days. I make a fresh pot of coffee and bring out the strawberry dessert. Everyone groans but takes a piece to try. I eat a piece and think I'm going to burst. I haven't drunk any wine and honestly don't care for an after-dinner drink either. I sip my coffee contentedly, while the others have a grasshopper. I stand up to start clearing away the leftover food. Jordyn and Haven immediately begin to help. Within minutes everything is put away and the dishes placed in the dishwasher. It's a beautiful evening.

Jordyn and Cam go to their cars for their guitars, and Matt goes to go get his from the front entryway. We all sit in a circle, and the three begin to play. I can't believe how well Jordyn fit in with the guys. She knows almost every song they suggest to play. Cam begins to sing "Me and Bobby Magee," and Jordyn joins in. It's as if they have sung together for years. Matt sings backup for them. When they finish, Cam looks at Jordyn and asks, "Hey, you want to join my band? Believe me, you'd fit in perfectly, and since I can't get Matt to come back, what do ya say?"

"Well, I'm busy with the store most of the week. I'd have to hire someone to run it if the practices were on nights we were open."

"Why not have Elise do it?"

Mack looks at me and agrees. "That's a great idea. She sits here all day long or is in that studio all the time. Maybe she could even set up and paint while she is down there."

I'm in shock.

"It's settled then."

"I'm sure you two can figure out what days or evenings she will be needed."

"I'm not sure. I know nothing about sales."

"You don't have to. I'll give you a rundown on the pieces I have in the store, and if you don't know something, just tell them the owner will be back at such and such time, and she will answer all your questions."

It's decided I will go to the store in the morning and get my feet wet in sales. Mack says he has some business to take care of so it will be a perfect time for me to go. The party winds down, and everyone starts to pick up their things and head for the door. Cam gives me another kiss on the cheek and says in my ear for only me to hear, "You are so unhappy, call me please."

I answer with, "I'm glad you enjoyed yourself." I wonder what would happen if I actually call him. With hugs and the goodbyes done, everyone piles into their cars and drives away.

I feel a loneliness deep inside, and I hug myself as I walk back into the house. Mack has gone ahead of me, and I hear the library door shut. I take Warrior and curl up on the living room recliner and turn on the TV. I wake up to the sudden slap to the bottom of my bare foot. I yell and scare the dog, who jumps from my lap and growls at Mack.

"Go ahead and bite me, you little asshole," he snarls at the pup. "I've told you I don't want the dog on the furniture. Do you ever listen?"

"He was on my lap, not of the furniture!" I shout back at him.

"I don't give a rat's ass if he was on your lap. Your fat ass was on the furniture, therefore so was his."

"You really are a piece of shit, Mack." Getting out of the chair and picking up the dog, I leave the room without another word.

As I'm getting ready for bed, I hear the library door slam. Warrior plops down on his teddy bear, and I lie watching the shadows on the wall until I fall asleep.

Chapter 75

I know it isn't a dream when I feel the hands around my throat. I don't have to open my eyes to know that it is Mack. I can smell the whiskey on his breath. I don't move, and I don't open my eyes.

"I could snap your neck, and I wouldn't even feel any remorse," Mack slurs.

"Go ahead, Mack." Opening my eyes, I see he is nude, and he is straddling me. I can't move from the weight of his body, and he's gradually tightening his grip around my neck. Still I don't give him the satisfaction of a struggle. He finally lets go of me and falls onto his side of the bed. He's snoring within seconds.

I turn onto my side away from him and try to calm my breathing and the pounding my heart is making. I'm not sure if I'm hearing my heartbeat or a drum beating in my ears. It's so loud and so out of rhythm I wonder if I'm dying. No, if I were dying, I would feel less pain I'm sure of it. I finally fall asleep thinking of Cam. It seems to soothe me to think of his kindness toward me. Maybe I will call him tomorrow. Maybe not.

I awake to Mack gargling in the bathroom. I look at the clock and can't believe that it's already six thirty. I spring from bed and grab my robe. Picking up Warrior, I head downstairs. The coffee is already on, and I chain Warrior outside before heading to the bathroom. I switch on the light and instantly feel ill. When I look in the mirror, I see a very tired, haggard woman. I brush my teeth and my hair and think of how exciting my day will be. I bring the dog in and pour myself coffee, still fighting the rising bile. I must make a doctor's appointment today. I can't go on with the nightmares and the feeling sick all the time.

Mack comes into the kitchen and pours his coffee. "I don't want breakfast and I don't want to hear a fucking word out of your mouth." I don't say a word. He gives me a deadly stare. "Don't wait up tonight. I have no desire to be anywhere near you."

"Don't worry, I hadn't planned on it," I snap back.

He stomps to the garage door like a two-year-old who's just been told he isn't allowed to eat any more cookies. I hear the garage door open and the engine roar. He's gone in a flash. I sit at the counter and finish my coffee. Then I call Warrior, and I go upstairs to get ready for my first day with Jordyn. I'm sure Warrior will be okay for a few hours alone in his pen.

I leave the house at eight and head for the bus stop. When I arrive at Jordyn's, I'm met at the door with a cup of cappuccino and a big smile from Jordyn.

"I'm so glad you decided to do this for me. Come, let's go in the back, and I will show you the book where I keep an explanation of all the things I sell in the store."

I'm on cloud nine until I see the size of the book. "Holy shit! Do you think I will learn all of this in one morning?"

"Oh, you don't have to. It's a guideline. Everything is in its own category. Statues, paintings, glassware, etc." She drags out another book the size of the old dictionary under glass in the city's library.

"Really? There is more than one?"

"Well, there is actually three. You will be able to find whatever you are selling listed in these three books. Easy-peasy," Jordyn assures me. "Here, for example, is a vase. Look at the tabs, see Vases, then check the number on the vase and match it to the number in the book. There will be the artist name and a description of the product. I'm sure you will catch on in just a few minutes. Plus, many of the pieces that sell are duplicates, so you will know right away."

"I have my doubts."

Just then the door jingles, and Jordyn says, "Let's go get your feet wet." I follow Jordyn back into the store area. The customer is a lady looking for a certain type of candlesticks. Jordyn introduces me as her new assistant, and we go to a corner of the store that holds several candlesticks. The lady is thrilled to find the ones she wants and makes her purchase and leaves the store singing her praises as she walks out the door.

"That wasn't so bad after all."

"Why don't you wander around and get your bearings of the place. You can cross reference pieces if you like or just familiarize yourself with where things are."

I spend the next couple of hours walking through the store and trying to remember where things are. I take a few items back to the books and look them up. I find it really isn't all that hard. Jordyn lets me wait on a couple of customers. Before I know it, it's already noon.

"Let's call it a day, go across the street, and have a salad, and then you can go home and let your dog out. If you want, you may come by tomorrow and help put out inventory. Otherwise, just come in on Wednesday morning to work with me again."

"If it's okay with you, I'll just skip lunch and go let poor Warrior out. He's probably making a big stink about being in his pen and all alone."

"No problem, hope to see you tomorrow if you can make it."

Chapter 76

Mack walks into the sheriff's department like he's still an active part of the place. Not one detective says a thing as he walks straight to the sheriff's door. He walks in and sits in the chair he had sat in many times before. Officer Potts has guts enough to walk past the window staring like a kid at a freak show.

"Why did you want to see me? I'm sure it's not because you miss me."

"The mayor and I talked to the board, and we all decided it would be better if you turned in your resignation."

"Really? Better for whom? Better for you, better for the mayor, or better for the citizens who voted me in?"

"Better for everyone."

"Well, I have news for you. I'm not turning in my resignation. So if you fire me, I will call in every lawyer I can buy to do a little research into this wonderful place you refer to as the sheriff's department."

"Now, Mack, don't be hasty. The mayor was supposed to be here a half hour ago to go over the details with you."

"Bullshit. You and the mayor can go to hell. I'm not bowing out until I solve the murders. Tell the mayor hello for me." Mack leaves without closing the door.

The sheriff doesn't try to call him back. He calls out for his secretary. "Have a couple of guys do some checking to see if they can find the damn mayor. Tell them to check the ditches."

"Really? You want me to tell them to check the ditches."

"I don't care where they check, just find him."

Mack walks through the detective department and notices that no one is in his office. He figures that's a good sign. At least no one is assigned his office or to his position yet.

Chapter 77

I can hear Warrior barking and whining from the sidewalk. When I open the door, the pup goes berserk. He barks, whines, growls, and wiggles as though he's filled with wiggle worms. He squirms as I pick him up and tries to get free. I set him down, and he runs to the patio door. As I let him out, he runs to the rose bush in the corner and squats to pee. I wait patiently while he roams the backyard, and when he finally comes to me, I put his chain on him. He doesn't even seem to mind the chain and proceeds to lie in the shade and gnaw on one of his toys. I don't talk to him but decide to try to leave him alone outside for a while. I turn silently and walk through the patio door. Sliding it closed behind me. I watch for a few seconds to see if Warrior will get upset and come to the door. He seems quite happy to just lie outside and chew on his toy.

I make myself a quick sandwich and grab a diet Coke. I peek at the dog before heading for my studio. I have to finish the paintings I've started, and I feel I have to paint more to keep up with the demand. I hope it won't change my love for painting, making me feel as though I'm a one-man assembly line popping out paintings for profit. I love to paint and never want the thrill of it to become clouded with the demand on the market. I feel better than I've had in weeks. I feel inspired and happy.

Warrior starts to howl, and I go downstairs to bring the pup inside. When I step outside, I hear the sirens blaring. It sounds like a parade of police cars all driving too fast and all running the sirens as high and loud as possible. The dog and I go back inside, and I wish that Mack is still working at the sheriff's department so he can tell me what's going on when he comes home. The draft that engulfs me comes swiftly, and I'm freezing from the inside out. I know instantly what has happened.

Feeling slightly ill, I walk into the bathroom and splash water on my face. I try to shake the icy feeling. It settles deep inside my soul, and I can't pull out of it. Stepping over to the commode, I lift the lid and spew out my sandwich and Diet Coke. The piercing headache is already seeping into the cavity behind my eyes. *God help me*, I think, *it can't be. Please let it be something other than what I already know it is.* I slowly walk back into the kitchen and sit at the breakfast counter staring out the patio door. Warrior plops down at my feet and lets out a sigh. I wonder if the dog can feel the death shroud that has invaded the house.

Chapter 78

Mack is driving around the town like he's in his squad. Checking out the little town that seems to be turning its back on him. He's met with three police cars whizzing past him like they're being chased by the devil himself. He pulls the car over to the side of the road to let them pass. The detective in him kicks into gear. He does a U-turn and follows the parade. He's surprised that they turn in the Get Away Motel parking lot. He follows close behind and parks a bit off to the side. The three officers run to the entrance and disappears into the ramshackle lobby of the ancient motel. He slowly follows. As he goes through the door, he can see a group of people huddled in the hall-way. One officer is instructing them to go back to their rooms or into the lobby. "Do not leave the motel," he's telling him in his most stern professional voice. Mack wants to burst out laughing at his novice technique but stays back and out of the way.

The cleaning lady is crying hysterically and making the sign of the cross as she begins to pray in Spanish. Mack catches bits and pieces of her gibberish and thinks she's saying Satan has done this evil deed. The owner of the motel is an elderly man that had built the place some forty years ago and hasn't put a dime into the upkeep since the doors opened. It's known in the area as the Easy Lay Motel to the kids in Flag Lake. Everyone knows you can get a room for a week, a day, an hour, or fifteen minutes if that's how long it takes for you to get your jollies off. Mr. Webster doesn't care who rents one of his dilapidated rooms. If you're tall enough to lay the cash on the counter, you can rent a room. Most out-of-towners who rent from Mr. Webster are those who are too damn tired to drive another mile to the better motel. Mr. Webster puts his arm around the cleaning lady and guides her to the lobby.

Mack slowly walks down the hall where the officers are gathered just outside an open door. Just as he comes to the open doorway to take a peek inside, Officer Stone looks up and says, "Thank God you are here, Detective Mackenzie." The other two officers look happy to see him too and quickly step aside so Mack can enter the room. What greeted him is a surprise and downright evil.

"Jesus. Has forensics been here yet to gather information?"

All three officers answer in unison, "No, that's why we haven't gone in."

"Good." Mack skirts around the outside edges of the room to get a better look. The mayor is hanging from an open beam. He has a black belt tight around his neck. There are nipple clamps cutting into his flesh nearly cutting his nipples from his chest. He has been sliced open from his throat to his groin. He has welts on his back obviously made by the whip still lying on the bed. At first glance it would seem the mayor had a masochistic encounter go bad. It's made to look like maybe a shafted lover had been seeking revenge. It's a bit over the top for that to be the case. Mack is just walking out of the room when the sheriff comes down the hall.

"Mack, what the hell are you doing here?"

"Just passing through, sir," Mack states as he tries to get passed the sheriff to leave.

"Wait, what do we have here? Do you think it's a lover gone mad or pure evil murder?" The sheriff is blocking Mack's path.

"I don't work for the department anymore, remember?" Mack states, trying to sidestep around the sheriff.

"Then why the fuck are you here?"

"I was just going past the old motel and thought, geez, maybe I should get a room for the night."

"Bullshit, Mack. You followed the squads. So now that you're here, what's your professional opinion on this mess?"

"I'd say you have yourself a mess. Why don't you ask the New Yorkers their opinion? I really need to get home and take care of my wife's puppy." He literally pushes the sheriff to the side and walks on out of the hallway and out the front door.

Once in the car, he realizes he's holding his breath. He lets his breath out in a loud rush and starts to shake. He's shaking and then laughing as he starts out of the parking lot. *Holy shit, that was a gruesome sight.* Even though he would have loved to string the mayor up himself, that was way too much to take in. The little dick bastard didn't deserve to die so violently. He wonders if the mayor agreed to be hung for a sexual high, or if he was threatened and afraid not to do the other's bidding.

He's pulling into the garage when he suddenly remembers Elise and her nightmare. Had she said the mayor was hanging on the other side of the bed, or that a man was hanging there? Either way, she had seen a murder. Had she seen the others too but just didn't say anything to him about it? He has to sit down and ask her a whole hell of a bunch of questions. What does the bitch really know? He has to know what she knows. It can be a matter of life or death.

Chapter 79

Mack finds me sitting at the breakfast bar. I feel like I've seen a ghost.

"Hey, didn't you tell me that the mayor was hanging in our bedroom last night?" he asks me before the door is even shut. I look at him and nod. "Well, you'll be happy to know your dream came true. How many of the other murders have you dreamed about?" I feel like a bug under a microscope and don't say anything. I still feel ill and want to lie down. My head hurts, and I'm not sure that I will be able to move without vomiting all over the kitchen floor. "Answer me, Elise. How many others have you dreamed? I'm beginning to think you are the cause of all of them. Who are you working with?" he screams at me.

His yelling at me is all I need to regrow my backbone. Warrior sits on the floor next to me and growls at Mack.

"Tell your killer dog to stand down or I'll slit his fucking throat." He's coming around the bar. Before I can get off the stool, he has his hands on my throat and begins to squeeze.

"Stop, you are hurting me," I cry, trying to pull his hands away.

"Tell me about your fucking dreams or I will choke you to death."

"I can't remember them after the first few minutes after I wake up. Most of them are just gruesome nightmares that don't make any sense."

He finally lets go of me. "You better be telling me the truth."

"Why? What has happened now?" I ask, even though I know exactly what has happened.

"The mayor was found at the motel a little bit ago. He told his wife he was going to a meeting yesterday but never came home. The cleaning lady found him in the room. It was not a pretty scene."

"How do you know all this?"

"I followed the squads and just happen to see the murder scene up close and personal. I wanted the bastard dead, but even for me his death was a bit of an overkill. It was made to look as if a sexual encounter had gone bad. The domineering one got the best of him and he died from hanging."

I really feel ill and faint now. "I have to go lie down before I pass out." I stand and call the pup.

"What the hell is wrong with you now?"

"I just feel sick, my head hurts, and I feel like I'm going to faint. Please just let me lie down for a few minutes." I leave and walk up the stairs with the pup in tow. I go into the bedroom and set the dog on the bed and then lay down beside him. It's as if the dog knows I need comfort. He curls up next to me with his paws resting on my arm. I pull him close and try to relax. I hear the library door slam shut and know that later in the night I will be in for another battle.

When I do wake up, the shadows on the wall indicate that I've slept longer than I'd planned. The pup is on the floor wagging his tail and squirming while expressing his need to be outside with little yips. I arise and pick him up and cuddle him. I hurriedly go downstairs and let him out the patio door. I step out on the cool tile and watch as he does his business next the rosebush. I wonder if the blossoms will smell like piss when it finally blooms again. I turn and meet Mack as he's coming through the door. He has a drink in his hand, and it's obvious that it isn't his first.

"Hello, Elise, did you have a nice nightmare?" he slurs.

"I didn't have a nightmare, thank you." I try to get past him. Only to be blocked by the bulk of his body. "Please let me through, Mack."

"No, you could use the fresh air, by the looks of you. You are quite pale and gaunt. You really need to see a doctor and start taking better care of yourself." He continues to slur his words.

"I decided to call a doctor in the morning. You are right, I need to find out what is happening to me and start feeling better." I try again to pass him.

This time he not only blocks the door but reaches up and takes my face in his free hand. Bringing my face to his. I start to resist, thinking he's going to kiss me. Instead he stares at me with a black blankness in his eyes.

"You are mine to do with however I please. Don't ever think you have a life of your own, because you don't and never will."

"Yes, master," I say between clenched teeth. He slowly brings his lips to mine and kisses me gently. Anyone watching would have easily thought he cherished his wife. I want to scream but stand there patiently waiting for the kiss to end. I then step through the door calling the dog. He stands there watching the dog happily run after me.

"Fucking little bastard," he mumbles under his breath.

I'm hungry and quickly make myself my go-to salad.

"Do you want a salad?" I ask him as he comes to the counter.

"No, I plan on getting my calories with another few of these. I've had one hell of a day today."

"Do you want to tell me about it?"

"Sure, why not. First I went to the sheriff's department and told Sheriff Assking that I had no intention of turning in my resignation until I find out who is doing the murders.

"Driving home, I see a parade of police cars coming at me. I pull over, and they pass, so I did a U-turn and followed them. They stopped at the motel, and all went running into the lobby. Of course, I followed. The maid was in hysterics, the cops were trying to tell the clientele to go back to their rooms or to the lobby but to not leave the premises.

"I just walked up to the open door, and there he was in all his glory, stung up like a freshly killed beefer. Only he wasn't so pretty. He had a belt of some sort around his neck and was hanging there. I can't tell you the number of times I wanted to see that fucker dead, but the gore actually made me feel sorry for him. The sheriff came just as I was leaving, and the dumb bastard had the nerve to ask me what I thought of the murder. I had to remind him that I no longer was working for the department. I told him to go ask the New Yorkers what they thought and could find. Then I come home to my loving wife that would sooner sleep with the fucking dog than me. There you have my day, Elise." Hate fills his eyes.

"I'm sorry, Mack. I had no idea what your day was like. What do you think of the latest murder?"

He walks to the sink and dumps the remainder of his drink down the drain. "I've had enough of these too. I need to start thinking more clearly if I am to figure out who is behind the murders. The mayor's death has put a new twist on everything. As many times as I have said to everyone I wish he was dead, I'm not too sure I won't be a suspect. I will need to be one step ahead of everyone working the case.

"That salad does look good. I think I will make myself one. Did you use up all the tomatoes, or are they hiding on me?" He rummages through the veggie crisper.

"No, they are in the basket on the counter. They weren't quite ripe, so I left them out."

Mack makes his salad and sits across from me and ate.

"Would you like some ice tea?"

"No, I've had enough to drink to last my body a while."

I notice his anger has seemed to ebb. I wonder if he would remain civil for the rest of the evening or would something set him off. I dread the thought of having any sort of sex with him. Maybe he would be too tired. Lord knows I am.

Chapter 80

The remainder of the evening goes by quickly. Mack says he's going to go over some files in the library so I decide to do some painting. Warrior goes with me. I close the studio door and give him some toys to play with. He seems happy to be free.

It's ten thirty when I hear Mack talking to someone, and he isn't happy. His voice is raised to a volume that nearly shatters the windows. Warrior starts barking, and I quickly pick him up so he will be quiet. I don't bother to clean up my painting supplies but go downstairs in a rush. Mack is standing in the kitchen having a very heated conversation with someone. He yells, "Fine, I'll come in, but I'm not happy about this." With that he throws his phone on the counter and looks at me for the first time. "That was Sheriff Assking, I mean Danking. He wants me to come in for questioning. The dumb ass said the New Yorkers are convinced that the murders are being done by someone who is either military or from the police force. He said they are questioning everyone. I am to go in first thing tomorrow morning. The dumb bastards want to pick my brain. I asked him if he was being interrogated too, and he said no. What the hell, he is the head of the whole damn unit, and he gets a free pass. It's all political, and it's all bullshit."

I hook Warrior up to his chain and return to the kitchen. Mack is sitting at the bar, looking as though he's ready to attack. "Maybe if you go in and tell them what they want to hear, they will leave you alone."

"Christ, the way things are going, they are probably going to use me as an escape goat and charge me. I want to make sure they interrogate the sheriff too. He shouldn't get a free pass. If I have to be questioned like a common criminal, then that bastard should have to go through the procedure just like the rest of us. He is just as capable as any of us on the force to commit a murder and cover up the tracks."

"Do you think that will really happen?"

"I have no idea, but I'm sure in hell going to try and get it done."

"Jordyn wants me to come in tomorrow and help her go through her incoming inventory, but if you rather I didn't, I'll stay home."

"No, you go, what the hell can you do for me staying home worrying whether I am going to jail or not. I don't think being Susy Homemaker will do me a damn bit of good."

"Okay, I'll go. I went today and learned a lot. She has tons of stuff, and she has it all written in books. Cross-referencing is easy and fun. It felt good to be able to get out and do something besides my painting."

"Well, at least one of us had a good day. I won't be able to sleep, so I might as well go in and check over the murder files. I kept a copy of everything. This time I'm not looking for an outsider, I'm going to try and see if it's one of the force. Who knows, maybe I will see a pattern."

I take Warrior and head up to bed. I clean my paintbrushes and put the rest of my things away. I go back downstairs and stop at the library door and knock.

"What?"

"Do you want me to set the alarm?" I ask through the closed door.

"Yes, normal time" comes back through the door. I continue up the stairs and into our room. A part of me wants him to come to bed so he'd be fresh in the morning, and yet a bigger part of me wants him to stay in the library the entire night.

As I crawl between the sheets, I try to think of who would want Mack off the force and who would threaten me. Although I haven't had a note or phone call for a couple of days, I'm sure I'd get one because of the mayor's murder. I drift off into a deep dreamless dream. I wake up with a start when I feel a hand caressing my breast. After a split second, my mind is wide awake, and unfortunately, so is my body. My nipples always disobey my thinking and respond to his touch. He knows they will and continue by rolling my nipples between his finger and thumb. When it's ripe and pouty, he replaces his hand with his mouth and tongue. Flicking at it with his tongue and gently sucking through the thin fabric of my nightdress.

With the expertise of a seasoned lover, he moves his hand down my body until it rests between my legs. Gently pushing on my legs to separate them, he rubs there through the sheer fabric. Still sucking at my breast, he works his magic on me. Soon I'm arching my back to give him better access to both places. As much as my mind says no, my body betrays me and says yes please. He slides my nightgown up and touches my hot flesh, and I can feel I'm moist. When his finger enters me, it's as if a bolt of lightning is running deep within me. It's so intense, and it feels so very hot and wonderful all at the same time. I'm more than ready for him. I need to feel him inside me. He moves above me, and I can feel his hot pulsing rod teasing me. I try to surge upward to receive him, but still he does not enter me. I open my eyes, and panic replaces the hot yearning I had felt just a second ago. I start to scream, but nothing comes out of my mouth. I hear him whisper in my ear, "You need me." And then he's gone.

I lie in bed shaking. It's so real, and how could I have been dreaming? Yet it was Cam who was pleasing my body, not my husband. I had wanted more. No, I needed more. I had nearly cheated on Mack in my dream.

My nightgown is up over my hips, and I'm wet. My nipples ache with a longing I have never experienced before. No one is lying with me in the bed. I can hear Warrior's little snores coming from his pen. I'm alone, and yet I can feel the heat of his body lingering with me. I roll over, half expecting to see him standing at the edge of the bed. I feel a pang of disappointment when I see for sure that I'm completely alone. I feel the tears sting my eyes and slowly slide down my face and onto my pillow. I feel lonely and sad. My satin pillow is absorbing my tears, much like a desert flower during a much-needed rain on a hot summer's eve.

Chapter 81

When the alarm goes off, I feel drained. I know I had slept, but my head feels foggy, and my body feels as though it had been badly abused during sleep. I remember my dream and feel guilty for enjoying the feel of another man. I slowly drag myself from the bed and go into the bathroom. Splashing cold water on my face does very little in making me feel better. I look like shit, and I feel even worse than I look. I take the dog from his pen and go downstairs to let him out. The coffee is done, so I pour myself and Mack a cup. I carry his cup to the library and knock on the door.

"Mack your coffee is done. I brought you a cup," I call through the locked door. I hear him coming to the door and step to the side.

"Thanks." He takes the cup and heads for the stairs. "I don't think I could eat a bite of anything this morning," he adds from the top of the stairs. I think the same thing about myself.

Getting the dog in, I hear the morning paper hit the mat at the front door. I absently open up the door and pick up the newspaper. There on the mat lies an envelope. I dread reading it. Yet I feel drawn to it. I pick it up and open it.

"Oh my, Elise, you are getting vicious in your killings. It would almost seem that you didn't enjoy the mayor's lovemaking. Was he really that bad that you had to kill him in such a manner? Your time is getting very, very close now. Soon, it will be all over, and you won't have to be looking over your shoulder. Ha ha, you won't have a shoulder to look over. Soon, my pretty, very soon."

This was the longest note I received. For a split second I thought about giving it to Mack. No, that would only make him angry. Not because I received a note, but because he'd think I'm just vying for attention. I rip it up and throw it in the kitchen garbage. I'm sitting at the counter once more, trying to think of who would do something like this to me. Mack has to be behind the notes. He's insanely jealous and wants me to suffer. I'm sure of it. Mack strolls into the kitchen looking fresh as a cucumber in a farmer's market. At that precise second, I hate the bastard. How dare he drink and then sleep on a couch and look refreshed and bright-eyed and bushy tailed. It's as if he's reading my mind.

"Maybe a couple of brandies before you go to bed at night would help you sleep," he says, pouring a second cup of coffee for himself.

"I doubt any amount of alcohol would help me sleep. I need to make an appointment."

"Well, at least I wasn't awakened by a bloodcurdling scream and the dog barking last night."

"No, I didn't have a nightmare last night." Even as I say it, I can feel my cheeks redden with the heat of embarrassment. Best not tell him I had the most sensational wet dream I had ever experienced.

"I'm not sure if I will be home to eat tonight, so don't worry about making anything. Who knows, I may be in jail," he says with no humor in his voice.

"Don't talk like that, Mack, it's ridiculous to think they would even consider you as a suspect. I just hate all this murder stuff. I wouldn't mind if you never went back to the department to work. I'd be happy if you became a mailman or something like that." I take a sip of my now cold coffee.

"I've never done anything other than worked for the sheriff's department. I'm not sure I could even deliver the mail without trying to find a clue of something going on in the neighborhood. Like why does the neighbor's dog only bark on Tuesdays?" He laughs at his own joke.

"I'm sorry, Mack, I just hate you having to put up with all the politics and shit that goes on there."

"Well, like I said, I have no idea what will happen today. I better get down there and get the show on the road." He heads for the garage door. "Have fun with Jordyn. I really like her, I think she is good for you."

I sit in silence, wondering what the day would bring for both myself and Mack.

Chapter 82

Mack enters the sheriff's department and goes directly to Danking's office. He doesn't bother to knock but just opens the door and walks in.

"Good morning, Mack," one of the New York investigators says as he comes through the door.

"Really? Who thinks this is a good morning? I think this morning sucks almost as much as the coffee you're drinking if you are drinking the shit Alice makes."

"We only have a couple of questions for you and everyone else that works here or interacted with the mayor."

"Shoot."

"Well, can you tell us where you were Sunday evening around seven thirty?"

"Why, yes, I can. I was at home entertaining my sister, her husband, their daughter Becca, and a bloke named Cam. Oh, and of course my wife was there, and so were two puppies. Although I doubt the dogs or Becca can honestly vouch for me. She does coo a bit, and the pups yip some too."

"How can we get a hold of these people?"

"I have all of their numbers here in my phone except for Cam's. Wait, Jordyn Kent was also there. She owns the shop downtown. I think its Forgotten Treasures. You can go there and talk to her." Mack reaches for his cell phone and goes to Contacts. He shows the investigator the numbers. "You can get Cam's number and last name from my brother-in-law. I can't for the life of me think of his last name. Is there anything else you'd like to know?"

"Yes, you stopped at the scene of the murder yesterday. What is your first impression of this new murder?"

"Ha ha, very funny. I no longer work for the department, therefore, I have no opinions to give. However, I do have a question of my own."

"What's that, Mack?"

"Are you asking the sheriff any questions? After all, he was at each crime scene, he has had years of experience, and would know more than many as how to cover up a crime."

"We were about to question him just before you showed up. He isn't too excited about having to answer questions from the investigating team that he hired to uncover the murders. But we feel we need to cover all the bases."

"Good."

"By the way, did you find anything of interest in your files at home?"

Mack laughs. "You knew I'd keep a copy of everything I had?"

"Any good detective doesn't just hand over their research."

"I'm looking at this a little differently now. I want to see if I can see any sort of pattern. I believe someone besides the dead mayor wants me out of the department."

"I hope you can find something, because we haven't found a damn thing. Usually our team has the ability to figure out cases because it isn't personal to us. We don't live where the crimes occurred. We are usually the fresh eyes. But these are completely beyond our ability to solve. It's like the guy isn't real. He leaves no clues whatsoever. It's unbelievable."

"If I'm done here, I'm going to go do a bit of research on my own."

"Yes, thank you for your cooperation. Keep us informed if you find anything that makes sense." They shake hands as Mack stands up to leave. "No matter what the mayor thought, you did a very thorough job."

"Thank you." Mack turns and walks out the door.

Not really knowing what to do with himself, Mack decides to take a quick ride out to the motel and have a look around. Maybe he can pick up something at the latest crime scene that will help him in some way. Pulling into the parking lot, he's surprised at the number of cars parked there. He walks into the lobby and sees that most of the people are just there to be nosy. He walks up to the desk, and the young girl asks, "May I help you? Do you want a room?"

"No, I'm a detective and would like to get into the room."

"Oh, okay here is the key. Don't let anyone else in, per the sheriff."

"I won't." Mack takes the key and heads down the hall. He opens the door and closes it on the foot of a reporter. While in the room, Mack looks for clues. Nothing but the body has been removed. The belt, whip, and other things are lying around. That means that forensics will be back. He decides he better leave before he leaves his own evidence. As he goes to the door, he sees something shiny under the edge of the dresser. He carefully picks it up and examines it. Slipping it into his pocket, he leaves the room. Giving the key to the young girl, he smiles and leaves the motel.

Once in the car, he takes the shiny piece out of his pocket and studies it closely. He knows of only one man who wears one of these little pins on his uniform. He laughs out loud and starts out of the parking lot. He's in a much better mood than he had been earlier that day.

Chapter 83

I take a long hot shower. Pulling my hair back into a ponytail, I put a few touches of makeup on and think it's good enough. Putting Warrior in his pen with toys, I'm ready to go help Jordyn. I'm excited to begin my new job. Even if it's only for a day or two a week.

Jordyn sees me coming through the window and meets me at the door. "Hope you like to write?"

"Yeah, I guess so. Why?"

"I received a double shipment of shit last night. Not that I don't want it and that it won't fly off the shelves, it's just that there is a ton of it to go through."

"Maybe we should get a cup of strong coffee before we start?"

"Oh, that's a marvelous idea." Jordyn grabs her wallet, and we head across the street.

We work well together, checking off all the merchandise that has been shipped to the shop. By noon we have finished most of it. Jordyn keeps thanking me for helping. I think I had better go home and let poor Warrior out, and leave shortly after noon. I plan on going back in the morning to work for a couple of hours to learn more about checking people out. The registrar keeps track of the items sold so the inventory will be correct at the end of each day. I just want to make sure I'm accurate in punching the right numbers.

Warrior is more than a little excited when I walk through the door. I take him out of the pen and outside. He does his business and then runs around the pool until he literally falls in. I have to laugh at his antics and let him swim a bit before calling him to the side of the pool to get him out. To my surprise, he's able to pull his body out of the pool all by himself. I praise him on what a big boy he is and think it would be nice to be able to let him loose on his own in the yard. Just to be safe, I chain him.

I grab an apple and a water and go up to the studio to finish my painting. I feel better than I had that morning when I woke up. I forget about calling the doctor for an appointment. I paint until I hear Warrior barking and I hear the garage door open. I'm not surprised at Warrior's racket, but I'm surprised that Mack is home so early.

Coming downstairs after putting my things away, I find Mack in the backyard talking to Warrior. He has let him loose and is watching him sniff bugs and pee on the rosebush.

"You're home early."

"Yes, it went quite fast and well today."

"Should I plan on making something for tonight to eat?"

"No, I thought maybe I would pick up Subway on my way back from Portsmith."

"Why are you going to Portsmith?" I ask, concern dripping from my voice.

"I just have to check something out, that's all." So he has no plans of telling me what the hell he's up too.

"Are you sure you will be back tonight at all?"

"Oh yes, my dear. I will be home before you know it, and we will have subs together, I promise." He stands up and pats me on the head and then pats the dog in the same manner and goes into the house and into the garage and drives away.

Chapter 84

The house phone rings, and I let it go to voice mail until Rebecca says to pick up. She skips hello and starts out with "Boy, do I have news for you."

"What news is that? Is Becca walking already?"

"No, this is about you."

"About me?"

"Yes, I entered your painting of Haven and Becca into an art contest in New York, and they just contacted me that you won."

"What?" I ask in a stupor.

"Honey you took first place in this contest in New York, and not only are they going to put your painting on display at the prestigious Paint and Perform on Eightieth Street, but you won a whopping hundred grand."

"Oh my god, Rebecca, Mack will be furious when he hears this!" A part of me wants to jump for joy, while another wants to cry and hide.

"You leave my son to me. I will handle him," Rebecca states firmly. "They also want you and Mack to go to New York for the big display they will be having in two weeks. Your painting will be in the center of the display, and everyone will see it. They asked if I would allow them to auction it off, and I said it wasn't for sale."

"This is just too much to take in at once. First my paintings start to sell here in Flag Lake, and now one is to be displayed in New York. Oh my, I think I'm dreaming."

"It's real, Elise, you are an artist. I will call Mack later and tell him. Right now I have to go tell my neighbor." Rebecca hangs up before I have a chance to say another word.

I'm shaking, but not from the news my mother-in-law has just dumped on me, but because of how Mack will react to me being the center of attention. I feel weak, sick, and scared as hell. Mack will be great with his mom, but as soon as he's alone with me, he'll turn into the other Mack and be angry and be the monster he really is. I have to be ready for the worse.

I spend the rest of the afternoon worrying about how Mack will react, and by the time he actually shows up, I have given myself one hell of a headache. I'm taking a handful of ibuprofen when he comes into the kitchen. He has a big smile on his face and a bag of subs.

"For someone who has just won big bucks and is going to New York in two weeks, you look like hell."

"I take it your mother called you." I down the pills.

"Yes, she was so excited about it I think she may have told most of Flag Lake by now."

"You aren't mad about it?" I ask with trepidation.

"Why would I be angry? It couldn't come at a better time. I have a leave of absence, so we can go on an extended vacation if we want to," he says, taking both of my hands in his.

"I've been so upset all afternoon thinking you would be angry that I have a terrible headache." Rubbing my temples, I sit down at the bar.

Mack comes over and starts to gently massage my shoulders. "You are so tense I can see why you have a headache. Why don't you go upstairs and lie down for a little while, and we can eat these when you get up. I have some work in the library anyway." Taking me by the hand, he leads me from the kitchen.

"Warrior is outside."

"Don't worry about the damn dog, I will take care of him. You just lie down and rest, I will come get you in an hour so we can eat."

"Please don't be mean to him, he is just a puppy."

He gently kisses my forehead. "I'll be nice." Covering me with the throw at the end of the bed, he leaves the room.

I'm not buying the nice guy act he's putting on. I know that he will explode, and I have to be prepared. I wish I felt better. This getting sick all the time and now this headache. These murders may be driving Mack crazy, but they seem to be taking a toll on me too. The dreams are getting worse and more vivid, and they are coming true. I should tell someone about them, but who? I want to sleep, but I'm afraid of having another dream. I lie there awake for a very long time. I can smell Mack before I feel his hands on me. I don't have to open my eyes to know he's ready to torture me with his idea of lovemaking.

"Wake up, my little bird, I have a big surprise for you." I open my eyes and see him standing naked. He rubs his engorged cock along my arm.

"Leave me alone, Mack. You've been drinking, and I still have a pounding headache," I plead with him.

"Oh come on, Elise, you know you want me to fuck your brains out. You know that once I enter you, you will be all mine," he says, still rubbing himself on me. I try to push him away, but he's already crawling on top of me.

"Mack, please get off of me."

He straddles me and begins to try to pull my shirt over my head. "Please stop, Mack."

He stops and looks into my eyes. I see the pure evil staring back at me. He grabs me by the throat and says, "I'll move, and you will remove your fucking clothes, then you will lie down and spread your legs like the good little whore that you are."

"No, Mack, I won't. I told you no, and I meant no." I try to pull his hands away from my throat.

"Oh yes, you will. I will not be second to your lover or to you, not ever." He tightens his grip around my neck and growls.

"You are an animal, not a man." I know as soon as the words leave my mouth I have pushed him over the edge.

He shifts his weight and slams his fist into my ribs. The next is a sharp slap to the side of my face. I cry out in pain, but that doesn't stop him. He places his knee on my pubic bone and kneels down. I would have doubled up in pain if he hasn't been holding me down. He rolls off me and the bed and grabs me by the hair.

"Get up and take your damn clothes off or I swear I will rip them off and then strangle you with them."

I stand up and try to pull my shirt up over my head. He grabs it and yanks it up over my face.

"Leave it there. That way I don't have to stare into your ugly face," he snarls at me.

I slide my pants down my legs and try to kick them free from my feet. With a quick hard shove, I find myself on my back on the bed. He immediately straddles me and tries to shove himself inside me. I'm not ready for him. He raises up and thrusts his middle finger inside me. He keeps thrusting in and out, making circles with his finger as he enters me, much like you would if you were stirring a cup of coffee with your finger. No matter how many times he does this, I'm still not wet enough for him to enter me. He's like a madman and again tries to enter me. This time he makes it, and I feel as if I'm being ripped wide open. I cry out in pain.

"See, I told you that you would enjoy it," he says between raspy breaths. I lie there motionless as the tears roll down the sides of my face. With one last thrust, he lets out an animal growl and comes inside me. He immediately slumps over my motionless body.

I can hardly breathe with the weight of his body on top of me and my shirt covering my face. I lie there, silently praying I would just die. No, I silently pray he would die. I want to get up and grab the poker and beat him to death. I want to slice his penis off and cram it down his throat. The hatred is so strong in me I'm afraid if he does get off me I would kill him. I want to escape from all this, and I want him to suffer. I vow I will get away from him, never to have to put up with his abuse again.

He eventually gets up, and when he does, he says, "Get up, bitch, and go get my sub ready so I can eat. You can at least do that much. You seem to fuck up everything else I ask you to do. Oh, and make sure that barking, biting mutt of yours isn't anywhere near me or I promise I will drown the little fucker in the pool." He walks into the bathroom and slams the door with enough force to make the pictures hanging on the wall rattle. I slowly get up and put my clothes back on. I feel as though I've been rolled down a hill in a crude barrel.

I feel dirty and bruised. I want to go into the bathroom and take a shower, but not while he's there. Instead I go downstairs and look for Warrior. I find him outside huddled under the rosebush. As I come closer, I see the dried blood on his face. He's hunched over and cowed down when I approach him.

"Come here, baby, what has he done to you?" I slowly pick him up to examine him better. He flinches when I rub over his ribs. I gently hold him close and speak low, soothing words to console him. I take him into the bathroom off the kitchen and put him down on the counter. I gently rub my hands over his fur to see if I can determine if he has anything broken. I'm sure his ribs are as bruised as mine. He has a small cut inside his mouth, and I think he's probably kicked there too. I place him on the floor and clean myself up. I carry him into the kitchen and place him in his pen. Then I pick him back up and take him quietly upstairs and put him in my studio. I go back down and get the pen and take it up there too. I place him in the pen and close my studio door. I wonder what's taking Mack so long in the bathroom. I peek in the bedroom and hear the shower going. I'm instantly angry. Why should he be allowed a shower after mistreating both me and the dog? I hate him even more.

Taking the subs from their wrappers, I place them on plates. I open the chips that come with them and add them to the plates. I open a can of Diet Coke for myself and take down a glass for Mack. I don't have any idea what he will want to add on top of his booze. I sit at the breakfast counter and wait for him to come down the stairs. I wonder if I poison him if it will be a slow and painful death, or if he'll just fall asleep. No, I think it will be more enjoyable to watch him slowly bleed to death. Yes, that will be better if I can see his face as he slowly dies.

Chapter 85

Mack enters the kitchen and never says a word. He sees the empty glass on the counter and goes to the refrigerator to get the ice tea. Pouring it into his glass, he finally looks at me.

"I suppose you would want my mother with you in New York instead of your failure of a husband."

I look at him for the first time since he has raped me, and what I see is a totally different person from just minutes before. He looks much older than his age, and he looks defeated and beaten. If I hadn't just been the object of his abuse, I would probably feel sorry for him.

"I guess that will be up to you. If you feel you don't want to come with me, then I will ask your mother if she wants to come."

"I would like to get away from this place for a while. I think I have had enough of the sheriff, mayor, and the investigating jerks to last a lifetime."

"I think we both could use some time away from everything." While thinking how I wish he would stay home.

"Okay, let's start planning a vacation. We can look at some brochures and decide if we want to stay in New York or go somewhere else." He never mentions he's sorry or that he abused the dog or anything. It's as if he never did anything of the sort.

After eating, he announces he's going back into the library. I go to my studio. I take Warrior outside, and he does his job. He walks around the backyard and then promptly jumps into the pool. I call him out, but instead of taking inside, I leave him out there while I go in and change into my swimsuit. I dive into the pool, and by the time I come up, Warrior is swimming around me. I laugh at him and then begin to swim laps in the pool. I swim until I'm tired and find it hard to catch my breath. I pull myself out of the pool and that's when I see Mack standing in the patio doorway watching me. I wait for Warrior to pull himself out of the pool, and when he does, I clap.

"Good boy."

He happily shakes himself all over my leg. I grab a towel and begin to dry him off. I figure it will do me no good to dry myself off first with Warrior still wet and dripping. I enter the house and go to my studio to put Warrior in his pen.

When I enter the bedroom, Mack is waiting for me. He has taken my nightgown out of the drawer and laid it on the bed. He has a fluffy towel hung over his arm like a butler. When I stop dead in my tracks, he says, "Your loyal servant is ready to be of service to your every wish."

"I wish to just take a shower and relax a little before bed."

He hands me the towel. "Enjoy your shower, my love."

I'm surprised when he leaves the room and quietly shuts the door. I wonder if that's his way of an apology for being such an ass before.

I take my sweet time in the shower and decide to even blow-dry my hair. Not sure of what I'd find once I open the bathroom door. Not sure of who I'd find when I open the door. A gentle Mack or a drunk and abusive Mack. What I find was nothing. There's a note on the table that reads, "I had to run out for a while. I found something in my files that I want to share with the investigators immediately. I feel it can't even wait until morning. Don't wait up. Love you, Mack."

What the hell? He can come home all excited for me, drink himself into an abusive ass, then go to work at a job he is suspended from? He truly is a bipolar man. I'm still angry but also filled with relief. I will be in peace for a little while.

Going to my studio, I take Warrior out of his pen. Letting him run along behind me on the stairs. He has really been growing fast, I think.

"I had better start teaching you some rules before you are too big for the pen and have no manners. Let's start with the living room. You are not allowed on the furniture and can only lie on the carpet in front of the fireplace. At no time are you to be near the TV. At no time are you to be anywhere but on the carpet in front of the fireplace. That is your home while in this room."

He promptly tries to climb onto the couch.

"No, down, that would be bad."

He stops, turns, and takes a flying leap toward the recliner. He's a bit short, but in a week, that will be no obstacle at all.

"No, down, that is not where you belong. You are allowed to be here."

Sitting on the small rug in front of the fireplace, he plops down beside me and starts chewing on the fringe of the rug.

"No, you only chew on your toys. This is going to be a lot harder than I thought." I try to get the fringe out of his mouth. That too turns into a game of tug of war. Giggling I scoop him up and decide that's enough for one night of rules. I wonder if he'll sleep in the pen in the studio by himself or if he'll pitch a fit. I think how lonely the house was before I added Warrior to the mix.

Chapter 86

Mack has called the sheriff's department to get the number of the head investigator. The dispatch operator is a bit skeptical on giving it out to Mack, but in the end, he sweet-talks her into it. He calls the woman and tells her he has found something that he thinks she should look at. She agrees to meet him at the department.

When he walks into the conference room, he's surprised to see all the investigators there and not just her.

"Let's hear what you have found."

Mack walks over to the table and shoves the folder over to her. "I think you may find this quite interesting. I know I overlooked it for all these years."

She opens the file and starts to scan the papers within. Looking up at Mack, she hands the first few sheets to the man next to her. "You know what this implies, don't you?"

"Oh yes, I do. I hate to say it, and I will be amazed if it pans out, but I think it's worth investigating further into it."

They all take turns scanning the paperwork. After they had all read it, she asks, "May we keep this folder and check into it thoroughly tomorrow? I'm sure we will be contacting you and letting you know what we think of these allegations. This will surely open one hell of a can of worms if you are correct."

"Well, do you really think it's a good idea to contact me? Seeing I am on administrative leave and all. Don't you think that it may actually drop a monkey wrench in the case?"

"Yes, I see where you are coming from. I will make sure you are included in this but won't imply that you brought it to our attention. Thank you, this is a great find. We too have overlooked this in our searching."

Mack feels higher than a kite, nods his goodbye, and leaves the department. He's sure no one pays attention to the fact that he's even in the building.

Not feeling ready to go home yet, Mack drives to the local watering hole. Hopefully no one from the department will be there tonight. He doesn't recognize any of their vehicles in the parking lot so feels safe having a drink or two. He takes a seat at the end of the bar so he can face the door, orders a brandy old-fashioned sweet, and smiles to himself. There are only six other people in the place, and they all are his dad's age. He sits alone and drinks his drink being very pleased with himself. Five drinks later and still feeling on cloud nine, he notices a pretty little brunette sitting all alone at the table in the corner. Grabbing his drink, he decides to walk over and introduce himself.

He stands in front of her so that her eyes will be just about level with his belt buckle. She looks up.

"Hello, Detective."

"So you know who I am already?" He pulls out the chair.

"Everyone knows who you are."

"Well, I am at a disadvantage here. You know who I am, but I have no idea who you are." He enunciates his words, making him sound hurt that he doesn't know her.

"I'm Maesyn Vane."

"Well, Maesyn Vane, I'm very glad to meet you." He reaches out his hand for a friendly handshake. "What brings you to our lovely little watering hole? I've never seen you here before." He notices her ringless hands.

"I am here for only a couple of days. I have an aunt who lives here, and she is ill."

"I hope it's nothing serious."

"Oh, she is just very mentally unstable. She shot up the downtown area last week or so, and I'm trying to get her into a facility before she kills someone."

"Yes, I know her well. She is a bit bonkers at times, but only when she is off her meds."

"Well, if she doesn't stay on her meds, she should be where she can't hurt herself or someone else."

They make small talk, enjoying their drinks, and when she says she has to leave, he makes a pouty face at her.

"I am in the motel just up the road if you want to come have a nightcap there." She takes his hand in hers.

"Well, I should be going home, but I don't see how one little nightcap will hurt any."

"I'm in room 304 in the back of the place. I'll meet you there." She walks out the side door and is gone.

This is my lucky night, he thinks as he throws some money on the table to cover the last round of drinks and a tip for the ugly bartender.

He tries his best not to look as though he's in a hurry to leave but practically bolts to the front door. He gets into his car and laughs at how lucky he has been today and how much luckier he is tonight. He pulls around the back of the motel and looks for where room 304 is. Pulling into a parking spot that's almost hidden from view, he gets out and locks his car. He knocks lightly on the door and about shits when she opens the door. There she stands in front of him naked as a jaybird. Instant hard-on.

"When I said nightcap, I meant I wanted to cap your cock off." She pulls him into the room. Her lips are on his before he can even think of anything to say to her last statement. She has no problem rubbing her full body up against his. As she's kissing him, she's undoing his pants.

He thinks, *Damn, this girl wants it bad.*

It takes two steps and two seconds for them to be naked on the bed. He tries to get the upper hand and be in control of the situation, but hell, she's good, and she just takes over. Her hands run down his body and cups his balls. She slowly runs her tongue down the same

275

path her hand has taken. He wants to taste those full hard nipples, but she doesn't give him a chance. Her mouth comes down on his big cock and sucks hard. He groans and thinks he's in heaven. When she comes up for air, he manages to flip her on her back.

He looks into her eyes and says, "My turn." Trailing kisses and licks from her slender neck to the hard peak of her nipple, he feels more alive and on fire than he has in a very long time. He spreads her legs and finds the hard nub waiting for his tongue. *Damn, she tastes great.* He licks and sucks her until she arches and gives way to an orgasm that he can tell rocks her to the very core. He raises above her and sinks his cock deep inside her. His first plunge is deep and hard. He stays there, letting her feel his throbbing cock.

She reaches for his head and brings it down to her breast. He licks and sucks and then raises to pull out almost to the very end. He enters his full length all the way in, only slowly this time. Only to do it again. He does this until he can't stand it anymore himself, and the rhythm becomes faster and faster. He can feel the pressure building up, and he can feel his own sweat drip off his body onto her skin. He explodes inside her like a cannon being shot off. Holy shit, does he feel good. He lies gently on top of her and breathes in her smell. It's a mixture of sweet perfume, hot steamy come, and his sweat. Damn, she smells good enough to eat. He thinks he may just have to do that after he catches his breath.

He rolls off her and takes her in his arms.

"That was nice, but you have to leave now."

"Why, I'm not done with you yet," he says, pulling her closer.

"Well, I have a big day ahead of me tomorrow, and you have a wife to go home to. So I think you better get up and get dressed and leave now." She's already breaking away from his hug and sitting on the edge of the bed. She picks up his shirt and tosses it over to him. He gets up and begins to dress.

"I'd really like to do this again when you and I both have more time." Zipping up his pants.

"Not going to happen. I have too much to do in a short time, and I won't be available again. This was just a fluke and probably a mistake." She's pushing him toward the door as she's talking. He stops in front of the closed door and takes her in his arms and kisses her deeply, almost devouring her. She says nothing, but she does rub up against him during the kiss. Then opens the door and says, "Goodbye." The door closes, and he hears the lock as he slowly walks to his car thinking, *Damn, that was good.*

Chapter 87

The drive home is over all too fast. He pulls into the garage and thinks of how good it feels to be appreciated in bed. If Elise fucks like that, he'll be hard pressed to ever leave the house again. Shit, he'll never get out of bed. He enters the kitchen and then goes into the bathroom off the kitchen. He cleans up a bit and splashes his face with cold water. He has quite a buzz on and has no intention of losing it with a confrontation with Elise. He goes to the library and stretches out on the couch and falls asleep thinking of how great his day had been.

* * *

I hear him come home and waited for him to come upstairs. I'm prepared for the negativity that he always brings with him. I'm ready for the fight that's destined to take place. I hear the library door close and sigh a sigh of relief. I know he will stay in there, and I know I can get some much-needed sleep. I fall into a deep sleep, not caring what he does or where he had been, only that he's leaving the forthcoming battle for the morning.

Chapter 88

"What's going on?" I ask as I enter the town square. Everybody who lives in the town seems to be packed into the small area. The streets are blocked off. I see police officers milling through the crowd wearing full riot attire. I stop a passerby and ask again, "What is going on?" He doesn't answer me. He just smiles and rushes forward. I'm being pushed to the middle of the crowd. Woman, children, old men, and people in wheelchairs are all heading for the end of the square. Even though I see faces I recognize, they all seem to be strangers to me. I see Cameron standing off to the side and push my way to him. "Cam, what is going on down here?" I'm feeling anxious.

"Haven't you heard? Your husband is about to hang the sheriff." He points to a scaffolding at the end of the street.

"What? Why? I don't understand."

"He was found guilty of the murders that have been taking place. Just this morning the judge sentenced him to be hanged by the neck until dead."

"There has to be a mistake. I know he didn't kill those people. This has to be stopped," I cry, trying to push toward the front so I can stop the horrendous injustice about to take place. I'm pushing hard to get forward but seem only to be pushed farther back and out of reach or earshot of Mack, who is leading the sheriff to the scaffold.

I watch as he's taken to the top of the platform. He's staring out into the crowd with eyes that are already dead. I hear Mack ask him, "Is there anything you would like to say before your sentence is carried out?"

He stares directly at me and says, "I am innocent, and you know it."

I hang my head and sob. I hear the crowd, but now it's a soft murmur. The trap door springs open with a loud bang. I can't help but look up. The sheriff is hanging just above the ground, staring into the crowd. He doesn't die in the fall. His neck isn't snapped. Nor are his hands tied behind his back. He reaches up, clawing at the rope around his neck. Mack runs down the steps and, with a machete, stabs it into the sheriff just below the neck. Bringing it down with such force the hilt of the knife digs into the bowels of the sheriff. When he pulls the machete out and away from the body, the guts and organs of the sheriff spew out and dangle from his body. Still the sheriff doesn't die. His eyes find mine, and they are silently pleading with me to stop my husband. I once again try to push forward, but the crowd around me is too strong. Holding me in place. I feel ill and try to cover my eyes. It's as if my hands are covered in cement, weighing them down. I can't move, I can't look away, and I can't speak. I watch in horror as Mack reaches into the sheriff's chest and pulls the still beating heart out of his body. He turns to the crowd and yells, "This black heart will never beat again, nor will it ever hurt another of my town's residents. I now will put an end to it all." After saying that, he throws the beating heart in the air and slices it in two. The crowd cheers for joy.

I awake and struggle to get out of bed to run into the bathroom and vomit. I'm tangled in the sheets. My feet are trapped. It seems to take me days before I free myself. Just making it to the toilet before I throw up. I slump on the floor of the bathroom and hug the porcelain god. The tile feels cold beneath me. It makes me shiver, sending a chill through me. I know what Mack has found or thinks he's found in the files. I also know that he's wrong. I somehow have to stop him before the sheriff is blamed for the murders he's tried so desperately to solve. I have no idea how to begin. I feel weak and tired as I rinse my mouth. My reflection is of a defeated woman. Pale and too thin, I look like my grandmother just before she died. Maybe that's what's going to happen to me. I'm going to free myself from Mack, and by dying, the dreams will finally stop.

As I go toward the bed, I see it's already six o'clock. I might as well stay up. I dress slowly, and with Warrior in tow, I head down the stairs. I can smell the coffee before I reach the kitchen. It turns my stomach into a nauseous pit of bubbling bile. Rushing to the patio door, I open it and practically throw the dog outside. Shutting the door with a thud, I run to the bathroom. Once again emptying my stomach's contents into the toilet bowl. I want to just lie on the floor and never move again.

Unfortunately, that's the precise second Mack walks into the kitchen. Seeing me on my knees, with my head hanging over the bowl, he says with disgust, "Oh for Pete's sake, Elise, get the hell up. I'm hungry, and I have a dozen things to do today." I'm not sure my legs will hold me when I try to stand. I slowly manage to wash my face and hands. I rinse my mouth once again and try to compose myself long enough to go back to bed. Knowing that isn't a real choice, I do my best to walk into the kitchen and start his breakfast. All the while he just stands there grinning to himself.

Chapter 89

Making Mack breakfast takes every ounce of strength I can muster. My stomach is so upset, and my head pounds like a drum in the Fourth of July parade, only without good rhythm. Warrior is at least being a good puppy and is chewing on something out in the yard. It's as if he knows not to fuss or Mack will do more harm to him.

"Did you call for a doctor's appointment yet?" he asks while filling his face with toast and a poached egg.

"No, I will call today as soon as the clinic opens up." Trying not to remember the dream and trying harder not to look at the eggs.

"This bullshit of you being sick has got to come to an end."

"You make it sound as if I want to throw up or have a headache."

"Well, my sweet whore, that is exactly what I think. Every time I have something good going on, you do something for attention. Like now, for example, I found a big lead in the murder cases and shared it last night with the investigating team. They are sure I am right, and things will start to happen as early as today."

"Really, so you worked with them until the wee hours of the night?" I raise my eyebrow with suspicion.

"Oh, I worked on something in the wee hours of the night all right." His sneer gives him away.

"You know I don't really care who she is or what you did with her anymore. I could care less, just so you leave me alone. I will not be one of your whores. I don't ever want you to touch me again." I feel as if a huge weight has been removed from my head and body.

"Oh, but you are my whore, and you will never escape me. Just remember that." He slowly gets up and comes to stand next to me. Grabbing my hair, he pulls me up and gently kisses my ear. "You are mine, to do with what I want and when I want and where I want. Remember, Elise, I can make your life a living hell." Shoving me back down in the chair, he turns and goes up the stairs.

Mack leaves shortly after the incident in the kitchen, and I take the phone book out of the drawer to find the number of the clinic. I have no primary doctor and wonder if the doctor that had checked me over in the ER and on the follow-up appointment would be willing to take me on as a patient. It's still too early to call for the appointment, so I go outside to sit in the morning sun. Warrior comes bounding over and drops a chewed-up old rag at my feet. I look down, and a wave of nausea flows over me. It's the dress off Maggie Mae. I look over to the place he has been lying to see if the doll has somehow been carried outside. I remember the doll was naked when it was in the pool. This had to have been placed in the yard sometime last night. I want to laugh and cry at the same time. Poor little naked Maggie's only dress all chewed up. I'm not afraid or angry; I'm was just tired and want it all to come to a head and end. What's to come to a head and what would end, I have no clue.

I go inside to start the day. I brush my teeth again and put my hair into a ponytail low at the base of my head. I think if I pull it tight it will only intensify my headache. I go into my studio and begin to sketch. I close the door so Warrior can be lose. I open the patio door but keep the screen closed. The dog is content to just lie in front of the open door and watch the birds in the trees. I feel as though my pencil has a mind of its own. The depth of the detail is amazing. I wonder what it will look like if I actually paint it. What would my followers think of this type of artwork? I laugh at myself for even thinking of bringing the sketch to life with paints.

I realize it is after nine, and I need to make an appointment. I go downstairs and call the clinic. I'm able to get in to see the same doctor at three in the afternoon. I take the appointment and decide I will leave early and stop off at Jordyn's to talk with her before the doctor's appointment. It's Tuesday, and the shop is closed, but I know

Jordyn will be there. I have so much to tell her. The art show, Mack's abuse, it all seems so unreal.

I toast myself a scone and add very little butter to it. I manage to eat it and wonder if I could brave a cup of tea. I make myself a cup of mint tea and take it outside to enjoy on the patio. Of course the dog wants to sit on my lap and cuddle while I'm sipping my tea. I laugh at his antics and let him curl up on my lap. I'm feeling much better by the time I've finished my breakfast and nearly call to cancel the appointment. I know I have to go in. Mack will check to make sure I have an appointment and make a fuss if I don't go.

The rest of the day flies by. I have no idea where Mack has gone so I leave him a voice mail message on his cell. I don't expect a response. With Warrior in his pen with toys and food inside my studio, I'm ready to leave. I lock the front door just as my cell rings. I answer, and all I hear is an evil laugh. I hang up and proceed to the bus stop.

Chapter 90

Jordyn is in the back when I knock on the door. She comes bustling to open the door.

"Thank goodness you are here. I just received a shipment of tiny little glass figurines. They are hand-blown glass and very fragile. I can use your help in unwrapping them and logging them in."

"Do you really want me to help unwrap? I will log them in, but I've been a bit clumsy lately and wouldn't want to break your shipment."

"Okay, you log and I'll break them."

We head for the back room. Jordyn babble all the way to the back room about how long she's waited for this shipment. I'm shocked at how someone could make these beauties by blowing into a tube.

"I have a doctor's appointment at three. So I will have to leave here by two forty-five," I share with Jordyn.

"That will give us plenty of time to shatter quite a few of these," Jordyn says, sighing. We work together on the shipment until it's all logged in and carefully put back into the crate. To take out and display just a couple at a time.

"Jordyn, I have some good news."

"Oh, you mean you winning the art show in New York?"

"How on earth did you find out?" I ask, totally surprised.

"Well, if you look on your part of the wall, you will see I haven't one painting of yours hanging there."

"What happened to them?"

"When your mother-in-law blabbed to the whole town that you won an art contest in New York, people flocked here to buy a painting before the prices skyrocketed from your fame."

"Holy crap, are you kidding?"

"Nope, they flew off the wall all day yesterday. Making you and me even richer."

"I am dumbfounded."

"You better have more paintings at your house."

"I do, but I don't think they are very good."

"Doesn't matter, they will sell now that your name is out there."

"I'm afraid to go to New York with Mack. He gets very jealous when he isn't the center of attention and then he gets very violent. He's liable to push me down a flight of stairs and tell everyone I was drinking and fell."

"Do you want me to come with as your distributor? It's done all the time. I would be the one who set up future sales, etc. You and Mack would just be there to look pretty."

"Oh, Jordyn, that would be fantastic." I hug her. "Oh no, I better leave so I'm not late." I grab my purse and head for the door.

"Hey, stop back and tell me the outcome of this appointment. Please." Jordyn stands at the door and watches me walk toward the clinic. Jordyn is pretty sure of the outcome already.

The appointment doesn't take too long, and before I can blink, the test results are in. The doctor is very kind and tells me that I need to get more rest, eat healthier, and try not to be so tense. He tells me he doesn't want to subscribe anything but does give me some vitamins to take and a couple booklets to read. I'm shocked at the diagnosis and wish I hadn't gone to the doctor at all. I cry all the way to Jordyn's shop. Jordyn sees me coming and opens the door and opens her arms for her pregnant friend.

Chapter 91

"Oh, Jordyn, what will I do? I can't have this baby. I don't want to have this baby. It might grow up just like the father." I sob while clinging to Jordyn like she's a life preserver and I'm drowning in a violent ocean.

"Don't worry, we won't let it grow up to be anything like its father. We got this. We just have to make plans, that's all. This is a turning point in your career and your chance to start living." Jordyn holds me tight until I'm completely cried out.

"What will I tell Mack? I can't continue to have morning, afternoon, evening, and middle-of-the-night sickness without him suspecting something is up."

"Don't tell him anything. I'm driving you to Ms. Hatters right now."

"Isn't she that voodoo lady at the edge of the river?"

"Yup and she will whip you up something to calm that belly of yours, and I'm sure she will also stop the nightmares."

"It won't hurt the baby, will it?" I ask skeptically.

"Nope, she loves babies." Jordyn grabs her purse and gently shoves me out the back door and into her car.

Ms. Hatters place is little more than a mud hut. It has colored bottles hanging from the trees and funny-looking plants growing in front of the house. They don't look like any flowers I have ever seen. Jordyn goes straight up the steps and knock on the door.

"Come in, my dears," a rather crackly old voice comes from within. Jordyn opens the door, and Ms. Hatters comes over immediately and gives Jordyn a hug and says, "I've been expecting you."

"This is Elise."

"I knows who she is, chile. I knows." Taking my hands in hers, she closes her eyes and says, "You be about nine weeks along, my little bird. Come have a seat and let me get you some herbs to make that baby stop making you sick."

Jordyn and I both take a seat at the table while Ms. Hatters scurries around, getting jars down off the many shelves she has in what I think is her kitchen. She fills small plastic bags with herbs she's mixed together. Then she writes out instructions on a piece of paper. I think I can't be more surprised when she writes the instructions in not only beautiful penmanship but also in French.

"How did you know I could read French? Even my husband doesn't know I can read it."

"I juss knows."

"How much do I owe you for these herbs?"

At first I think the old woman is angry with the look she shoots at me.

"You don't know me, do you? Ifin you did, you'd knows I don't take money for my medicines."

"Well, how do you survive out here if you don't receive payment for your work?"

"I get by all right. Come here, my chile." Taking me by the hand, she takes me to another room that's divided off the main room by only a dark curtain. On this side of the curtain, she has another table. Sitting me in one chair and she takes the other, she reaches across the table and takes both of my hands in hers. "You gots the gift, chile. You gots the gift."

"I don't know what you mean." I try not to pull my hands away. I don't want to know what she means.

"You know very well what I mean. You see things ahead of time. You know before they happen. You gots the gift, all right." I'm shaking while I sit there. "No need to be afraid of the gift. You just need to know how to channel it and bring it to life before the event happens. You need to learn to control it and make it work for you and for the good of others. Like the one you saw last night. It's not too late."

"How do I stop my husband from putting the blame on the sheriff?" I ask in a whisper. "I know he is innocent, but I don't know how to prove it without making a mess of it."

"I can't help you with that. You have to see it for yourself. The answer will come to you. Let it come naturally in its own time. I know your dreams are violent, but that is because you are in a violent stage in your life. Once you are free of this stage, you will not have the violent dreams but helpful dreams. You must learn to embrace them."

"I am afraid of my dreams." I'm crying now.

Ms. Hatters stands and puts her arms around me and says a few illegible words while holding me tight. I immediately feel a calm surround me. I don't understand what has just taken place, but I know Ms. Hatters is right.

Chapter 92

Jordyn drives me home from Ms. Hatters.

"Elise, I want you to come discuss the trip to New York with me before you let Mack try to make plans for you."

"I'll come tomorrow morning, I promise." I step out of the car and wave goodbye to my only friend other than Haven. I'm surprised Haven hasn't called to discuss the winning.

I don't expect Mack to be home when I come through the door. He's standing in the hallway with a pleased look on his face.

"Hello, Elise, how was your day?" he asks, coming toward me. I back against the door and wait for whatever he's about to befell on me. He stops just a foot in front of me and asks again. "How was your day?"

"It went well. The doctor suggested I get a restful sleep, eat healthy, and try not to stress out over everyday life. He said there is nothing wrong with me. All the tests came back okay. I'm a bit low on iron and so he gave me vitamins to take. He said I should feel the difference in a week or so. Then I stopped at Jordyn to help her." I know I'm talking ninety miles an hour but can't seem to slow down.

"Good, I'm glad it isn't anything serious. I have a surprise too," he says, guiding me into the kitchen. I look around for the dog.

"Where's Warrior?" I ask with alarm.

"He's wherever you stuck him, I haven't had time to look for him. I just got home myself."

I see something run up to the patio door and look at Mack. "Please tell me you let him out? I left him in his pen."

"Yes, you caught me. I let the little asshole outside. He was barking up a storm, and I didn't feel like cleaning dog shit out of his pen. Now for my surprise. I found several things in the file that points directly at the sheriff. The investigating team checked it all out, and they have called in the Portsmith's deputy sheriff, and they have arrested Sheriff Danking for the murders that have taken place these past couple years. It's all very hush-hush yet, but it should be on the news in the morning. I will probably be instated as the new sheriff in a couple of days." He sounds so happy and pleased with himself.

"That is wonderful. You must be pleased."

"You don't sound too fucking pleased. Can't you be happy for me just once in your life?" he says as he shoves me into the counter.

"Mack, I am happy for you. I was just thinking of the last time you were so sure you had the right man. I wouldn't want this to fall through like that one did."

"Oh, it won't. The whole investigation team is on board with this one. There is enough evidence to hang the asshole." Cracking open a beer, he takes a long swig. "Did you want a beer too?" he asks, smiling from ear to ear.

"No, I think I'll stick with water today. My stomach is still a bit queasy. The doctor thinks I should lay off the Diet Coke or anything with a lot of caffeine. That may be the reason for all my throwing up." I'm lying through my teeth.

"Before I forget, I was hoping you wouldn't mind if I went to the shop tomorrow to help Jordyn out. I believe she is to do her first practice with the band after the store closes. I want to be sure I have the hang of it down pat before I am actually needed."

"No, by all means, go. I will be busy with the investigating team. I'll probably be busy the rest of this week. I need to get everything in order. Geez, first the mayor getting offed, and then it being the sheriff who did it all along. Kind of funny in a way."

"I don't see any humor in anyone's death. Especially as violent as all of these were." I can see the humor in his eyes. He's actually enjoying all this. The death of the mayor and the demise of the sheriff is just up his alley. "It all frightens me."

Mack goes off to the library whistling a merry tune as he practically skips to the room. *Jesus, he is a bloodthirsty bastard* is all I can think. Before he closes the door, I ask, "What do you want to eat later?"

"Whatever the hell you want to make. I don't really care what we eat!" he yelled back. Going to the freezer, I take out chicken breasts for stir-fry. I have no desire to eat anything.

Taking my bags of herbs and Warrior, I go into my safe haven. I reread the directions and look closely at each bag full of the different weedy-looking concoctions. If the directions would have said to smoke one of them, I would have been sure it was pot. Maybe it is. I really have no idea what are in the bags. I only know one is for nausea, one for sleep, one for anxiety, and one for the health of the baby. I don't know why, but I know I can trust each and every one of them to do their job. Putting them in my locked file cabinet, I think of what Ms. Hatters said about stopping what Mack is doing. Nothing comes to mind, and I'm afraid nothing will. I'm afraid it's already too late.

I decide to call Haven and see why I haven't heard from her since her mother-in-law called about the art contest.

"Hello, beautiful momma."

"Oh, Elise, I am so happy you called. I've been dying to call you, but Matt said to let it all sink in before I called to talk about it. He can be such an old fuddy dud." I had to laugh at her referral to Matt as a fuddy dud. "I suppose he was just trying to be considerate, but I found it nerve-racking to have to sit and wait for you to call. How are you handling it?"

"I have to admit, it was shocking to hear at first, but I think I am finally getting my brain wrapped around it."

"Oh, I am so proud of you. Mack must be elated. Well, hopefully he is."

"He's managing to get his head wrapped around it too. He has been very busy on his own." I want to say "being a bloodthirsty ass" but stop before I blurt it out.

"Is he back working on the case?"

"He never really stopped. You know Mack." I'm on the brink of telling Haven what he's about but think better of it. I also want Haven to know about the baby, but I know that will be all over town faster than the plague if I tell her. Haven can't keep a secret if her life depends on it.

"Well, I for one am so excited for you. I wish I could go along and just be a fly on the wall at that big doings."

"I wish you could go too. Jordyn said she will go with and be my director. That is someone who does all the legwork for the client. That way I don't have to worry about anything but showing up and acting like I know what the hell I am doing."

"Oh, I am sure you will do great. When do you leave?"

"I don't really know. Your mother has all the details. I really need to get with her so I can plan. If you don't mind, I will call her right now."

Chapter 93

"Hi, Rebecca."

"Well, hi there, love. I was going to call you in the morning. I received everything in the mail today. You and Mack will be staying at the Inn New York City on Seventy-First. It's a five-and-one-half-star hotel and supposed to be wonderful. All your meals and transportation will be covered and provided by the art company. You will fly first class and be picked up at the airport, etc. Damn, this sounds wonderful. You two will stay there for four full nights and fly back on the fifth day." Rebecca is rattling off things so fast I can hardly understand her. "You will leave Portsmith on the fifteenth and return on the twentieth."

"Wait, Rebecca. I need to get the dates and times so I can run it past, Mack. He might be busy those days."

"I'll bring the info over tomorrow so you two can go over it. I'm going to call him on his cell right now and run it past him before I even bring it over."

"Oh, you don't have to do that," I say into dead air, for Rebecca has already hung up. Quickly telling Warrior to hurry up, I run down the steps just as Mack is flying out of the library like an evil demon.

Throwing the dog outside, I turn to see a red-faced Mack coming up to me. Shit, shit, shit, he's going to explode right there at any second. He keeps trying to get a word in edgewise, but Rebecca isn't letting him. I can see by the look on his face that he's very upset.

Finally he says, "Okay, Mother, I will make those days work, and I won't spoil anything for your loving daughter-in-law." Tossing the phone on the counter, he turns and glares at me. "You conniving bitch. You just have to find some way to make it all about you, don't you?"

"Honest, Mack, I would have never entered the painting into any art contest. If I would have known she would have done something like that, I would have never given her the painting in the first place. You have to believe me." I try to calmly put the counter between us. He's too fast for me, and he reaches me before I have a chance to move more than a step. Slapping me across the face and then grabbing my face in both hands, he pushes my head back. I would have fallen backward if not for him holding me upright. He lets go so fast I do stumble backward and fall over the stool that's out of place. He reaches out and snatches me by the arm before I fall completely to the floor. This time it's an even harder slap to the face. I feel the sting and taste the blood in my mouth. My eyes are watering from the blows, and I'm having a hard time not crying out in pain. Still he hangs on to me. I try to pull away in vain. He only tightens his hold on my arm. He takes both of my arms and begins to shake me. My head snaps back and forth like a rag doll's head being shaken by some naughty boy who's tormenting his little sister. I can see the darkness slowly taking over. I welcome it.

I wake up lying in a heap on the kitchen floor. The dog is barking in the backyard. I crawl to the patio door and let him in. He begins to lick my face and whine.

"I'm okay, boy," I tell him. I manage to stand up, and I have to hang on to the counter and wait for the dizzy spell to ebb. I hear the garage door close or open and look out the kitchen window in time to see Mack in his convertible drive down the street. Taking deep breaths, I turn my head both to the right and left to see if my neck hurts. I figure he shook me just enough to make me pass out, but not enough to hurt me. I go into the bathroom to look at my face. It's red on both sides, but in an hour or so, it will also show no signs of abuse. He's a cleaver bastard.

Chapter 94

I know that Mack won't be home until late or probably not at all. He has been on a high, and his mother's call has slammed him into the earth. I decide I won't make the stir-fry. The chicken can just sit in the refrigerator for another day. I don't think I can keep anything down if I try. I remember the tea and decide to try the one for nausea. I make myself a cup as directed and find it to be very good. Within minutes my stomach starts to settle. I know I have to start making plans. Big plans and I know that Jordyn will be my lifesaver.

I spend the rest of the evening in my studio and paint like a mad woman. I want to get as many paintings done as I can before going to New York. Although I have years of paintings in my studio just gathering dust, I want at least three new ones to give to Jordyn. Tomorrow I will talk with Jordyn. I doubt Mack will like the idea of Jordyn coming to New York, but I need her there. He may even be able to skip out on a few of the showings and doings if she's along. Yes, I will present Jordyn's participation to him in that manner. It might just work after all.

I eat a small fruit salad and drink my tea for sleeping. I don't care whether Mack comes home or not. Putting Warrior in the pen in the studio, I go to bed. I crawl into bed and feel very relaxed, and the bed feels more comfortable than it ever has. I drift off into a wonderful deep sleep. Although it's a deep sleep, it's not dreamless.

I'm standing on an all-too-familiar cliff. The waves are violent, and the clouds overhead are dark and menacing. The lightning strike comes straight down into the rolling waters. It's as if the water follows the lightning into the sky and showers down in bright, luminous drops. It's both beautiful and evil. I stand there watching the waves crashing onto the rocks. I feel an urge to let myself fall onto the jagged rocks and into the turbulent water below. I lean into the wind, and it lifts me from the cliff. I'm floating above the water and can feel the lightning bolts surge through me. I feel it gives me the strength I need. I look below and see the waters begin to calm. I see the lightning change from frightening streaks of power into a gentle rainbow. The sun is shining through the clouds, making the sky a beautiful hazy blue. I'm at total peace and know I will survive.

I awake to the weight of Mack crawling in beside me. I feel calm and not at all angry. Turning my head, I see it's nearly four o'clock. He turns, and I'm sure he says I'm sorry. I don't answer for I'm not sure I'm awake or dreaming. Mack never apologizes for his anger. I drift back into a gentle, peaceful sleep. I know I'm on the right path and that my journey will bring me the peace I need.

When I become fully awake, I can hear Warrior whining, and I'm surprised that it's after seven. He's probably anxious to start his day. I slowly crawl from the bed, trying not to disturb Mack. I slip my robe on, and as I reach the door, he says, "Please come back to bed after you let him outside." I don't answer and leave the room. Warrior is delighted to see me, and after letting his feet hit the floor, he runs as fast as he can into the bedroom and, with a mighty flying leap, lands right in the middle of Mack's stomach. Holy shit, I run after the dog and miss grabbing him by inches before his ill-planned launch and landing. With an *ooof* and a groan, Mack sits up in bed.

"I'm so sorry, Mack, I tried to catch him, but he was just too fast."

The dog is licking Mack in the face as if he were cleaning off a child's face that has smeared food all over it. Mack starts to laugh and begins to pet the dog.

"You are really a pain in my ass," he says in a loving manner. "I guess this is one way to stop me from making love to your beautiful owner. I will just have to wait on that notion and do it when you are outside or in your pen or maybe staying at Aunt Haven's."

"What do you mean 'staying at Aunt Haven's'?"

"I thought maybe we should drop him off there a few times before we go on our trip to New York. That way he can get used to Issy and Becca and his surroundings."

"Oh, I guess that would be a good idea. He and Issy got along beautifully here, but he was in his own territory." I gently pick the mutt up and set him on the floor and tell him to be a good boy. Mack is crawling out of bed. He seems happy and not at all like he was the night before.

He heads into the bathroom and says, "I hope the coffee is made. I could really use a cup."

"I'm sure it is. It always turns on earlier."

I pour myself a cup and then remember the tea. I push the cup aside and start up the stairs to get my tea. Mack is coming out of the bedroom dressed and ready for the day.

"I don't need breakfast, and I will be going into the department right away. I have things to catch up on and to set into place before we leave. I was hoping you'd agree on an extended vacation to somewhere besides New York. Lord knows we both deserve one."

Surprised at his offer, I jump at the chance to tell him my idea. "I was thinking the same thing. But what about the case, and what about taking over the sheriff's position?"

"I decided not to take the position and keep doing what I am good at. Being a detective is what I trained for, and I love it. So I will have a while before the investigation team is finished, and I plan on spending it away from this fucking mess with my beautiful wife." He kisses me on the forehead like I'm six and bound down the stairs. Yelling into the air, he says, "I'll be leaving right away. Love you."

Completely shocked at his manner, I answer, "Love you."

I drink my tea and eat a bagel smeared with cream cheese. I feel better than I have in days. I decide to check out a few vacation sights on the internet and maybe find a nice place in the Bahamas or somewhere tropical. I'd have to call Haven later, and I want to go to the shop to talk with Jordyn too. Finding the perfect place on a lovely island in the Bahamas, I write down all the info to give to Mack when he returns home. In the meantime, I have some shopping and planning to do on my own. God, it feels good to be alive.

I take a quick dip in the pool before I go upstairs to get ready for her day. My call to Haven is a success, and Haven is actually coming to get Warrior later that day for a sleepover. So far the plan is right on track. I also make plans with Haven to go to Portsmith to buy a few new outfits. I will use some of the payment I received from Jordyn. I feel wonderfully alive and free. Free, but not quite.

Chapter 95

Jordyn is working on a display that's made up of actual rock statues. Not carved, but someone took many tiny rocks and glued them into awesome statues of people, animals, and abstract figures.

"Hi, I have a few things I'd like to discuss with you if you have the time."

"What's the matter?"

Immediately I can see the concern on Jordyn's face. "Oh, I'm sorry, I'm fine, probably better than fine. I want to discuss some business, some pleasure, and some scheming."

"Oh, I am always up to discussing all three of those things. Come and let's get a coffee or something and sit in the sunny room in the back."

We take our drinks and sit at the table in the back where the sun shines brightly and makes the place shimmer in the light.

"What's up?"

"Well, I want you to take all of the paintings I have in my studio. I want you to keep them in storage, and if anything happens to me while I am on a vacation with Mack, they are to be your property to do with whatever you want."

"Okay, but I don't quite understand."

"I plan on explaining it all to you, but you must not mention it to anyone. Not my family, not Cam, not even the statues in this place."

"Oh, Elise, should I be concerned for your well-being?" She reaches for my hand.

"No, you should be happy for me."

As the hour passes with no customers to interrupt, Elise explains her plan to Jordyn. It's a bit crazy, but in the end, Jordyn agrees.

"You know I think we can make this happen. You really are a brilliant woman."

"I sure hope it will work. You and I both know I need this to happen. It's a matter of life or death, or at least a matter of me keeping my sanity." I have tears running down my face.

We continue to plan, and when a customer enters the store, Jordyn knows everything. She's more than willing to make it happen. She wants to include Cam, but I insist that it has to be just the two of them knowing what's to happen. Jordyn confesses that she actually works for some time with an agency she's sure will be more than happy to assist. As she puts it, she has several favors that need to be repaid.

Chapter 96

Haven stops over and picks up Warrior. He seems very happy to be taking a road trip with Issy and Becca. I doubt he realizes he'll be spending the night with his friends, and I hope he will be a good boy and not give Haven any trouble. With him out of the house, it seems so quiet and almost too peaceful. I go up to my studio and begin to sort the rest of the paintings out and set them aside in stacks of the same size. Jordyn has to come get them later in the week. Haven and I are to go shopping in the morning. I no longer care what Mack will say or think about my comings and goings. He will just have to deal with it.

I know there will be more abuse before the trip to New York. I have to tell him about Jordyn coming with. Jordyn has already booked a flight for herself and made reservations to stay at the same hotel as us. I offer to pay for her way or some of the cost of the hotel, but Jordyn won't hear of it. She says she'll be making a name for herself while she's there. She's so happy to be able to this for me it's as if she has won a prize herself, and in a way, she has.

Mack comes home to find stir-fry ready and a bottle of wine chilling in the ice bucket. The table outside is set, and everything is ready for us to enjoy a lovely romantic meal. He's flying high, and this is a nice surprise for him. He walks in and finds me standing in front of the TV, listening to a special broadcast telling of the sheriff's arrest and that Mack has been taken off his leave. I turn as he puts his hands gently on my shoulders.

"I just don't like all this," I say and switch the boob tube off.

"Oh, honey, it is just beginning. You just have no idea of all the shit the sheriff has been pulling. Besides the murders he has committed." Mack pulls me back against him and starts nuzzling my neck. I shiver, not because of his kisses, but because I know he's lying through his teeth, and I don't know how to stop it all. Why didn't Ms. Hatters give me more direction?

We sit outside and enjoy our meal and wine. Mack is once again like the old Mack I had loved so long ago. It seems like a lifetime ago to me. I tell him of the resort I have found in the Bahamas. We discuss the cost and the length of time we should spend on vacation. He agrees that the island sounds perfect. I show him the pictures on the laptop as we sip more wine. He loves the idea that it's a smaller place and that there are charter boats and lovely secluded, quiet beaches and yet an active nightlife environment if you wanted to eat, dance, and well, be merry. He suggests that I book the place tomorrow and that we will fly right from New York to the Bahamas. I agree to do it first thing in the morning before Haven comes.

I then drop the bombshell that Jordyn is coming along to do all the legwork. "I suppose that is a good idea, seeing she is the one that will be handling the majority of your work," he says slowly, like he's a bit unsure of the idea.

"She will be my director, and she will be doing any setting up of future paintings for art showcases, etcetera. That is, if there really is an interest in my artwork."

"Oh, I'm sure there will be many who will be interested in your work and probably a fortune to be made."

I don't answer him. I'm just happy he accepts the fact that Jordyn is coming too. Now to tell him Haven and I are going shopping in the morning when she comes to drop off Warrior.

"Haven and I are going to Portsmith in the morning to get a few things for the trip. She will be dropping Warrior off by about ten, and we are leaving then. I'm not sure what time we will actually be home. Your mother is watching Becca." I try to sound nonchalant about the whole thing.

"I will leave the credit card for you when I leave in the morning. Try not to spend over five hundred." He's staring off into space as if he really hadn't heard what I had said. I want to laugh and tell him I could spend a lot more than that.

"Are you sure I can spend that much?"

"Yes, I'm sure. We haven't been anywhere for a long time. We can afford to spend a bit on ourselves."

All seems to be going just the way I had hoped. It all seems too unreal, and I'm sure he will throw a monkey wrench into the plans sometime along the way. The old Mack will surface. He never goes for more than a day or two before his mood swing changes and will come out in full force. This time I don't care. He can't hurt me any worse than he already has. He had beaten me, sodomized me, raped me, and verbally attacked me. He made me feel useless, dirty, dumb, and less than human. What more could he possibly do to me. I know what he's capable of doing, and that does frighten me, but I must not go there in my head. I must think only positive thoughts. I must keep moving forward. Hopefully the dreams will stay away until it's over. So far, he has agreed to everything I had planned.

Chapter 97

The evening ends with him going into the library, and I take a bath in the whirlpool tub. I refuse to turn on the television and see what's happening with the town. I just don't care. I'm now in my own world. A world I've created, and I'm going to stay in it as long as I can.

After my bath, I knock on the library door and tell him through the massive carved oak door that I'm going to bed. He mumble something, and I know he has continued to drink. He doesn't even seem to notice that I've only sipped a bit out of my glass of wine. He's too busy taking in the plans for New York and the Bahamas. I had made the tea for sleep before relaxing in the tub, and now I feel very tired and ready for a good night's sleep. I fall sound asleep before my head hits the soft down pillow. No dreams, no terrors, no fear of Mack, only a peaceful rest. I vaguely feel his body touch mine as he slides in beside me.

He tries to arouse me sexually but fails miserably. I seem truly dead to the world in a sleep he envies. He gives up after touching and rubbing me in all the places I usually respond to with an uncontrolled wanton fashion. Rolling over, he fall into a restless sleep. Waking up often in a cold sweat with an anxious feeling deep in his gut. He's afraid to close his eyes. He's afraid of what he will dream. Never having this happen to him, he now is beginning to understand my fear of dreams. He almost feels like praying.

I wake when the alarm buzzes, but it doesn't annoy me as it usually does. I feel refreshed and alive. To my surprise, Mack, instead of just shutting it off, he throws it on the floor. I want to giggle but instead just rise and go into the bathroom to relieve my over full bladder. I quickly do my morning toilet and hurry to go down to the kitchen. Mack slowly enters the kitchen rubbing his aching head. He manages to get dressed and grab his to-go cup and pour himself his coffee.

"I think I would barf up any food I tried to put into my stomach this morning. My head feels as though it is filled with a hundred little bastards all beating on my brain with hammers. I want to put my head in the freezer and just freeze what living brain cells I may have in there. I doubt I have any that are alive and actually working correctly. I have no idea when I will be home. Enjoy your shopping spree with Haven. God, I want to just die." With coffee and briefcase, he goes into the garage, and soon I hear him leave. I laugh out loud after he's gone and hum a little Irish ditty.

Drinking my tea for nausea and eating my bagel, I look up the resort in the Bahamas and begin to reserve a room for us to live in for a week. The hotel has all the amenities we need. They even have a private balcony. Having done that, I text Jordyn with the details of the place. Jordyn will be there on the same island, but not in the same hotel. Mack will never even know she's there. How exciting and fun this is going to be. I realize I can be just as sneaky and secretive as my evil husband. I hope the rest will fall into place as easily.

Haven arrives right on time with Warrior. He's very excited to see me, and he doesn't want to stay in his pen and tells me so with a lot of barking and whining. I feel bad leaving him alone, but I have things to get done.

Chapter 98

The trip to Portsmith is filled with a lot of talking, laughing, and just plain silliness. By the time we pull into the mall, I have to pee so bad I'm worried I won't make it to the mall bathrooms. My side hurts from all the laughing, and having a full bladder doesn't help.

"Wait 'til you're pregnant, then you'll know what it is to have to pee."

The mall isn't too crowded, and we are able to shop without fighting other women for the same outfit. Haven is a big help in picking out the evening dress and the casual dress. I had to have a dress for each day of the showing and clothes for the Bahamas. I spend only four hundred on the credit card Mack has given me but a ton more on the card I have from my money from Jordyn. Haven helps me pick out a couple swimsuits, some short outfits, and some sundresses. Not to mention the heels for the evening gown for the banquet. Heels for the dresses for the exhibit showings, the sandals and the flip-flops for the beach. Of course, I have to have a new jacket, a shawl, a couple sweaters, and a few light sweatshirts. I then stop and pick up new luggage for the trip. Mack will never believe I got all this for just four hundred dollars, so I think I'll just tell him that Jordyn paid me. Not the real amount, but enough to cover my shopping. Can't let him know the real amount. I'll need that money. I just hope I can get away with putting the award money into the joint savings account so I can easily get at it without him knowing.

Or maybe they'll just give me a check and I can sign it, and Jordyn can take care of it all. Yes, that is what I'll do, if possible.

We shop and have lunch and shop some more. We spend most of the time laughing and talking as though we're in our late teens. It's so much fun to have a free day and a friend to enjoy it with. I'm on top of the world when we're driving back to Flag Lake. Stopping at the root beer stand for an ice cream float is the frosting on the cake.

Haven drops me off and helps me carry in all the things I've bought. I have more than I had planned on and wonder if I really need it all. Maybe I should take some of the things back. Haven leaves and I take my things to the bedroom. I'm hanging up my new things when I hear Mack come into the kitchen. I haven't even let Warrior out yet. I'm so excited about my shopping spree. I immediately stop and run down the steps.

"Hi, I just got home a bit ago, and I haven't even let Warrior out yet," I state as I pick the squirming dog up and let him out into the backyard.

"I take it by your flushed look that your shopping trip with Haven was a success?"

"Yes, but I think I bought too much, and I should decide on what I really want and take the rest back."

"Just keep it and don't worry about it. We will be gone for a while, and we deserve some new things. Plus, I plan on going tomorrow and getting a few things myself. We need new luggage."

"I picked mine up today. I was going to get you some, but I thought you'd prefer to pick it out yourself."

"Smart thinking, I don't think I'd like them to have big colorful butterflies on them."

"Hey, how in the world do you know I bought luggage with butterflies on it? Were you following us in the mall?"

"No, I ran into Haven downtown, and the girl would not shut her mouth. I could probably tell you everything you bought and what size, if I could remember everything that spewed out of her mouth. She said you two had a splendid time and she ached from laughing so much. She was picking up carryout at the café when I saw her and stopped. I'm not too sure that was a good idea. Are my ears burned a little from her jabbering?"

"Oh, Mack, we had an absolutely wonderful time. I had forgotten what it was like to have a crazy girl's day. I'm sorry, Mack, how was your day?" I ask, going to the refrigerator and holding up an unopened beer to him.

"Yes, don't mind if I do." He reaches for the beer. I take out a decaffeinated ice tea bottle and open it. "Well, my day was a cluster fuck of questions and answers. First from the investigators and then from reporters. They all wanted to know how I figured the case out. The investigators knew how, but I provided them with a bit more insight. The reporters are like a group of hungry vultures flying around a dead corpse. Jesus, they are relentless in trying to get info out of the department.

"The investigators called a mandatory meeting of all employees so they could go over everything. The new officers were in awe of all the information that was uncovered. The older ones are still skeptical of the whole thing. I can't really blame them." He talks while he drinks his beer, and I just listen.

"Who do you report to now? There is no sheriff, does the chief deputy take over his duties until one is elected?" I ask, really not knowing the procedure.

"Yes, he will be the stand-in sheriff until an election is held or the county board appoints one. I already told them I was staying right where I am."

"Did you tell them we were going on vacation?"

"Yes, and they wanted to know if I could postpone it for a month. I told them that my wife won an art award in New York and we were going come hell or high water. I added that I hadn't been on vacation for years and I was going to take one after the awards thing."

"Ooo, how did that go over?"

"There is nothing they can really do about it."

"Do you want to come upstairs and see what I bought?"

"Sure, why not see where my hard-earned money went."

"I only spent four hundred on the card. The rest is from the money I earned at Jordyn's shop. So I kind of saved you money."

"It's nice to know you actually decided to spend your own money on this damn trip." He sits on the bed and patiently waits as I show him everything that I bought. Right down to the new underwear. "I was hoping once we get to the Bahamas you would think about not wearing underwear or anything at all most of the time." He raises his eyebrows.

"Maybe if you are a good boy, I can arrange that."

Today has been fun. I'm not sure if it's because Mack is in a good mood, or if it's because I finally have a real plan. I do feel sad for the sheriff and wish I can stop the travesty about to happen.

"Let's run to the café and get a couple of burgers. I feel as though we need a night of just relaxing. We can take Warrior and walk there. It isn't that far, and as long as we aren't going to be carrying anything, it will be a fun walk."

I want to say I'm tired of walking. "Yes, let's."

We change into more comfortable shoes and clothes and put Warrior on his leash and start out. After a couple of blocks, I realize that I'm getting my second wind and I'm happy I agreed to walk.

The café is jumping by the time we arrived. A group of teenage boys are making googly eyes at the group of teenage girls, and the girls are giggling and doing the hair flip. I think how wonderful it would be to be that innocent and young again.

"Talk about an overabundance of testosterone and hormones." I giggle just like the teenage girls, and he has to laugh out loud at my response. The girls come rushing over to pet Warrior, and the boys follow in pursuit. They all ooh and aah over the dog and ask a million dumb questions only teenage girls can dream up. The boys think the dog would be a good hunter. Finally making it to the order window, we are rid of the gaggle of teens. We order our food and find a table off to the side of the crowd.

We eat in peace and just enjoy the start of the evening, with the sky turning into a beautiful sunset.

"We need to do this more often," Mack suggests with a mouthful of burger.

"Yes, this is nice." Warrior is happy too with the occasional french fry that comes his way. After the meal, we order malts and start the walk back home.

We're only two blocks from home when a squad car pulls alongside of us.

"I'm sorry to bother you and your wife," he begins, "but the sheriff, I mean the inmate sheriff, I mean the old sheriff, has requested to speak with you, and he is making one hell of a ruckus in the cell block."

"Shit. Can't it wait until morning? Put the goofy bastard in holding away from the rest of the inmates and let him make noise. The jail staff should know the procedure. No mattress until ten tonight and only a small Bible to read, no cups, and only bag lunches until he behaves. I'll talk to him in the morning."

"Boy, he ain't gonna like being treated like a common criminal."

"Well, that is what he is, and a bad one at that."

"I don't think he is going to take any of this lying down."

Chapter 99

The rest of the evening is filled with making plans for the trips. Mack is excited to get away and to be able to go out on a charter to fish or snorkel or just lie in chairs on the deck. We go to bed together, which never happens anymore. He holds me close, and we both fall asleep in a matter of minutes. Of course, I drank tea and knew I would have a peaceful sleep. Mack hope for a good night sleep and not to have any dreams.

He wakes in a sweat and to me gently calling his name. "Mack, wake up, you are yelling in your sleep." Yelling isn't exactly correct. It's more like begging and crying in a tortured voice. Boy, is this a change in role-play. It's usually me having the nightmares and screaming, but not tonight. Mack is embarrassed by what's happening, and as soon as he's fully awake, he jumped from the bed.

"I have a stomachache. I think the burger was tainted." He rushes to the bathroom. I lie there remembering what he had said while still asleep. I try to piece it all together, but it isn't clear to me. He had said some things that just don't make sense. He was talking or begging another person to help him and yet he was telling that person to keep his mouth shut. I find it hard to believe the other person knows what I did about Mack, and I just can't wrap my head around it. Mack returns to bed and lies on his back, not saying a word. He stares at the shadows on the wall, afraid to shut his eyes. This has never happened to him before, so why is it happening now? He should be elated that his plan has worked.

Morning comes slowly for Mack. He tosses and turns the remainder of the night. He can't get comfortable and he can't get over his dream. He's a bear when the alarm goes off.

"Make damn sure the coffee is hot and strong this morning. If I'm to confront that fucking idiot right away, I need to have some caffeine in me. I didn't sleep for shit last night. How the hell you can fall asleep and be so peaceful is beyond me."

"If you remember, I don't always sleep peacefully, and I am usually the one who is screaming in the throes of a nightmare," I state, knowing he will be pissed with me for saying it.

"Yeah, well, I don't like it, and it's as if you are enjoying this."

I suppress a giggle as I go to the studio to get Warrior and make sure the coffee is hot and strong. It's always hot and too strong for me. I haven't told Mack I've been making decaf since I found out I was pregnant, and I'm not about to tell him now. It's another secret I'm enjoying.

He comes into the kitchen like a raging bull and grabs his travel mug. Fills it to the brim and slams the lid on it. Spilling coffee all over the counter. "Fuck, this is going to be a beautiful fucking day." He heads for the garage. I think, *At least he didn't kick the dog or choke me.* I sit and enjoy the decaf cup of coffee and think of just how good it will feel to be away from here.

Cleaning up the mess and after taking care of the dog, I decide to get ready and go to the shop. Jordyn and I have a lot of planning to do. I decide to walk there and slip into my comfortable Nikes and a soft short breathable cotton outfit. It promises to be a warm, sunny day. Warrior is in his pen, but his pen is pushed up against the back patio door. Leaving the door open but the screen locked. That way he will be inside but he will be able to enjoy the nice weather. I turn the air off in the house. I'll be back in plenty of time to cool the rooms down before Mack shows up. I doubt in his mood that he'd show up until late or at all. I know his moods all too well. But this morning I just don't give a rat's ass about Mack or his mood swings. I'm happy.

The walk to the shop is invigorating, and I feel even more pumped that I had been earlier in the morning. Jordyn is in the process of selling a very ugly wooden dog to an equally ugly older man. He smiles at me when I enter and continues telling Jordyn that his wife is just going to love the piece. I go behind him and make a gagging jester to Jordyn behind the man's back. Jordyn starts to laugh and turns and rings the piece up, asking if he wants it wrapped. He says no, it would be fine the way it was. After he leaves the store, we laugh until tears roll down our cheeks.

Chapter 100

We spend the rest of the morning making plans for the trip. Jordyn books a later flight from New York to the Bahamas and also reserves a room at a motel about a mile away from ours. She also shows me the body padding she has to make her look heavier than she is.

"Aren't you going to be hot in that damn thing?"

"Probably, but it will be worth it. Here is the wig I will wear, and I will have sunglasses on all the time." She flops the wig on her head, and she looks like a graying woman. With sunglasses, Elise doubts anyone will recognize her.

"I am so excited, and I pray that this works. For if it doesn't, I will be a dead woman and never leave the island. They will never find my body."

"It will work. I know it will."

We talk for a bit longer and double-check the reservations and recheck the plans to be sure it's all ready to go.

"How will you get in contact with me while we are on the island?"

"Never fear, my dear, I will get all the plans and details to you when the big guy is not anywhere around you."

"How can you be so sure?"

"Relax, Elise, this will work, and everything will turn out as we plan it. Now try to act calm and give me some credit that I know what to do. I have done something similar before."

She walks over to a customer who is eyeing herself in a gilded mirror. "It's a Louis XVI replica. It was handcrafted by a gentleman in England a few years ago. His work is the best."

"It's a bit pricey for what I planned to spend, but I do love it. I don't suppose you have something similar but less expensive that I could look at?"

"I do have a slightly smaller one in the back. It is not quite the same, but it was handcrafted by the same artist. I can get it for you if you like." Just then I come into the shop carrying the mirror from the back.

"Is this the one you were speaking of, Jordyn?"

"Yes, it is. This is my assistant, Elise, she is the artist who did the beautiful paintings on the far wall."

"I was admiring them before I found the mirror. If this was for me, I'd prefer a painting, but it is a present for my in-laws' fiftieth wedding anniversary. I thought the gold would be appropriate."

"I do have a couple of gold frames we could put on a painting if you really would like one of those." She nods at my work.

"I better stick with the mirror. My mother-in-law is a weirdo and wouldn't appreciate fine art if it bit her in the ass."

After the sale of the mirror, I decide I better head home. The plans are pretty much all made except those I'll be making with the lawyer.

I enter the house, and I'm met with a red-faced, hostile husband. "What the fuck are you thinking? Leaving the air off and the damn door open for that stupid dog you insist on having?"

"Where is he now?" I'm afraid Mack may have harmed him.

"I kicked his fucking whining ass outside, and I hope he drowns in the fucking pool."

"I thought it would be nice for him to be able to enjoy the fresh air and yet he'd be safe in the house." I back away from him. I know the slap is coming before he even raises his hand to strike me. Only this time instead of standing there and taking it, I hold up my purse, and he hits it with such force it flies out of my hand and smashes into the vase of flowers on the side table. Crashing to the floor and

316

shattering into a thousand pieces. He turns to stare at it for only a split second and then comes thundering toward me.

"Look what you did. My mother bought that for us on our first anniversary." To his surprise, I still don't back away, and I yell right back at him.

"You did that, I didn't! It was you who tried to hit me. It was you who broke it, and it will be you who will clean it up." I turn and start toward the stairs. He stands stunned for a split second and then comes charging after me. I make it to the staircase, and he reaches for my hair. I duck, and he misses. Turning as fast as I can, I kick at the inner side of his knee. Much to both of our surprise, he goes down like a ton of bricks. "No more, Mack. You will not ever touch me again. Do you understand? If you so much as think of hitting me, slapping me, choking me, I will kill you in your sleep or turn you over to the investigating team. I know a lot about you that they would love to know." Shaking, I turn and go up the stairs. Not bothering to turn around and look at him.

He lies on the floor, rubbing his knee for several minutes before getting up. He wonders what the hell I'm talking about. What do I know that the investigators would like to know? He thinks back, and he thinks hard, standing at the bottom of the stairs. He remembers how I had said the mayor was hanging. Just what do I see in those dreams, just how much do I know? He isn't sure what I really know. He would have to be very careful around me. He doubts I have the balls to kill him, but he knows I have the balls to talk to whoever would listen. He will have to change his tactics with me until Danking is prosecuted. He will have to keep his temper in check, and he will have to keep an eye on me at all times. It's probably a good thing we're going to be flying out in a week. Yes, it will be a good thing to get me away from here and play all nicey nice with me.

I'm sick again and run into the bathroom, just barely making it before I empty the contents of my stomach. I will have to make a cup of tea, but I don't want to go back downstairs. I hear the vacuum running and know he's cleaning up the vase. I never really liked the damn thing anyway, but I'm sorry it's broken. I have no plans on explaining to my mother-in-law how it broke. He can make up a story for all I give a shit. I'm done with it all.

I go into the studio and take out the bag of tea. It's going down quite fast. I will need to go back to the old voodoo woman soon to get enough to last the trip. I look for something to put a pinch of it into so I can take it downstairs to make a cup of tea. I decide to go back downstairs to face the music.

As I come down the steps, Mack is putting the vacuum away. He looks at me and says, "I think I managed to get it all out of the carpet. It was an ugly vase anyway." He smiles at me and adds, "I'm so sorry, Elise, I had a bad day at the department, and when I came home and it was hot in here, I lost it. I didn't hurt Warrior, if you are wondering. I did however put him in the backyard. Last I saw him, he was coming out of the pool. He has no problem getting out now. He has grown quite a bit. I think it would be okay to leave him out there while we are gone for a few hours. I'll get him a comfortable doghouse tomorrow."

I look at him and never say a word. My stomach is still upset, and I'm afraid if I open my mouth, puke will flow out freely. I walk past him and into the kitchen. I proceed to make my tea. While the water is getting hot, I go into the backyard to check on the dog. He is sprawled out on the grass sound asleep. I leave him there and go back in to drink my tea.

"What are you making?" he asks, watching me.

"I have a special tea to drink when my stomach is upset. It seems to help almost instantly," I say not looking at him.

"I've noticed you seem to be better since your trip to the doctor."

I almost laugh out loud. "Yes, I am." Thinking, *You mean my trip to the voodoo doctor.*

I don't talk to him for the rest of the night unless he asks me a question. It's driving him crazy and I know it. I walk away from him several times and talk to the dog as though he isn't even in the room. The dog seems to sense my mood and stays his distance from Mack. He finally gives up and goes to the library, quietly shutting the door. I go to my studio and begin to paint like a fire is in my brush. I paint until hunger forces me to stop. Not having anything in my stomach but tea since being sick, I decide I better eat for my own health and the baby's. I have no intention of cooking a meal for Mack. He can starve to death for all I care. I make a salad and a sandwich. Probably not the healthiest, but at least it's food. I even pour myself a glass of chocolate milk, thinking how I hate milk in general. I'm just about to go into the backyard when Mack enters the kitchen.

"That looks good, I think I'll make myself one too," he says, looking at my plate. Not saying a word, I go into the backyard. Warrior comes charging over to see if I will share.

Mack makes himself a sandwich and grabs a beer. Coming into the backyard, he thinks he'll try again with the apology.

"I'm sorry, Elise, do you plan to ignore me for the rest of the time we are here before we leave for New York?" He is sitting in the vacant chair next to mine. Warrior lies down between us, taking turns looking from one to the other. Not a crumb is dropped.

"No, I just want to make it clear to you that I am done with your bullshit." Getting up and calling to the dog, I go back into the house. Leaving my plate and glass in the sink, I go back up to my studio.

Chapter 101

The week seems to fly by. Jordyn and I clean out my studio of all the paintings we think is worth selling. All the others stay stacked like they have for years. Jordyn is thrilled to help me. We decide to wait on an account for the monies earned from the paintings. I feel better and happier than I have for years. My appointment with the lawyer is a success. A trip to the voodoo lady is made. With tea packed along with all the other things one needs for a double trip to two separate climates, I feel ready.

Finally the day arrives for us to fly to New York. Mack has been overly nice the past week. His actions are so fake all it does is send up many red flags. I know he's worried, and I make sure I keep alert and don't fall for his tactics. The flowers, the offers to make dinner, the early evenings would have been wonderful if they were sincere, but it's too late. I'm not about to fall for his shit. I just hold on to my plans.

Warrior is the last thing that I have to take care of. Packing everything he needs into the jeep, I head for Haven's. The dog seems to know something is up and is very vocal and restless on the short trip. Haven meets me in the driveway with Issy.

"Oh, Elise, you are radiant. You look amazing. I think I need to go on a trip, I feel like a saggy old lady next to you."

"I don't feel radiant, but I do feel better than I have in years."

The dogs immediately start to play and run around. Haven helps me unload the car, and we go in the house so I can spoil Becca for a bit.

"I can't believe my brother didn't come along to play with Becca for at least a few minutes."

"I guess he had some last-minute stuff to take care of at the department before we leave. I can't believe how fast Princess is growing. She will be a teenager before you blink an eye." I hold Becca tight. I have tears in my eyes, and I know I better get myself together before Haven thinks something is going on. After Haven assures me that Warrior will be fine, I hug Becca one last time and leave.

With everything finished, we are ready to take off for the airport. It's an exciting time in my life for many reasons. Mack packs the car and then calls his mom. They are to meet us at the airport and pick up the car. I make one last cup of tea to be sure I won't be ill on the flight. Flying has never bothered me before, but I don't want to take any chances. The drive to the airport is a blur. Walking to the gate, I wonder how Mack will act in New York. I wonder if he will keep the facade of Mr. Nice Guy, or would the real Mack emerge? Would he be the loving husband in public and the asshole he usually is in the privacy of our hotel room? Gerald and Rebecca are waiting for us at the gate. After handing over the keys and checking in, we have time for a quick cup of coffee before boarding.

"Elise, you look fantastic. Did you do something different with your hair?" Rebecca asks, giving my hand a quick squeeze.

"No, I think I'm just excited. I am so glad Jordyn will be there to answer questions because I'm sure I will be shivering in fear and tongue-tied."

"I'm sure you will do just fine. You deserve this award, and you deserve some time away from all the turmoil that has happened the last few months in Flag Lake." Mack returns from the counter in time to hear the last part of his father's statement.

"I don't think the turmoil has affected my dear Elise one bit. I, on the other hand, have been stuck right in the middle of the bucket of shit."

"Well, I'm sure you haven't been the perfect person to live with since all this has started," Mack's mother states.

"Just what the hell has she been telling you?"

"She hasn't said a damn thing, Mack. It's just been all over the news every night, and so has your face. You act like you are the only one affected by all this. It's been a strain on everyone in the family," Rebecca retorts.

"I'm sorry, Mom, I guess I am a bit touchy about the subject, and I guess I'm nervous about this trip too. I want to make a good impression standing next to my lovely wife. I want her to be proud of me," he says sheepishly.

"I'm sure the two of you will take New York like pros. The city will never be the same after you two leave. Then down to the Bahamas." Just then our flight is announced.

I have tears in my eyes as I hug Rebecca and Gerald. They are mixed tears. Tears of joy and sorrow together spill out and down my cheeks. They are mistaken for tears of happiness, and I don't correct them. To do that will just create questions I can't answer.

Once on the plane, I begin to relax. Flying first class is really a pleasure. I'm sound asleep practically before the plane takes off. I'm startled when Mack shakes me awake with a murderous glare on his face.

"What?" I ask, confused.

"You were starting to scream in your sleep. Don't tell me I will be having to put up with your fucking dreams while on vacation." I can smell the whiskey on his breath and know he has had a couple of drinks while I've been asleep.

"I'm sorry, I don't remember what the dream was about."

"Maybe you should have a drink or two before we land." He drains his glass.

"No, I think I'll just go to the bathroom and splash some water on my face."

Looking at myself in the mirror, I remember the dream, and it frightens me to the point of my knees buckling. I have to get away. I saw my own death in that dream. I was murdered, and it wasn't by Sheriff Danking.

The rest of the flight goes smoothly. There was a car and driver waiting for us when we deplane. The city of New York is a jumble of people, cars, buses, subways, and so many buildings, I wonder how anyone remembers how to get from point A to point B. I'm looking out of the windows, trying to take it all in, when I feel the sharp slap to the back of my head. Turning with fire in my eyes, I say as calmly as possible, "I warned you never to touch me again. I will not ever again put up with your abuse. Remember that, Mack, I am no longer your punching bag."

He looks at me as if seeing me for the first time in a long time. "What ya going to do, bitch, kill me in my sleep? Because you sure in hell don't have the guts to do it while I'm awake."

"Mack, I don't have to kill you, you have already done that to yourself. I just have to wait." Turning, I look out the limo's window. Mack sits there wondering just what the hell I'm up to. I know he's about to do something to be rid of me.

Chapter 102

The limo pulls up in front of a large building, and immediately a doorman opens the door for me to exit. Mack gets out on the other side of the car without assistance. The driver pops the trunk, and another man from the hotel begins taking our luggage from the trunk and placing it on a cart.

"Right this way, Mr. and Mrs. Mackenzie, your luggage will be waiting in your suite when you are finished checking in at the front desk."

Taking my hand, Mack is the perfect husband as we enter the massive lobby. After checking in, another bellhop appears. "Follow me and I will escort you to your rooms." Once again Mack takes my hand, and together we follow him into the glass elevator.

Our suite is a penthouse suite and unbelievably beautiful. After tipping the bellhop, Mack turns to me, "Holy shit, this is something else. Don't go thinking you are the queen of Sheba, because you are still a nothing from Flag Lake."

"Oh, I'm sure I will never forget where I come from. You will never let me forget it."

The phone rings just as Mack is heading for the bathroom. "I'm sure it's for you, probably your fucking boyfriend." I answer with a cheery hello that I don't feel at all. This is to be a wonderful few days, and yet I'm filled with sadness and dread.

"Hi there." Jordyn giggles. "I just got to my room, and I had a note from the gallery waiting for me. Your mother-in-law took all the guesswork out of everything for us. They know I will be handling the business part of the deal and want to meet with the two of us over cocktails at eight tonight in the Voltage lounge at the hotel."

"Wow, so soon? I thought maybe they'd wait until tomorrow."

"Nope, they are excited to meet the artist and see what else they may be able to get out of you. They really want to put the painting up for auction."

"That can't happen. I gave it to Rebecca."

"No worries, I packed two others that they can auction. If this goes as I plan it to, you will be set for a long time."

"What are you wearing tonight?" Suddenly I'm feeling apprehensive.

"Just black slacks and a blue silk blouse. I'd wear the deep blue pantsuit you bought. It's dressy but very professional."

"Okay, will you come up to the room before eight so we can all walk down together? I'd just feel more comfortable with you beside me."

"Sure, but Mack will probably protest."

"No, no, he won't."

"Who was on the phone? I heard you say something about coming up to the room first."

"It was Jordyn. Your mother notified the gallery that she is taking care of the business end of this showing. We are to meet the gallery people tonight to discuss the event in the Voltage lounge downstairs at eight. Jordyn is coming up to the room to walk down with us."

"I'm sure you'd rather I stayed out of the picture."

"Why would you think something like that?"

"Because, this is your event, and I'm just your hick husband."

"Don't be an ass, Mack, of course I want you with me."

I finish unpacking the clothes I plan on wearing for the rest of the days in New York. Thank goodness I had the foresight to pack the Bahama clothes separate. Mack does his own wardrobe and walks into the bathroom for a shower. I sit in the comfy chair and begin to read the pamphlets in the room showing all the wonderful places to check out while visiting New York. I hope we have time to experience some of the sights.

Chapter 103

The Voltage lounge is just as beautiful as the rest of the hotel. Jordyn is a blessing and seems to know immediately whom we're to meet. After the initial introductions, we're taken to a small private room to discuss the business side of the trip. Drinks are served, and I have a club soda. Mack, on the other hand, has doubles. He's pretty much silent during the conversation regarding the showing. He's surprised that Jordyn steps in and does most of the details. He's also surprised to hear that his mother refused to let the painting be auctioned off.

"I find that just stupid. I can't believe my mother would insist on holding on to the damn thing if she could make that much money."

"Well, she made it very clear the painting was not to be auctioned and had better be returned to her intact," Mr. Ride, who is the head of the showing, informs Mack.

"Let me talk to her, I'm sure I can get her to change her mind."

Jordyn shakes her head and adds, "I doubt it, Rebecca was quite adamant about keeping the painting."

"Oh, for fuck sake, you don't even know my mother," Mack slurs.

I want to crawl under the table. Mr. Ride just nods at Jordyn.

With all the details figured out regarding the showing the next day, everyone decides to get a bite to eat and call it a night. We order food and continue to talk mostly about the city and what sights to see. Mack continues to drink doubles and becomes louder with each drink. After the meal, Mr. Ride excuses himself for the evening.

"A car will be sent for you in the morning." He and Jordyn walk out together, leaving Mack and me sitting at the secluded table.

"I suppose you think you are important."

"I don't think I'm any different than I ever was." I begin to leave. Mack's hand reaches out in a flash and grabs my arm. "Let go of me, Mack, you are drunk, and I am tired. I'm going to our room, and I'm going to try and get a good night's sleep before tomorrow. I suggest you do the same."

"Oh, now you think you can tell me what the hell to do? You fucking ugly bitch. I'll come up to the room when I am done having a couple more drinks. I suggest you be ready because I plan on fucking your brains out."

"Mack, I told you that you will never treat me like your whore again, and I meant it."

"That's exactly what you are and will always be." After he lets go of my arm, I walk away without looking back.

Chapter 104

I reach our room, and when I enter, I find a bottle of wine and a dozen roses on the table. The card in the flowers reads, "So very proud of you, Love Rebecca and Gerald." I stare at the card for a long time while the tears roll silently down my cheeks like tiny rivulets of water sliding down the pane of a window on a rainy day. I smell the beautiful roses and think of how loving my in-laws are. I wish their son is a bit like his parents and sister. How and why had he become so calloused? What made him into the tyrant he is now? Had I been such a poor judge of character when I was younger and didn't see him as he really is, or was I just too in love to see it? I decide to go to bed.

I drift into a sweet slumber. The flash of lightning comes out of nowhere. I jump and I'm surprised to be knee deep in water. The clap of thunder comes with a violence not to be matched by anything man made. Something has made Mother Nature strike out with a vengeance. The warm water seems to be filled with tiny needles pricking my skin. I turn around and around, searching for a way out of the water. It seems to be endless. It has no beginning and it has no end. It's getting deeper, and the current is becoming too strong for me to stand or wade back. Wade back to where? Which way am I to go to get to safety? The needles are now sinking deeper into my flesh, causing the water to turn a dull red. The noise of the thunder vibrates through my body, taking my breath away. The lightning breaks the darkness and bounces off my wet skin, making a multitude of brilliant colors reflecting in both the water and the sky. The needles are no longer pricks to my skin but long slashes, tearing my flesh into ribbons, and they are floating away in the blood-colored water. Soon I will be standing there as a skeleton, with only eyes to see my life being taken from me. I struggle to keep my head above the surface of the raging, violent sea of my own flesh and blood. It seems fruitless to try to fight a battle I'm losing. It will all be over soon. All I need to do is relax and let my life seep away. It's far easier to let go than to try and keep struggling to stay alive.

I feel a new flutter deep inside me. A movement like no other I have ever felt. A strong desperate feeling of hope and survival. I awake in a silent room with only a dim light glowing from the foot-light next to the bathroom door. My breathing comes in deep gasps, like those breaths taken when you have swum underwater a bit too long. Coming up, trying to fill the lungs to the max with fresh sweet air. It stings as it enters me, bringing me wide wake. I feel the move-ment deep within me, and I'm surprised that it's a real feeling, not part of the dream. Placing my hand over her lower belly, I feel the hope within me move again. My eyes fill with tears, and they spill freely down the sides of my face.

"Oh, little one, for you I must live, and I must escape this hell I have put us both in. I promise I will keep you safe, and you will never feel the wrath of your father. I will do everything in my power to give you the love and protection you deserve." Lying there, I stare at the shadows running across the ceiling. I go over the plans I had made. Saying a silent prayer, I roll over and fall back to sleep. This time a dreamless sleep, a restful sleep that my body absorbs like the desert does during a gentle rain.

Chapter 105

I smell his breath before I see him standing over me. He has switched every light on in the suite and looks like a dark ogre with the bright light behind him. I don't say anything, and neither does he. He just stands there staring at me. I want to shout at him to get out but know that's what he wants. He wants a fight. He wants me to grovel at his feet. He wants this to be all about him and only him. I will not give him that satisfaction. He finally reaches down and gently runs his hand over my cheek. Still I don't move or say a word.

"You know you really are quite beautiful when you sleep. You sleep so soundly I could have easily choked the life out of you before you even knew I was here." Still I do not move or say a word. He staggers a bit as he tries to straighten up. "You may be beautiful when you sleep, but when you are awake, you are a fucking ugly bitch." I can tell my silence is making him even angrier than he had been when he entered the room.

"What do you want, Mack? I really am tired, and I don't feel like arguing with you." I sit up against the headboard.

"What do I want? I want no part of you. I don't want anything to do with your little spotlight of fame here in New York. Just for once in my life, I want to get the respect I deserve without you trying to upend the cart and pushing into what should be my limelight. That's what I want."

"If you don't want to go tomorrow or the next day, then don't go. Stay here at the hotel or go see some sights here in New York.

I'm sure you will be bored to death just standing around the gallery, watching people looking at pieces of art and talking about each piece. Take some time for yourself."

"What? And look like an asshole who doesn't support his wife? You'd like that, wouldn't you? You'd like for me to look bad in front of all those snooty fuckers that will be falling all over themselves to meet the winner of this goddamned contest. No, Elise, I will not give you the satisfaction of making me look like a country bumpkin that doesn't understand the first fucking thing about art. I will stand there all fucking day right beside you, acting the doting art lover!" he screams into the air as if he were addressing a crowd of people.

"Really, Mack, you don't have to go if it bothers you that much."

"Fuck you, Elise, just fuck you."

Falling onto a stool at the bar, he tries to get the stopper out of the bottle of expensive brandy sitting on the bar. Tipping it over, he's about to sweep the whole top of the bar clean with one swipe of his arm. Luckily, I read what's about to happen and have quickly followed behind him. Grabbing the bottle of brandy, I reach for a tumbler.

"Do you want ice or right from the bottle?" I'm holding both bottle and glass out of his reach.

"I'll drink it right from the bottle if you hand it to me." He's teetering on the edge of the stool, and I'm sure that at any second he will crash to the floor.

"Why don't we just go to bed and try to get some sleep?" He looks at the bed as if it's some faraway island that he isn't sure he can swim to. He stands and wobbles to the bed. He throws himself facedown on the bed and groans as though he's in great pain. I walk into the bathroom and gently close the door. I look at myself in the mirror and wonder what he will be like in the morning. Which Mack will I wake up to face? I come out to hear his even breathing and loud drunken snores. I look for the earplugs I had packed and place them in my ears. Rechecking the alarm, I turn the lights off in the suite and return to my side of the bed. I finally fall asleep, pretending his snoring are waves crashing against the rocks below the cliff I often stand on in my dreams.

Chapter 106

It seems only a matter of seconds, and the alarm starts its loud annoying beep. I wait for Mack to reach out and turn it off and then remember where I am and that the alarm is on my side of the bed. I turn it off, and at the same time I feel Mack's breath on my neck. He smells terrible. The stale whiskey and cigarettes turn my stomach. With the speed of the Mad Hatter, I shoot out of bed and run to the bathroom. I barely make it before I spew the contents of my stomach into it. I hear Mack swear under his breath, but I can't help it.

"What the hell is wrong with you? I sure in hell hope this isn't going to happen every time I come close to you. I wanted to make love to you on your big day. I guess that is out of the question. You aren't much of a turn-on with your head in the toilet." He gets up and is drinking out of the orange juice container. The thought of orange juice brings on another wave of nausea. I need my tea to calm my rolling stomach.

"I'm sorry." I try to stand up without being dizzy. "I guess I'm nervous about the next couple of days. I should be okay after I have a nice cup of tea and maybe a piece of toast. I'll call for room service."

"Don't bother to order anything for me. I plan on going downstairs after my shower to eat without listening to you puke up your toast and tea." He takes his clean underwear out of the drawer and goes into the bathroom and slam the door a bit too hard.

I take my special tea out and start to warm a cup of water in the microwave. I call for toast and then wonder if I will make it through the day without incident. My toast arrives in a matter of minutes, and I sit at the small table and sip my tea and try to eat my toast. Mack is actually humming when he comes out of the bathroom. Looking at my toast, he reaches out and grabs a piece and takes a huge bite.

"I feel great."

I notice he's putting on his suit and tie. He really does plan on standing next to me in the gallery. Deep down inside I wish he'd just go see the sights of the city and leave me alone.

"A car will pick us up at nine thirty. They said to be downstairs in the lobby to meet the driver."

"Don't worry about me, I'll be there with bells on." I think to myself that he's such a handsome man. Too bad his personality doesn't match his looks. He leaves shortly after he's dressed, and I sit for a few minutes, waiting for my stomach to settle down before getting ready for my big day. I giggle as I rub my belly.

"Thank you, little one, for saving me from being raped."

Chapter 107

The driver walks through the hotel's front door precisely at nine thirty. He nods to the two of us and asks if we're ready. I'm shaking with excitement, and Mack looks murderous. I pray he will not be a monster in the limo or at the gallery. I realize I'm more afraid of his actions than I am facing a gallery full of people I don't know and being the center of attention.

The ride to the gallery is short and uneventful. As we enter the gallery, we're met by the director. I'm surprised to see Jordyn already there standing off to the side, speaking with an elderly gray-haired gentleman. After a few minutes of greetings and small talk, the director leads us over to Jordyn and the gentleman.

"This is Mr. Ross Webster, he has an extensive collection of art pieces. He is looking for raw natural talent and believes he has found it in you, Elise."

"I'm not so sure of that, but I am flattered," I say, shaking hands with Mr. Webster.

"Oh, don't be so modest, you have more talent in your little finger than most artists do in their entire body. Jordyn has told me she brought a couple other paintings to be auctioned off, seeing the prize winner is not for sale. I'm very anxious to see them later today."

"Did you get a chance to convince your mother to sell the painting?" Mr. Ride turns to Mack.

"I tried, but she said if I allowed the painting to sell, she would disown me on the spot."

"Well, I guess we will just have to be content in auctioning off the other paintings." Mr. Ride has a pouty look on his face. I look at Mack and can tell he's rip-snorting mad, but I'm not sure of the reason. Is it because he isn't the center of attention or because he failed in convincing his mother to sell the painting?

"Shall we all go in and go over the events of the day?" Mr. Ride suggests. Mack takes my arm possessively.

The gallery is exquisite. The artworks on display are beyond my wildest imagination. I can't believe my piece is actually hanging somewhere in this building, much less actually taking first place in the contest. There has to be a mistake or it's a dream I would wake from at any second. We enter a large room off the pillared hallway, and it feels as if I were walking into some sacred place. The cathedral ceiling has paintings on them, the walls are covered in art pieces that look to be from all over the world. I'm truly in awe. Mack follows the men, turning his head in all directions, trying to take in the whole essence of the place. We come to the front part of the room, and there on a pedestal in the middle is a painting covered in a rich black velvet throw.

"This is your painting, and this is where you will be standing or sitting. The chairs are here because it becomes a very long day after a while. Of course, you will be escorted to the restaurant for lunch. The gallery will be closed from twelve until two, to allow everyone to have a nice lunch before returning."

Out of a doorway near where we are standing comes an elderly woman bustling over to our small group. "Oh no you don't, you old lecher," she cries, coming over to Mr. Webster and giving him kiss on the cheek. "You will not snatch up any paintings of this beautiful young artist if I can help it."

"Oh, Beatrice, calm your jets. They brought a couple of pieces, I'm thinking one for you and one for me."

"This is Beatrice Gold. She is a curator for her uncle's estate, and these two often fight over the same paintings at auctions."

"Oh, Ride, you know you love it, because it's usually here that we bicker, and it makes the sale of the piece just that much higher. Your cut in all the auctions has made you a multimillionaire, so just shut that lovely piehole of yours." One can see immediately that they are all close friends and probably closer enemies when it comes to the art world.

"Well, we better get ready, the doors open in about ten minutes."

Jordyn gives me a reassuring hug and whispers in my ear, "We are on our way."

I just nod and take hold of Mack's hand and asks, "Are you ready?"

"Yes, my dear," he answers in a voice only I will recognize as being insulting. Jordyn winks at me, and we all stand together as the doors to the gallery opens. Let the show begin! People begin filing into the place like ants at a picnic. There are several who stand beside some of the paintings hanging on the walls, obviously the artist of the painting. A couple walks up to me and extends their hands. Looking at the attire the woman is wearing, I feel frumpy and out of place. It's obvious that money is standing all around me, and I suddenly feel small.

"You must be Elise Mackenzie? I am so pleased to meet you." The woman is shaking my already shaky hand. "I'm Linda Morhead. I have a small gallery here in New York and love seeing the works of fresh new artists."

"I'm very happy to meet you, and this is my husband, Mack," I say, turning the attention to Mack.

"Oh, you lucky man. To be a part of this astounding adventure in your wife's life. It's always wonderful when you have a great support behind you. Welcome to New York."

Mack smiles his charming smile. "Yes, it is wonderful to be a support to my dear wife." I can see he's near to exploding into a million pieces. I'm afraid what the rest of the day will bring but more afraid of the night alone with him in the motel room.

The next few hours fly by. The gallery closes for lunch. Jordyn, Mack, Mr. Ride, and I all ride together in the same limo. Mack makes himself right at home and pours himself a liberal amount of bourbon into a crystal glass from the limo bar. No one else has a drink while riding the short distance to the restaurant. He downs the remains as the car pulls up to the place. Everyone pretends not to notice.

The restaurant is located in a turn of the century building with a European flair to its decor. We are led to a secluded area where the table has already been set up for us. After being seated, the waiter comes with a bottle of wine. He pours each of us a glass. I don't know how to reject it without being questioned, so I decide one small glass of wine with my meal will be okay. We have a lovely meal, and the conversation is of course all about the paintings and the auction. Mack sits seething beside me but is pleasant enough to everyone around him. He orders another bourbon for an after-dinner drink, while everyone else has something nonalcoholic. No one seems to notice how he practically chugs it like he were a college student in a drink-off. I begin to feel more and more uncomfortable with Mack's pent-up anger. Jordyn gives me a reassuring look and reaches over and squeezes my hand. Mack doesn't miss the exchange at the table, and when walking out to the limo, he leans into me, looking all the part of a loving husband, and whispers in my ear, "Maybe you aren't fucking some guy, maybe it's that bitch who seems to be everywhere in our lives." I ignore his remark and get into the limo. The first thing I notice is that the bar is closed and probably locked. I sigh in relief and look at Jordyn, who just smiles in return.

The afternoon seems to go by faster than the morning did. Several art investors stop to ask if the painting is really not being auctioned off. Jordyn takes care of most of the answers and assures them that other paintings will be at the auction later that evening. I do have to sit down a couple of times to just catch my breath. Mostly from the excitement of the day. Mack stays next to me fuming but acting the supportive husband when needed. When Annette Patrick comes walking over to check out the painting, Mack perks up like a puppy about to be adopted. She's just his type of woman. Tall, willowy, large breasts, and long jet-black hair that hangs past her waist. She has on a tight red skirt that clings to every curve from her tiny waist down. Her blouse is of a soft off-white silk buttoned down the front but open far enough down to show off the tops of her creamy breasts. Mack is practically drooling watching her walk toward us. She immediately extends her hand to Mack.

"Hello, I am Annette Patrick. I work for the European Art Institute here in New York. When I heard there was a showing here of a young, talented artist, I knew I must come check it out."

Mack looks at her with devouring eyes. "Yes, that would be my lovely wife, Elise. She is the artist in the family, I am just a detective in our small hometown."

"Oh, how exciting that must be for you, to have a job that is filled with suspense, intrigue, and danger. I would love to tag along with you for a day to see what it is truly like to be able live on the edge every day." She is still holding his hand.

"I'm sure if you really wanted to, it could be arranged, but I'm afraid you would find it not all that exciting and be bored to death." Mack makes no effort to remove his hand from hers. After a very awkward few seconds, she finally turns to me and greets me. I feel as if I somehow had interrupted a very intimate moment between a loving couple.

Annette doesn't seem too interested in the art around her, but she sure seems interested in Mack. She doesn't hold back at all and makes it quite known that she wants him. He suddenly seems in a great mood and chats and laughs with her much like lovers do. Although I feel embarrassed by their camaraderie, I also feel relief. I know if things go right, Mack will not spend much time in our hotel room. Annette may be a blessing after all.

Chapter 108

The gallery closes exactly at five. The limo is waiting to take us back to the hotel to change and rest for a bit before going to dinner. The preview of the auction is to start at eight.

Once in the room, Mack turns into his old self. Taking me by the arms, he shakes me hard. "I will not be made a laughingstock for the whole world to witness." I try pulling away from him, but he just holds me tighter.

"I don't know what you are talking about," I grind out between clenched teeth. I feel as if my head is about to snap off and roll across the plush carpet. I'm not expecting his mouth to come down on mine hard and demanding. It's a kiss of punishment, not of love. When he raises his head, he pushes me so hard I hit the edge of the bed and fall backward. Just as he's about to cover my body with his, there's a knock on the door. As he turns to look at the door, I scoot off the bed.

"Coming!"

He grabs my arm and turns me back toward him. "You lucked out this time, bitch, but I can guarantee your time is running out."

"Who is it?"

"Room service" is the voice from behind the closed door. "A package arrived for you earlier today."

Peeking out through the peephole, I can see the uniformed man standing outside the door holding a package. I open the door and sign the receipt for the package and bring it into the room, closing the door.

"What do you have there?" Mack asks with a sneer.

"I have no idea. There is no return address, but it is postmarked Portsmith." I start to open the package.

"Let me guess, a present from one of your fucking lovers," Mack states coldly. He's at the bar, pouring himself a large glass of bourbon straight up. I tear open the box and freeze. There lying in a bed of rose petals is my beloved doll Maggie Mae. "Well, what in the hell did your lover send you? You look like you've seen a ghost." Mack walks over to see what's in the box. "What the hell is that? It looks like an old doll. Is it a symbol of your love?"

I feel ill and turn to look at him. "Did you do this before we left? Why are you doing this to me?" I freely let the tears slide down my face.

"I have no idea what the hell you are talking about. Why the hell would I send an old doll to you? You are a fucking fruitcake." Mack continues to look at the doll in the box, and taking a sip of his drink, he smiles to himself. I take the box and put it in the closet. I begin to pick out an outfit for the preview. There will be a banquet the following night, so I choose a simple pantsuit to wear tonight.

I really don't care if Mack comes along tonight or not. I hurriedly give my face a fresh look and change into my clothes. Pulling my hair back into a messy bun on the lower part of my head, I place a simple jeweled clip in my hair to hold it in place. Pleased with the look, I'm ready to leave. While I'm doing my hair, Mack changes into a deep-blue dress shirt and looks like a million bucks. He has a way of looking handsome in just about anything, but blue is his dominant color. The limo arrives, and we are joined by Jordyn, who is wearing a stunning navy-blue long dress. Mr. Ride is to join us at the restaurant. This time we dine in a place on Broadway. The lights on this street from all the marques could blind a person. I can't wait to go sightseeing after this is over. I'm surprised to see Mr. Ride waiting at a large table with Beatrice, Mr. Greene, Ms. Patrick, and Mr. Webster. I hadn't realized we would be joined by the others. Of course, Annette makes sure she's seated next to Mack. She makes no bones about the fact that she finds him fascinating. She looks as if she would devour him at any time. The others seem not to notice her antics, or they choose to ignore her. I have to suppress from giggling at her ludicrous behavior. The evening turns into a lovely time. There's mostly talk of the auction and how it's going to be packed and how exciting it will be. Mack seems too lost in the front of Annette's dress to be paying much attention to the talk around the table. Having finished the meal, we all begin to leave. Mack excuses himself and says he will not be attending the preview but will be taking a taxi to the hotel. No one seems to think it odd, and they all shake his hand and hope he has a great rest of the night. As he leans in to kiss me on the ear, he says, "See you in the morning."

The ride to the gallery is filled with talk of the preview, which helps me forget that my husband is about to have sex with Annette. Once at the gallery, I'm surprised to find Annette actually there. The place is set up completely different than it had been previously that day. Most of the pieces are displayed on easels or pedestals. The group goes from display to display, bickering over who's to bid on which pieces. I can't believe the pieces on display, and I'm in awe of the talent that's gathered into one showing. When they come to my pieces, I'm astounded that I have six pieces all sitting there among the other artists' finest work. I look at Jordyn, and she responds with, "I had a few more pieces shipped in this morning. Can't have the other artists outdo you."

The bickering and the chattering about my work overwhelms me. I never in a million years would have thought my work would be discussed like it's a Rembrandt. I feel weak, giddy, excited, and suddenly ill and shaky. Jordyn takes one look at me and says, "I'm afraid all this excitement may be a bit too much for Elise. If it's all right with everyone, I will call a cab and have her taken back to the hotel."

"Oh no, the limo will take her, we will be here a bit longer and can wait for his return," Mr. Ride insists.

I was never so happy to see a hotel room in my life. Jordyn comes in and helps me get settled. She makes me a cup of tea and sits with me as I drink it. It quickly helps to settle my stomach, and I begin to get the color back in my face.

"You had me worried there for a minute." Jordyn smiles at me.

"I really thought I was going to lose it and pass out right there. I just can't believe this is happening to me."

"Well, believe it. You are going to be rich. I have an account all set up, and Mack will never be able to touch it or any sales of any of your other work. Not traceable."

"Oh, Jordyn, I have no idea what I would do without your friendship and help."

"Don't you worry about a thing, my sweet little friend, it will all turn out great. This I promise you."

Jordyn stays for a bit longer and then leaves to go back to her hotel. She advises me to get some sleep and reminds me that we're to be up and in the lobby at eight o'clock sharp tomorrow morning. I'm feeling sleepy and decide to just curl up in bed and maybe read the paper that's lying neatly on the bar. The silk sheets feel fantastic, and I can hardly finish the first article before I reach over and shut off the bedside lamp.

Chapter 109

I wake to the door being slammed and the light being switched on. The brightness brings a wave of nausea, but it's more from fear than from the pregnancy. Mack stands in the middle of the room disheveled and obviously intoxicated. I lay my head back onto the pillow and stare at him, wondering if I'm in for one of his outbursts. Would he just rant and rave, or would he try to rape me? I have made up my mind he will never do that again, but I know he can easily overpower me.

He staggers to the bed and leans over me. "I just had the best piece of ass I have ever had. Holy shit can that girl fuck. If she'd be willing to give you lessons, I would gladly pay her anything to teach you. I doubt if you could ever hold a candle to her or even learn that skill in bed. But it sure would be fun to have her show you how a real woman pleases a man." He slurs his words and belches a belch of pure bourbon. I don't answer him. Really, what would I say? He pushes himself off the bed and staggers into the bathroom and slams that door too. I turn onto my side and pretend to be asleep when he returns to bed. He isn't lying down for two seconds when the snoring begins. I peek at the clock and see it's five.

The alarm goes off at six, and I turn it off immediately. Not wanting to wake Mack until I absolutely had to. I pray he will not go to the gallery until later. It's a few minutes after seven and I'm done getting ready for the auction. I quietly call Mack's name to wake him. He rolls over and stares at me like I'm a demon from hell.

"Shit, is it that time of day?" he asks, rubbing his face with his hands. "I feel like shit. What time did I get home?" he asks still rubbing his face.

"It was just before five this morning. So you should be tired. If you don't want to go to the gallery until later, I will understand," I say, trying to sound like I'm not wishing he'd just stay there in bed.

"Oh yeah, you'd like that very much, wouldn't you? To be the star of the show, without me being there to take some of the spotlight from you. Hell, if that will ever happen. You, my dear, belong to me, and I will be there to guide you and make sure that bitch Jordyn doesn't try to grab all that beautiful money." He now isn't rubbing his face, but he's greedily rubbing his hands together. I shudder to think how pissed he will be when he finds out the truth. I hope things will be in place by then.

The limo driver is waiting when we walk out of the elevator and into the lobby. Thankfully I had downed a cup of tea before we left the room and brought a small paper cup and some more with me. I think I might pee myself with excitement, and the day hasn't even started. When we arrive at the little café, we are met by Mr. Ride. We are to have a quick breakfast and then head straight to the gallery. I'm surprised to hear that Jordyn is already at the gallery. Thank God for my friend. Also much to my surprise, Mack is the perfect gentleman and husband. I think maybe he should get laid by Annette every night and then my life wouldn't be a living hell.

The gallery is buzzing when we arrive. It's mostly staff running around, setting things up. The buyers will be allowed to do a quick walk-through with the paintings set up the way they had been last night. After that, there will be an hour break. The buyers can do whatever they like in another part of the gallery or leave. The artists that are there will be taken to a lounge to relax before the actual auction is to begin. I'm thankful for the break. Jordyn comes over to greet us and squeezes my hand for assurance.

"The way you to carry on, one would think you were lovers."

"I'm sure if we were, that would just be a turn-on for you."

Mack gives her a bloodcurdling glare and stomps off.

Chapter 110

What a maze of excitement and what a mass of cackling people. I'm sure I'm going to get lost. I notice that there are ropes up forming aisles around the paintings so no one can actually touch them. They also have uniformed guards standing at all the exits and also milling around with the crowd. The time seems to just fly past. Mack and Jordyn stand next to me most of the time. Of course, Mack will introduce himself to the attractive women in the gaggle of prospective buyers. I find it entertaining to see how he conducts himself with the mostly stodgy older crowd. It seems like only minutes before the crowd is escorted out of the room. Jordyn, Mack, and I are taken to the second floor, where we find ourselves in a most ornate lounge. There are few in the room, and no one is mingling but sitting in their own little groups. Jordyn makes me another cup of tea, while Mack pours himself a large cup of rich black coffee.

When we return to the gallery where the auction is to begin, the place is completely different than it had been just a short hour ago. We're seated in front of the rows of many cushioned chairs set up so the lighted stage area is easily seen. A podium is off to the side of the stage, and a painting covered in black velvet stands on an easel. I'm surprised when Mack actually reaches over and holds my hand. The whisper in my ear completely erases the loving gesture.

"Here we go, baby. I can see the bank account filling up just sitting here."

"I don't think the money from a sale is deposited immediately. I was told it could take weeks and even months before we see any of the money from the sales."

"Why the hell would it take more than a day or two to wire money from one fucking account to another?" he growls in my ear.

"That's just their policy."

Just then Mr. Ride steps to the podium and asks for everyone's attention. A hush goes over the crowd.

"Today we have some exceptional pieces to be auctioned off. I would like to express my appreciation to the artists that were able to attend today and also to you buyers. I have some sad news but also some great news to tell you potential buyers. First, the bad news. The painting that won our contest is not for sale." A groan is heard throughout the crowd. "However, there are six other paintings from the artist here. I think you will find them equally as fine as the *Mother and Child* painting." Everyone claps at the announcement. "Without further ado, let the bidding begin."

I'm surprised at the amount of money spent on many of the paintings. To hear "one hundred fifty thousand dollars" and "sold" is becoming almost a chant. The auction goes much faster than I think it will, but I'm relieved when it's lunchtime. I have to use the bathroom really bad and don't want to embarrass myself and have to get up in front of everyone to leave the room. The tea does a wonderful job at keeping me calm, but it seems to be traveling in a straight pipe from my mouth to my bladder. While Mr. Ride is explaining that the limo is out front waiting for us to take us to the restaurant to eat, I excuse myself and practically run to the ladies' room. Jordyn joins me and asks, "How are you holding up, little one?"

"I'm fine, except the tea went right through me today. I suppose all the excitement didn't help matters."

"It won't be long after lunch before your paintings are auctioned off. I heard what Mack said about the money. That was a great answer you gave him. He will be waiting an eternity for the funds to hit his bank account."

"I don't know how to thank you."

Chapter 111

The rest of the auction whizzes past in a blur. I'm surprised two hours have passed when my first painting is placed on the easel. It's one I had done several years ago, and I didn't think it was a wise idea to even bring it out of the closet, much less show it at an auction of this magnitude. The first words out of the auctioneer's mouth nearly knocks my socks off. Well it would have if I had been wearing any.

"We are starting this painting off with bids higher than one hundred thousand."

"Is he nuts?" I say, leaning into Jordyn.

"Nope, just sit tight."

The painting sells for a whopping two hundred and twenty-five thousand. The next three sells for right around the same amount. Then the painting of the mare and colt is brought out and placed on the easel. A low murmur of whispering can be heard throughout the gallery. The first bid is for one hundred fifty. I feel the tears swelling up in my eyes and can't stop them from spilling down my cheeks. I know my makeup is a mess already but really don't care. When the final bid is placed and the auctioneer does his "Going once, going twice and sold," I'm sobbing uncontrollably. The painting sells for three hundred and ninety-five thousand dollars. All I can think about is how I'm going to use that money.

When the auction ends, everyone stands up, and Mack gives me a rib-cracking bear hug. "Elise, we are on our way." The laughter in his voice tells me that if he could, I would never see a cent of the money my paintings have earned today.

"Yes, I believe we are."

Jordyn quietly slips away to complete the transactions of the sales. Mack doesn't even seem to notice she's gone.

"What do we do now?"

"I think we are to go to the reception area and just talk with the buyers and have champagne for a little bit."

Just then Mr. Ride and Annette come up to us. "Shall we join the others in the reception room? There are several people who want to meet you." Taking me by the arm, with no notice of the glare Mack gives him, he begins to walk out of the room. Annette takes Mack's arm and whispers in his ear, "No worries, love, I've got you."

There are not as many people in reception area as I had thought there would be. I don't know if that's a bad thing or a good thing. I'm beginning to settle down from the actual auction, and I'm happy to not be swarmed by a bunch of eager people. I'm also worried no one liked my paintings enough to come meet with me in person. That, I learn, is not the case. These people are representatives of galleries from all over the world. Only the top of the line are admitted into this tiny celebration. I'm handed a flute of champagne, and I bring it to my lips, feeling the bubbles tickle the end of my nose. I pretend to take a sip. A round of cheer goes up, and I'm saluted. I notice Mack is the only one who doesn't salute me. Instead, he downs his glass and is reaching for another off a tray held by a servant. Annette stands stoically at his side. They make a handsome pair. Jordyn joins the group and winks at me. I know that she has taken care of the financial end of the sales, and it will all be safely out of Mack's reach. This makes the rest of the afternoon fly by with ease.

Mack and Annette keep to themselves, giving Jordyn and me a chance to roam the room and talk with the representatives. I find out that Jordyn knows many on a first-name basis and is able to answer most of the questions thrown at her. The representatives are given cards with both Jordyn and my names on them, but only Jordyn's contact information is on the cards. Which is good, because I'm not sure how they will be able to contact me in the near future. All in all, it has been a very productive and lovely day. Jordyn suggests that they head back to the hotel for some rest before the banquet that night. I'm more than ready to do just that. Mack tells me he will meet me at the hotel later.

The ride to the hotel is uneventful. Jordyn says everything has been handled and that things are a go. I just sigh and close my eyes.

Chapter 112

I wake to Mack's whistling, and I'm surprised it's coming from the shower. I had fallen asleep as soon as my head hit the pillow. I can't believe it's already six, and the banquet will start in just an hour and a half. I sit up and feel better. It seems as though a huge load of rock has been lifted off my body. I can smell freedom. As I sit on the side of the bed, I rub my lower abdomen and smile to myself.

Mack is still whistling when he enters the bedroom. "I see you had a nap while I was gone."

"Yes, thank you, I did. I feel much better now. How about you, Mack, did you have a nice nap with Annette?"

"Jealous, Elise? You should be. She is fantastic in bed, and she is sweet and intelligent."

"I'm sure she is everything I am lacking."

"Why, yes, she is."

He parades around the room with just a towel wrapped around his waist. I look at him and wonder why I had fallen so hard for him. He was worse than any con man I had ever heard about. Shaking my thoughts from my head, I head for the shower. The hot water beating against my bare body feels like a million fingers giving me a much-needed massage. It feels wonderful. Maybe it's because I knew Mack will not enter the shower and force himself on me. He's fully content having had sex with someone else and letting me know I was lacking. A couple of months ago, no, a few weeks ago, I would have felt sad, mad, and ready to crawl into a hole, knowing my husband purposely had sex with another woman. Not today. I feel fantastic.

I do my makeup carefully and take extra time on my hair. I smile at myself in the mirror, satisfied with whom is reflected back at me. My deep-blue dress with silver shimmers fits me perfectly. It enhances my natural curves and makes me look like a million bucks.

"You do look beautiful, Elise. Too bad you are such a cold bitch and suck in bed. I'd be all over you."

"Why, thank you, Mack, I'll take that as an endearing compliment."

"You really are a bitch."

We enter the lobby, just as the driver is walking through the door. He nods to Mack and takes my arm and says, "Ma'am, if I may? It would be a real pleasure to escort you to the limo." Mack gives him a look that would curdle most men's blood. The driver just grins back at him and starts walking toward the hotel door. The ride is uneventful, with the exception of Mack downing a glass of bourbon. The driver opens my door and helps me from the limo. Mack is left to get out of his side of the car on his own. That burns him more than the bourbon does when it rushes down his throat, like a raging river.

Shortly after entering the banquet hall, we are met by Mr. Ride and Jordyn.

"Hello, Elise, you really look stunning. We have a table near the front, waiting for you and your husband. You will join Jordyn and a few others you already met." Mr. Ride escorts me. Jordyn giggles and takes hold of Mack's arm and begin following me and Mr. Ride to the table reserved for us.

"This is bullshit," Mack mumbles to himself. He perks right up when he sees Annette sitting at the table. Unfortunately another man is sitting next to her. As we are seated, I catch a wink between Annette and Mack. Mr. Ride introduces the gentleman next to Annette as her fiancé, James Cloud. I watch as the blood drains from my husband's face, and I snicker into my hand, trying to cover it with a cough. Mack shoots me a glare and orders a bourbon on the rocks from a waiter walking past.

What a night. There's dancing, champagne, hors d'oeuvres, and very elite art collectors in swarms. It seems that every one of them wants a painting of mine. Thank goodness Jordyn knows what she's doing and takes calling cards, numbers, and notes by the dozen and puts them in her small briefcase. Apparently, she knew that this was going to happen, and it isn't just a banquet in my honor but a springboard for my art career.

By the end of the night, Mack is pleasantly pickled, and I'm ready to fall asleep standing up. As we say good night to Mr. Ride and are escorted to the limo, Annette comes up to Mack and kisses him on the lips.

"Later, baby."

I'm shocked and appalled at her open perusal of my husband with her fiancé standing only feet away. Mack surprises her even more by saying, "No, thanks, honey, I have all that I need right here." Shit, that means he plans on taking out his frustration on me in the form of sex.

The limo ride is done in silence. No words are spoken, only the clinking of ice and the sipping of bourbon can be heard. I'm once again escorted by the driver to the door of the hotel. Mack follows behind like a sulking puppy. The doorman lets us in, and we walk to the elevator. No one is in the elevator, and as soon as the door slides close, Mack grabs me by the face.

"You are in for a night of pure pleasure." His lips crush mine as he presses me up against the wall of the elevator. I try to push him away, but it only seems to excite him even more. The bell dings, and he backs away from me as the door slides open. Another older couple steps into the elevator and says hello to us. I answer, "Hello," but Mack only grunts toward the couple. At our floor, Mack walks out without even looking at me. I nod a goodbye to the couple and follow Mack from the elevator. I dread entering our room.

Chapter 113

Mack takes his suit jacket off and throws it on the back of a chair. Making a beeline to the bar, he dumps ice into a glass and fills it to the brim with bourbon. I slip out of my shoes and head for the bathroom. I don't make it that far. Mack steps in front of me and takes me by the shoulders.

"If you hadn't just made me rich, I'd snap your fucking neck right here. Remember, Elise, I am your owner. I rule you, you do as I say, and you do whatever I want. You are little more than a pawn in my world. Now, my darling, take that god-awful dress off before I rip it off your ugly body. I am about to show you how it feels to be fucked." His face is only inches from mine, and he's smiling. A chill of terror runs down my entire body. I had vowed I would never let him control me again, but I don't know how I can possibly stop him without harming the baby. I pray for some miracle to happen to save me and my unborn child.

Just as I'm taking my dress off, the telephone rings. I jump from the sound and look at Mack, waiting for his outburst. Instead he answers the phone with a calm, steady voice.

"Hello. Yes, Mother, the whole trip has been wonderful and has turned out even better than I ever thought it could. Yes, the auction went splendidly, but it would have been a whole hell of a lot better if you would have agreed to sell that damn painting. Shit, it probably would have sold for half a million. Okay, I get it. It was a fucking present from Elise. Well, when you croak, I'm going to sell it off.

You what? You already put it in the will so Princess will get it? Isn't that just like a loving grandmother. Elise is right here." Handing the phone to me, he walks into the bathroom.

"Hi. It is so good to hear from you. Oh, this trip is honestly the most exciting thing that has ever happened to me in all my life. I have met so many people and shook more hands than a politician. I swear my teeth dried out from all the smiling I had to do. Oh, the auction was fantastic. I have never seen so many wonderful art pieces, and the buyers were so intense. The walk-through was hilarious. Listening to them bicker over who was going to bid on what piece. They seem to be the best of friends and yet the worst of enemies. Haggling over prices and paintings. They seemed territorial at times. I so enjoyed myself. Thank you so much." I hadn't realized that I hadn't let Rebecca get a word in edgewise.

"Well, honey, I am so happy you had a good time and that the auction went well. We are excited to hear all the details when you get back from your vacation. When are you leaving for the Bahamas?"

"Tomorrow in the evening. The flight leaves at seven fifteen."

"Okay, call when you are all settled in. Goodbye, dear."

I hang up the phone and have tears in my eyes. Mack comes out of the bathroom and stares at me.

"Now what the hell is wrong with you?"

"Nothing, I guess the day is just catching up to me."

"Well, you are a buzzkill. I'm going down to the hotel bar. I may be up later, but if I'm lucky, I won't see you until it's time to go sightseeing." He takes his tie off and checks his wallet and walks out the door. I sigh a sigh of relief and decide to soak in the bathroom hot tub. I need to calm down so I can get some sleep. I truly hope Mack didn't come back until the plane is about to leave. I'm exhausted and have had enough of his bullshit for one day.

I turn on the water to fill the hot tub, and after picking out a nightgown, I decide to send our dirty clothes down to be washed by the hotel. I ring the front desk and ask if someone could please pick up our clothes to be cleaned. The lady at the front desk says she'll send someone right up to get them. I pick up the clothes from the closet floor, and that's when I see my doll lying in the box. I pick it up and hug it much as I did as a little girl. "It's going to be all right," I tell the doll and decide to have it sent to Jordyn. I don't want Mack to know what I did with the doll. Let him think I threw it away. While waiting for the cleaning lady to arrive, I text Jordyn and tell her I will be sending the doll to her and ask her to please take care of it for me. It's the only thing of my past I will be taking with me. I feel it's the right thing to do.

After the clothes are picked up, I slip into the luscious bubbling bath. The hot water feels fantastic, and the water jets seem to massage my body in all the right places to help me relax. I lay my head back on the built-in pillow and close my eyes. I wonder if I can afford one of these in the bathroom. I'm sure I'd get my money's worth out of it. It's something I would have to consider doing. As I'm enjoying my bath, I daydream of my future. I can almost taste the freedom. I'm in a floating dream state when the door to the hotel room slams. I jump and call out Mack's name.

"What? Were you expecting your lover?"

"No, you just startled me, and I didn't expect you until later."

"Don't worry, I'm not staying, I just stopped to give you a message that was left for you at the front desk."

"What does it say?"

"How the fuck do I know? I didn't open it."

"Well, open it," I say as I stand and reach for a towel to dry myself off with. Instead of opening it, he comes into the bathroom and hands it to me. I immediately know who it's from. I recognize the envelope. I tear it open, and all it says is "Your Time Is Running Out." Dropping it to the floor, I walk with shaky legs to the bed and sit down. Picking the note up, Mack reads it and smiles to himself.

"What does your lover mean by this?"

"Shut up, Mack."

"Well, I'm not going to worry about you anymore. You are a big girl. Maybe you should come to the bar and find a new lover." He walks out the hotel room.

I curl up in a ball on the bed and weep. Why can't I just be free of all of this? I think, just when I'm beginning to get a grip on my life, this has to start again. First the doll and now another note. Mack has to be behind it all. I can feel it in my bones. Not bothering to put my nightgown on, I crawl under the covers. I don't even bother to shut the lights off. Instead, I cover my head with the comforter and continue to weep. Falling into a restless sleep.

Chapter 114

The cliff is so high I'm sure I can reach the dark clouds. The pebbles are sharp beneath my bare feet. The wind is cold and whips my hair away from my face. I can smell the salt from the sea below me. It's almost suffocating as it rises up from the waves that are violently crashing against the rocky cliff. I look into the dark clouds just above my head. They are a deep red. Such an odd color for clouds, I think as I reach high above my head to touch them. Even though my hands easily sweep through them, they have a feeling of fullness. They are so thick and oppressing, I know if they engulf me, I will surely suffocate. I feel the drops of rain falling on my face. As I look out to the sea, I see the deep red drops falling from the blood-filled clouds. I know they are drops of my own blood. With each drop of blood that falls from the clouds, I feel weaker and weaker. I turn away from the cliff and can see a sliver of moon peeking through the clouds. I know I have to run toward the moon. It's beckoning to me. It will be my salvation.

The stones are sharp and hurt my bare feet. Still I run toward the moon. The crescent moon seems to be smiling in the dark sky. I'm not sure if it's mocking me or pleased that I'm trying to run to it. I feel my feet being sliced by the sharp stones. Yet I continue to run away from the cliff and toward the smiling moon. The farther I run from the cliff, the smoother the path becomes. It's soft sand that I'm running in now. The tiny grains are becoming embedded in the cuts, and they stop the bleeding but make my feet sting and burn.

Still I keep running toward the moon. The raindrops lessen and at last stops completely. The sand slowly turns cool, and eventually I realize I'm running in snow. My feet doesn't sting anymore; they feel healed. I can feel my body becoming stronger with each step in the cold snow. I can see my breath as I run. I begin to feel as though I can conquer anything that tries to pull me down. I feel strong, and a sense of calm engulfs me instead of the darkness. I have reached my destination and stop my running. I wake and realize I'm lying in bed naked. Then I remember the note that had arrived. I no longer feel trapped and afraid. I know what has to be done, and I know where I have to go to find peace of mind.

I get up and put my nightgown on. I feel refreshed and decide to start packing up my things. I lay out the clothes I will wear tomorrow and take the clothes from the closet and fold them neatly in my suitcase. I think about packing for Mack, but decide no matter how I do it, it would somehow not be right. After packing the clothes and accessories I won't be using until on the island, I decide to get dressed and go down to the gift shop in the hotel. I haven't been in there yet, and it stays open twenty-four hours. I slip into a pair of jeans and a light sweatshirt, pull my hair back into a low ponytail, and leave the room.

Passing the front desk, I decide to see if the clothes are washed. If they are, I could have them delivered up to the room and pack them too. The lady behind the desk makes a call and says they will be delivered within the hour. I thank her and head for the gift shop. I pass the lounge as I walk to the shop. I'm tempted to look in but decide I don't want to see my husband doing his stuff to try to snag a late-night piece of ass. I enter the gift shop, and I'm met by a young man in his early twenties.

"May I help you find something?"

"No, I'm just browsing."

"Well, if you need help or advice on one of the pieces, please don't hesitate to ask."

"I will." I walk around the gift shop and think of Jordyn's. Many of the items on display in the shop are very similar to the ones in Jordyn's shop, only more expensive. I find a cute little china princess doll and think how it would fit Becca to a tee. I'm holding it, when I hear my name.

"Elise?"

I'm startled and nearly drop the doll. Turning, I'm surprised to see Mack standing behind me.

"I thought that was you who walked past the lounge door, but I had thought you'd be fast asleep by now."

"I did take a short nap. When I woke up I wasn't sleepy, so I decided to come down here and check out the shop. I already packed most of my clothes for tomorrow's flight, and they will be delivering our washed clothes in a little bit."

"Boy, you have been a busy beaver. What do you have there?" He takes the doll from me.

"I was just thinking of Becca and how it was so much like her."

"Let's get it for her." I'm surprised at his suggestion and even more surprised at his attitude toward me. He seems completely sober.

"It's rather pricey."

"Nonsense, it's the perfect gift for her." Taking it toward the checkout counter, he says over his shoulder, "Is there anything else that you think we should get? Like for my mother?"

"I hadn't thought about buying for her, but it would be a nice gesture of thanks to get her something."

"Okay, let's look around."

We settle on a nice crystal vase for Rebecca, a plate with a stand for Haven, and a gold necklace that they had engraved with Becca's name on it. He suggests that we ship the gifts to them instead of lugging them to the Bahamas and then back home. We pick out an appropriate card for each one and give the address to the young man behind the counter, who promises they will be shipped right away in the morning.

Much to my surprise, he comes with me back to the room. I'm afraid of what his next move will be and begin to feel the anxiety creep into my body. Once in the room, he removes his clothes and slides under the covers just as the clean clothes are delivered. I answer the door and receive the neatly pressed clothes. Turning from the door and walking to the dresser, I catch Mack's reflection in the mirror. He looks so at ease and comfortable. I almost wish I could join him and feel safe and loved like I used to when first married.

"Leave the packing until in the morning," he suggests. "Elise, I need to just feel you beside me. Please come to bed and let's just hold each other." His suggestion almost thrills me more than it scares me. I go into the bathroom and brush my teeth and put my nightgown on. When I start to climb into bed, he says, "No, Elise, come lie with me naked. I want to feel all of you next to me." I slide out of my nightgown and crawl beneath the covers. Pulling me close to him, he whispers, "That's better, I love you, Elise."

I don't answer him, but he doesn't seem to notice. He just holds me, and soon I can hear his breathing change to that of a sleeping man. I awake to the ringing of the phone. Checking the time, I can't believe it's already seven thirty on the day we are to leave on our vacation.

Chapter 115

Mack answers the phone, and I know it's Matt.

"Hey, old man, what you doing up this early? Oh yeah, you have to go to work," Mack says, laughing into the phone. "How is everything back in Flag Lake? Anything new that we need to know about? How is Becca?" I can tell that Mack is happy to be talking to Matt. After a few minutes of bullshitting, Mack hands the phone to me. "Here, Haven wants to talk to you."

"Hi, Haven. I feel like it's been forever since we last talked. I know, the time is just flying by. How is Becca? How is Warrior? I hope he hasn't been too much of a pain in the ass." After Haven has answered all my questions, I feel a stab of pure heartache and do all I can do not to break down and cry. Saying goodbye is so hard.

Mack has gone into the bathroom, so I'm able to compose myself before he walks back into the room. "That was nice of them to call this morning."

"Yes, it was really good to hear Haven's bubbly voice. I swear she can bring the brightest sunshine to any gloomy day."

"You think today is gloomy?"

"No, not at all, I just meant she is always so bubbly."

We decide to ring for room service and have a quick breakfast in our room before going on a scheduled tour of the city of New York. Weather permitting, it will include a trip to the Statue of Liberty. I'm happy to be able to down a cup of tea before the day actually gets underway. I don't want to get ill on the ferry or on a tour bus.

After a quick bite to eat, we dress in jeans and simple T-shirts and comfy shoes for the day's excursion. After finishing the packing, we call for the bellboy to come get our luggage. It will be waiting at the airport for us when we arrive later to catch our flight. At ten o'clock sharp, we enter the lobby. Mr. Ride is standing with the driver.

"I won't be tagging along today. I have a ton of things to do at the gallery. Joe here will take you to the tour guide agency and drop you off. The tour includes lunch and a light afternoon tea. After it is concluded, Joe will drive you to the airport in plenty of time to catch your flight to your vacation. I did want to thank you and also assure you that Ms. Kent has taken care of the financial end of everything, and the funds will be transferred into the designated account in a couple of weeks. It has been a real pleasure meeting you and doing business with you. I'm sure I will be seeing a lot more of you."

"The pleasure has been all mine," I reply, shaking Mr. Ride's hand. Mack sticks out his hand, and Mr. Ride shakes his hand.

"Thank you for bringing this lovely, talented young lady to New York."

"Like Elise said, the pleasure was all ours." Mr. Ride nods and turns to leave. Joe takes me by the arm and escorts me to the limo. Once again Mack is left to follow. This morning he cocks an eyebrow at me and winks. I think he never ceases to surprise me with his many moods.

The tour agency is the elite of the elite. It isn't just a brightly painted open bus, but a very plush, sophisticated open bus, with a bar and a smartly dressed young woman as a guide. I think, *Oh great, Mack will have her in the back seat, with her legs in the air before we've gone a block.* She greets us and asks our names. After checking them off the list, she takes us to our assigned seats in the upper tier. It's open, and you can see three hundred and sixty degrees. It's wonderful. Mack goes to the bar and brings back two cups of coffee. It smells delicious, and I'm eager to sip mine. It takes about fifteen minutes for the rest of the tourists to be loaded on the bus. As the bus begins to move, the guide speaks over the speaker in a natural New York accent. It just makes the experience that much more interesting.

Seeing we are not that far away from Broadway, it's the first street we conquer. It's just as spectacular in the daytime as it is in the night. The marques, the thousands of people all rushing to and fro. I wonder how they manage not to get lost on the sidewalk. It seems that no two people talk to each other as they walk. Everyone seems to be alone in their own little world and walking very fast. I'm happy I don't have to walk to work in this atmosphere every day. We stop many times while the guide explains the different theaters and shops. She also mentions where movies have been filmed and who stars in them. It's past noon when we find ourselves on Madison Avenue. I'm overwhelmed with all the glamour and glitz in the shop windows. The tour guide tells us which stores are which star's favorite place to shop. She states that many times a star can be spotted going in or coming out of the shops. As if on cue, someone shouts, "Oh, look, it's Reese Witherspoon with her daughter!" The bus nearly tips with everyone going to that side of the bus to see for themselves. Fortunately, we are seated where we can see Ms. Witherspoon and her daughter clearly. I snap a photo with my phone, and as many are calling her name, she turns and waves at the bus. It really is thrilling to be in the city. The bus pulls into a bistro parking lot, and everyone piles off the bus and into the restaurant. We are ushered into a private room. We are seated four to a table. I can tell that Mack would have rather dined without another couple at the table but doesn't make a scene.

We are coupled with newlyweds from Michigan. It turns out to be an enjoyable lunch. He's a young professor at the University of Michigan, and she's a financial consultant at the college. They have only been married for a week, and this is the first time they have been on a trip together. They are intrigued with Mack's detective stories, which makes him King on the Hill. The food is wonderful, and I'm afraid I will have to roll out of the bistro and onto the bus. I have eaten way too much. After a quick potty break, we hustle into the bus again for more of the tour.

We stop at a museum of history and are guided through a portion of the place. The guide explains it will take all day to actually cover the whole museum. Many pictures are snapped of the displays, and many sigh, wishing for more time. We also stop at a recording studio and are able to watch an actual recording for the record company. I don't recognize the name of the young singer, but many say he's a great up-and-comer. All I can remember is Adam someone. I take a picture of him so I can ask Jordyn if she knows who he is. The tour hits all the hot spots of the city, and we are allowed a short walk in Central Park. The end of the tour is the Statue of Liberty. It's so majestic that I have goose bumps just looking at it from afar. Actually, being able to go inside is breathtaking. To me, that is the highlight of the whole tour. Mack says about the same thing on the way back on the ferry. It isn't until we are once again seated on the bus that I realize how exhausted I really am. I'm almost happy that the tour is ending soon. We stop for our quick afternoon tea, and it's time to head back to the agency.

Chapter 116

Joe is patiently waiting with the limo to take us to the international airport. It feels like heaven to be in the limo, and when Mack pulls me close to him, I gladly lay my head on his shoulder and close my eyes. The ride to the airport is far too short for my way of thinking. I'm so comfortable I don't want to ever move, much less go through the lines at the airport and fly to the Bahamas. Then I remember what's going to happen, and the life seems to pump back into my weary bones.

As Joe escorts us to the proper airline and checks on our already waiting luggage, Mack puts his arm around my waist and asks, "Well, did you enjoy your visit to New York? It sounds like it may be the beginning of many visits, if the art deals start rolling in."

"Yes, I enjoyed most of it very much." I hope he knows which ones I didn't enjoy. He says nothing as we sit waiting for our flight to be called to begin boarding. Joe bows his goodbye and is gone in a flash.

"Arrogant bastard," Mack comments as he watches him disappear into the crowd. I just giggle.

Our flight is called, and the stewardess making the announcement calls for a Mr. and Mrs. Mackenzie to please report to the flight check-in desk. We are both confused as to why we would be paged. Reaching the desk, the stewardess tells us that our seats have been updated to elite first class. I ask her by whom. She says that information is not available, but we can board immediately. Mack takes me by the arm, and we walk down the corridor to the plane. We are met at the door by another stewardess and taken to our upgraded seats.

"Holy shit, this is awesome."

I sit down and start to laugh. "This truly has been an experience I will never ever forget."

"Me neither."

I have my shoes off before the door to the plane closes. The stewardess checks seat belts, and the announcements are made, and the plane is ready for takeoff.

The light dings off, and the refreshments are being served. Mack takes a bourbon, and I have a lemon water. It isn't long after takeoff when I can no longer keep my eyes open. I put my seat down and lie back. I'm sound asleep within minutes. Mack watches me sleep, thinking how much money I will be providing him. He almost laughs at how naive I am and how easy it will be to be rich and free. Patience, my dear old boy, he says to himself. He gently wakes me when it's time to eat. The food in first class is superb. It's catered in and delicious. I eat all the bourbon beef tips served over what tastes like home-made noodles. I even manage to put away the dessert of fresh strawberries over a white cake. I drink a whole glass of chocolate milk, and I don't even like milk.

Mack looks at me when I sigh and says, "Man, was that good. Maybe we should just stay on the plane and fly all over the world. What the hell has gotten into you this trip? I have never seen you eat like this in all the while I've known you."

"I guess it's all the excitement lately. It makes me extra hungry."

"You'll weigh four hundred pounds before we get home."

Feeling totally refreshed, I decide to watch a movie for the remainder of the trip. I get up and head for the toilet before starting the movie. Mack watches me leave and is once again hit with the fact that he's rich, or will be shortly. He knows he married me for a reason. He's still smiling when I return to my seat.

"You seem in a good mood," I state as I sink into the luxurious seat.

"I am," he says, taking my hand and bringing it to his lips. I'm not fooled at all by his mood. I know it's because of the money he's so sure will be in the bank account soon. I also know that his mood can switch in a blink of an eye. I'm always on alert when it comes to his many moods. I decide to enjoy the rest of the flight and not worry about what will come next.

The stewardess announces our descent. We both fasten our seat belts and prepare for the landing. The weather is a balmy eighty degrees, and the time is nearly midnight. Tomorrow's weather promises plenty of sunshine, and the thermometer may reach into the nineties. I can see the lights of the city below. My stomach does a quick flip-flop. *Oh, please stay calm, stomach,* I pray. It takes another forty-five minutes before we are actually on the ground. We are allowed to deplane ahead of the rest of the passengers and quickly find the baggage area where our luggage will be coming down the conveyor. Walking to the baggage area, I notice several stations offering transportation to the hotels. I see the name of our hotel on a flashing sign and think how convenient it is to the baggage claim area.

Our luggage is some of the first that come shooting down to the carousel. It only takes about fifteen minutes to get our bags and load them onto a cart. We immediately head to the transportation area to catch a ride to our hotel. The van used to take us smells of cigar, and I'm happy the windows are open, because I think I might add to the smell of the van by throwing up in it. The ride is nearly hour, or it seems that way. Once the driver stops in front of the place, I practically shoot out of the van. The Royal Hotel is a regal-looking place on the outside and even better once inside. The bellhop comes and takes our luggage to the check-in desk.

We tell the pretty woman behind the counter our name. She checks her computer and says, "Oh yes, by mistake, your sea shore room was doubled booked."

Mack looked at her with a look of death. "Just what the hell does that mean to us? We paid for a seaside room here, and I demand that we get one," he grinds out between clenched teeth.

"No worries, sir. We have moved you to a bungalow right on the beach. It is a lovely two-bedroom suite. No extra charge because of our error. More privacy and still all the amenities of the hotel."

"Thank you, that sounds wonderful." I'm a bit worried being out of the actual hotel building but think there's nothing I can do about it. "Will we be moved back into the hotel after our room opens up?" I hope we will.

"I doubt you will ever want to leave the bungalow, ma'am, but if you truly want to, it can be arranged."

That makes me relax a little bit.

We are loaded into a golf cart and taken a short distance from the hotel to the bungalow. The pathway is illuminated with both footlights and streetlights every few feet. We pass a thatched roof bar with several people at the bar and some at tables. I think it will be a perfect place for lovers. We reach the bungalow, and the bellhop unlocks the door and turns the lights on. I immediately understand why the desk clerk says she doubts we'd ever want to leave. It's beautiful. The decor is done in sea horses and, of all things, peacocks. It blends wonderfully with the wicker furniture and the flowing curtains covering the screened windows. The bellhop explains the bedrooms have windows that can be closed, and they are air conditioned. The main room has only screens and isn't air conditioned. After giving us a quick tour, he stands next to the door, waiting for a tip. Mack reaches into his pocket and hands him a twenty. The young man nods and leaves.

"I think I'll walk to the bar and have a nightcap."

I'm not surprised with Mack's announcement. "Enjoy, I'm going to take a shower and turn in. I'm beat from all the things we did today." He's out the door, and I doubt he even heard my last sentence.

Chapter 117

I fall into bed exhausted and don't hear another thing until the sound of the tropical birds in the morning. Mack is not in bed with me, and I wonder if he came back to the bungalow at all last night. I have to pee and crawl out of bed, checking the time. It's a little after six in the morning, and the sun is very bright in the sky. I see that Mack is sprawled out on top of the bed in the smaller bedroom. He's snoring almost louder than the birds outside. After freshening up and dressing in a short outfit, I step out on the back deck. It's several feet above the sand and faces the beach. It's breathtaking. Going back inside, I find a coffeepot on the counter and coffee sitting next to it. I decide that coffee is just what I need. I also find a covered plate of sweet rolls. I wonder how I had missed them sitting there last night. But then I didn't even unpack. I just went to the shower and then to bed. Taking a roll and my cup of coffee, I go back out on the deck. The beach is roped off farther down the beach. Apparently, the bungalows have their own private beach area from the main hotel. Just then I hear my phone ding with a message. Looking at the screen, I see it's Jordyn. Opening it, I read, "How was your first night? Mine was peaceful. I'll keep in touch. Have a good day."

I answer with "I slept like a baby" and "okay."

I'm just about to get a second cup of decaf when I hear Mack coming out onto the deck.

"Good morning, Elise." He's bending down and planting a fatherly kiss on my forehead.

"Good morning, Mack. Isn't it beautiful here?"

"Yes, do you really want to go back to the hotel if a room opens?"

"No, I love it right here."

"Good, then we agree on something."

I go for my second cup of coffee, and we sit in the morning sun, enjoying the gentle breeze coming off the ocean. The birds and the swaying palms add to the beauty of the place.

"Can we just enjoy the beach and the ocean today?" I ask him after finishing my coffee.

"I was thinking the same thing. We have five more days to go sightseeing and shopping."

"I would like to take a jaunt around the islands on one of the many cabin cruisers they are renting out of the main hotel," I plead.

"That does sound relaxing. Let's do it. How about the beach and ocean today, sightseeing and a little shopping tomorrow, and a cruise around the islands the next day, and then maybe just sit and relax here on the fourth day?"

"Sound's great, we do leave the next day, and we have a bit of time that day to do whatever is left."

I think this will be perfect.

Chapter 118

We spend much of the day walking along the beach. At noon we stop at a little food stand on the main course of the beach. We see many Americans sitting together, enjoying each other's company while vacationing. It's hard to tell if they had been friends in the States or if they met while vacationing. We order a salad. To both our delight, it's served in a melon bowl and topped with not only a bit of chicken but fresh fruit and a dressing to die for on the side. We drink a tropical concoction of fruit in a glass, blended with just the right amount of ice. It's refreshing and a thirst quencher all in one large glass. Fruit hangs along the rim of the glass. If anything, the baby is definitely getting his dose of fresh food.

Another American couple asks if they can join us at our table. The outdoor seating is full, and there are very few chairs open. The woman, a petite little blonde, smiles at Mack, and I know he'll jump at the chance to let her sit anywhere, even on him if it had to be. They had been on the same plane, but in coach. They admit they had saved up for three years to be able to come for a vacation. Mack of course takes over the conversation. He tells them of how he solved many murders and then, as if an afterthought, mentions that I'm an artist and had just won a contest held in New York City. The woman is thrilled to meet a real detective and an artist. You can just tell by looking at her she's small-town America and hasn't been farther than thirty miles out of her hometown in her life. Just Mack's type. Too bad she's very much in love with her husband. She asks, "Do you have any children?"

"No."

"We hope to in the very near future." Mack takes my hand in his.

"We have a little boy at home staying with my mother. I had him when I was a senior in high school, and it was the best mistake I have ever made." She beams ear to ear.

"How wonderful for you both."

Mack and I talk for a bit with the couple and then excuse ourselves to continue enjoying the beach. We stop at the hotel to make reservations in the main dining room for dinner that night. We also order rolls to be delivered every morning at the bungalow. As we're leaving the main entrance, an older lady accidentally bumps into Mack.

"Sorry, mister, how clumsy of me," she says in a very Italian accent.

"No problem."

I stifle a giggle as I recognize Jordyn's getup from when she had showed me at home. Mack has no clue. I feel better knowing Jordyn is nearby.

Once back at the bungalow, I decide to take a nap in a lounge chair in the shade of the rollout awning on the deck. I spread a blanket on the chair and settle in for a nice late-afternoon nap. Mack decides he would rather go to the bar and have a couple of drinks before our dinner date. It doesn't take long before I'm sound asleep. Once again I wake to my phone ringing. Checking the screen, I see it's Jordyn.

"How did you know I'd be alone?"

"I have been tailing you all afternoon. Actually, I have several disguises. and I have used two already today. Check the beach right in front of you."

There straight ahead on the beach is a beautiful long-haired woman walking a large black dog. The lady waves as she slowly strolls along the edge of the water.

"Oh, good grief, that doesn't even look like you."

"That's the idea. Now erase the call history and go back to taking your nap."

"I feel so much better knowing you are near," I admit before I hang up. I quickly erase all the call history on my phone and settle back in for another short nap.

I sleep for a good hour, and when I wake, I feel very refreshed and hungry. Mack isn't back yet, and I hope he wouldn't be too intoxicated when he does return. I hate being subject to his abuse in private or in public after he's had a few drinks. I check the time on my phone and decide to take my shower now and then Mack could have the bathroom when and if he returns. I decide to wear a skirt and loose-fitting blouse for dinner. It's brightly colored, casual, but still dressy enough for a nice leisurely dinner in the hotel. I have just stepped into the shower when I hear the door to the bungalow open. It isn't two seconds before Mack steps into the shower with me. I can smell the bourbon on his breath and the perfume on his body. The stench sickens me. He reaches for me and pulls me into his arms.

"Didn't you have enough with the girl you spent the afternoon with?"

"Listen, Elise, when I tell you, too much is never enough for me." He begins to kiss me on the neck and trails a path of hot kissing down to my nipple. There he suckles, and I'm upset that I have no control over my reaction to his manipulation. His fingers find my secret garden, and as he gently rubs and finally inserts his finger, I'm feeling sickened and excited all at the same time. He lifts me up and pushes me back against the shower wall. The thrust inside me comes hard and sudden. I tense and wrap my legs around him and let the ride begin. It doesn't take either of us long to find our release.

I feel like a traitor to myself and don't say anything when the deed is done. I mentally scold myself for my behavior with him. He begins to wash his body, and I finish with my hair, and we step out of the shower together. He says nothing to me as he wraps a towel around his waist and leaves the bathroom. I dry myself and my hair. I notice a slight bump as I dry off my stomach. My breasts seem overly sensitive as I pat them dry. I feel warm and loving inside and wonder what it will be like to hold my baby to my breast for the first time. It gives me a sense of purpose, and a new drive seems to fill me.

Chapter 119

We arrive at the hotel dining room a little early and, when we check on the reservation, are told they are running a bit behind. We are given tickets to have a free cocktail as we wait for our table. We enter the bar, and the couple we had met at the beach food stand waves at us. Not wanting a drink, I choose water with lemon, giving Mack my drink ticket. We join the young couple at their table. They are so excited to see us I feel honored.

"It's so nice to see you two again."

"We are having dinner here, but they are running behind. Isn't it just wonderful how they take care of their guests?" the young woman exclaims, taking a sip of her exotic drink with more fruit hanging off the glass than alcohol in it. We sit and listen to more of Mack's heroic deeds as a detective until I want to slap him. Soon the other couple's name is called, and they excuse themselves. Mack turns to me.

"Remember when you loved me like she does her husband?"

"Remember when you didn't screw anything that was female?"

"Remember when I didn't have to, because you were willing to let me fuck you?"

"Yes, well, times have certainly changed." Just then our name is called.

As we sit down to the table, a beautiful young dark-haired woman comes to take our drink order. I know immediately by the way she looks at Mack that she was whom he had spent his afternoon with. He openly winks at her as he tells her he'd like a bourbon on the rocks. I want to grab the metal wall art next to me and beat both of them in the head with it. I think I would've if I'm not so damn hungry.

The meal is superb. The company is lacking. We are certainly waited on to perfection. I think to myself that at least his afternoon rendezvous paid off in service for our table. After a light dessert, we walk back to the bungalow. It's a beautiful night, and it would have been a great night for lovemaking under the stars, if only we were still in love. Mack drops me off and leaves to go back to the bar. I sit on the deck just listening to the soft sound of the waves and the swish of the wind in the palm trees. Daydreaming of a life of freedom, without Mack and his abuse.

Chapter 120

I have lost all track of time and can't remember ever feeling so relaxed in all my life. When I lived with my parents, there was no relaxation allowed. My father was not one to let anyone sit idle, and my mother wore the brunt of his constant badgering to get things done his way. I realize I haven't spoken to my parents since the day after I was married. I had never felt close to them, and I don't miss them at all. I wonder if they ever think of me. I doubt my mother has time to think about anything but making my father happy. I feel a sadness sweep over me. Is it sadness for missing out on having the love of a normal family? Is it a sadness knowing I will probably never talk to them again? I think I must not think of things like that now. Now when things are finally coming together. No, I must think only of myself and my baby. I vow I will be the best parent I can be, and the baby will never want for love.

It's nearly two o'clock when I decide to go inside and go to bed. I don't expect Mack to come home soon. Even though the bar closes down at two o'clock, I know he will be with the dark-haired beauty or possibly another one. He isn't choosey; as long as she's beautiful and willing, she'd be his type. I fall into a wonderful dreamless sleep and never hear Mack stagger in. He stands next to the bed and watches me sleep. Saying out loud to himself, "You are such a stupid little bitch. You have no idea what is about to happen. All that beautiful money will be all mine, and you, my dear will be *poof*, gone." He staggers into the other bedroom and flops on the bed, laughing all to himself. Soon snoring can be heard from his room, and yet I sleep on.

I awake to another beautiful day. I'm feeling amazingly refreshed as I step out onto the deck. All the flowers are open already, and the blooms smell so sweet and fresh. I go inside to get my cup of coffee and roll. I hear Mack groan in the other room.

"Elise, can you bring me a cup of coffee? I'm not sure I can even crawl to the counter to pour myself one." He lets out a painful groan. I pour his coffee and take a roll and carry it to him. His hand is shaking when he reaches for the coffee. "Oh god no, I'll surely puke if I so much as smell that roll." He groans while sipping his coffee.

"So I take it you had fun last night with your little waitress?"

"I honestly don't know what you are talking about. I just know I drank a lot and it'll be a bit before I am well enough to go sightseeing."

"Well, I'm going to enjoy the start of the day on the deck." I turn and walk out of the bungalow with a broad smile on my face. *Serves the bastard right,* I think as I nibble my roll and sip my delicious coffee.

It's already eleven when Mack finally is ready to meet the day. He still moves at a snail's pace but isn't in a foul mood, so that's a plus. We decide to walk down to the main street and see if we can find some sort of tour or a guide to take us inland to other villages and the surrounding countryside. We are bombarded with locals trying to make a buck off the tourists by transporting them anywhere they please. We pick one that looks reputable, and his prices are very reasonable. I notice an older woman across the street, and when she nods good day, I realize it's Jordyn. How many disguises did this girl have? I wonder as I climb into the open jeep to start our adventure for the day.

We are taken to a small village just a short distance from the city. It's a beautiful place with quaint shops and small children playing everywhere. Mack suggests we eat at one of the open cafés on a street that has crushed gravel on it instead of being paved. I notice that hardly any of the streets are paved and wondered what it will be like to live here. We order a pigeon peas and rice and conch fritters, along with ice tea. The food is delicious, and as we eat, the driver explains about the quaint little village. Most of the villagers ride crude busses to work in the city. They are happy to see the tourists pour into the islands because it means they can feed their families. He explains it's a poor village, and without the tourists, many would be hungry. I'm quickly changing my mind about living in a place like this.

After finishing our lunch, we drive farther out into the country. The road becomes narrower, and the trees become thicker on both sides. I'm beginning to wonder if we are going to be kidnapped, robbed, and maybe even killed. We go around a sharp curve, and the roadside instantly transforms into field of lush tropical flowers and blossoming trees. The driver pulls into a small parking area off the road and asks if we would like to walk among the flowers and trees. I'm delighted to walk in the luscious foliage. I don't expect Mack to enjoy our jaunt among the trees and flowers, but he even holds my hand. I practically skip along the path. The driver keeps his distance to let us enjoy our time together. I think he probably figured we were in love and enjoyed each other's company. I want to laugh out loud at my thought. I come down to earth when Mack pulls me into his arms and snarls.

"You had better give me a great piece of ass when we get back. I am letting you have your little romp in the woods and flowers when I could be enjoying myself at the bar."

I look lovingly into his eyes and answer, "No, you can get your great piece of ass from some slut that you pick up in the bar. I will no longer be your whore." I pull away from him and start back the way we came.

So much for the lovely day of sightseeing. I hate him even more now than I have before. The driver is surprised when I ask to be taken back to the city. He says there's another village just a few miles off that had wonderful gift shops and trinkets. I'm about to say no when Mack says it sounds like a splendid idea. We don't speak for the remainder of the trip to the other village. Once there, I fall in love with the many outside shops and the vendors in the street. The colorful dresses hanging outside and the fresh-cut flowers being sold are breathtaking. I find myself looking at little outfits for Becca and can't resist buying a couple. I buy a scarf for myself and one for Jordyn. We spend the rest of the afternoon just walking the streets and enjoying the atmosphere. Even though we have very little to say to each other, we do enjoy the time spent in the tiny little village.

We ride back to the city in silence. I can't believe how tired I am and decide all I want to do is lie on the deck and enjoy a glass of tropical fruit punch. I'm also starving. I ask Mack if he has plans for dinner, and he says his only plan is to drink his dinner. I plan to order a chicken salad and more conch fritters. I seem to be hooked on them.

Once back in the city, the driver suggests he drives us to the hotel. We agree it will be easier, seeing we have packages to carry. He takes us right to the bungalow. Mack pays him and then tips him for bringing us to the bungalow. The man is so pleased and happy I think he's going to cry. What a shame people have to rely on assholes like Mack to feed their families.

Mack never says a word to me when we get back. He changes his clothes and leaves faster than he moved all day. I order my salad and change into my swimsuit and decide to walk on the beach until it's time for my salad to be delivered. I stroll along the lonely beach, just enjoying the solitude. I watch as a couple comes toward me. I immediately recognize the woman as Jordyn but have no idea who the handsome gentleman with her is.

Jordyn stops in front of me and says, "Hello, senora."

I nod and answer, "Hello, senorita."

Chapter 121

Jordyn giggles as she introduces me to her companion. "This is Senor Marino. He and his brother have agreed to be at your service when you go on your exertion tomorrow."

"Oh, and just what will he be going on during our outing on the boat?"

"Senor Marino's brother, Marco, will be piloting the boat. Gorgio here will be with him but out of sight. When the time is right and everything is perfect, you and Gorgio will quietly slip into the sea."

"But how will we manage to get back to shore without being noticed? I'm afraid I will be recognized when I get back to land."

"No worries, Elise, you will be taken to a remote part of the island and change into your disguise. Believe me, no one will recognize the young woman. Everything is in place. You will be off the island within the hour after you are discovered missing. Have faith, Elise, it is all arranged."

"I'm so afraid he will find out, and he will kill me for sure."

"It is all in place. You will be gone, and he will never find you, and he will never get a penny of your money. My lawyers have arranged everything. You will be free of him for good."

"How will I ever thank you?"

"We better be on our way."

"Yes, I have a salad coming, and I'm famished."

I arrive back at the bungalow just as my salad does. I'm so hungry I don't think the salad will come close to filling me up. I devour it, and I'm amazed that I feel full. I make myself a cup of my special tea and settle down on the deck to just enjoy the rest of my evening and night. I realize I can honestly live like this for the rest of my life. I doubt I will ever get bored. Thank goodness for the tea, for once I'm settled on the deck, I start to worry about tomorrow. "What ifs" arise all around me. What if he finds out about my plan? What if I can't go through with it? What if I don't make it to the airport? What if I'm recognized? I begin to feel panicky and drink my tea in one gulp instead of enjoying it. It seems like forever before I start to calm down and feel drowsy. I try to think of a new life and how much love I will have for my baby. I decide I don't want to know the sex of the baby. I want it to be a surprise, just like the unplanned pregnancy had been. I finally feel calm and at ease and know I'm ready for my new adventure.

I have been out on the deck for three hours, and it's after nine when I finally go back inside. I take a quick shower and climb into bed, hoping for a peaceful night. Praying Mack will not come back drunk and in a foul mood. The tea does its job on me, and I fall into a dreamless sleep. I awake to Mack crawling in beside me. I don't move a muscle and try to keep my breathing steady.

"I know you are awake, Elise. No need to pretend. I have no desire to touch your ugly body. In fact, I don't think I ever want to touch you again. You disgust me just as much as I disgust you. I'm seriously thinking of a separation once we get back home."

I don't answer him but think, *Oh, we will be separating all right.* I soon hear his breathing ease into a rhythm of slumber. I feel a deep feeling of relief sweep over me just as I fall asleep next to my husband for the last time.

Chapter 122

I awake to the sounds of the birds singing and the toilet flushing. I roll onto my back as Mack comes strolling out of the bathroom scratching his crotch. Not exactly what I'm hoping to wake up to, but then I will never have to see his display of crude behavior again in the morning. The thought of freedom gives me a feeling of euphoria.

"What time is our little outing on the bay?"

"We are to be there at one sharp." I slowly drag myself out of bed. "Why? You haven't changed your mind, have you?" I'm praying he will stick to the plan.

"No, I just wondered how long we had before we are going out to sea. It's early, and I don't feel like doing anything. I was hoping to just sit and relax and enjoy the morning on the deck." He pours himself a cup of coffee. "Want a cup of coffee?"

"Sure, just let me freshen up, and I will be right out." I'm thankful he's in a good mood and even more thankful that I'm not experiencing any morning sickness. I will be sure to drink my tea before going on the outing today. I don't need to throw up while trying to breath underwater. If that's even possible.

We spend an uneventful morning sitting on the deck and enjoying the view of the bay. It really is a sight to behold. We speak briefly about what we need to do as soon as we return home. I say I miss everyone so much and especially Warrior. Mack agrees he can't wait to see Becca and even his mother. I'm surprised that he misses his mother. I didn't think he had feelings for anyone but himself and maybe Becca.

Soon it's time for us to leave for the dock. I put my one-piece on and cover it with a short pullover beach dress. He takes my hand as we step out of the cab that had taken us to the dock. As we approach the many cabin cruisers along the dock, I see the one that's to take us for our adventure. Mr. Marino approaches us and guides us to his lovely cabin cruiser. As we board, he says there are complimentary drinks and a small tray of brownies and appetizers on the table beside the cushy seats on the main deck. He shows us where the bathroom facility is and winks as he says there's a nice bed behind the curtain under the deck where he will be piloting the boat. He shows us where the life jackets are laid out for our convenience and safety. He also shows us the small inflatable raft in case of an emergency. We will be going close to the coastline until they round a small peninsula. There they will venture farther out to sea. Many dolphins can be spotted in that area, and it promises to be secluded for us to enjoy ourselves without prying eyes.

I look for his brother but see no sign of him. I choose a seat and open a bottle of water. Mack sits in the opposite seat and opens a bottle of beer. We head out to sea. Keeping to his word, we stay within sight of the coastline. You can easily see the busy activities that take place on a daily basis in the small villages that line the coast. After about an hour of skirting the coast, we head around the peninsula Senor Marino had mentioned earlier and head out to sea. It's absolutely breathtaking. I'm feeling both relaxed and anxious at the same time. I laugh out loud at that thought. How can one feel relaxed and anxious? I'm surely losing it. Mack seems to be lost in his own world too. I wonder at his thoughts.

He looks at me, and I think, *I wonder if the guy at the dock is ready for this.* He smiles to himself and then eats a brownie.

"Damn, Elise, these are great. You should have one." He gobbles down a second one.

"No, I'm really full from the sandwich and tea I had before we left the bungalow." I'm looking out to sea. "Look, there is a school of dolphins swimming straight for us."

Mack stands up and yells for Senor Marino to cut the motor. Senior Marino nods and cut the engines. The dolphins swim so close to the cabin cruiser. I fear one will accidently leap into the boat. They are marvelous to observe. They seem to be putting on a show just for us. Both Mack and I laugh at their silly antics in the great sea.

Suddenly Mack swears. "Damn it, I have got one hell of a stomachache. I guess I shouldn't have mixed beer with the brownies. I feel as though I am about to shit my pants. Oh my god." He cries as he runs down below to the windowless bathroom.

I look at Senor Marino, and he nods. His brother appears next to him. He quickly descends the stairs and takes me by the hand. We quickly walk to the back of the cruiser, and he steps over the edge and onto the rung of a ladder. He goes down a couple of steps and reaches for my hand, and I follow him into the sea. I hold my breath as he guides me under the hull of the boat. I'm able to see where we are as the water is quite clear. I see two scuba tanks attached to the underside of the hull. He quickly turns on the oxygen, and I know what to do next. I'm thankful I had taken scuba lessons years before while in college. After we both are breathing from the tanks, he helps me strap mine on. He fixes his and takes a spear gun that's attached to the boat. Taking my hand and motions for me to follow him.

I have to keep telling myself to breathe evenly. I'm so afraid Mack will come up and discover me missing before we can get far enough away from the cruiser that he won't see us or our air bubbles. We seem to swim for hours, but I realize my fear of being spotted is warping my sense of direction and time. Finally we surface, and I see we are headed toward a remote part of the island. I scan the sea and see no sign of the boat. Giorgio takes his mouthpiece out of his mouth and in perfect English says, "No need to worry, they are just on the other side of that piece of rock jutting out from the mainland."

I remove my mouthpiece and struggle to get my footing as we begin to wade toward the rocky beach. I'm chilled to the bone, but I'm not sure if it's from the swim in the cool water or the excitement that's engulfing me. We manage to crawl between several larger boulders and come to a very secluded part of the beach. It's covered in boulders, where anyone can easily hide. I begin to wonder if the Marino brothers can be trusted.

Giorgio seems to read my mind and says, "You can trust us. Ms. Jordyn has hired us, and we will do our job most efficiently."

"Thank you."

We walk for about a quarter mile when the terrain changes and becomes wooded. I'm so busy following and watching my step that I don't notice the trees until I'm amid them. He drops the tanks he has been carrying and says we will wait there until Jordyn comes for us. He tells me to sit on the tanks and try to catch my breath. We aren't there but a minute when I hear a vehicle in the distance. I jump up and immediately look for a place to hide. Giorgio laughs and touches my shoulder.

"It is your friend, little one." He picks up the tanks and starts to walk over a rise in the leafy undergrowth. Just beyond the ridge is a small dirt road. On the road is a covered jeep. Jordyn leaps from the driver's side and runs to give me a hug.

"Come, we must hurry if we are to get you to the airport in time."

I follow Jordyn into the back seat of the jeep, while Giorgio climbs into the driver's seat. We are moving before I have a chance to take a second breath.

Jordyn hands me a padded belly belt. "Well, you are pregnant, not just this pregnant, that's all." I strap it onto my belly.

"Won't it show up as I go through security at the airport?"

"Nope, it will go through the scanner just fine. I tried it out on the way down here."

I slip the maternity top on and the pants Jordyn is holding for me. Strapping on the sandals, I'm set in the clothes area.

"You look fantastically pregnant. Now for the rest of your disguise. Here, let's put some makeup on. Let me put some color on your cheeks and some contour. Can't have you not look the part of a pregnant Latino."

"I have blue eyes, Jordyn."

"Yes, but the contacts I had you try on at my shop will take care of that."

"What, you honestly have contacts? What if they irritate my eyes?"

"You will have to keep blowing your nose and bear with it until you arrive where you are going. Makeup is done, now put your sassy wig on. Here's your hat."

After the final touches are added, I look in the hand mirror Jordyn hands me and can't believe it's really me. The contacts are dark brown to match my hair. They aren't too bad, and I hope I can stand them. We're arriving at the airport already, and I begin to feel ill. It's as if Jordyn can read my mind.

"Here, drink this down. It will stop the jitters you are having."

Giorgio pulls up in front of Gate 12 and stops. Jordyn gets out of the jeep and helps me out. She goes to the back of the jeep and takes out a single suitcase and an over-the-shoulder purse. Handing it to me, she says, "Everything you need is in the suitcase and in the purse. You are now Elizabeth 'Lizzie' Martins. After checking in, be sure to read everything." With that, Jordyn gives me a quick hug. "I will be in touch. Oh, by the way, you will be landing in Milwaukee, Wisconsin, there will be a plane change, and from there you will be flying into a tiny airport in North Central Wisconsin. You will have a car waiting for you."

To anyone watching us, it looks like two sisters saying their goodbyes.

Chapter 123

Mack has been in the bathroom for a good half hour. His legs have fallen asleep sitting on the toilet. They feel like rubber, and he isn't sure he can walk up the staircase to the main deck. When he reaches the fresh air, he looks around for Elise. She's nowhere to be found. He goes back down the stairs and checks behind the curtain to see if maybe she has decided to wait for him in the bed. Not finding her there, he rushes back to the main deck. He spots the dress she had been wearing in the seat she had occupied before he had to use the toilet. He yells to Marco and sees that the man is sound to sleep.

"Where the hell is my wife?" he growls out to him.

"Is she not with you?"

"Does she look like she is with me?"

"I thought she joined you in the bed, senor. I did not want to disturb your lovemaking, so I took a siesta."

"Did she tell you she was going to join me? Did she say anything to you about swimming? Did you even see her at all?"

"No, senor, I was reading a couple of the charts, and when I turned back to the main deck, no one was there. I assumed you both went below," he says with a worried look on his face. Mack scans the water around the cruiser. He calls her name. He yells into the wind in vain.

"Call the local police and tell them to get their asses out here with scuba gear and start looking for my wife."

Marco can be heard talking in Spanish to the coastal police and sounds as though he's about to have a panic attack. Mack paces the boat until he thinks he would wear a hole in the damn thing.

It seems to take hours for the coastal police to arrive. They immediately come aboard and begin to ask both Marco and Mack a million questions. Mack is very frustrated with their technique and begins to tell them how to do their jobs. That does not go over very well with the captain of the police.

"I don't care if you are a detective in the States. Please answer our questions and let us do our jobs."

"Just do your goddamn job then. Find my wife."

After answering all the normal questions—When was the last time you saw her? What were you doing together last? Did she get ill too? How long were you below?—and asking Marco much the same questions, the captain instructs the divers to begin searching for clues in the water.

"Did your wife have any suicidal tendencies? How was your marriage relationship?"

"Our marriage was just fine, and she was nuts, but I doubt she committed suicide!" Mack screams at the captain. The divers begin their search. Coming up periodically to report that there's no sign of Elise's body.

Chapter 124

I enter the airport, without looking back. When I checked my bags, the woman had asked when the baby was due. I wasn't expecting the question, and I hesitate before saying two months. I had sat alone after that, waiting for my flight to be called. I carefully sit with my back to a wall and take out the envelope with the papers I need to become Elizabeth Martins. I'm headed to Milwaukee. I have never been west of the Ohio River so I'm excited and scared to death. I study the paperwork and return it to the envelope. Keeping my new passport out, I look at the picture, and it depicts me with long hair instead of the sassy cut I have now. I don't remember having the picture taken. I hadn't. Jordyn had doctored it with one taken from the gallery. Damn, she's good. I think Jordyn will make a great thief or fine arts or a CIA agent. Hell, maybe she is.

My flight is called, and I follow the crowd boarding the plane. I give my ticket to the stewardess, and she tears the boarding pass off and hands it back to me. I find my window seat halfway down the plane and sit and stare out the window at the airport workers getting the plane ready for takeoff. Shortly after the safety announcements begin and the plane begins to taxi onto the runway, I hold her breath until the plane is actually in the air. As I stare out the window, I'm shocked to see we're flying directly over the cruiser I had just escaped from. It has two coastal police boats next to it. I can almost make out Mack, or at least I think I do. I'm suddenly ill and reach for the bag in the pocket of the seat in front of me. Thankfully, no one is seated next to me. A stewardess comes to aid me, and I'm given Sprite to help settle my stomach and asked if I want anything else. I remember my tea and ask the flight attendant for a cup of hot water. Once I down the tea, I begin to relax, and my stomach feels almost normal for the remainder of the flight.

I try to watch a movie but end up feeling very tired, so I recline my seat and soon fall into a dreamless sleep. When I awake, I found it hard to believe that in just two more hours, I'd be landing in Milwaukee. The temperature there is sixty degrees, and the skies would be cloud covered. Sitting upright for the remainder of the flight, I once again go over the paperwork in the envelope. I'm nervous and scared to death. How on earth did I think I could actually live on my own and take care of a baby? I feel like crying and know I have to get myself together before the plane actually lands. Trying to think positive, I think of how good it will feel to be free. By the time the plane is descending, I feel much better. Scared but better.

Chapter 125

Finally the search is called off, and the captain orders Marco to return to dock. It's then he tells Mack that he will be coming with them to the police station for more questioning. Mack wants to kill them all.

The cruiser is taken into custody along with Marco and Mack. The boat will be processed for fingerprints and blood or any other evidence that may have been left behind. Marco will be questioned separately from Mack. The captain doubts that the pilot had done any wrongdoings as he had known him for years and had even used his cruiser for luncheons with other police departments in the area. As for Mack, the captain feels he's lying through his teeth and can't wait to get him into an interrogation room. He may be a bigshot detective back home, but here he is a murder suspect.

The boat is processed thoroughly, and nothing is found to be out of place or unusual. The brownies are analyzed and found to be just that, brownies. The beer is also tested and is found to be untainted. There's no evidence that anything had been tampered with. Marco is questioned and is even given a lie detector test. He passes with flying colors. He had not seen Elise after he had cut the motor. He had no idea what may have become of her. He had kept his eyes on the maps and charts as his brother slipped into the water with Elise. Therefore, not knowing a thing.

Mack refuses to take the lie detector test, which makes him look even more suspicious. The police captain holds him in the holding cell for two days while the tests are being run. He thinks maybe Mack will be more willing to cooperate after he spends a few nights with some of the local drunks and thieves that are arrested on a nightly basis. Mack is spitting bullets by the third morning and threatens to take the whole department down. It does nothing but make the police even more suspicious of him. When he's brought out of the cell, he smells of stale beer, sweat, and feces. The captain smiles to himself when he walks into the small room with the cameras and recorders in every corner to record every move and sound that takes place in the room. Mack immediately lawyers up and asks for a phone call.

"You can hire a lawyer from here or fly one in, but you will still be questioned, without a lawyer present. That is how we do things here." The captain pulls out a chair for himself. Mack stands in front of the table with his hands handcuffed behind his back.

"I have nothing to say to you. I want to call my lawyer in the States *now*!" he screams.

"No need to raise your voice. You will get your phone call in due time. Now, I'd like for you to sit down and start at the beginning."

"Fuck you, I will not answer another one of your fucking questions until my lawyer is here."

"Suit yourself." The captain gets up and starts to leave.

"My phone call?"

"Ah, yes, all in due time."

"You can't hold me here. I've done nothing. My wife has disappeared, and you are treating me like a criminal. I demand to be released."

"You will be released when I believe you had nothing to do with her disappearance. You will get your two-minute phone call after lunch." The captain leaves the room, leaving Mack in the custody of another officer. Mack turns to the officer and growls like a wild dog at him.

"Fuckers, I'll have all of you fired by the time I'm through with you." His threats are wasted on deaf ears.

After a lunch of flour tortillas and something that resembles fried beans, Mack is allowed his two-minute call. He is advised ahead of time that after exactly two minutes, he will be cut off. He places the call to his lawyer and quickly explains the situation and tells him to notify his brother-in-law immediately of the details. He's then taken to an individual cell. It's at least clean, and he's told he will be allowed to shower in a few hours. Mack doesn't want to sit on the bunk as he feels filthy, and so he huddles on the floor in the corner of the cell. He never realized how desolate a suspect could feel until that moment. He almost feels sorry for some of the ones he had arrested. The key word is *almost*.

Chapter 126

Mack think of what's really happening to him. He had had a plan all along to do away with Elise. He was sure all the phone calls, notes, and packages would drive her over the edge. All he had to do was have the papers drawn up that she was incompetent, and all that money would have been his. He was sure she was close to cracking. Just a couple more months and it would all be his. This, however, turns out better than he had thought. The bitch had truly done him a favor. He begins to laugh all alone in his cell. He quickly composes himself, thinking of the cameras and how it would look if he's happy about his poor little wife being lost at sea. Now he hopes they never find her body. He just wonders what the hell really did happen to her. He hopes she was eaten by a shark. It would serve the ugly bitch right to be torn apart piece by piece. He would have paid good money to see it. He chuckles to himself, thinking of all the money he will now have, thanks to his dead wife.

He lies on his lonely bunk and falls into a sweet dreamless sleep. The guard who walks past his cell to check on him thinks how Mack has a youthful look about him. He seems to be in a sweet slumber without a care in the world. Not at all like a man who has just lost his wife in the bay. The guard doesn't like Americans, and this one makes his skin crawl. He feels an evil aura dwelling in the cell. He hurries his step to get away from him. He will go to his priestess and have her say a cleansing prayer over him when he's off duty. He wants nothing to do with the prisoner. The more he had to be in contact with him made him feel he would also be in grave danger. Shaking the evil feeling that has overcome him, the guard leaves the room. He's thankful he doesn't have to bring him any more meals.

Mack is suspicious when the police officer comes to his cell and opens the door.

"You are free to go," he says sadly.

"What? Did you find my wife? Is she all right?" Mack is afraid of the answer.

"No, her body is still missing, and we are assuming she is lost to the ocean for forever." The police officer leads the way to the central booking area.

"You are just going to quit looking for her? How can you just give up after only a day of searching? How can you be sure she has been lost to the ocean? I don't understand how you can be so sure she will never be found?" Mack continues to follow the policeman, still asking him questions. "What am I supposed to do now? I can't just go home and not know what happened to my wife!"

"Sir, we have done our investigation. You are free to hire investigators to continue to search for your wife, but we have no reason to believe she will be found dead or alive. The ocean tides have already gone out, and her body or body pieces could be halfway to Europe by now. There is no sign that she ever reached the shore anywhere along the coastline, and nothing of her remains have shown up anywhere. As far as we are concerned, she is dead and gone out to sea."

Mack thinks the officer is an asshole and is about to tell him that when he hears Matt's voice. "Mack, Mack, are you all right? Man, I can't believe this has happened."

"Oh my god, Matt, am I ever happy to see you." Matt gives Mack a quick hug and a pat on the back.

"Your lawyer called me, and I jumped on the next available flight. Jesus, man, did they actually think you may have had something to do with her disappearance?"

"I guess they did as they interrogated me and kept me here."

"What are they going to do now?" Matt asks as he watches Mack get his personal items back.

"They are doing nothing. They say their investigations are done, and they are convinced that she is dead and gone."

"It's only been a day of searching, and they are convinced she's dead?"

"Yup, that's what this asshole told me just before we entered this room."

"Watch your mouth, Mr. MacKenzie, I can arrest you for disorderly conduct."

"My apologies, I'm just shocked that you have stopped the search. Am I free to get out of here?"

"Yes, the door is open to you. Good luck on your search for your wife. I can give you names of a few local investigators if you'd like."

"No, thank you, I will find my own people to search for my wife."

Chapter 127

"Did you tell my parents?" Mack hails a cab.

"Yes, they are devastated, and Haven hasn't stopped crying since she heard of the accident. I did call Elise's parents. They acted as if they could care less whether she was alive or dead."

"They didn't really like each other much, and I doubt they are concerned unless they will get some money from her death."

They arrive at the bungalow, and Mack pays the cab.

"Holy shit, this is awesome. I could learn to love living here." Matt casually walks through the rooms and onto the deck overlooking the bay.

"Yeah, and I found a couple of hot willing senoritas at the bar. It was a great getaway. Elise really got away." Mack chuckles at his last statement. Matt looks at him and busts out laughing.

They decide to grab a bite to eat and then call the folks back home.

"I don't think I will tell them that nothing was found of her."

"What are you going to tell them? You know they will be upset if they think we didn't do everything possible to find her."

"I have a plan. We will buy a coffin, fill it with weights, and ship it home. We will tell them that it will have to be a closed casket because she was badly banged up when she was washed ashore on the rocks. They don't have to know she was never found, and they sure in hell will take my word that it is her in the coffin."

"Sounds like it just may work."

"Plus I have her wedding set, because she took it off when we went out on the cruise. She didn't want to lose it. I will say I took it off of her finger and was hoping to make it into a necklace for Becca, in remembrance of her loving aunt."

"Shit, that will make Haven happy and your mother."

"Okay, that's what we will do."

They go back to the bungalow for a quiet place to call home.

"Hello," Rebecca answers in a very shaky voice.

"Mom, it's me."

"Oh, Mack, is there any good news?"

"No, I'm afraid they found her body washed up on shore this morning a few miles down the beach. I had to go in and identify her. Oh, Mom, it was horrible." Mack sobs into the phone. "Her body was badly bruised and cut from scraping against the rocks. I could hardly look at her. It's something I will never forget."

"Oh, honey, how terrible for you. What will happen now? Do the authorities have to do an autopsy or whatever they do?"

"No, they are satisfied that she drowned. I will be shipping her body home in the morning. Matt and I will be returning with it. I just feel so lost and empty. I can't believe this has happened. Things like this happen to other people, not to me. Thank God Matt is here to help me."

"Let us know what time your flight will be in and Dad and I will meet you at the airport. Shall I call the funeral director and have him there too?"

"Yes, if you could please do that for me. God, I just don't know where to begin. Has anyone contacted Jordyn? There will be the new accounts and everything to go through." Mack sounds as if he's about to lose it.

"Don't be worrying about all that now. There will be time to straighten things like that out later. Just come home. Love you, Mack."

"Love you too, Mom." After hanging up, Mack takes a big swig from the glass of bourbon Matt hands him.

"Let's see if I can hire someone to come in and pack all this shit up, while we go buy a coffin and arrange for it to be at the airport in the morning."

"How are we going to keep the undertaker back home from snooping in it?" Matt asks, sipping his drink.

"We will have it sealed here and tell him the body was already embalmed and all he is to do is set up the funeral. I'll pay him extra to just make the funeral a lovely event."

Matt goes in to shower, and Mack call the front desk and explains the situation and asks for a maid to please come and pack for him. After downing another bourbon, he heads for the shower. He has a lot of things to get done before they're to leave in the morning.

Chapter 128

They hire a cab and tell him they need to go to a funeral parlor that sells caskets, etc. The driver looks at them as if they have lost their minds. Without seeming too nosey, he asks what sort of casket they're looking for, a plain one or a more ornate one? Mack tells him price is no option and that it's for his dead wife. He just smiles and drives them to the other side of the city. Mack asks him to wait and says he will make it worth his while. Once inside the immaculate parlor, they're greeted by a beautiful woman in her late fifties. Mack thinks to himself, she must have been a great looker and a great fuck in her younger days.

Matt's voice interrupts his thoughts. "Hello. We are looking to purchase a coffin for his late wife."

"Oh, I am so sorry to hear of your loss. Did you have anything specific in mind?"

"We will need it right away, and we will need it sealed for delivery to the States."

"We don't usually seal the casket until the body has been viewed at the ceremony." She hands them a brochure of many different styles of caskets.

"Well, my dear wife was lost at sea, and there will be no body. However, to save the family more heartbreak, we have decided it best for them to think she is in the coffin when it arrives in the States. They would only worry and wonder for the remainder of their lives if they thought something terrible had happened to her and she was never found. They must never know that she wasn't found."

"Oh, Mother Mary, I see where that would be most upsetting to her family. We will do everything to fulfill your wishes."

Mack can see the dollar signs lighting up in her eyes. He's sure this is going to cost him a small fortune.

"Take your time in picking out what you like. My husband will be in shortly to help with the arrangements that need to be made." She leaves them to look over the brochures.

"I like the one with the carving of the sea on it. It seems to be fitting for the occasion," Matt says, giggling like a girl.

"You are quite right. That is perfect. The bitch died at sea and will be buried in a sea-themed coffin. Excellent choice," Mack agrees.

The lady and her husband walks in together speaking in Spanish but quickly change to English when they are completely in the room.

"Have you made a decision, sirs?" The wife looks sad.

Mack thinks, *Like you really give a shit about my loss.* "Yes, I have decided on the one carved with the sea on it. I thought it fitting seeing she was lost at sea."

"That is a most beautiful piece. My brother-in-law hand-made it for our facility."

"Now, I do have a rather unusual request." Mack taps the brochure on the counter. "I will need it to be weighed with something at about one hundred and twenty pounds, and the casket sealed. It is to represent my wife's weight. I don't want the family to think she was never found. They would go crazy knowing she was lost to them forever. This way they will think their lovely daughter and sister is lying peacefully inside this beautiful casket, to be with the Lord forever." Mack sobs.

"I handle all the, how do you Americans say it, Jane Does? I have a young woman who was stabbed yesterday. She can be placed in the coffin for you."

"Won't the authorities find out?"

"No, once I receive the body, it is up to me to dispose of it. I will seal the casket as you requested."

"Yes, that way, no one will know our little secret."

"No problem, we will be happy to do those things for you."

"It must also be at the airport tomorrow morning so it can be shipped back to the States on the plane that we will be on. Can you guarantee that it will be there to be transported?"

"Yes, that will not be a problem."

After Mack gives them the final instructions and the flight information, he's shocked at how inexpensive this all will be. He expects thousands and thousands of dollars. The total bill is around two thousand American dollars. He uses his credit card and adds another five hundred dollars as a tip for all their hard work. The couple are very happy and smiles gratefully at the two men as they leave the parlor. Once inside the waiting cab, Mack laughs out loud.

"Well, if I'd have known it would have been this easy, I'd have done this years ago."

"Yes, but remember, years ago you weren't a rich fucker."

"You are so right. I can't wait to see just how much money I will be getting."

Other than Matt and the insurance company, no one knows of the five-hundred-thousand-dollar policy Mack had taken out on Elise a year ago. Both men sit back and are silent the rest of the trip back to the bungalow.

Chapter 129

Once they've called home and told them of the flight details, they decide it's time for a bit of fun before they leave. After all, it has been a very trying day. Having to arrange for Mack's poor dead wife's body to be shipped back home and packing all her shit. They head for the bar on the beach.

They discuss what they will say and do once they're Stateside. The family is so shaken up that it shouldn't be a problem pulling off the sealed casket and the funeral. Mack will call her parents and let them know when the funeral will be just in case they decide to show up. He doubts they will, but he will let them know that they are not receiving a fucking penny of his money. That would ensure that they will never bother him again. They drink until after midnight. Each deciding not to pursue a piece of ass. Needing to be alert in the morning.

The alarm goes off at five, and both Matt and Mack are ready to get to the airport in a matter of minutes. Mack wants to make sure everything goes smoothly with the coffin.

The flight leaves on time without a hitch. The coffin has been loaded, customs read the paperwork from the funeral home and scans the coffin through. It passes with flying colors, and they are on their way back to the States. Mack feels happier than he has in years. It turns out to be the best vacation ever.

Chapter 130

The flight is uneventful, and they land in Miami and go through customs in a matter of minutes. They are on their flight to Portsmith in less than an hour after arriving in Miami. Mack has checked to make sure the coffin is on the plane before they take off. Everything is going as planned, and he's quite pleased with himself. He and Matt just smile a knowing smile and drink a bourbon on the rocks. Soon it will all be over, and they can do whatever they feel like doing. Mack is sure he will continue being a fantastic detective, and maybe he will somehow get Matt a job in the department. It will make things so much easier for them.

It seems only a matter of minutes before the plane is descending and will be landing. Mack actually feels nervous about lying to his parents and Haven. What the hell is coming over him? He's happy the bitch is dead and all that money will be his. He mentally scolds himself and tells himself to get it together.

The plane lands, and when they depart the plane, Matt is happy to see Haven holding Becca in the receiving area. He hadn't realized how much he had missed his little girl until he sees her. Haven has dressed her in a little pink dress with a matching hat. Damn, that girl is cute. Mack's parents meet him with open arms and tears. His mother is sobbing into her Kleenex, and his father's eyes are all red, proving he has been crying earlier. He hugs his mother first and tells her everything will be okay. She sobs into his shoulder.

"How can anything ever be okay again with Elise gone? She was so sweet and just a wonderful girl. I miss her so much. I should have never entered that painting into the contest." She moans, still hugging Mack.

"It's not your fault if that is what you are implying. We planned on going on a vacation anyway." He lies. "It would have probably happened anyway."

"I just feel so bad."

"We all feel bad," Haven pipes in. "I just can't seem to wrap my head around the fact she is dead."

"I know what you mean," Mack says in his most sullen voice. "One minute we were enjoying our time on the bay, and the next minute, she was just gone. We notified the authorities as soon as I discovered she was missing from the cruiser. I had a horrible stomachache and went below for maybe twenty minutes. It all happened so fast." He sobs.

"The damn police thought Mack had something to do with her disappearance and actually held him in their jail. I had to damn near call the army to get him released. They were so sure he pushed her overboard. The captain of the cruiser told them repeatedly that Mack was below. He said he saw him go below but then was working on some things and did not see Elise leave the cruiser. He thought she went below to be with Mack."

"I don't know, that just sounds fishy to me. Maybe he did away with her," Mack's dad offers.

"No, nothing was taken or moved from when I went down below deck. I believe him. Besides, like he said, it is bad for business to lose such a beautiful lady from his cruiser."

"You say there was no trace of her, until her body was found several miles down the coastline?"

"Yes, they did quite an extensive search for her." Mack waits for their luggage.

After grabbing his suitcase and the couple that contains Elise's things, he turns to his parents. "I just want to go home and sleep for a day or two. Can you make arrangements for her funeral?"

"Yes, of course we can. I'll go to the claims department right now. I'll have the coffin sent to the Jewel Funeral Home before we leave." Matt and Haven follow close behind as Mack makes for the parking lot.

"Did you all ride together?"

"No, I drove our van," Haven answers. "I thought you could ride with us and even stay the night at our place if you wanted to."

"If it's all right with you, I'd rather just go home." He waits for the van to be unlocked.

"I just don't like the idea of you being there all by yourself. I worry about you."

"For Christ sake, Haven, I'm a grown man, and I'm sure I can stay at my own house. It's not like she is going to come haunt me."

"Mack, what a horrid thing to say about Elise. You don't even seem upset that she is gone. Maybe you are in shock and I just don't think it's a good idea to be alone."

"Listen, little sister, I was in shock, I was interrogated like a common criminal, I couldn't believe she just disappeared, but I have had time to process it all. Believe me, I am fine. I will grieve her my way. Just leave it at that." He climbs into the back seat next to the car seat. He watches Haven strap the baby in, and after she shuts the door, he starts to relax and talks to Becca. He thinks, what a lucky little girl, she's having a rich uncle to buy her things.

Chapter 131

They drop him off at the house, and after making sure he wants to stay alone, Matt and Haven leave.

"He will be fine," Matt says after they're back into the car. "He was a mess when I first saw him in the jail," he lies. "He could hardly talk, and it looked as if he had been up for days on end and had cried all the time."

"I suppose you are right. I realize he has dealt with so much death in his life that he probably can handle this. I still can't come to terms with her death." She wipes at her eyes and blows her nose. He gently kisses her cheek.

"I don't think I could live without you."

Mack goes directly to the bar and pours himself a drink. He swallows the hot burning liquid and picks up the bottle and goes into the library. He finds Jordyn's number and dials it. She answers on the first ring.

"Hello."

"Hello, Jordyn, this is Mack. I'm sure by now you heard what happened to poor Elise?" He pours another drink.

"Yes, of course. Your mother called me right after she got the news from you."

"Did you know we found her body?"

"No, where?"

"It washed up a ways down the coast." He almost sounds happy.

"Really? Were you able to bring her home with you?"

"Yes, and there will be a funeral soon. But I want to go over the financial details with you as soon as possible. Will you be available in the morning?"

"Yes, but don't you want to wait until after the funeral and you are in a better frame of mind? You must still be reeling from all that has happened."

"No, I want this done and done as soon as possible."

"Fine, I have everything that was set up. Her lawyer also has a copy. I will call to see if he can meet us at his office."

"You mean my lawyer has a copy of what was set up in New York?" Not believing that she had already sent everything to him.

"No, Mack, her lawyer, not yours."

"What the fuck are you telling me? She had her own lawyer? Why the hell would she need a lawyer when I have a lawyer?"

"I'm not sure of the details. All I know is she felt with the artwork selling like it has been that she wanted to be sure the profits were invested and put in accounts. I'm sorry, Mack, all I can tell you is what I set up for her and that she gave me the paperwork in a sealed briefcase."

"It's almost as if she was planning something before we went on the trip. Tell me, was she planning on getting a divorce when we got back? It's obvious she talked to you about our life." He now is drinking bourbon straight from the bottle.

"I have no idea what her plans were. We really only talked about her artwork and what we were going to do with it. We were too busy trying to figure out which paintings to put on display and which ones to hold off on. Her work is flying off the walls."

"Well, that's just great. Who is this lawyer? And make damn sure he is ready to have a meeting bright and early in the morning. Let's try for nine o'clock. Call me when you have it all set up."

"Okay, I'll let you know if he is available. His name is Kevin Redman."

"I know that asshole. He better be ready." Mack slams his fist down on his desk. It doesn't give him the relief he wants, so he sweeps all the things on the top of his desk off onto the floor in one swift movement of his arm. Lying on the carpet staring up at him is a picture of Elise he had taken of her on their honeymoon. He grinds his shoe into the glass frame and stomps out of the library.

Chapter 132

I watch out the window as the plane lands in Milwaukee, Wisconsin. I'm one of the last to deplane and have my passport and everything ready to hand to the authorities. I go to the baggage claim area and pick up my bag. Going through customs is a breeze. Nothing to claim makes it easy. The airport is larger than Portsmith, and I hope I can find the domestic flight that will take me to North Central Wisconsin. I walk down the corridor, looking at the informational signs, and soon come to the area where my next flight will be taking off. I see that the flight is on time and that it will leave in an hour and twenty minutes. I check my luggage in and then run my boarding pass through one of the newfangled automatic boarding pass machines. I'm shaking by the time I finish. I look for a place where I can sit and maybe have a bite to eat.

Sitting on a stool at the counter of a McDonald's, I carefully eat my chicken fillet and french fries. I order a Sprite to help wash it down. I watch as people rush this way and that way through the busy airport. Children are trying to free themselves of their parents' hands to look at all the things in the little gift shops along the corridor. I see a woman carrying a tiny baby, and I'm thankful that my baby is still inside and I don't have to worry about luggage and caring for a baby while trying to get booked in. After my meal, I sit in the waiting area where my flight will leave. I watch out the window as the flights come and go. Finally my flight is called, and I line up with the other passengers to board the plane.

It's a much smaller plane with only about seventy-five people aboard. I wonder just what sort of place I will be going to. I sit in my window seat feeling a bit apprehensive. No, scared to death would better explain the feeling I'm having. A young man sits down in the seat next to me and politely says, "Hello."

"Hello."

He doesn't say anything more, and I'm happy I don't have to explain myself to him.

Soon the flight is in the air. It will take a little more than an hour to reach my destination. For some reason, I'm thinking it will be another flight of hours in the air. I hardly have time to think about my life or anything else when the announcement comes that the flight will begin its descent. I do manage to drink a bit of my tea while in the air, so my stomach isn't quite as upset and queasy. The plane circles the airport, and I can see the farms and fields around the airport. It looks as if the airport has been dropped in the middle of nowhere. This seems to be about as remote as one can get if one is hiding. I realize that hiding will be a part of my life from now on. I hope it will be worth it.

The plane lands, and everyone scrambles for their things in the overhead compartments. I wait until the aisle is clear behind me before getting out of my seat. I will be the last to get off the plane. I'm a wreck and hope I don't show how nervous I really am. Once in the very small terminal, I go to the only baggage claims area there. I patiently wait for the luggage to be put on the belt and go round and round. Once I have my one suitcase, I head to one of the two car rental counters. The lady behind the counter asks if I wish to rent a car.

"I believe one should be waiting for me to pick up."

"Name?"

"Elizabeth Martins," I say, much slower than normal.

"Oh, yes, you have a Ford Fiesta waiting for you in the lot, and here is a package I was instructed to give to you when you picked up the car."

I take the large envelope and wonder what's inside. There's no name or marking on the envelope, and remembering the ones I received at home, I'm almost afraid to open it. The woman gives me two sets of keys to the car and instructions to where it's parked.

The car isn't at all hard to find as it is the only red car in the whole damn parking lot. I giggle, thinking, *Let's not be conspicuous, let's drive around in a sporty red car. Boy, if this isn't just like Jordyn, put me out there in plain sight. Yet hiding from the world.* Once I've placed my suitcase in the trunk, I sit down in the driver's seat and quickly open the new envelope.

"Holy shit."

There inside the envelope is a new Wisconsin driver's license, a birth certificate that said I was born in Madison, Wisconsin, a Social Security card with Elizabeth Martins on it, and a new passport that matched everything else. The directions to a small town about forty miles away, with a house key to a house just outside the town. I would be living about nine miles out of the town of Merrill on Spring Lake Road. If I feel too tired to go there now, I could stay at a motel in Wausau.

I'm so pumped up I think I could drive all the way to the Coast and not be tired. I start the car and put the address into my new phone's GPS. Just then, the phone rings and literally scares the daylights out of me. It's Jordyn.

"Hi, Lizzie" comes the cheerful voice on the other end of the phone.

"How did you get all of this stuff for me?"

"Oh, it was nothing."

"Nothing, my god, girl, you thought of everything. How will I ever repay you?"

"Don't worry about that. I have friends who owe me in just about every state. If you don't like Wisconsin, we can move you to another state or another country. The choice will be up to you. By the way, your artwork is flying off the walls."

"Well, I don't know if I want to know what these people owe you for, but I am sure thankful that they owe you. I'm about to leave shortly for my new home."

"You sure you're not too tired?"

"No, I'm so pumped I couldn't sleep if I tried."

"Okay, I'll let you go. Call me when you get there."

I pull out of the parking lot and start toward my new home. It's as if the baby knows something exciting is happening because he or she kicks, and I automatically reach down and rub my belly. We're going home.

Chapter 133

Mack had spent most of the night raging and drinking bourbon. Falling asleep on the leather couch in the library, he awakes to one of his own snoring snorts. He had drooled on the leather seat, and his face sticks to it as he raises his aching head. It's already seven. He groans as he sits up and tries to desperately shake the cobwebs from his head. Dragging his body out of the library, he heads to the bathroom and starts a scalding-hot shower. As he steps into the water, he thinks he will surely pass out before he's done. Wrapping only a towel around his lower half, he goes into the kitchen. Coffee, strong, black, and about a gallon of the shit is what he needs. While he rarely makes coffee or anything for himself, he manages to make a pot and laughs at the fact that he would have to hire a maid. He hopes she will be a better piece of ass than his wife was. Pushing open the patio door, he steps out into the cool morning air. He sees Warrior's leash and swears out loud.

"Shit, I'll have to get rid of that asshole today too." He sits in the chair next to the pool and sips his coffee. Thinking of how nice it will be to have all that money. Maybe he will just keep the detective job long enough to see Danking be sentenced to life for the crimes. Yes, that is what he will do.

He arrives at Attorney Redman's office just as Jordyn is getting out of her car.

"Hello."

"Good morning, Jordyn, I assume you have everything ready for this meeting."

"Yes, I'm sure Attorney Redman is prepared."

They walk into the building, and Mack announces to the receptionist, "MacKenzie and Kent to see Redman."

"Yes, he is waiting for you in his office." She leads them to a double door and opens for them to enter. The office is more like a suite.

"Mr. MacKenzie, Ms. Kent, have a seat at the conference table, I have everything set out for your review." He gestures to the table. "Would you like something to drink while we are going over the files?"

They answer simultaneously, "Coffee, black."

The receptionist immediately goes to the sideboard and pours two cups of piping-hot coffee and sets the cups down in front of them. She then leaves the room.

"Shall we begin?" Redman nods toward the folders.

"All I really need to know is the account number and which bank the money she is making off of the paintings is going into."

Attorney Redman pays him no heed and proceeds with the paperwork in front of him. "If you will open the folder in front of you, you will see a letter that your wife wrote before going on the trip to New York. In fact, she wrote it a good month before the trip."

The letter reads as follows:

> Dear Mack,
>
> If you are reading this letter, then something terrible has happened and I am dead. I have hired Mr. Redman to take care of my estate, should I actually have any money from my paintings. Fortunately, none of my estate will ever reach your hands. A small portion of my earnings will go to Becca, and the rest will be going to a worthy cause that I have left up to Jordyn to decide. You, my dear husband, will get nothing, nil, zippo, zilch. This decision you brought on yourself. All of the meanness, cheating, and lying you did during our marriage made it easy for me to make

the decisions as to what to do with my estate. I hope you are as pleased with my decision as I am. Oh, and you can contest all you want, but the legality of it will stand up in any court. It will only cost you money to fight this. Money you won't want to spend. I hope you enjoy the rest of your life, and I pray that no other woman will have to suffer under your hands. Mr. Redman will give you all the legal paperwork, and you can go on with your life. Oh, and one last thing. I hope you rot in hell.

Your loving wife,
Elise

"I will fight this, and I will win. No way in hell will I allow you or anyone else take what is rightfully mine. You and she must think I am an idiot!" Mack screams at the lawyer and Jordyn.

"Mr. MacKenzie, you have no rights to any of your dead wife's money. Seeing you had no children, she was allowed to do whatever she wanted with her money, paintings, and any other personal items. You, sir, have the house and any other properties that you may have acquired while you were married. She filed all the proper paperwork, and I am sorry for your loss, but this is an airtight will."

"Bullshit, there has to be a way around this. You just don't know. I will have my lawyer contact you. As for you, Ms. Kent, I hope you die." Having said that, Mack picks up the folder and storms out the door.

"He can't really break this will, can he?" Jordyn asks, worry filling her voice.

"No, it is airtight. No worries, there isn't a judge or court that would reverse her will."

"Thank you." Jordyn leaves the office. She's almost afraid for her life. She's familiar with men like Mack. They will stop at nothing to get what they want. She will have to make a call to the agency and have them investigate Mack more thoroughly.

Chapter 134

Mack has his lawyer on the phone before he reaches the outside door.

"I have the paperwork from my late wife's will, and I need for you to break whatever the hell this is. All her money from the sale of her paintings is going to wherever the hell Jordyn Kent decides they should go. I have nothing. I'm bringing them to you right now, and I expect you to work on it exclusively. I pay you enough to get results, and to get them *now*."

After thoroughly looking over the will, while Mack is pacing a rut in front of his desk, he raises his head and says, "Your wife was no dummy. There is no legal way to break this will. You can take it all the way to the Supreme Court, but you will never win. Sorry, Mack, but you would be wasting what money you use to fight this. She covered all her bases. It is a lock-tight contract. Jordyn Kent is her choice to distribute her profits from her paintings, and she is to get all her paintings, artwork, etc. You can't even keep a painting for a keepsake."

"What the fuck would I want anything of that bitch's? So you are saying I am fucked. There is no way to break this? What if Ms. Kent falls off the face of the earth? What happens then? Not that I'm planning on doing her in. I just want to know, will it then go to me or Becca?"

"Well, as it is stated, Becca will continue to get her share, and the designated foundations will get the rest."

"Who are the foundations?" Mack asks, thinking maybe he can get something from them.

"Unfortunately, that is a confidential agreement only Ms. Kent has access to."

"So you are telling me I can't even find out where the damn money is being used?"

"That's right."

"This is just fucking bullshit."

Mack leaves his lawyer's office feeling sick and mean. He wants to hurt somebody. He heads straight to the sheriff's department. Maybe seeing his work pals and seeing Danking behind bars will make him feel better.

Chapter 135

I pull into a long driveway that has tall pine trees on either side. The headlights shown on a small ranch-style house with a detached garage. It's nestled in a small clearing that's surrounded with woods. It will be a perfect place to paint and raise a child. I'm really not able to see much of the town as I drive through it, but it has a Walmart, a Walgreens, and a McDonald's. That's a good start. I get out and take my suitcase out of the trunk and walk to the door. A motion sensor light comes on as I drive the car up to the house. I walk directly into a mudroom. That's nice, no muddy tracks going into the kitchen. The kitchen is a U-shaped one, not too big but very modern with an eat-in area that has a nice oak table and chair set. Suddenly I hear a yip and a growl. I nearly lose my footing as I'm walking down a short hall. Flying out of one of the rooms comes Warrior. He jumps on me full force, knocking me into the wall.

"What are you doing here?" I cry as I hug my dog. He's busy licking my face and wiggling all over. I begin to cry.

After a full five minutes, I manage to compose myself and walk into the end bedroom. It's spacious with a huge four-poster bed and very large furniture.

"Wow, this place is amazing and it's all ours." I explore the other two bedrooms and a small office area. I pick one that has large windows for a studio. I open the back door to a large deck and a swimming pool. The yard light doesn't allow me to see all the yard. I tie Warrior to the leash hooked to the side of the house and let him do his business. I go to the refrigerator and cupboards and find them to be stocked with food and everything I need to start my new life. Letting Warrior in, I make a sandwich and sit in the living room to eat and watch a late-night news show. I remember to call Jordyn.

"Hello. Does everything meet your requirements and standards, Ms. Martins?"

"Oh my god, yes. And how did you get Warrior here?"

"Oh, he must've got out of Haven's backyard and just ran off the other day."

"Poor Haven must be just sick."

"She'll get over it. You better get some rest. You have a lot of exploring to do in the next couple of days. You have only a few neighbors on your road, no one to be worried about. The place has been for sale for a while, and no one asked any questions when the moving van went in and out. You should be good to go. All the emergency numbers and important numbers you may need are on the refrig. Have a good night sleep. I'll be in touch."

I take my suitcase into the bedroom and place it on a chair. I do my nighttime ritual, and soon I'm tucked neatly under the covers. Warrior has jumped up on the bed and is now lying on the half that I'm not using. Gently patting his head, I fall asleep.

Chapter 136

The next few months fly by. I've made a few friends at a local café. Jordyn and I speak often. Warrior keeps me company, and I'm happy and content. The doctor says the baby is due anytime, and I feel fat and heavy. It has shifted to rest upon my bladder, so the toilet has become my best friend. Sitting on a stool in my studio, I work on a painting of Warrior. It's going to hang above my small fireplace. I don't hear the car drive up, nor do I hear the door open.

When I hear the familiar voice say "Is anyone home?" I practically fall of my stool. Warrior is barking a greeting when I come running out of the room. Jordyn is already standing in the hallway. I run to her and throw my arms around her.

"Oh my god, you are here. I can't believe you are here. I didn't think I was lonely, but gosh, I missed you." I'm crying and laughing at the same time.

"Well, I sure in hell wasn't going to miss the birth of my godchild."

"Hey, where am I supposed to put the suitcases?"

"Are you kidding me?" I let go of Jordyn to run to Cam. "You are here too?"

"I don't like traveling alone." Jordyn laughs.

The rest of the afternoon is spent catching up on the happenings in Flag Lake. I realize I don't miss the place at all. During their supper meal, I announce that I've been having contractions most of the afternoon.

"I thought you looked pale and were experiencing some discomfort. How far apart are they?" Jordyn demands.

"Right now, I'd say about ten minutes. I want to wait a while to make sure they are real." I flinch as another one hits me. "I'll call the hospital and see what they suggest I do."

"Good idea, and I will clean up our dishes."

"What am I supposed to do?" Cam asks, feeling helpless.

"Take care of Warrior."

We arrive at the hospital an hour later with me in hard labor.

Chapter 137

Mack and Matt are cleaning out the rest of the things in the house. The house has only been on the market a few days when it sells. Mack will be moving into a nice little place next to the river. It's closer to the department, and he likes the idea of not being on a busy street, filled with nosey neighbors.

Prying open a locked file cabinet, Matt takes out a stack of sketchbooks. He starts leafing through them.

"What do you want me to do with these sketches?"

"Well, seeing they all belong to Jordyn, I suppose we better put them in a box for her. She probably knows everything that was left in this fucking room."

"Um, you may want to look at these." Matt is staring at the sketches laid out before him. Mack looks at the drawings.

"What the fuck. How in the hell did she know what the crime scenes looked like? Look at the details. She knew everything. I never told her anything. It had to be her damn dreams. I remember her coming out of one of them saying something about blood all over the bed and him hanging."

"I thought we were lucky when Danking hung himself before his trial came up. I was really worried about him. But these could hang us. Yes, these would be our death sentence."

"Thank god the bitch is dead."

Chapter 138

At that precise moment that Matt and Mack discover the sketches, I give birth to a beautiful dark-haired baby girl. As I'm holding her in my arms for the first time, I smile down at my daughter and say, "You are my life now. You are what gave me the strength I needed to survive. You gave me faith in myself and the hope of a future. You are my precious Gem. I will name you Gemma Faith."

The End

About the Author

Judy grew up in North Central Wisconsin in a very rural area. After graduating from Medford High School, she moved to Racine, Wisconsin. While living there, she attended technical college and met her husband. Judy moved to several large cities in several different states and even lived in Japan for three years. She returned to her hometown to raise her two daughters and retired from working as a correctional officer. While taking a memoir-writing class, she decided to challenge herself by writing a novel. Judy enjoys the peacefulness of the rural community and the excitement of watching her grandchildren grow into fine young adults. A sequel is in her future.

www.ingramcontent.com/pod-product-compliance
Lightning Source LLC
LaVergne TN
LVHW021156030225
802714LV00001B/4